# NEW PERSPECTIVES ON ARABIAN NIGHTS

Adopting a multi-disciplinary approach, this comparative study of a selection of *The Arabian Nights* stories in a cross-cultural context, brings together a number of disciplines and subject areas to examine the workings of narrative. It predominantly focuses on the ways in which the *Arabian Nights* have transformed as its stories have travelled across historical eras, cultures, genres and media. Departing from the familiar approaches of influence and textual studies, this book locates its central inquiry in the theoretical questions surrounding the workings of ideology, genre and genre ideology in shaping and transforming stories. The ten essays included in this volume respond to a general question, 'what can the transformation of Nights stories in their travels tell us about narrative and storytelling, and their function in a particular culture?'

Following a *Nights* story in its travels from past to present, from Middle East to Europe and from literature to film, the book engages in close comparative analyses of ideological variations found in a variety of texts. These analyses allow new modes of reading texts and make it possible to breach new horizons for thinking about narrative.

This book was previously published as a special issue of *Middle Eastern Literatures* entitled *Ideological Variations and Narrative Horizons: New Perspectives on Arabian Nights.*

**Wen-chin Ouyang** is a lecturer in Arabic at the School of Oriental and African Studies. She works primarily on narrative and storytelling in classical and modern Arabic Literature.

**Geert Jan van Gelder** is Laudian Professor of Arabic in the Faculty of Oriental Studies, University of Oxford.

# NEW PERSPECTIVES ON ARABIAN NIGHTS

## Ideological Variations and Narrative Horizons

Edited by
Wen-chin Ouyang &
Geert Jan van Gelder

LONDON AND NEW YORK

First published 2005
by Routledge
2 Park Square, Milton Park, Abingdon, Oxfordshire OX14 4RN

Simultaneously published in the USA and Canada
by Routledge
711 Third Avenue, New York, NY 10017

First issued in paperback 2014

*Routledge is an imprint of the Taylor and Francis Group, an informa company*



Typeset in Plantin by Infotype Ltd, Eynsham, Oxfordshire



*British Library Cataloguing in Publication Data*
A catalogue record for this book is available
from the British Library

*Library of Congress Cataloging in Publication Data*
A catalog record for this book has been requested

ISBN 978-0-415-36698-4 (hbk)

ISBN 978-0-415-75915-1 (pbk)

# CONTENTS

# ACKNOWLEDGEMENTS

This book grew out of a three-year project on 'Genre Ideologies and Narrative Transformation' (2001–2004) funded by the AHRB and run under the auspices of the AHRB Centre for Asian and African Studies SOAS-UCL. The essays in this book were originally read at the four Project workshops run over a period of two years. We take this opportunity to acknowledge the support of the Arts and Humanities Research Board in funding the project, and allowing for the creation of a genuine interdisciplinary space. We would also like to thank the SOAS-UCL AHRB Centre for hosting the workshops and providing all the necessary administrative support. We thank Stephen Hart, co-leader of the project, for his presence and support, and Stephanie Jones, research assistant assigned to the project, for her indispensable role in conceptualizing the project and organizing the workshops. Special thanks also for Stuart Woodman, Jonathan Manley and Amber Bulkley at Taylor & Francis, whose initiative, efficiency and discipline made this book happen. We are, above all, grateful to all the contributors, without whose contributions this book would not have been born.

Wen-chin Ouyang
Geert Jan van Gelder

# Foreword: Genres, Ideologies, Genre Ideologies and Narrative Transformation

**WEN-CHIN OUYANG**

*Layālī alf layla* (translated into English by Denys Johnson-Davies as *Arabian Nights and Days*, 1995), the re-writing of *The Thousand and One Nights* in a novel by Naguib Mahfouz, the 1988 Egyptian Nobel Laureate, appeared in Arabic in 1979. Viewed from the post-colonial perspective, this novel may be considered both a symptom and symbol of post-colonial identity politics. An imported literary genre from the 'West', the novel is integrated into the indigenous tradition of storytelling. The process of 'authenticating' imported literary forms—novel, play and short story—has been a familiar feature of contemporary Arabic literature. Arab writers have evoked, adapted and appropriated pre-modern Arabic storytelling, its stories and main characters in the newly imported literary genres from the West since the turn of the twentieth century. However, locating the 'authenticity' of modern Arabic story-telling in the *Nights* is interestingly problematic, for the discovery of the *Nights* and, in fact, the final shape of the text were to a great extent the results of the interest, initiative and efforts of European 'Orientalists'. Ever since Antoine Galland (1646–1715) discovered and subsequently translated the *Nights* into French, beginning in 1704, the tales contained in it have fascinated the world; they have been translated first into English and later into virtually every major language in the world. The *Nights*' influence outside the Arabic-speaking world has been so pervasive in the arts throughout history that, according to Robert Irwin, it is easier to name those who have not been influenced than those who have. Its narrative techniques are constantly emulated, its stories adapted and retold, miniatures are created to illustrate the luxurious editions of the book, music is composed in honour of Scheherazade, and films based on scripts adapted from its stories are made.[1] Arab interest in the *Nights* is, in a way, triggered by Orientalist enthusiasm and the contemporary efforts of authenticating the Arabic novel manifest in re-writing the *Nights* may be considered a process of re-possession too, an attempt to reclaim ownership of this corpus of stories.

The twin issues of 'ownership' and 'influence' have thus far been the pre-occupation not only of Arab writers caught up in post-colonial discourses of identity politics, often framed by East–West cultural politics, but also of scholars of the *Nights*. *Nights*' scholarship has in part been engaged in 'influence studies', looking at influences on or of the *Nights*. It traces horizontally the spread of *Nights* across diverse geographical areas and cultures, by locating in one instance the extra-Arabic–Islamic origins of the *Nights*[2] and identifying in another the influence of the *Nights* on non-Arabic literatures.[3] It also examines vertically the impact of the *Nights* on contemporary Arabic fiction and looks at the use of *Nights* narrative techniques (such as frame-within-frame, arabesque or repetition, and the 'marvellous') or the recasting of *Nights* characters (such as Sindbad, Scheherazade and Shahriyar) in contemporary Arabic storytelling, be it novel, play or short story.[4] A more important part of *Nights*' scholarship is perhaps what may be termed 'textual studies', or studies driven by close scrutiny of the *Nights*' 'text,' including typology of stories and motifs based on current printed editions of the *Nights*,[5] analysis of one or a number of stories, including description of storytelling techniques in these stories[6] and, above all, identification of the 'original text' of the *Nights*.[7]

Textual and influence studies make the assumption that it is possible to locate 'cultural origins' of stories and that knowledge of 'cultural origins' is crucial in the understanding of these stories. Bruno Bettelheim thus asserts in his book on *The Uses of Enchantment: the meaning and importance of fairy tales*: '—one especially crucial limitation must be noted: The true meaning and impact of a fairy tale can be appreciated, its enchantment can be experienced, only from the story in its original form'.[8] (Of course, he goes on to give a psychoanalytical reading of *Sindbad the Sailor* and the frame-tale based on a translation made for children.) If 'cultural specificity' were significant in the process of reading or understanding texts, then what would make a story 'culture-specific'? In other words, is there such a thing as 'cultural specificity' and, therefore, 'literary ownership'? If there are such things as 'cultural specificity' and 'literary ownership', how can we articulate the components that would explain such specificity and legitimate such ownership? More importantly, would such an articulation necessarily contribute to theories and methods of literary analysis? Or are these issues simply irrelevant to reading stories, especially where the *Nights* is concerned, given its multi-cultural context?

## The Multi-cultural Context of the *Nights*

The *Nights*' scholarship tells us that the stories it contained may be traced to diverse origins, such as Indian, Persian, Greek as well as Arabic–Islamic, and that the 'text' took its current shape across a number of historical eras. We have, for example, earlier Baghdadi cycles and later Cairene cycles in the earlier manuscripts. We also find that older and newer tales seemed to have been incorporated into this infinitely expandable 'text' in the cross-cultural exchange between East and West during the age of European Empires, especially between the eighteenth and twentieth centuries. The obsession in current scholarship with locating that definitive 'original text' is, in a way, a statement on the entanglement that bespeaks the complex collaborative effort that went into this multi-cultural product.

In the process of Muhsin Mahdi's reconstruction of what he calls the 'archetypal text', it has become even more evident that there are different recensions of the *Nights*. In addition to the manuscript based on which Antoine Galland provided his own version of the *Nights* in French, which Mahdi identifies as belonging to the Syrian family, there is the Egyptian family of the *Nights*, the 'archetypal text' of which would have to be extracted from, for example, the 1835 Bulaq edition. There is also Maghrebi version called *Mi'at layla wa-layla (One Hundred and One Nights)*, which the editor (Ṭarshūna) claims to be part of the North African, particularly Tunisian, recension of the *Nights*.

More importantly, European translations seemed to have played an instrumental role in shaping the 'text' of the *Nights* we have today. The story is now a familiar one. It all began with Galland, who discovered a manuscript of *The Voyages of Sindbad* and translated and published it in 1701. Inspired by the success of *Sindbad*, Galland obtained a three-volume (some say four) manuscript, dating from the fourteenth or fifteenth century, from Levant (now Syria, Lebanon, Jordan and Palestine) and began translating it. His fruition took the form of the twelve-volume *Les Mille et une nuit*, the first two of which were published in 1704 and the final in 1717. The popularity and influence of Galland's translation were immediate and pervasive in Europe. For almost a century translations of this translation, not of any Arabic version of the *Nights*, were made into other European languages, especially in English. In the meantime, an earnest search began for the Arabic manuscripts of the *Nights* and consequently, or subsequently, a series of Arabic texts, drawing on 'translations', and perhaps even 'pseudo-translations' so popular in the eighteenth century, were put together and published. There are at least twenty-two surviving Arabic manuscripts of the *Nights* of either Egyptian or Syrian origin, most of which come from a late date, leading some scholars to conjecture that they may have been produced in the eighteenth and nineteenth centuries in order to meet the demands of European manuscript-hunters in the Near East. Whether this is true or fictitious, there remains lingering doubt regarding the 'authenticity' of the four sets of *Nights* texts in print (excluding the Mahdi edition): Calcutta I (1814–1828), Breslau, or Habicht (1824–1839), Bulaq (1835) and Calcutta II (1839–1842). If the Arabic 'texts' were the product of cross-cultural exchange, the pervasive global influence of the *Nights* underscore even more the multi-cultural dimensions of their stories.

The so-called 'full' translations of these texts are in many ways texts of their own right; they are distortions of the Arabic texts, dependent on the personality of the translator and the era to which he belonged. Edward Lane, for example, was a Victorian scholar, and his translation betrays that: he cleaned up much of the 'vulgarity' of the Arabic text, provided copious footnotes to explain the 'Oriental Culture', or what he calls 'manners and customs' of Egyptians, for example, and more importantly, omitted stories contained in the 'texts' he worked from and removed the story-within-story structure that is so much a feature of the *Nights*. John Payne, similarly, did not adhere to the narrative organization of the Arabic texts, nor to their 'integrity'; in fact, he integrated freely into his 'translation' stories from all Arabic 'texts' available to him. At least he did not expunge the 'vulgar' parts of the Arabic versions. Richard Burton, who preserved the story-within-story structure of the *Nights*, was an adventurer of the 'Romantic' persuasion taken with exoticism and eroticism of the 'Orient' and his translation inevitably exaggerated the exotic and erotic. These translations are effectively European literary artefacts of a specific era that have a life of their own away from the Arabic 'texts' and tradition of storytelling.

They, as well as the eighteenth-century pseudo-translation of 'Oriental' stories unleashed by Galland's translation, ushered in a new era of fiction writing in Europe, starting with the 'low-brow' 'Oriental Tale' in the eighteenth and nineteenth centuries and culminating in the 'high-brow' novel in European languages in the nineteenth and twentieth centuries. The influence of the *Nights* in Europe was not limited to fiction writing only, but also extended to cinema. Many *Nights* stories were and continue to be made into films. The *Nights*' popularity in the 'West' in turn created within Arabic culture an interest in this corpus of stories, which has until recently been marginal to the Arabic literary and critical tradition. Arab writers are now turning to re-writing the *Nights* stories as part of their engagement with cultural and identity politics as well as ways of producing 'authentic' Arabic novel.

That the *Nights* stories travel well across historical eras, cultures, genres and media explains perhaps their enduring popularity. In their travels, however, they all seemed to have been subject to transformation. What can this transformation tell us about narrative and storytelling and their function in a particular culture and, more importantly, point the way to new modes of reading texts, in addition to the already prevalent inquiries into the migration of the *Nights* narrative techniques, the workings of the 'fantastic', or Todorov's 'marvellous' and Bettelheim's 'enchantment' and gender politics in the frame tale? In a case where no fixed 'text' can be found, what would we learn from bringing together a variety of versions of the same story across cultures, eras genres and media? Would this endeavour provide us with insights regarding notions of 'text' and its function in a particular culture? Would these insights in turn help us understand better the culture that produced these stories, therefore these stories? The three-year Arts and Humanities Research Board (AHRB) Project (2001–2004) on Genre Ideologies and Narrative Transformation is inspired by this set of theoretical questions raised by the multi-cultural context of the *Nights*. Given the complexity of the multi-cultural context of the *Nights*, the project necessarily focused on one area of inquiry. It looked at the role of 'genre ideologies' in 'narrative transformation', an issue that gave the project its theoretical focus and definition.

## The AHRB Project on Genre Ideologies and Narrative Transformation

Even though the scope of the Project is not limited to *The Thousand and One Nights*—in fact, it covers diverse literatures of Asia, Africa and Europe—the *Nights* remained at the heart of the Project. The issue central to narrative transformation, therefore, narrative, appears to be genre and its implicit ideology, the worldview embedded in a genre, which often surfaces as generic expectations in our reading of literary texts: 'genre ideology'. 'Genre ideology' is a compound of two terms, each of which raises its own set of problems. Genre, a term denoting 'types or kinds of literature', is fluid, ambiguous and at times controversial. At the outset, there are debates about whether there is such as thing as genre, or whether it is possible to speak of such a thing in the context of the study of literature. Some argue that a text should be studied in its own right because each text is unique and it is pointless to produce typologies, for as soon as one is produced its limits are already transgressed. Moreover, there does not seem to be any agreement on what literary genres may be. Classical genres, those derived from Aristotle, seem to serve little purpose where non-Western classical literatures, as well as modern literatures, both Western and non-Western, are concerned. There are necessarily other serious reservations about any kind of typology, for we are always in danger of being imprisoned in the types we construct and of overlooking the fluidity of such things as genre. Despite all these reservations the idea of 'genre' is useful, if not indispensable, in speaking of narrative and storytelling as long as Todorov's advice is heeded and room is made for the 'interlacing' of genres. 'Ideology' is an equally charged term. Here, it denotes the political meaning of the word, but even more the sense defined by Terry Eagleton in his works; that it is a paradigm of knowledge, which determines the way we look at or respond to the world around us—our 'worldview'. 'Genre ideology' then means the paradigm of knowledge implicit in a genre of storytelling which often manifests itself in the text as generic expectations.

The Project began with looking at the 'cultural trans-mutations' of the *Nights* stories and attempting to explain the changes occurring in stories in terms of genre, ideology, genre ideology or, inevitably, subjectivity. The Project then went on to ask broader theoretical questions, such as: In what ways do paradigms of knowledge inherent in narrative genres inform and shape cultural and literary texts? Does narrative in turn generate new paradigms of knowledge? The papers collected in this special issue of *Middle Eastern Literatures* on the *Thousand and One Nights* are part of the research outcome of the AHRB Project. They follow four tracks of inquiry:

1. transformation of stories when they travel from one genre to another in the same period and in the same culture (e.g. history to literature);
2. transformations of stories when they travel from one culture to another (e.g. Sanskrit to Arabic, or Arabic to English);
3. transformation of stories when they travel from one period to another (e.g. pre-modern to modern); and
4. transformation of stories when they travel from one medium to another (e.g. literature to film),

and more particularly they seek to answer the following questions:

1. How do stories change in their travel from one culture to another, from one era to another, from one genre to another, and from one medium to another?
2. In what ways may the changes be attributed to genre ideologies? Are there other factors?
3. What can these genre ideologies tell us about the culture, genre or medium that produce the story?
4. Can genre ideologies explain the formations of literary, or other, canons and traditions?
5. What can narrative transformations tell us about the function of 'tradition' in the ways texts, literary or otherwise, are shaped?
6. Why are the seemingly same stories re-told in a variety of ways?
7. Are genre ideologies an invented category by critics and are of no concern to writers?

Wen-chin Ouyang sets up the theoretical parameters of the Project in 'Whose Story Is It? Sinbad the Sailor in Literature and Film'. She examines the role of ideology, genre ideology and subjectivity in shaping the various reincarnations of the story of 'Sindbad the Sailor' across cultures, historical eras, genres and media and explores the interpretive possibilities of applying insights gained from such an examination to a re-reading of the famous *Nights* story within the medieval Arabic–Islamic context.

The first three articles have in common their concern with the medieval Arabic–Islamic context of the *Nights*. Aboubakr Chraïbi, arguing that the kernel of the *Nights* was an organized and integrated collection of stories belonging to medieval Arabic literary tradition, discusses in 'Texts of the *Arabian Nights* and Ideological Variations' the ways in which the ideological priorities and literary considerations of medieval Islamo–Judaeo–Christian culture went into the re-formulation of two *Nights* stories of ancient Indian and Near Eastern origins. Julia Bray considers the usefulness of ideological analysis of medieval Arabic texts, looking closely at two versions of the *Nights*' 'The Steward's Tale' found in al-Tanūkhī and Ibn al-Jawzī, and interrogates the distinction between 'story' and 'history' in 'A Caliph and His Public Relations'. Ulrich Marzolph ponders the connection between narrative strategies and ideological messages in a comparative analysis of adaptations of three *Nights*' stories in 'Narrative Strategies in Popular Literature: ideology and ethics in *Tales from the Arabian Nights* and other collections'.

The second set of three articles take us beyond the immediate world of medieval Arabic storytelling and look at the implications of the migration of some of *Nights*' narrative techniques to the European novel for the interpretive process. Richard van Leeuwen focuses on the nights-division as an organizing principle that allows for a dialogical confluence of multiple worldviews in one textual space. This democratic narrative principle, he argues in 'The Art of Interruption: *The Thousand and One Nights* and Jan Potócki', is central to the *Nights*' influence on the European novel. Peter Caracciolo traces the narrative structures of the *Nights* in the English novel between the eighteenth and twentieth centuries in 'The House of Fiction and *le jardin anglo-chinois*'. Evelyn Fishburn offers a playful reading of 'Traces of *The Thousand and One Nights* in Borges', the presence of which she finds both constitutive and subversive of 'Western' culture.

The third set of two articles break further new grounds for *Nights* scholarship. They interrogate the by-now familiar notions of 'Orientalism' by looking at the transformation of *Nights* stories in popular film and theatre. In '*Arabian Nights* in Film', Robert Irwin locates European and American cinematic adaptations of *Nights* stories in the realm of a popular form of orientalism that is driven not so much by a will to dominate but rather by a repertoire of visual cliché giving a sub-genre of film its visual identity. In telling the story of the development of the repertoire of a commercial Malay-language theatre from colonial Indonesia in '*One Thousand and One Nights* at the Komedie Stamboel: popular theatre and travelling stories in colonial Southeast Asia', Matthew Cohen relates the draw of the spectacular and comic elements of the *Nights*. More importantly, his article opens up a new vista for a reconsideration of the definition and workings of 'Orientalism'.

And finally Stephanie Jones traces inter-textual allusions to the *The Thousand and One Nights* in a number of contemporary novels written outside the immediate Arabic context and looks closely at the on-going conversation between the ideology of the *Nights* and that of the novel in 'Emboldening Dinarzad: the *Thousand and One Nights* in contemporary fiction. Locating her inquiry in the slippage between the seemingly polarized 'abstracted Shahrazad' and 'emboldened Dinarzad'; she posits that the relative silence and absence of Dinarzad in the *Nights* frame-tale, as well as contemporary re-writes of Shahrazad, is paradoxically a fountain of creative energy and narrative generation. It also allows for novel ways of interrogating ideologies. Ideologies and genre ideologies in the liminal space betwixt the beginning and end of a story's journey from one culture to another or one historical era to another are open to more than one form of dialogism. Tracking ideologies and generic expectations in texts does not have to produce restrictive or reductive readings; on the contrary, it can give voice to silence and make present what is absent.

During the deliberations of the four workshops of the Project, the 'articulated category of knowledge' that is genre proved to be difficult to grapple with. It is vague, shifty, indescribable and often seems to be 'an abstraction' from the perspective of hindsight. It becomes more manageable when 'ideology' entres the picture. Ideology, it seems, figures everywhere and can be more easily grasped than genre. Ideology makes it possible to speak of changes in an 'approximated' genre, especially when the discussion is located in the particular changes of a story, and when it is possible to relate these changes to shifts in ideology, whether ideology at large or genre ideology. Narrative transformations seem to come hand-in-hand with ideological shifts. Genre ideology is necessarily (or is it?) part of a specific culture, and seems to play a role in shaping the story and can tell us a great deal about the culture that produced the story.

There is, however, an operative ideology that is often left out of the picture because it is hard to pin down: ideology of the audience, or readers of both verbal and visual texts. Texts do have built-in mechanisms for recognition. This raises also the nagging question about our own practices. As readers of texts, should we begin to examine our own ideologies before we embark on any kind of textual analysis?

In pondering these questions in relation to the 'cultural trans-mutations' of the *Nights* stories the Project gained significant insight into the workings of narrative, the arts of storytelling and, more importantly, notions of the 'text' and the ways in which this 'text' may be read. Mono-cultural literary theory, such as Harold Bloom's 'anxiety of influence', may now be interrogated in a multi-cultural context. It cannot account for the kind of 'intentional' re-writing of pre-modern texts such as that of Mahfouz's *Arabian Nights and Days*. Julia Kristeva's 'intertextuality' and Gérard Genette's 'palimpsest', despite their fundamental importance in looking at the historical layers of a text, cannot explain the changes that occur in a story when it migrates across cultures, historical eras, genres and media.

This said, the theoretical strands of thought these theorists initiated, especially their advocacy of comparative analysis, are crucial in paving new ways towards interpreting texts. In the particular contexts of the Project on Genre Ideologies and Narrative Transformation, the close, comparative scrutiny of ideological variations, whatever their sources may be, as they are manifest in a variety of texts have made it possible to discover new epistemological horizons delineated by narrative and uncover novel horizons for thinking about narrative.

## Notes

1. See Robert Irwin, *The Arabian Nights: A Companion* (London: Allen Lane, 1994).
2. See, for example, Domenico Comparetti, ed., *Researches Respecting the Book of Sindibad* (London: E. Stock, 1882); and B. E. Perry, *The Origin of the Book of Sindbad* (1960). These two works trace the *Story of Sindbad the Philosopher* to Indian origins. A popular version of this cycle of stories appears in the *Nights* as the *Story of the Seven Viziers*.
3. See, for example, Peter L. Caracciolo, ed., *The Arabian Nights in English Literature* (New York: St Martin's Press, 1988); and Muhsin Jassim al-Musawi (aka Ali), *Scheherazade in England: A Study of Nineteenth-Century English Criticism of the Arabian Nights* (Washington, DC: Three Continents Press, 1981); and *Anglo-Orient: Easterners in Textual Camps* (Tunis: Centre de Publication Universitaire, 2000).
4. See, for example, Muṣṭafā 'Abd al-Ghanī, *Shahrazād fi al-fikr al-ʿarabī al-ḥadīth* (Cairo: Dār al-Shurūq, 1985 [1995]); Muḥsin J. al-Mūsawī's *Thārāt Shahrazād: fann al-sard al-ʿarabī al-ḥadīth* (Beirut: Dār al-Ādāb, 1993); and Mohammad Shaheen, *The Modern Arabic Short Story: Shahrazad Returns* (Houndsmills: Palgrave Macmillan, 1989 [2002]).
5. See, for example, Mia I. Gerhardt, *The Art of Story-telling: A Literary Study of the Thousand and One Nights* (Leiden: E. J. Brill, 1963).
6. See, for example, Ferial Ghazoul, *The Arabian Nights: A Structural Analysis* (Cairo: AUC Press, 1980); *Nocturnal Poetics: The Arabian Nights in Comparative Perspective* (Cairo: AUC Press, 1996); Sandra Naddaff, *Arabesque: Narrative Structure and the Aesthetics of Repetition in the* 1001 Nights (Evanston, IL: Northwestern University Press, 1991); David Pinault, *Story-telling Techniques in the Arabian Nights* (Leiden: E. J. Brill, 1992); Eva Sallis, *Sheherazade Through the Looking Glass: The Metamorphosis of the* Thousand and One Nights (Richmond, Surrey: Curzon, 1999); and Daniel E. Beaumont, *Slave of Desire: Sex, Love and Death in the* 1001 Nights (Madison: Fairleigh Dickinson University Press, 2002).
7. See, Muhsin Mahdi, *Kitāb alf layla wa-layla min uṣūlihi al-ʿarabiyya al-ūlā*, 3 vols (Leiden: E. J. Brill, 1984–1994).
8. Bruno Bettelheim, *The Uses of Enchantment: The Meaning and Importance of Fairy Tales* (New York: Vintage, 1977 [London: Penguin, 1991]), 10.

# Whose Story Is It? Sindbad the Sailor in literature and film

**WEN-CHIN OUYANG**

Where would *The Thousand and One Nights* be today had it not been for Sindbad the Sailor? In the all too well-known (hi)story of the *Nights*, Antoine Galland's discovery of the *Seven Voyages of Sindbad the Sailor* was what started his search for and translation of the corpus of stories known to us as the *Arabian Nights* today. It is no wonder then that the *Story of Sindbad the Sailor* has remained one of the most enduringly popular *Nights* stories around the world. It is especially suitable for adaptation into children's stories and action adventures. Children across the world have long enjoyed the intriguing adventures of a sailor who seems to be able to survive all kinds of ordeals at sea and return to his homeland a rich, happy man. The story is simply full of ingredients that can, in an infinite variety of concoctions, go into the making of a good adventure. It was the first story I read in Chinese when I was learning my 'mother' tongue as a child in Libya. The Japanese animated series in thirteen episodes made in the 1970s was so popular that the Arabic version is still being sold in video form in Arab communities everywhere. The status of the series in the Arab world is evident in the investment the Arab producers made in dubbing it into Arabic. Prominent Lebanese actors, who were professionally trained in the *fuṣḥā*, were employed to provide impeccable Arabic for the characters. When broadcast during the month of Ramadan, it brought public life to a halt in Tripoli before the cannon was sounded to signal the end of fasting. Streets became eerily silent as children and adults disappeared into their living rooms to immerse, perhaps even partake, in Sindbad's adventures.

The story's capacity to draw its readers and viewers into its world has ensured that fictional re-writings and cinematic remakes are in regular production. There is, it seems, no cure for Sindbad's wanderlust. From children's stories, to Hollywood films, Arabic poetry and modern American and Arabic fiction, Sindbad has travelled across cultures, historical eras, genres and media. Whether called Sinbad or Sindbad, he has endured many more journeys than his 'original' *Nights*' assignments, and somehow managed to transform himself from a medieval Baghdadi merchant into a personality with global appeal. He may be a young boy, a dashing pirate, a majestic prince, a disgruntled old man or an Arab Odysseus condemned to eternal wandering, reliving the same but recast seven *Nights*' journeys, or embarking on new adventures. He is a shape-shifter who always manages to survive and emerge a different person, persona. That Sindbad is transformed through his various reincarnations is obvious; however, what remains to be unravelled is the workings of the narrative, verbal or visual, which effect such transformations. Where do we locate the kernel of these transformations? What does Sindbad's globetrotting tell us about the role of ideology, genre ideology and subjectivity in driving narrative and shaping story? More important, in what ways will his travels inform a new reading of the 'original' *Nights*' story? In the following, I trace the sources of 'trans-mutations' of the *Story of Sindbad the Sailor* in Hollywood films and contemporary American and Arabic fiction, examining more particularly the role of ideology and genre ideology in narrative transformation. I then return to the *Nights*' story to look at one possible new vista for reading, or re-reading, this popular *Nights* story.

## A Pirate Prince in Hollywood

The 2003 DreamWorks' animated version of the story, *Sinbad: legend of the seven seas*, is the latest of a long tradition of adapting *Nights*' stories into films in Hollywood. Like the Japanese television series, translated into Arabic as *Mughāmarāt al-Sindbād* (the adventures of Sindbad), this film is addressed mainly to children. It, too, focuses on the fantastic (the roc bird and the whale island) and the journey(s) of the hero and his entourage. In the Japanese television series, Sindbad is a young boy who, because of a momentary lapse in responsibility, is separated from his family and forced to embark on thirteen adventures in the company of Yasmin, a princess-turned-bird, and Ali Baba, a thief-turned-mentor. *The Adventures of Sindbad* is perhaps more appropriately described as an amalgamation of *Nights*' fantastic stories of adventure. Stories suitable for the consumption of children including, for instance, *Aladdin and the Magic Lamp*, are integrated into the series, and the seven voyages of the 'original' *Nights*' tale grew into thirteen adventures. Constrained by the format of feature length films and considerate of the attention span of young children, DreamWork's adaptation tells the story of one adventure, centred more particularly on Sinbad's journey to a place called Tartarus, home of Aeries, Goddess of Chaos, to retrieve the stolen *Book of Peace* that is essential for maintaining peace in the twelve cities of Syracuse.

These animated versions are, for obvious reasons, mindful of their young audience and many of the gruesome and adult details of the *Nights*' tale, such as the rampage of the cannibals or Sindbad's polygamy, are toned down or omitted. Romance is kept at a level deemed appropriate for children of the 'modern world'; friendship grows into love and love leads to happily-ever-after marriage. Values such as freedom, justice, loyalty, responsibility and, more importantly, pursuit of dreams, are endorsed. These adaptations take great liberty with the tale and this is especially true of *Sinbad: legend of the seven seas*. Departures are already anticipated in the title in which the name 'Sinbad' and the number 'seven' evoke the *Nights*' tale but the term 'legend' and the phrase 'seven seas' point to a world radically different from that of *Nights*' medieval Islamic world. Sinbad is more of a pirate than a sailor. In one of his piratical ventures he runs into his old friend Proteus on a mission to bring home to Syracuse the *Book of Peace*. Instead of stealing the book, he helps his friend fight off a giant squid sent by Aeries to intercept Proteus' ship. His adventure begins when Aeries steals the book from Syracuse and frames Sinbad for her transgression. Sinbad is tried and sentenced to death. Proteus steps in to stay the execution in the nick of time, pledging his life in exchange for Sinbad's retrieving the book from Aeries. Sinbad sets off reluctantly and with the help of Marina, Proteus' fiancée who falls in love with him and eventually decides to join him in his life at sea, and his crew, he overcomes the sirens, the whale island and the roc bird and finally Aeries. He returns the *Book of Peace*, saves Proteus, and sails away with Marina.

The story of this film is likely to be more familiar to viewers of *Nights* films than readers of *Nights* stories, for despite the roc bird and the whale island, it resembles little the Arabic story known to connoisseurs of *The Thousand and One Nights*. Its portrayal of characters and the development of its plot are only part of the story. It is not simply that the cast and setting are Greek rather than Oriental, but also that the values imparted are modern secular rather than medieval Islamic. Its political correctness cannot disguise its genealogy. It is true that it does not exoticize or eroticize the Orient (the Greek cast and setting help) nor marginalize women (Marina is as capable, self-sufficient and free as Sinbad); however, it derives its narrative paradigm not from the *Nights*, as I shall demonstrate, but from the Sinbad films made in or for Hollywood. Since 1924 many of the *Nights*' stories have been subject to Hollywood treatment, beginning with Raoul Walsh's silent masterpiece, *The Thief of Bagdad*, going through a plethora of B-films, and culminating in the 2003 *Sinbad: legend of the seven seas*. *The Story of Sindbad the Sailor* has been one of the most popular *Nights* stories in the film industry, perhaps ranking even above Aladdin[1] and Ali Baba.[2] The Sinbad films[3] are all variations of the same theme, following a narrative paradigm established in *The Thief of Bagdad*; even the set of three films known better for their Harryhausen special effects are not immune. The story is inevitably about Sinbad, both pirate and prince, who rescues a 'damsel in distress' as he battles an 'evil prince' in a 'quest' for a 'treasure' that will 'save the world'. *Sinbad the Sailor*, the first of the series of Hollywood style Sinbad films, is paradigmatic of this action-adventure genre.

Made in Hollywood in 1947, *Sinbad the Sailor* was meant as vehicle for Douglas Fairbanks Jr, son of the star of *The Thief of Bagdad*, Douglas Fairbanks. It accentuates the swashbuckling qualities of the star and the exotic and treacherous features of the Orient and Orientals and, more importantly, it pays homage to the first *Nights* film. Like its predecessor, the hero of *Sinbad the Sailor* is a pirate who chances upon a ship and sets out on his eighth voyage in search for the treasure left by Alexander the Great on the Island of Deriabar. He has two evil contenders: Jamal and the Amir of Daibour. The latter has as hostage the Princess of Persia, Shreen, who of course falls in love with Sinbad. As the story unfolds Sinbad turns out to be Prince Ahmed, the long-lost son of the King of Deriabar, who sent him away when he was still an infant in order to keep him safe, for he knew that many evil men will use his son to force him to disclose the location of Alexander's treasure. When they all converge on the Island of Deriabar Sinbad comes to the realization that, as his father also believes, real treasure can be found only in the heart and mind and, above all, a 'pair of bright eyes'. He abandons the hunt for treasure, rescues his beloved Shreen and his crew, who were enslaved by the Amir of Daibour, and in the end manages to eliminate the Amir of Daibour, who has already killed Jamal. In the final scenes we see Sinbad telling this story to a group of onlookers, then throwing precious gems at them, only to chastise them for not having learned the lesson he himself has learnt so well. He then runs up the deck and holds Shreen's hand and together they disappear behind the transparent sail to seal their fate with a kiss.

Sinbad, a princely pirate or piratical prince, cuts a 'Romantic' figure in Hollywood films that is reminiscent more of the hero of European oriental tales, whether pseudo-translations pervasive in the eighteenth century or creative works popular in the nineteenth century,[4] than the seafaring merchant of the Arabic *Nights*. Sinbad, and his story in most Hollywood films, embody the values of an individual-centred worldview that was at once seductive and scandalous in the 'Western' world of the eighteenth and nineteenth centuries but has become commonplace in the twentieth century. This emerging worldview has been accompanied by changing gender politics that would gradually come to define notions of love, relationships, marriage and gender equality as we know them today. More important, perhaps, is the central role of the individual will in mapping human destiny. However, individual will is necessarily supported by a set of attendant values that would ensure the coherence, and continuity, of community. The difference between *Sinbad the Sailor* and *Sinbad: legend of the seven seas* is that while the former could indulge in the post-war optimism (or is it escapism?), the latter must contend with the perceived threat to world peace today. The broader ideology, or politics, plays only a partial role in shaping the story. Generic expectations, or genre ideology, contribute vital ingredients to the story. In Sinbad films we find all the structural functions of an action-adventure genre, including *Indiana Jones*, *Star Wars* and even *James Bond* films. The hero predictably swashbuckles his way through an action-packed adventure, defeats evil, saves the world and gets the girl.

## An American Tycoon in John Barth

These workings of genre ideology may be underscored by contrasting *Nights*' films to fiction written in the 'West'. In 'The Thousand-and-second Tale of Scheherazade' (1845), Edgar Allan Poe recasts two *Nights*' stories in the form of a short story in the middle of the nineteenth century. This story is about modern discoveries and technological advances which were, during his time, mind-boggling. The quote of an old saying appearing as subtitle of the story, 'Truth is stranger than fiction', sets the tone. The 'fantastic' elements are in fact 'real' phenomena, whether they are natural discoveries or industrial wonders. The characters of the frame-tale, Shahriyar, Scheherazade and Dunyazad, and the characters of the Sindbad cycle, the Sailor and the Porter, are all present. However, each is given a newly defined comical role. Sinbad the Porter, who actually carries the Sailor's merchandise to the harbour, is portrayed as greedy and cowardly. As soon as he sees the 'fantastic' submarine he runs away, leaving the Sailor to fend for himself.

Otherwise, the story is a simple one. It parodies the life-saving function of storytelling in the *Nights* and its implicit gender politics. Poe uses the frame-within-frame technique of the *Nights* and re-writes the fate of Scheherazade, making her fate dependent her telling the story of Sinbad's eighth voyage. At the end of the story, Shahriyar reverts to his former bloodthirsty self and throttles Scheherazade. This 'regression', or reverse transformation of Shahriyar, is obviously the 'plot' of the story and is played out in a way that simultaneously evokes and transforms the *Nights*. It rather locates itself in gender politics derived from a 'Western' version of the story of Adam and Eve. This is how the story of Sinbad is framed: 'At all events, Scheherazade, who, being lineally descended from Eve, fell heir, perhaps, to the whole seven baskets of talk, which the latter lady, we all know, picked up from under the trees in the garden of Eden.' Here, Scheherazade's 'prattle' is her downfall, and the justification and mechanism for Shahriyar's reverse transformation. Gender politics are no stranger to modern re-writings of *Nights*' frame-tale, and they change with the tides even among 'Western' writers. John Barth's *Dunyazadiad* (1972) rectifies Poe's rather misogynistic outlook and tries to restore female subjectivity to the story. In both cases, subjectivity of the author, internalized and externalized in the narrative, is defined in the main by aesthetic priorities.[5] Poe's whimsical employment of *Nights*' frame-within-frame technique points to a departure in narrative and an affirmation of the importance of such a move. Scheherazade dies in the end because she no longer tells 'fantastic' tales; rather, the eighth voyage of Sinbad comprises a record of stranger-than-fiction 'real' phenomena devoid of imagination or drama. Re-writings of *Nights*' stories in the 'West' often signals the arrival of new aesthetic sensibilities. This is especially true of contemporary American John Barth's re-writings of two *Nights*' stories: the frame-tale and Sindbad.

In critical assessments of John Barth's career, both as writer of contemporary American fiction and theorist of narrative, *Dunyazadiad* is examined in the context of discussions of *Chimera*, a trilogy of which *Dunyazadiad* is the first part. *Chimera* signals Barth's transition from 'modernist' to 'post-modernist' writer in his creative work. Three features of the novel—textualized self, direct engagement with mythology and multiplicity of narrative voice—are seen as signs of this departure. The necessity for this departure is located in Barth's crisis as a novelist suffering 'writer's block' and his response to it creatively and critically. Creativity lies not in inventing new stories necessarily from scratch but rather in finding new perspectives for old stories. Intertextuality comes to symbolize post-modernist reconciliation with 'literary tradition' and a cure for 'exhausted narrative possibilities'.[6] *The Last Voyage of Somebody the Sailor* (1991) is another, albeit considerably longer, playing out of 'post-modernist' creative possibilities grounded in layering of narrative and voice in a story. '*Alf Laylah Wa Laylah*, The Book of the Thousand and One Nights', according to Barth himself in the epilogue to *Dunyazadiad*, 'is not the story of Scheherazade, but the story of the story of her stories' (p. 55). *The Last Voyage* is a 'post-modernist' story about 'post-modernist' storytelling. It has not achieved the success of *Dunyazadiad*, which perhaps explains the critical silence on the work, and in fact it repeats to a great extent the kind of 'tricks' he plays with words, notions of fiction, narrative techniques, and modes of expression familiar to readers of his earlier work(s).

In an interview Barth explains that the novel is the meeting ground for medieval Islamic world (Sinbad) and the word of twentieth century America (Simon William Behler) structured around two alternating series of tales. The six fabulous voyages of Sinbad alternate with the cyclic tales of Behler's six voyages, literal or figurative, until they come together and become one story.[7] The plot unfolds in the interstices. Sinbad the Sailor is preparing to set out on his seventh and final journey when a mysterious stranger, Behler, Baylor or Somebody the Sailor, arrives in his house. Behler finds himself in medieval Baghdad after a mishap at sea. Over the course of six evenings they take turns recounting their voyages, merging the two narrative worlds of the *Nights* and contemporary American novel. The 'fantastic' and the 'realistic' are not mutually exclusive; in fact, they tell similar stories, even though we may not be aware of that. 'The high ground of traditional realism, brothers, is where I stand!', a member of the audience exclaims after hearing one of Behler's stories, 'Give me familiar, substantial stuff: rocs, rhinoceri, ifrits and genies and flying carpets ... Let no outlander imagine that such crazed fabrications as machines that mark the hour or roll themselves down the road will ever take the place of our homely Islamic realism, the very capital of narrative'.[8] But what happens to the *Nights*' Sindbad the Sailor in this narrative marriage?

*The Last Voyage* spotlights both the nocturnal world of storytelling and the stories of adventure. The evening gatherings are positively 'carnivalesque', crowded with notable guests, female companions, food, music, dance, story and intrigue. Sindbad woos the male guests as potential financiers for his last voyage, and the female companions are his seductive baits. As the story unfolds doubt is cast on his past accomplishments and the veracity of his stories. In the end he is exposed as a fraud, prohibited from leading the anticipated expedition to legendary Serendib, where the alleged treasure will be found, and Behler is sent in his stead. Behler of course returns to America. Never mind whether America is the fabulous Serendib or not, the adventures of *Nights*' Sindbad are savagely sabotaged. Indeed, the 'fantastic' creatures are all there, but the seven voyages all seem to have gained additional twists and turns. Sindbad is not the happy-go-lucky seafarer of the *Nights*; he is rather a disgruntled old man full of greed, tricks and malice. His relationship with the men and women in his life say as much. The family, or families, in the background of Sindbad's adventurous life is brought to the foreground. He falls in love with Marjānah and marries her. He sadly loses her soon after she gives birth to their daughter, Yasmīn. He learns of her death only after his return from his journey. He then has a son with his wife's maid Jaydā, whom he treats like a servant. His adopted son, Umar al-Yom, in love with his daughter, meets a similar cruel fate at sea—he is sacrificed so Sindbad may live when their ship sinks and they find themselves hanging onto the same piece of log. Then there is Yasmīn's mysterious loss of virginity, pregnancy and miscarriage, or is it abortion? Is her father the culprit? There is more than a hint of incest here.

The liaison between Simon and Yasmīn signals that everything is not what it seems. We are now reading a different kind of story. In an interview originally published in *The Johns Hopkins News-Letter* in 1991, Barth speaks of the title of the novel, and the beginning and the end of the story, as suggesting and echoing the 'possibilities that these voyages have been more or less rites of passage: birth, initiation into sexuality, marriage, parenthood, divorce, remarriage, middle age, peaking of ... career ...'. It seems likely that the voyages of Sinbad are recast as 'mirror' versions of Behler's rites of passage, themes prevalent in contemporary American fiction.[9] One critic, protesting loudly, calls it a 'replica of' of Burton's 'classic work of Orientalism in the imperialists, racist and sexist sense', in which '[t]he world to which [Barth] consigns Simon Behler is a territory of infinite license where storybook characters in turbans and djellabas wield scimitars and deflower maidens with cries of "*Ai yi!*" and "*Pfwah!*"—it is the old, mystic, irrational, "feminine" East of Occidental colonial mythology. Unlike Maryland, it is necessarily lacking in credible contingent details. It is made for pantomime. Its 20th-century author is not *composing* Burton as Menard composed Cervantes and Mr Bloom composes Genesis; he is copying him'.[10] Is he right? There may be some truth in this critique of Barth's noisy, and chaotic comic book Orientalism, but this does not explain the transformation of Sinbad or his journeys in the novel. The parallel journeys, as the author himself explains, point to the intersection of Sinbad and Simon's life stories, their rites of passage, as both process and narrative.

There is no uniform rite of passage, therefore no single way of telling the story. The narrative is structured around Behler's story, Somebody's Voyages which frames, or is framed by, Sindbad's story, from the first set of six Interludes to the final one Interlude, each interlude being a story told by or about Sindbad. The first-person narrative of the rites of passage of Behler, a small town boy who becomes an international New Journalist, from coming of age to failed marriage, success in career and remarriage, is juxtaposed to the multi-voiced narrative of Sindbad's journeys. Sindbad's adventures are now supplemented with additional details and perspective from Jaydā, Yasmīn and his adopted son, Umar al-Yom. His problematic familial relations characterized by self-interest and exploitation of others only highlight his equally self-serving attitude towards his potential sponsors. The story told here is that of the rise and fall of an American business mogul punctuated by digressions, or sexual diversions, which only accentuate the 'scandals' of corporate America, Serendib Limited. Medieval Baghdad is, for instance, New York City, and the lavish dinner parties and glamorously clad and properly behaved guests are but a smooth veneer concealing a world brimming with greed, malice and plotting. Similarly, the 'Oriental flare' of Barth's narrative cannot disguise the Americanness of the story he tells. He simply tells it differently from the tradition of American fiction and narrative (such as John Updike, Saul Bellow and Gore Vidal) which he tries to transcend. He does this by bringing together not only the two narrative worlds of 'East' and 'West', but also the two fictional universes of 'small-town America' and 'corporate America', each with its own rites of passage. These are paradigmatic. They also define two rather separate strands of American novel and film.

The 'Americanization' of Sindbad is inevitable in the fictional world of Barth, for what is at stake here is not the fate of Sindbad the Sailor or the future of *Nights*' stories, but rather the trajectory of Barth's journey as a writer of American fiction. Barth's authorial self is typically textualized in this novel and, like *Dunyazadiad*, this work is more about storytelling than story. Revisiting *The Thousand and One Nights* twenty years after his breakthrough from his 'writer's block', Barth re-emphasizes both his identity with American fiction and his departures from its narrative. What drive and shape the story here are aesthetic priorities, which determine an author's sense of himself and his place in the American tradition of fiction. Sindbad is what Behler, Barth's textualized authorial self, is not, fashioned not so much in the image of *Nights*' Sindbad, but the counter-image of Behler. Barth's Sindbad is a creature born out of the author's vision of his place in the world of American fiction. He is given an American passport that legitimates his residence in and gives him licence to travel with American narrative. Is there avoiding this kind of narrative re-fashioning, that for his survival Sindbad must always shed one identity for another? Can he be spared distortion? There seems no escape, not even when he stays 'home' in Arabic literature. The decision, it seems, is always up to his new hosts, heirs to Arabic storytelling.

## A National Allegory in Naguib Mahfouz

Sindbad the Sailor has made many guest appearances in modern Arabic poetry, short story[11] and novel,[12] and in each form he inadvertently dons an allegorical disguise, always incognito. His name conjures up not the fearless seafarer travelling willingly around the world wilfully seeking adventure, but a battle-fatigued wanderer condemned to exile; he is an Arab Odysseus in perpetual search for a way home. His journeys are motivated not by a call for adventure but a need to leave the familiar world behind in order to find a cure for its ills, and to leave behind the past in order to find a future for the postcolonial Arab world. Sindbad and his world have been reincarnated in Arabic literature as a paradox. In Badr Shākir al-Sayyāb's poem, 'Madīnat al-Sindibād'

(Sindbad's city, 1954?), the contemporary state of decay is contrasted to the splendour of Basra (and perhaps Baghdad) in the world of the *Nights*. In Khalīl al-Ḥāwī's 'al-Sindibād fī riḥlatihi l-thāmina' (Sindbad on his eighth journey, 1958), the world of the *Nights* is the past that must be given up, even though the search of a new future has alienated the contemporary Arab intellectual from his present. More importantly, his journey to the West in search for answers and solutions, which comprises Sindbad's eighth journey, has left him betwixt two seemingly irreconcilable worlds. Sindbad is reduced to a metaphor of a bygone time and place. This kind of 'literal' engagement with the *Story of Sindbad the Sailor* tells only a part of Sindbad's story in modern Arabic literature. He is assigned a different role in Naguib Mahfouz's 1982 novel, *Layālī alf layla wa-layla*,[13] an allegorical re-writing of the *Nights*.

Mahfouz's re-writing of the *Nights* picks up where the *Nights* left off in the story of the education of Shahriyar. Now that the crisis is averted he must learn about the nature of power and the responsibility that comes with it. Various re-written *Nights* stories are consolidated into one, dismantling the frame-within-frame structure of the *Nights*, to tell the story of Shahriyar's transformation from a bloodthirsty tyrant into a wizened man. The ways in which the *Nights*' stories are re-written point to the political allegory spoken of by critics of the novel. This political allegory is grounded not only in the context of the contemporary Arab reality, but also in the ways Mahfouz reads the *Nights*. The intersection between the fantastic world of the *Nights* and the contemporary political allegory in Mahfouz's novel, as I have demonstrated elsewhere,[14] makes a statement about the nation-state that is Egypt. The novel imagines a community as a nation-state and at once subverts its own imagining. The novel mimics the nationalist discourses and imagines a community that secularizes and democratizes in a painfully bloody experience. It begins with humanizing power and ends with popularizing it. Power, and more particularly political authority, follows the movement of two counter-narratives: one of Shahriyar's descent from power and the other of the 'folk's' ascent to positions of authority. These two narrative movements are in turn mediated by the story of Jamaṣa al-Bulṭī's metamorphosis from instrument of tyranny to means of justice. By choosing political power as his subject, Mahfouz creates a world akin to Benedict Anderson's 'imagined political community'. Anderson's definition of the nation calls for two more criteria: it must be imagined 'both as inherently limited and sovereign'.[15] The community is defined by the all-too-well-known realist Mahfouzian *Ḥāra* located in the heart of old Cairo, and its members are all citizens of this *Ḥāra* who, like the characters of his realist novels, congregate evenings in the Café of the Emirs, where news of the community is disseminated.

However, the novel does not only make ideological statements about political authority but also provides diagnosis and prognosis of the nation-state. This is effected on Mahfouz's play with the paradigm of knowledge inherent in the *Nights*' love stories. Scheherezade saves Shahrayār's kingdom not only by putting a stop to 'gynocide' but also by giving him three sons, making sure that the genealogy of the kingly family is not interrupted. More importantly, she teaches her king the meaning and power of love. Lessons of love are, however, fleshed out in the enframed tales, which inform and are informed by the frame-tale. Stories of love in the *Nights* are more often than not about the fate of a 'nation' effected on the interplay between 'erotic romance' and 'patrimonial romance'.[16] Survival of the nation often depends on the resolution of stories of love in *Nights*' romances. *Nights*' love stories are about the propriety, suitability and legitimacy of a love match guided by loyalty and endurance. An appropriate love match, such as the successful union of a prince and princess conducted within societal codes of propriety after a series of misadventures, leads to the coherence of the royal household and, therefore, the nation. Our understanding of the skeletal pattern and unjustified happy ending of the *Nights*' frame-tale are premised on our understanding of the pattern and resolution of the love stories it enframes.[17] Mahfouz's reformulation of the *Nights*' frame-tale and love stories is informed by but wary of their inherent paradigm of knowledge, or their genre ideology; it disrupts this paradigm. As the marriages dissolve in separation or death, the imagined community falls short of cohesion and the legitimacy of the political authority is brought into question.[18]

However, all is not lost. There are important lessons to be learned from the journeys Shahriyar undertakes in the novel. He is now a benevolent king rather like the famous ninth-century ʻAbbasid caliph Hārūn al-Rashīd, who tours the city at night and inspects his subjects. In his nocturnal wanderings he comes to understand the incompatibility of wisdom and power, as the heart-breaking story of humanity's yearning, search and failure in finding the Utopian 'state of fantasy' unfolds.[19] More importantly, he now sees that the transformation of power from despotism to something closer to democracy must be grounded in knowledge defined by 'experience of power'. The transformation is summarized neatly by Sindbad, who leaves at the beginning of the novel and returns only at the end. The story of Sindbad parallels that of Shahriyar, and the lessons they learn from their respective journeys are mutually confirming.

> The first thing I have learned, Your Majesty, is that man may be deceived by illusion so that he thinks it is the truth, and that there is no safety for us unless we dwell on solid land (first voyage) … I also learned, Your Majesty, that sleep is not permissible if wakefulness is necessary, and that while there is life, there is no reason to despair (second voyage) … I also learned, Your Majesty, that food is nourishment when taken in moderation but is a danger when taken gluttonously—and this is also true of the carnal appetites (third voyage) … I learned too, Your Majesty, that to continue with worn-out traditions is foolishly dangerous (fourth voyage) … I also learned, Your Majesty, that freedom is the life of the spirit and that Paradise itself is of no avail to man if he has lost his freedom (fifth voyage) … I learned too, Your Majesty, that man may be afforded a miracle, but it is not sufficient that he should use it and appropriate it; he must also approach it with guidance from the light of God that shines in his heart (seventh voyage).[20]

These vague statements may be interpreted as a discourse on power. Truth about power is necessarily derived from on ground experience, vigilance in curtailing power's abusive tendencies leads to optimism, naked desire for power is dangerous, power must guarantee freedom, and political authority must be tempered with wisdom. *The Story of Sindbad*, it seems, is integrated into the story of the education of Shahriyar, and his voyages, short of seven and shorn of details, are recast in order to serve as 'mirror' journeys of Shahriyar's transformation. Sindbad, now a secondary character, is subordinated to the plot revolving around the main protagonist, and once this is done his stories lose their previous characteristics. Rather, they take on the characteristics of the new genre in which it is now cast.

The effects of the transformation of *The Story of Sindbad* are, however, premised on our familiarity with the *Nights*' version. That this is true of all the re-writings of Sindbad goes without saying. In these re-writings both the protagonist and his story look familiar yet unfamiliar. Distortions may be attributed to the cultural context and its accompanying worldview, in which the story is recast, as well as to the paradigm of knowledge inherent in a genre of storytelling and, on occasion, to authorial subjectivity. Whatever the source of transformation may be the story necessarily loses parts of itself in the process. Can these missing parts tell us as much about the story as about their reincarnations? There is some urgency in considering such a question because pre-modern Arabic storytelling remains wanting in the kind of literary analysis that will unravel the workings of its narrative and the consequent meanings these produced. It needs more particularly to be related in a sensibly intimate fashion to the culture that produced it. How do we explain the particularity of Arabic storytelling? Perhaps a good place to start is genre ideology. What is the source of this ideology? In what ways can the parts of the story absent from its reincarnations help to relate the story to the culture that produced it?

## A Storyteller in the *Arabian Nights*

Of all the reformulations of *Sindbad the Sailor* Hollywood action adventure films, perhaps unsurprisingly, preserved the premise and structure of a journey. A crisis precipitates departure, followed by adventure and ending with return upon resolution of crisis. This pattern of journey seems fairly universal. *Sindbad the Sailor* follows a similar blueprint. There is, however, a rather different ordering of the functions of the journey; Sindbad's journeys are not always preceded by crisis; rather, crisis is often synonymous with adventure in his case. It is cast in a narrative paradigm specific to medieval Arabic–Islamic culture: the well-known genre of '*faraj baʿd shidda*'. *Jullanār* and *Abū Muḥammad al-Kaslān*, two *Nights*' stories, appear in *Al-ḥikāyāt al-ʿajība wa-al-akhbār al-gharība* (discovered and edited by Hans Wehr, 1956) with the term '*faraj baʿd shidda*' at the end of each story title. *Faraj*, literally openness, refers to a state of emotional and material relief after a period of hardship, *Shidda*, which means tightness. The pieces collected in the numerous compendia under the general rubric of '*al-faraj baʿd al-shidda*', whether in classical[21] or vernacular[22] Arabic, tell the stories of hardship followed by relief. The structure of this Arabic genre seems more elastic than that of Hollywood action adventure. There is no need for a crisis to motivate a protagonist to embark on a journey, and no adventure is necessary for the resolution of a crisis. The literal and figurative overlap in a *Nights*' journey. The journey is that which takes the protagonist from hardship to relief, whether or not he actually travels.

The *Nights*' frame-tale, as well as a majority of the enframed tales, exhibits the same narrative patterning. In the frame-tale Shahriyār and Shāhzamān as well as their kingdoms clearly fall on hard times, when the betrayal of their respective wives unleashes the 'gynocidal' wrath of the two kings. The kingdoms are thrown into crisis not only because women are being killed on a nightly basis, but also because 'gynocide' will result in the discontinuity of the kingdom. Who will bear the heirs to the kingdom when the virgins are all killed on their wedding night? Scheherazade resolves the crisis when she is able to postpone her death for one thousand and one nights, during which period she bears Shahriyār three sons. She saves Shahriyar's kingdom by first putting a stop to 'gynocide' then making sure that the genealogy of the kingly family is not interrupted. Dunyāzād, it is inferred, works a similar kind of miracle with Shāhzamān and saves the other kingdom.

The seven voyages of *Sindbad the Sailor* in the *Nights* (nights 536 to 566 in Bulaq and Calcutta II) tell the same story of hardship followed by relief. Indeed, each voyage takes place in a different place and involves different 'fantastic' events and creatures, but all the seven voyages follow the same pattern and have the same ending. Except for the first adventure, which is initiated by Sindbad's need to make a living after squandering his inheritance, the rest of the adventures are set off by Sindbad's restlessness, consistently phrased as his 'need to see the world'. Each story consists of three parts: departure, danger and survival. All stories have one mechanism for survival, which in turn consists of a trinity: faith in Allah and Allah's compassion, *ṣabr*, patience as well as endurance, and the will to survive, manifest in actions taken by Sindbad under duress.

In the first journey Sindbad lands on an island that is in fact a sleeping whale. The whale moves and many of his shipmates run away or drown. He does not make it back to the ship. He finds a trough, hangs on to it until he drifts to an island. He stays there until a ship sails by and picks him up. Lo and behold, he also recovers his merchandise, makes a load of money and returns to Baghdad a rich man. In the second journey he falls asleep on an island and is abandoned again. He sees a roc nest, climbs in and ties himself to the gigantic bird, which flies him to the Diamond Mountain. He fills his pockets with diamonds, ties himself to the sheep that diamond collectors throw down to gather diamonds, and when the roc bird picks it up he is recovered by the diamond hunters. He lives with these people until a ship sails by and returns him to Baghdad again a rich man. In the third journey he is shipwrecked at an island where serpents and a carnivorous giant live. He and his shipmates manage to blind the giant then escape, but he alone survived the serpents. He is finally rescued by a ship, recovers his possession and returns to Baghdad. In the fourth journey he encounters a tribe of cannibals, who fatten then roast his shipmates. He survives by starving himself, then runs away and finds his way to a kingdom where he becomes a courtier by making a saddle for the king. He marries the princess, the princess dies and he is buried alive with her. He again survives by killing those who are thrown into the 'tomb' after him and by stealing their few-days' supply of food. He is finally rescued and returned to Baghdad. In the fifth journey he ends up on an island where there is a parasitic old man who sits on his shoulders and locks his legs around his neck. Sindbad makes him drunk, kills him and escapes to a community of coconut gatherers. He stays with them until a homebound ship picks him up. He makes a great deal of money on spice trade and again returns to Baghdad a rich man. In the sixth journey he survives another shipwreck and drowning by holding on to a raft and following a cavern until he comes upon a kingdom. He becomes a courtier and when the king hears that he is from Baghdad, he is sent home to Hārūn al-Rashid with abundant gifts. In the seventh journey he ends up in a community of flying men hostile to Islam. He even marries there. However, when he sees their ungodliness he runs away and returns to Baghdad.

Inherent in this narrative pattern is an Islamic paradigm of knowledge that informs both the structure of the story and its narrative movements and, more significantly, speaks to the function of storytelling in this culture. The parts of the story missing in the contemporary reincarnations are crucial in an understanding of the narrative paradigm and function of storytelling in the medieval Arabic–Islamic culture in general and the *Nights* in particular. The original title of the story in Bulaq and Calcutta II is *Ḥikāyat al-Sinbād al-Baḥri maʿ al-Sindbād al-Ḥammāl* (the story of Sindbad the Sailor and Sindbad the Porter). Like the *Nights* in general and many of its stories there are two stories, one framing another, a feature not duplicated in any contemporary reformulation of the story. The story of the Porter frames the story of the Sailor. Sindbad the Porter, a poor labourer making do with carrying heavy loads for rich people, chances upon Sindbad the Sailor's opulent palace one day and in a moment of exhaustion and weakness complains of the injustice of fate by reciting a poem aloud outside the gates.

Sindbad the Sailor hears the recitation and invites the Porter to the feast he is giving in his house. He then tells him a story and sends him home with 100 gold dinars. For seven consecutive nights, the Sailor tells the Porter a story and sends him home with 100 gold dinars every night. By the end of this cycle of stories, not only did the Porter become rich but also good friends with the Sailor. The Porter, the listener, reaps the benefits of storytelling. This is true of the *Nights*' frame-tale. Shahriyār is the beneficiary of Scheherazade's stories. More importantly, this narrative paradigm may be traced to the Qur'ān.

The stories of the prophets (*qiṣaṣ al-anbiyā'*) are perhaps the most popular stories in the Qur'ān based on which at least two distinct, albeit overlapping, genres of religious stories are derived: *qiṣaṣ al-anbiyā'* integrated into the known historical chronicles, such as al-Ṭabari's *Tārīkh al-rusul wa-al-mulūk* and Ibn Kathīr's *Al-bidāya wa-al-nihāya*, which are later extracted and compiled into a single-volume work; and the more popular strand, such as al-Kisā'ī and al-Tha'labī's works carrying the same title. Regardless of the differences between the two genres, which pertain primarily to details not found in the Qur'ān and, for instance, 'unorthodox' explanations for these details, all the stories of the prophets contain 'fantastic' or 'extra-ordinary' elements, known in Qur'ānic exegesis and commentary as '*gharā'ib wa-'ajā'ib*', which showcase the miracles performed by the prophets, their gifts from God as proof of their prophecy. These stories are inevitably about the prophets whose endurance is tested but whose patience, indeed their faith in God and their mission, ensure their survival and triumph. These are the precursors of the *faraj ba'd shidda* genre, as al-Tanūkhī tacitly asserts by beginning his collection of stories with them in *Kitāb al-faraj ba'd al-shidda*.[23] The purpose of telling these stories is clearly to teach that faith is the guaranteed winner. The beneficiaries are clearly the Muslims who had, at the time, fallen upon hard times. The story of Joseph in *Sūrat Yūsuf* epitomizes the *faraj ba'd shidda* paradigm of both narrative and knowledge.

*Sūrat Yūsuf* is the only chapter in the Qur'ān that consists of a story in its entirety.[24] It tells the story of Joseph's 'exile' or departure from home—thanks to his brothers' jealousy and betrayal—then various ordeals he has to survive while exiled in Egypt, including Mrs Potiphar's failed attempt at seduction, her accusation of his improper behaviour and his imprisonment. However, he survives. His faith and endurance turn 'duress' into 'triumph', poverty into wealth, powerlessness into power, separation into family reunion and exile into homecoming. This journey from crisis to resolution overlaps interestingly with the paradigm of the 'journey in search of knowledge' (*riḥla fī ṭalab al-'ilm*). In fact, the latter frames the former. The Sūra begins as follows (Verses 1 and 2): 'Alif Lam Ra. Those are the signs of the Manifest Book. We have sent It down as an Arabic Koran; haply you will understand (*la'allakum ta'qilūn*)', which is followed immediately by 'We will relate to thee the fairest of stories (*naḥnu naquṣṣu 'alayka aḥsana l-qaṣaṣ*) in that We have revealed to thee this Koran, though before it thou was one of the heedless (*kunta lamina l-ghāfilīn*).'[25] The end of the Sūra (Verses 102–111), once the story is told, takes us back to the lesson implied in beginning:

> We sent not forth any before thee, but men We revealed to of the people living in the cities. Have they not journeyed in the land? Have they not beheld how was the end of those before them? Surely the abode of the world to come is better for those that are godfearing. What, do you not understand (*afalā ta'qilūn*)? Till, when the Messengers despaired, deeming they were counted liars, Our help came to them and whosoever We willed was delivered. Our

> might will never be turned back from the people of the sinners. In their stories is surely a lesson to men possess of minds (*laqad kāna fī qaṣaṣihim ʿibratun li-ulī l-albāb*); it is not a tale forged, but a confirmation of what is before it, and a distinguishing of every thing, and a guidance, and a mercy to a people who believe (Arberry I: 266).[26]

Knowledge in this context is, of course, knowledge of God, therefore, faith in Allāh. The last verses of the Sūra (102–111) define the knowledge to be learned—conveyed in the verb *taʿqilūn*, *ʿaql* being the instrument of knowledge, *ʿilm*—as the nature of Allāh's power and mercy. The *Nights*' story of *Sinbad the Sailor* is an articulation of this article of faith. The horrors he encounters, the wonders he witnesses (referred to as *gharāʾib wa-ʿajāʾib* throughout the seven voyages), and the miracles he receives culminate in one resolution in Sindbad's last journey: God has shown him what calamities greed brings and he repents. His wilful escape in the seventh voyage, in which the only horror he experiences is the discovery that he is living in a community of non-Muslims, confirms his realization that Islam is the ultimate goal for a Muslim. He returns to Baghdad, settles down, and lives contentedly among the Muslims.

However, the 'journey in search of knowledge' is undertaken not only by the prophets (Joseph or Muḥammad) and Sindbad the Sailor, for they already know the content of this faith, but also by those who listen to the story; the 'you' in the Sūra. Sindbad the Porter in the *Nights*' story embodies the 'you' of *Sūrat Yūsuf*. He is given the task of listening to Sindbad the Sailor's stories. Sindbad the Sailor's narration is the knowledge Sindbad the Porter ought to learn and his reward. The Porter is poor at the beginning of the cycle but becomes rich by the end of the story. The only thing he does is to listen to the Sailor's stories. The monetary reward makes no sense unless it is interpreted symbolically. This makes even more sense when the Sindbad cycle is read in the context of the frame-tale of the *Nights*. The crux of the matter in the frame tale is a crisis that needs to be resolved. The resolution of this crisis is found in storytelling. And in the Sindbad cycle, the solution suggested is faith and patience. When the lesson is learned, the crisis in the frame tale is also resolved. Shahriyar spares Scheherazade, who embodies faith and patience, has a family with her, and harmony returns to their 'community'.

The emphasis on a harmonious, coherent 'community' of Arabic storytelling past and present seems to frame the stories of individuals. This may be juxtaposed to the more individual-centred 'American' storytelling, whether in literature or film, in which the integrity of individualism seems to frame the stories about community. The differences in the two sets of existential priorities have produced genre ideologies, as well as subjectivities, which conform to as well as subvert these priorities. However, these priorities necessarily engage with ideologies having to do with a subject's negotiations for power in relation to others and to the world. Stories we tell are subject to these pressures and often take the shape of the various discoursing ideologies. These ideologies seem to be products of specific cultures within particular contexts. Story inevitably changes when it travels across cultures, historical eras, genres and media. That ideology is form shaping is obvious. The benefit of an inquiry into the relationship between ideology and form in an intercultural context is gradually becoming evident as well. Tracing influence seems superfluous to the understanding of story or the culture that produced it. When a story travels it absorbs the priorities of, or is absorbed into, the new host culture, genre or medium and comes to 'represent' them. This, however, does not explain why some stories travel and others do not. There is, it seems, much work to be done.

## Notes

1. E.g. *Aladdin and His Lamp* (1952; dir. Lew Landers) and Disney's animated films: *Aladdin* (1992; dir. John Musker and Ron Clements) and *The Return of Jafar* (1994; dir. Toby Shelton, Tad Stones and Alan Zaslove).
2. E.g. *Ali Baba Goes to Town* (1937; dir. David Butler), *Ali Baba and Forty Thieves* (1944; dir. Arthur Rubin), *Son of Ali Baba* (1952; dir. Kurt Neumann) and *The Sword of Ali Baba* (1965; dir. Virgil Vogel). The Story of Ali Baba and the forty thieves is also integrated into the second Disney *Aladdin* film mentioned above, as well as *The Thousand and One Nights* (2000; dir.?).
3. E.g. *Sinbad The Sailor* (1947; dir. Richard Wallace), *Son of Sinbad* (1955; dir. Ted Teztlaff), *The 7th Voyage of Sinbad* (1958; dir. Nathan Juran), *The Golden Voyage of Sinbad* (1974-British; dir. Gordon Hessler) and *Sinbad and the Eye of the Tiger* (1977, British; dir. Sam Wanamaker).
4. There is need for a more comprehensive analysis of the eighteenth-century pseudo-translations of oriental tales into French by François de la Croix (*Turkish Tales* and *Persian Tales*) and Thomas Simon Gueullette (*Chinese Tales, Mogul Tales, Taratian Tales* and *Peruvian Tales*) and the subsequent translation of their concoctions into other European languages in order to work out their influence in popular 'Orientalist' storytelling.
5. I have discussed gender politics in modern re-writings of the *Nights*' frame tale and the question of subjectivity in Barth's novella at length in 'Metamorphoses of Scheherazade in literature and film', *Bulletin of SOAS*, 66, 3 (2003), 402–18.
6. See Jac Tharpe, 'Toward the Chimiracle', *John Barth: The Comic Sublimity of Paradox* (Carbondale and Edwardsville & London and Amsterdam: South Illinois University Press and Feffers & Simons, Inc., 1974), 105–10; Charles B. Harris, 'The New Medusa: Feminism and the Uses of Myth in *Chimera*', *Passionate Virtuosity: The Fiction of John Barth* (Urbana and Chicago: University of Illinois Press, 1983), 127–58; Stan Fogel and Gordon Slethaugh, *'Chimera', Understanding John Barth* (Columbia, SC: University of South Carolina Press, 1990), 131–48; M. F. Schulz, 'The Eraton Transactions of *Chimera*', *The Muses of John Barth* (Baltimore and London: The Johns Hopkins University Press, 1990), 16–32; and Patricia Tobin, '*Lost in the Funhouse* (1968) and *Chimera* (1972): The Hero Minors in Metaphor', *John Barth and the Anxiety of Continuance* (Philadelphia: University of Pennsylvania Press, 1990), 84–102. See also Bruce Allen, '*Chimera*', Jerry H. Bryant, 'The Novel Looks at Itself—Again', Cynthia Davis, 'The Key to the Treasure: Narrative Movements and Effects in *Chimera*', and Jerry Powell, 'John Barth's *Chimera*: A Creative Response to the Literature of Exhaustion', in *Critical Essays on John Barth*, ed. Joseph J. Waldmeir (Boston: G.K. Hall & Co., 1980), 211–40.
7. In an interview with Dave Edelman, 'An Interview with John Barth (1991)', published at http://www.dave-edelman.com/barth/interview.cfm.
8. John Barth, *The Last Voyage of Somebody the Sailor* (Boston & New York: Houghton Mifflin Company, 1991 [2001]), 136.
9. In an interview with Dave Edelman, 'An Interview with John Barth (1991)', published at http://www.dave-edelman.com/barth/interview.cfm.
10. Jonathan Raban, 'The Sloop of Araby', The New York Times (February 3, 1991, Sunday, Late Edition). http://www.nytimes.com/books/98/06/21/specials/barth-voyage.html.
11. See Mohammed Shaheen, *The Modern Arabic Short Story: Shahrazad Returns* (Palgrave Macmillan, 1989 [2002]).
12. Samīr ʿAṭallāh, *Awrāq al-Sindibād* (Beirut: Dār al-Ḥāḍir, 1998).
13. Translated into English by Denys Johnson-Davies as *Arabian Nights and Days* (Cairo: American University Press, 1995).
14. See, 'Theorizing Narrative, Narrativizing Theory: Mahfouz interprets the *Nights*', http://www.cpge-cpa.ac.ma; and 'Metamorphoses of Scheherazade in literature and film', *Bulletin of SOAS*, 66, 3 (2003), 402–18.
15. Benedict Anderson, *Imagined Communities: Reflections on the Origin and Spread of Nationalism* (London, New York: Verso, 1983 [1991]), 6.
16. See Andras Hamori, 'An Allegory from the *Arabian Nights*: the City of Brass', *Bulletin of SOAS*, 34 (1971): 9–19; 'A Comic Romance from the *Thousand and One Nights*: the Tale of Two Viziers', *Arabica*, 30: 1 (1983): 38–56; 'The Magian and the Whore: Readings of Qamar

al-Zamān', *Mundus Arabicus*, 3, *The 1001 Nights: Critical Essays and Annotated Bibliography* (Cambridge, MA: Dar Mahjar, 1983): 25–40; 'Notes from Two Love Stories from the Thousand and One Nights', *Studia Islamica*, 43 (1976): 65–80; and *On the Art of Medieval Arabic Literature* (Princeton: Princeton University Press, 1974).

17. See my two articles, 'Romancing the Epic: 'Umar al-Nu'mān as Narrative of Empowerment,' *Arabic and Middle Eastern Literatures*, 3, 1 (2002), 5–18; and 'The Epical Turn of Romance: Love in the Narrative of 'Umar al-Nu'mān,' *Oriente Moderno* 83; 2 (2003) 485–504.
18. For a detailed analysis, see my article 'Metamorphoses of Scheherazade in literature and film', *Bulletin of SOAS*, 66, 3 (2003), 402–18.
19. I borrow this term from Jacqueline Rose, *States of Fantasy* (Oxford: Clarendon Press, 1996).
20. Johnson-Davies, pp. 210–16.
21. E.g. Abū Bakr 'Abdallāh Ibn Abī al-Dunyā, *Al-faraj ba'd al-shidda*, ed. Ḥasan 'Abd 'Āl (Ṭanṭā: Maktabat al-Ṣaḥāba, 1987), and Abū 'Alī al-Muḥassin Ibn 'Alī al-Tanūkhī, *Kitāb al-faraj ba'd al-shidda*, ed. 'Abbūd Shāljī (Beirut: Dār Ṣādir, 1979).
22. *Al-ḥikāyāt al-'ajība wa-al-akhbār al-gharība* (Bibliotheca Islamica), ed. Hans Wehr (Wiesbaden: Franz Steiner Verlag, 1956), which includes many of the *Nights* stories.
23. A number of stories in al-Tanūkhī's compilation have been examined in Julia Ashtiany Bray, 'al-Tanūkhī's al-faraj ba'd al-shidda as a Literary Source', *Arabicus Felix, Luminosus Britannicus: Essays in Honour of A. F. L. Beeston on His Eightieth Birthday*, ed. Alan Jones (Exeter: Ithaca, 1990), 108–28; 'Isnāds and Models of Heroes: Abū Zubayd al-Ṭā'ī, Tanūkhī's sundered lovers and Abū 'l-'Anbas al-Ṣaymarī', *Arabic and Middle Eastern Literatures*, 1, 1 (1998), 7–30, and 'Figures in a Landscape: the Inhabitants of the Silver Village', *Story-telling in the Framework of Non-fictional Arabic Literature*, ed. Stefan Leder (Wiesbaden: Harrassowitz, 1998), 79–129; and Andras Hamori, 'Tinkering with the Text: Two Variously Related Stories in the *Faraj Ba'd al-Shidda'*, *Story-telling in the Framework of Non-fictional Arabic Literature*, ed. Stefan Leder (Wiesbaden: Harrassowitz, 1998), 61–78.
24. Mustansir Mir has looked at the literary dimensions of this Qur'ānic story in 'The Qur'anic Story of Joseph: Plot, Themes, and Characters', *The Muslim World*, 126, 1 (1986), 1–15. However, he does not deal with the narrative paradigm implicit in the story.
25. A. J. Arberry, *The Koran Interpreted* (New York: MacMillan, 1955), I: 254.
26. Arberry, I: 266.

# Texts of the *Arabian Nights* and Ideological Variations

**ABOUBAKR CHRAÏBI**
**Translated from French by Natasha Romanova**

What are the texts of the *Arabian Nights* today? There are manuscripts which constitute the foundation of the work's existence and which inscribe it in the patrimony of medieval Arabic civilization, by their language as by the social, cultural and ideological codes in use. There are also editions, scholarly or popular, whose purpose is first of all to make the content of these manuscripts available to modern readers of Arabic. Finally, there are translations based on the former or the latter source. Their purpose is to make the *Nights* available in other languages and for other cultures. The most reasonable course of movement from one of these categories of text to another would be from manuscript to edition, then from manuscript or edition to translation. However, in this case things did not happen in this way. The status and shape of the collection of stories that came to be known as the *Arabian Nights* and also, no doubt, the specific circumstances determining the creation of each version of the *Nights* played a decisive role.

If we consider, for example, *The Story of Scheherazade*, *The Voyages of Sinbad the Sailor*, *Aladdin and his Magic Lamp* and *Ali Baba and the Forty Thieves*, which are doubtlessly the four most famous tales of the *Arabian Nights*, we notice that only the first two stories are recognized in the Arabic manuscript tradition as part of the collection. The two others, *Aladdin* and *Ali Baba*, at first presented a mystery as no edition, no manuscript includes either of them. There is no written Arabic source. Antoine Galland, it was discovered later, obtained it orally from a monk from Aleppo and was the first to introduce it in French at the beginning of the eighteenth century, in his famous translation of the *Arabian Nights*.[1] In this situation, to attempt to study *Ali Baba* from the point of view of Arabic literary tradition proves to be difficult: where is the Arabic text? If we find one, for example a version from Syrian folklore, the question is: what connection has it with the *Nights* stories as they existed in the medieval Arabic–Islamic world? To which the answer probably is: none. This difficulty does not only concern translations, but also and no less problematically editions and manuscripts that are clearly marked as the *Arabian Nights*. I am not speaking of fabricated editions, such as that made by Habicht (1825–1843) or the earliest of all, so-called Calcutta I (1814–1818) to which stories were added in order to reach the figure of one hundred nights per volume. I am referring, rather, to editions as respected and well-known as those of Būlāq (1835), Calcutta II (1839–1842), or Beirut, and of others that more or less reproduce them.

Short anecdotes about lovers who die of love, *Al-Mutawakkil and Maḥbūba*, *The False Madman*, *ʿUtba and Rayyā*, *The Lovers and the Lion* and others found in these editions clearly come almost without modification from classical Arabic literature, from the collections of *adab*.[2] They are representative of the literary genre that very early on gave birth to treatises such as the epistle of Al-Jāḥiẓ (d.255/868) or the book of Ibn Dāwūd (d. 294/909) and that was continued in the following centuries with al-Washshāʾ (d. 325/937), al-Kharāʾiṭī (d. 327/939), as-Sarrāj (d. 500/1106) and his very substantial collection of anecdotes of this genre, *Maṣāriʿ al-ʿushshāq*, and others later still. Therefore, a study of the ʿUdhrite lover or any other *khabar* of this kind inscribes itself first and fully in the tradition of learned literature and in reality engages very little with the *Arabian Nights*, except as one of the many additions that the collection was subject to in the later periods.

As for the manuscripts it suffices, for instance, to note the presence of the major romance of *Sayf Ibn Dhī Yazan* in MS Reinhardt (University of Strasbourg, Arabic, 4278–4281) to understand how foolish it would be to treat a story as representative of the *Arabian Nights* based on its presence in a given manuscript. *Sayf* is not a typical tale, and the same could be said of some other romances that are found in the same manuscript.

The significance of the choice of a text—a manuscript, an edition, or a particular translation—is therefore not negligible. Moreover, in the selected text the choice of a particular tale is equally important, as all do not have the same value and all are not representative of the *Arabian Nights* in the same way. For example, if one wishes to study the collection as it circulates and as it is perceived nowadays outside the Arab world, it would be indispensable to include *Aladdin* and *Ali Baba*. On the other hand, if one wishes to study the collection as an *organized* and *integrated* example of medieval Arabic literature, as I propose to do here, it seems reasonable to begin by having recourse to particular tales, the most characteristic and the most ancient, that marked its constitution as a book, for they alone might be able to give an idea of the initial unity that the collection represented.

Before becoming an enormous assemblage of tales, the collection did in fact circulate in written form as a complete book and not as a collection of popular or oral literature. This book, it is said, comes from Persia, where it was called *Hezār afsāne*, that is *alf khurāfa* (thousand tales). It was translated subsequently into Arabic, in all likelihood in the ninth-century or even as early as the eighth century. The summary of the frame narrative (the tale of a resourceful woman-storyteller) given by al-Masʿūdī or in even more detailed form by Ibn an-Nadīm could today be applied to different works: *One Thousand and One Nights*, but also *One Hundred and One Nights*.[3] The latter represents a more archaic form of the frame narrative but gives a list of tales very different from that of the *Arabian Nights*. So, what happened when the book entered the medieval Arabic–Islamic world? Evidently it was imitated, reworked and recast. Ibn an-Nadīm states this explicitly. It is also obvious, given the success of the former and the relatively discreet life of the latter, the *Arabian Nights* survived this reworking better. Nevertheless, both works preserve undeniable traces of their origins: Persian and, more distantly, Indian.

If we wish to recover the origins of the work and the process through which the book of *One Thousand and One Nights* established itself in Arab culture, we must obviously study some of the archaic layers, taking into account that there can be ancient tales, such as those of the lovers who die of love, that were introduced later. It is possible to restrict our scope to what constitutes the nucleus of the *Arabian Nights*. This nucleus is represented by around thirty stories (a kind of common trunk) that are present in the majority of the manuscripts. It could be identified in a large part of the incomplete so-called Galland manuscript (BNF, Arabic, 3609–3611, ed. by Muhsin Mahdi, Leiden, 1984). They are, roughly, the following tales: *The Two Kings Shahriyār and Shāhzamān* (the frame narrative and the inset tale); *The Merchant and the Genie* (plus three inset tales); *The Fisherman and the Genie* (plus three inset tales); *The Porter and the Three Ladies* (plus six inset tales); *The Three Apples* (plus one inset tale); and *The Hunchback* (plus eleven inset tales).

From this relatively large selection I have chosen two tales for detailed analysis: *The Ass, the Ox, the Farmer and his Wife* and *The Merchant and the Genie*. The first is situated before the beginning of the *Nights*; it is included in the frame narrative and is told to Scheherazade by her father the Grand Vizier. The second opens *The Thousand and One Nights* themselves; the first night of Scheherazade's narration begins with *The Merchant and the Genie*. Both tales have a very interesting history, as we shall see, and will help us to understand better the organization of the collection.

## 1. The Ass, the Ox, the Farmer, and his Wife

> A farmer who understands the speech of animals hears an ass advising an ox, who complains about having too much work, to pretend to be sick. The farmer then sends the ass to do the ox's work. To avoid the work the ass tells the ox that he has heard the master ordering that the ox be sent to the butcher: the news cures the ox immediately. The farmer's wife hears her husband laughing about this matter and wants to know the reason for his cheerfulness. He refuses to answer because he cannot, under pain of death, divulge what animal language reveals to him. She insists. Unable to resist, the farmer prepares to die. At this moment he hears his dog blaming the cock for being cheerful when their master is going to die. But the cock responds that the man is of little intelligence because he is unable to make one woman obey him, when he himself rules over fifty hens, and that the man should take a cane and thus make his wife die or bring her to her senses. The farmer makes use of this advice.[4]

From an external point of view this tale has two particularities: it is the only inset tale in which Scheherazade is not the teller of story but the one who listens to and receives it; on the other hand, it is situated before all other tales, and belongs to the frame narrative itself. What also attracts attention, from an internal point of view, is that knowledge of animal language is not a simple gift, because it is accompanied by an obligation to keep it a secret or face a threat of death in case of disclosure (and the question remains of how this death will happen?) This extraordinary knowledge evidently has its own history of which we are not told. I will begin by examining this particularity of the text, that is, by reconstructing as far as possible the internal coherence of the tale. In fact the text informs us: '*wa kāna yaʿrif bi-lughat al-bahāyim wa-l-ḥayawānāt, wa-s-sirr idhā fassarahu li-aḥad māt* [He knew the language of beasts and animals, and he kept his knowledge a secret, for if he were to tell anyone about it, he should die']. It is shown later that the secret to be kept is neither his knowledge of animal language nor the way he learned it.[5] He is simply not allowed to translate to another person what he alone hears: '*wa-akhāfumin as-sirr idhā buḥtu bihi fīmā yaqūluhu l-ḥayawānātu bi-lughatihim* [I am afraid to disclose the secret (and communicate) what animals say in their language].'[6] To put it briefly, whatever the situation and whatever the animal says he does not have the right to tell it to anyone else, otherwise he dies. But he can say that he understands animal language.

Our tale belongs in fact to the narrative tradition classified by students of folklore under the title of *The Animal Languages* (AT 670). Italo Calvino gives a Sicilian version in his *Fiabe italiane (Italian Folktales)*. An Algerian version can be found in the *Contes Maghrébins* collected recently by Nadine Delcourt and Naïma Louali-Raynal.[7] In all versions there is a section explaining more or less convincingly the acquisition of animal language and the obligation to keep that a secret. This section is absent from the *Arabian Nights*. One of the most ancient tales of the AT 670 type, to my knowledge, dates from the fifth century, and may even date back to the third century BC.[8] It is also the most coherent version. It comes from the same archaic source as the *Arabian Nights*, that is, from India. It is a *jâtaka*, an anecdote linked to one of the previous lives of Buddha. Here is its summary:

> King Senaka saves the life of the king of the nâga (a fabulous snake with magical powers), and after some adventures the nâga made the king the gift of a magical formula that allowed him to understand animal language. 'This *mantra*, great king', he added, 'is priceless. If you were to reveal it to anyone else, you would have to enter the flames and die.' Later in the text the king laughs at what different animals say. This attracts the attention of the queen, who learns about the existence of the mantra and asks to know it. The king prepares himself to give in and kill himself, but he is delivered in time by the intervention of Sakka, the king of the gods, who takes the appearance of a he-goat covering a she-goat (cf. cock and hens in the *Nights*). Following Sakka's advice, the king claims that in order to learn the mantra one has to submit to a ritual and receive a hundred lashes without complaining, but 'she had received only a couple of lashes when she started screaming, I do not care about this *mantra*.'

In this story there are several elements that could not have been accepted by other cultures, Christian or Muslim, without modification. The gift of understanding animal language is in fact related to snakes, and the Sicilian and Algerian tales conserved this element. More importantly, the particular threat hanging over the holder of the secret in the *jâtaka* is very difficult for other religious beliefs to contemplate: if he communicates to someone else the means of understanding the animal language, he has to sacrifice himself, to kill himself. Such a serious act could not be justified from a Muslim or Christian point of view. This part was thus either erased or replaced (in the Sicilian tale): we no longer know where the threat comes from. Another interesting point that allows us to understand better the wife's insistence is that she wants not only to satisfy her curiosity, but also to obtain and share a useful knowledge, the *mantra*, the magic formula that grants understanding of animal language, and that only the husband seems to have the right to possess. She wants to share this power. The sequence of events linked to the actions of the farmer and to the reaction of his wife in the *Nights* can thus be understood in the light of the *jâtaka*, which must be very close to the original version of the tale. As I have mentioned before, the tale originated in India, as did many components of the frame narrative, the story of Shahrayar and Scheherazade.

Now let us consider, from an external point of view, the function of this tale in the *Nights*: how does it influence the development of the narrative that frames it, what purpose does it serve? The Vizier tells it to his daughter at first, in order to convince her not to behave like the ass, who brings trouble onto himself, when he wants to help his neighbour. The story parallels that of Scheherazade, who wants to marry the king in order to save the other young women of the kingdom. Later, the story is meant to persuade her to obey her father for fear of a similarly severe punishment. Scheherazade's answer to this is: 'Nevertheless, it shall be as I have decided'.[9] The Vizier wants to use the tale (as it is used in *Kalīla and Dimna* for example) to communicate a certain rule of behaviour, a moral lesson that would have been understood by his daughter and immediately put into practice; but, obviously, the tale does not fulfil the function attributed to it. In this new context, the tale cannot support the argument.

Let us now consider the next story and its inset tales.

## 2. The Merchant and the Genie

The essence of the story consists of, on the one hand, the astonishing sequence of events involuntarily initiated by the merchant who provokes the death of a young genie and, on the other hand, the strange bargain made by the father of the genie and the three old men who offer to ransom the merchant's life by each telling an extraordinary story.[10]

The first part of the tale is characterized by unusual details of the narrative and by its dramatic qualities, these latter reappearing in the other tales of the *Nights*. From the point of view of detail, the motif of the 'fatal date stone' is rarely encountered in literature; no other version of it, to my knowledge, has been found. From the thematic point of view the death sentence imposed on the poor merchant for an insignificant act (throwing a date stone) strikes us as excessive, unjust and absolutely unexpected, and therefore shocking and interesting to tell, according to the antithetical principle: 'little causes, great effects'. From this perspective it can be classed with other tales of the *Nights*, such as *The Fisherman and the Genie* (also based on antithesis and injustice, the fisherman being condemned to death by the very person he had saved), *The Hunchback* (a piece of fish causes a death sentence for four innocent people); and, to a lesser degree, the *Porter and the Three Ladies* (because of an indiscreet question, several people are threatened with death), as well as *The Three Apples* (if he does not succeed in his investigation, Ja'far and forty Barmacides will be executed, and all, as we discover later, because of an apple). This thematic grouping does not seem accidental, the more so because we are talking here of the tales that are situated at the beginning of the book and are its most ancient components, the tales that constitute the archaic kernel of the *Arabian Nights*.

The question to be asked now is: why choose these tales? More specifically, why choose the first among them, *The Merchant and the Genie*? For the other tales that follow it present themselves as part of the same family, forming a thematic unity. In order to provide a satisfactory answer, I need to show that the two propositions that follow are acceptable: first, that the *Arabian Nights* was understood as a collection of *khurāfāt*; and secondly, that *The Merchant and the Genie* refers back to the eponymous story of Khurāfa.

The first point presents no difficulty: Ibn an-Nadīm cites the collection as one of '*kutub muṣannafa fī l-asmār wa-l-khurāfāt* [books composed about *asmār* and *khurāfāt* (sing. *khurāfa*)']. He goes on to say: *awwal man ṣannafa al-khurāfāt* [the first to have composed *khurāfāt*]'; then translates the title of the Persian book that lies at the origin of *The Thousand and One Nights*, the *Hezār afsāne*, as *one thousand khurāfa*. One could give many similar examples from the works of al-Mas'ūdī, at-Tawḥīdī and other authors. To sum up, the first proposition appears to be acceptable: *The Arabian Nights* was seen as a collection of *khurāfāt*.'[11]

At the beginning of the twentieth century,[12] D. B. Macdonald noticed the connection between *The Merchant and the Genie* and the story of Khurāfa, the term *khurāfāt* being derived from this story at the beginning of the twentieth century. What is this story? Khurāfa, a Bedouin, is captured in the desert by three genies who cannot decide whether to kill, enslave or free him. Three people appear, who tell an extraordinary story each in exchange for the liberation of Khurāfa.[13] In this plot we recognize the second part of the story of the merchant, whose life is saved in the same way. The points of divergence concern, on the one hand, the beginning of the story where *Khurāfa* is incoherent, because it is not clear why the genies want to do the hero harm (what has he done to them?), and on the other hand, the three inset stories that are not the same, except for the last which presents a few similarities. In both stories, in both *The Merchant and the Genie* and *Khurāfa*, the third man who comes to the rescue of the protagonist rides an animal that is none other than an adulterous wife transformed into a mule, and at the end of both tales the animal nods to attest that all that has been said is true.[14]

The common points concerning both structure (a man is ransomed with three stories) and detail (the desert, demonic creatures who act arbitrarily and an adulterous woman transformed into a mule) are sufficient to establish a close connection between *The Merchant and the Genie* and *Khurāfa*. Moreover, a double urge towards rationalization (justifying the aggressive behaviour of one or several genies toward the merchant) and normalization (offering the same type of character, all old men, all accompanied by a metamorphosed animal) seems to explain the passage from one tale to the other. Put together, these arguments appear sufficient to show that someone familiar with the story of *The Merchant and the Genie*, like Macdonald, will certainly see in it a version of the story of Khurāfa.

One can therefore argue, on the one hand, that *The Thousand and One Nights*, a book of *khurāfāt*, begins with a story referring back to the origins of the genre, that is to the story of Khurāfa, and on the other hand that the first and the most ancient stories of the *Nights* are united by the theme of injustice, the principle of 'little cause, great effects'. Giving unity to a newly compiled book and beginning it with an explanation of its subject matter are scholarly techniques, the work of an expert in Arabic philology (what is *khurāfa*?). Their presence shows that the *Arabian Nights* have been carefully reworked and rewritten after they made their entry into the medieval Arabic–Islamic world.

Another innovation that characterizes the group of tales introduced by *The Merchant and the Genie* is the role that these tales give to stories. Scheherazade, for example, uses stories to stall, to gain time. In the texts which have a clear Indian origin, such as *Kalīla and Dimna*, or certain other parts of the *Nights*, stories are used to support an argument (as the Vizier tried to do, or the second Qalandar or else to teach and transmit some sort of wisdom. Here stories appear as elements in an exchange. What is their value? It is the pleasure that they can bring. Who are the characters sensitive to this pleasure? Genies, demonic creatures or kings whose behaviour is unjust and tyrannical.

There are, however, other stories that are addressed not to demons but to God, and that have a structure very similar to that of *The Merchant and the Genie*. I am speaking of the Prophetic Tradition, Hadith, as it can be found for example in the *Al-faraj baʿd ash-shidda* [*After trials comes relief*] by at-Tanūkhī (d. 384/994). Here is its summary:

> Three men of the tribe of Israel are caught by a violent storm and take shelter in a cave. A huge stone falls and blocks the exit. After a discussion, they decide each to recount their best deed, invoking God and asking Him to rescue them. After the first story (chastity) the stone moves by one third; after the second (filial respect), it moves by another third; after the last (respect of others' goods and property) the stone moves away completely and the passage is free.[15]

It is interesting to note, for example, that in this anecdote, as in the story of Khurāfa, the misfortune that befalls the protagonists appears as random (the genies capture Khurāfa for no reason; the stone just falls), there is no motivation for the fateful events. Even more remarkable is the similarity of the function of the narratives. The three old men and the three Israelites use their tales to the same purpose. They tell their tales in the hope of reward from their audience: in exchange for a wage, a service (freeing the merchant; moving the stone). They are 'narrateurs à rétribution'.[16]

Of course, the audience being different, the narrators do not stress the same aspects of the text. The three old men hope to save another man, and to do so they offer extraordinary tales that are of particular interest for the audience, and more exactly represent a source of *pleasure*. Those who appreciate this 'pleasure of the text' are morally deficient characters, opposed to the good: genies, demons and tyrants. The three Israelites, however, do not offer the pleasure of the text but underline the *ethical aspect* of the text, as, on order to achieve their purpose (that is to be able to leave the cave) they tell about their most virtuous actions. It is not to a demon but to God that they appeal, and God cannot be impressed by what brings pleasure but by good deeds. In other words, 'pleasure to a demon, virtue to God'.

*The Merchant and the Genie*, as well as other tales, such as *The Porter* and *The Hunchback*, appears to be part of a cultural and social system based on the ideology of barter, of exchange. The story is a product that is immediately cashed in, like any other action that calls forth remuneration: reward if it is good, punishment if it is bad. By contrast, the Vizier who tried to convince his daughter using the story of *The Farmer, the Ass and the Ox* did not use it in this way. This tale, as we saw earlier, belongs to the tradition of *Kalīla and Dimna* and probably that of the book of *Hezār afsāne* before its reworking. Rather than obtaining a reward or provoking an immediate and definitive action, the Vizier's arguments seek to bring his daughter to a progressive understanding of truth, according to an ideology that favours gradual change through an infinity of intermediate stages.

It appears that those who reorganized the *Arabian Nights* and modified them were not very convinced by this 'long-term' function of the tale. Those tales that use stories for the purpose of argumentation that were retained or reinserted in the collection, such as that of the second Qalandar or of the Vizier, result in failure. This means that the most effective narrators, such as the three old men, are those who obtain profit from their actions and satisfy immediately the demon, God or the pleasure of the audience.

When one compares the texts of *The Thousand and One Nights* one comes to two conclusions: first, they are constructed around a common part, a kernel of stories, which is extremely old. More importantly, starting from the Persian book *Hezār afsāne* (*Thousand Tales*), one composed another book, giving it a new title (*The Thousand and One Nights*), new contents (Khurāfa) and a 'commercial' ideological orientation. This currently dominant ideological orientation, similar to the Judeo–Christian or Muslim model, is based on a final exchange (good deeds are exchanged for paradise; good stories are exchanged for life) and not on an argumentation or a long training during several successive lives, according to the Buddhist model. Secondly, the technique used in this new composition is a literary one (beginning a book of *khurāfāt* with the story of Khurāfa). More importantly, the material and language used, and the evolution of different manuscripts show that the *Nights* belonged to a much vaster middle literature (not popular or oral) that uses literary material as well as folklore (which is between the two), and that brings together hundreds of other similar manuscripts. This middle literature is a genre that has its own rules of composition. The study of *Thousand and One Nights*, *The Hundred and One Nights* or other collections of *Astonishing Stories and Surprising Tales* will, in the future, undoubtedly require better understanding of these rules of compositions, their mode of production and reception, and therefore this 'middle genre' to which all these books belong.

## Notes

1. M. Mahdi, *The Thousand and One Nights*, vol. 3, Leiden, 1995, pp. 32–3.
2. V. Chauvin, *Bibliographie des ouvrages arabes ou relatifs aux Arabes publiés dans l'Europe Chrétienne de 1810 à 1885*, 12 vols, Liège, 1892–1922, vol. 5, pp. 105, 111, 115, 116–17.
3. See www.univ-tours.fr/arabe, section *Mille et une nuits*, article 'Témoignages des auteurs arabes'.
4. V. Chauvin, *Bibliographie* ..., vol. 5, pp. 179–80.
5. M. Mahdi, *Alf layla wa-layla min uṣūlihā al-ʿarabiyya al-ūlā*, Leiden, 1984, p. 67.
6. M. Mahdi, *Alf layla* ..., p. 69.
7. Anti Aarne & Stith Thompson, *The Types of the Folktale*, Helsinki, 1964, no. 670: I owe this important information to Ulrich Marzolph; *Italian Folktales*, selected and retold by Italo Calvino, tr. by George Martin, New York, 1980, pp. 639–41; *Contes maghrébins en situation interculturelle*, ed. by Nadine Delcourt & Naïma Louali-Raynal, Karthala, Paris, 1995, pp. 43–6.
8. *Choix de Jâtaka, extraits des Vies antérieures du Bouddha*, trans. from Pali into French by Ginette Terral, Coll. UNESCO, Gallimard, 1958, p. 7 for the dating, and pp. 65–71 for the history of king Senaka; an equally ancient witness, of the second century, indicates the acquisition of animal language through the ingestion of the heart or the liver of a snake *S* by the Arabs: '(*S*) la science selon laquelle, selon la manière des Arabes, (Apollonios) parvint à entendre le language des animaux. Il l'apprit au cours de son voyage à travers ces populations arabes (*S*) Car c'est une pratique commune chez les Arabes d'écouter ce que prédisent les oiseaux, tels les devins. Ils acquièrent l'intelligence du langage des bêtes en se nourissant, les uns disent du cœur, les autres disent du foie des serpents'. Philostrate, *Vie d'Apollonios de Tyane*, trans. by Pierre Grimal, in Romans grecs et latins, Gallimard, Bibliothèque de la Pléiade, Paris, 1958, p. 1049, 1.20.
9. *Les Mille et une nuits*, trans. by J.E. Bencheikh & A. Miquel, vol. 1, Paris, 1991, p. 46.
10. M. Mahdi, *Alf layla* ... pp. 72–86 and 689–701; Būlāq edition, I, pp. 6–10; V. Chauvin, *Bibliographie* vol. 6, pp. 22–3.
11. Ibn an-Nadīm, *al-Fihrist* ed. by Y. A. aṭ-Ṭawīl, index by A. Shams ad-Dīn, Beirut, 1996, p. 475. Also see www.univ-tours.fr/arabe, section *Mille et une nuits*, article 'Témoignages des auteurs arabes'.
12. D.B. Macdonald, 'The Earlier History of *The Arabian Nights*', in *JRAS*, 1924, pp. 353–97, particularly pp. 372–5.
13. Al-Mufaḍḍal Ibn Salama, *Kitāb al-fākhir*, ed. by C.A. Storey, Leiden, 1915, entry 'ḥadīth Khurāfa'; al-Ḥarīrī *Maqāmāt*, sharḥ ash-Sharīshī, 4, al-Maktabat ash-Shaʿbiyya, Cairo, 1979, particularly vol. 1, p.91, in 'al-maqāma ar-rābiʿa ad-dimyāṭiyya'.
14. I owe this observation to Claude Bremont.

15. At-Tanūkhī, *Kitāb al-faraj baʿda ash-shidda*, ed. by ʿAbbūd ash-Shāljī, 5 vols, Beirut, 1978, vol. 1, pp. 125–8; *Qiṣaṣ al-ʿArab*, ed. by M. Jād al-Mawlā, A. M. al-Bijāwī and M. Abū al-Faḍl Ibrāhīm, 4 vols, Cairo, 1963, p. 299 (after Majmaʿ al-amthāl by al-Maydānī).
16. See A. Chraïbi, «Les à-côtés du récit ou l'enchâssement à l'orientale» in *Poétique*, no. 117, 1999, pp. 1–15, especially pp. 5–6.

# A Caliph and his Public Relations

JULIA BRAY

A recent book (1995) by Marc Zvi Brettler, *The Creation of History in Ancient Israel*, has been given a most misleading blurb by its publisher. Is the Old Testament true? it screams, and supplies a sensational answer: '[This study] demonstrates how the modern historian ... can start to piece together the history of ancient Israel using the Hebrew Bible as a source.' This makes the book sound like a literalist reading of the Old Testament—a handbook for treasure seekers or a charter for fundamentalists. In fact, it is nothing of the sort. Brettler picks his way discriminatingly through a range of discussions of the nature of historiography; and as a text scholar fully aware that in most cultures what is offered up as history is something other than the bare recording of data, he works from the position that the Hebrew Old Testament must be approached through ideological analysis.[1] This type of approach, he argues persuasively, gives a closer and fuller account of the significant components of an uncorroborated historical narrative than does formal literary analysis. In seeking to identify functional structures, it will not enable us, any more than literary analysis does, to determine where the kernel of factual truth, if any, lies; but it may make it possible to frame controlled hypotheses about the *Sitz im Leben* of an ostensibly historical text—its probable purpose and the kind of milieu in or for which it was produced—and in some cases to discover to what extent a historian is 'creating' history rather than recording it. Brettler goes on to show

how the author of the Book of Chronicles 'radically reshaped'[2] and even changed his sources—that is, earlier biblical narratives—'by introducing certain *patterns* of history [my emphasis] for ideological reasons: his [the Chronicler's] new history emphasises issues of collective significance, such as the continuity between the Second Temple, the First Temple and the Tabernacle, and the legitimacy of David'.[3] Similarly, the Deuteronomist can be shown to have 'restructure[d] his sources, ... fill[ed] them out, and, if necessary, ... modif[ied] them radically', all this, ironically, 'within a work that emphasizes that the Israelite community should neither add to nor subtract from YHWH's teaching.'[4] The implication of this is that ideological analysis can be a genuine hermeneutic tool: properly conducted, it can uncover inconsistencies and discover the unexpected.

Brettler is dealing with unidentifiable authors who can be fitted only into the broadest of time-frames. The purported actors in these shadowy writers' narratives may or may not be mythical. Given the nature of his sources, genuinely retrievable history therefore consists, for Brettler, not in the subjects of the historical narratives, the originators of alleged events and institutions of which there is no independent record, but in the attitudes that historians adopt towards them. Historical content, in this sort of case, is to be identified not in a topic, but in how it is treated. It may be useful to compare this kind of strong definition of ideological historical content with a weak definition of factual historical content such as we find in a contribution to a volume which links up neatly with the *Thousand and One Nights* theme. The volume in question is *The Thousand and One Nights in Arabic Literature and Society*,[5] and the contribution is Muhsin Mahdi's article 'From history to fiction: the tale told by the king's steward in *The Thousand and One Nights*'.[6] This posits the fourteenth-century *Nights* version of the steward's tale as fiction, and its prototype, set in the Baghdad of the first decades of the tenth century AD (fourth century AH) and committed to writing in the latter half of the tenth century, as history, on the basis that the prototype has historically identifiable narrators in its frame and that the story proper contains references to contemporary landmarks and to some real personages.

The first part of this article will take Mahdi's comparison further and will question his notion of factual historicity. In comparing the two versions of the tale, the *Nights* version and its tenth-century prototype, I shall not follow Brettler's approach as a blueprint, for it is not intended as such, dealing as it does with a group of texts which present very particular problems of authorship and contextualisation. Brettler's general approach to comparing sources on the basis of the way they treat common themes is, however, broadly applicable to medieval Arabic writings, which are characterized to a very high degree by the repetition and reshaping of earlier narratives and by their recombination in new patterns and series in such a way as to emphasize certain themes which, one may suppose, seem particularly significant to the reorganiser. I will assume that it is this latter aspect—selection, patterning and sequence or context—that serves to carry ideological content, and in the second half of the article I will look at the broader setting of the prototype of the *Nights* tale and the themes there emphasized, and compare these with the use made of the same or similar materials by a later author. I use the term 'author' with the familiar caveat that, whether or not they invoke named sources for their materials, medieval Arabic writers usually present themselves as mere transmitters or editors, not as producers of new material. The second half of the article also explores the possibility that the actual authorship, the production of the ideological message of this corpus of stories, may in fact originate with the hero of the stories, the ʿAbbasid caliph al-Muʿtaḍid, and may form part of a caliphal propaganda programme.

My conclusion is that it does not, but the fact that our 'authors' suggest that it does has implications for our understanding of their own ideologies.

The *Nights* version of the tale discussed by Mahdi, usually known to English readers as 'The Steward's Tale', is set in the late second/eighth century, or rather in legendary time, in the reign of the mighty Hārūn al-Rashīd and his high-born consort Zubayda. It opens with a description of a Qur'ān recitation followed by a meal, at which one of the guests refuses to eat a certain dish (called *zīrbāja*, translated by Husain Haddawy as 'ragout spiced with cumin') and then reluctantly consents, complaining that 'If I must eat, then I will first have to wash my hands forty times with soap, forty times with potash, and forty times with galingale, all in all one hundred and twenty times'.[7] As he eats, clumsily, 'his hand and indeed his whole body ... shaking', it is revealed that his thumbs are missing. They have been cut off, and so too have his big toes, as he shows his fellow-guests; and he goes on to explain how this came about. His injuries mark the final stage of his prolonged and perilous courtship, and are the emblem of his wife's authority over him.

The protoype of the story is found in al-Muḥassin ibn ʿAlī al-Tanūkhī (329–384/940–994), *al-Faraj baʿd al-Shidda*,[8] an anthology which contains many stories, themes and techniques which later resurface, with modifications, in the *Nights*. A comparison between stories common to the two works not only highlights some of the fantastic features of the *Nights* but also brings out what seem to be deliberately structured thematic patterns in the *Faraj* stories, which need to be taken into account in any evaluation of their historical content.

The two versions of the story considered here are very close, in outline and even in small details, but there are equally significant differences. One difference is that the *Faraj* version is set in a period close to al-Tanūkhī's own time, indeed within living memory for some of his readers, in the reign of the weak caliph al-Muqtadir (reigned 295–320/908–932). Another is that in the *Faraj* version it is not the caliph's wife, but his mother (herself a former slave, as al-Tanūkhī's readers would have known) who helps her favourite slave girl smuggle the poor young merchant with whom she has fallen in love into the palace after she has repeatedly tested his devotion by taking away his most expensive goods without either paying for them or revealing her identity. So far, all is plausibly in keeping with historical fact: the caliph's wife is not mentioned because the Queen Mother dominated her son to the exclusion of his other women. She was also notorious for surrounding herself with female cronies, and it is not improbable that her favourites would have had free rein to roam the shops of Baghdad in search of luxuries for her or for themselves. The development of the story is, however, posited on qualities—benevolence and a sense of decorum—for which the Queen Mother was less well known than for her wilfulness. Her good nature, and its pervasive influence, being taken as givens, the power play between women and men is subtler and less claustrophobic than in the *Nights*, and although both the hero and the caliph are manipulated by women, appearances are preserved: having once gained the approval of the Queen Mother after being rather ignominiously conveyed to her in a box, the hero is reimbursed by her and his suit is openly acknowledged, and she makes the caliph conduct his betrothal in public audience instead of usurping his prerogative and conducting it herself inside the palace, as Zubayda does in the *Nights*.

A further significant difference is that though both the *Nights* and the *Faraj* versions are stories of mystery, suspense and fear, the elements are not distributed in the same way nor with the same emphasis. In the *Nights* version, dread overshadows the anticipated happy ending when the young merchant's beloved turns on him in the marriage bed just as he has embraced her. The sole object of real fear in the *Faraj* version is the caliph who, in his capacity as a man and the figurehead of the state, must be kept from discovering that his harem has been penetrated. The differences affect the frame as well as the story embedded with in it; thus the frame of al-Tanūkhī's version is intriguing, but not disturbing: the hero merely insists on washing his hands forty times but he does not lack his thumbs, cut off by his bride in the *Nights* version as a punishment for eating *zīrbāja* on his wedding day without washing afterwards. Unlike the *Nights* version, this is not a tale of cruel sexual dominance, and there is no expectation of horror in its unfolding (contrast the *Nights* hero's reminiscent and premonitory trembling). The *Nights* makes the slave heroine behave against all normal expectation: after whipping the hero for his sin 'on my back and buttocks until her arm was tired', threatening to send him to the chief of police to have his hand cut off, and leaving him in suspense for ten days, 'When the lady finally came in, she looked at me and said ... "I will not make peace with you until I punish you ..." Then crying out to the girls, who surrounded me and bound me, she took out a sharp blade and, coming up to me, cut off my thumbs.'[9] Al-Tanūkhī's heroine is, on the contrary, comically but predictably feminine according to the conventions of her period—so refined that, as soon as she smells *zīrbāja* on her husband's kiss, 'she promptly kicked me, toppling me off the bridal throne' (an unrefined dig at the contemporary craze for *ẓarf*, exquisiteness of manners and sentiment). Romantic as she is, she is easily won over by her groom's promise to wash forty times in future, and seals their reconciliation by sitting down to eat with him. True, she holds the purse-strings of the household; but this is a male fantasy about women of a quite different sort from that of the *Nights* version. Marriage makes the hero rich; but far from being his wife's mutilated prisoner, he fathers sons on her and goes back into the outside world where, in obedience to his father's dying wish and his own conscience, he makes his own way and becomes a respected merchant.[10]

I think that, like most modern readers, the original audience of the *Faraj* story would have seen this elaborate tale of steadfast love rewarded with a perfectly happy ending (and with proper masculine social standing being restored to the hero) as a story of a familiar literary type, which uses factual details, such as local landmarks and contemporary turns of phrase or sentiment, for purposes of verisimilitude and emotional truth. Mahdi none the less refers to it as a historical report or historical account.[11] It certainly draws on fact, to the extent that in a variety of historical and biographical sources we find passing references, which would repay study, to men who bettered themselves by marrying palace women. Nevertheless, the bizarre details (the hand-washing, the journey in the box) would, if anything, have strained credulity less than the idea of a palace connection leading to an independent, trouble-free career. If its grounding in certain selected and improved aspects of reality is enough to make the *Faraj* story broadly plausible, it is not enough to stop one noticing that it is a rags-to-riches romance which can be viewed not only, in its action, as a tale of love and adventure, the heading under which al-Tanūkhī himself classes it, but also, in its outcome, as a fable of social and political harmony in which the love interest has the function of uniting the palace and the people. Mahdi, however, does not deconstruct the story's message, which is more wishful than realistic (be honest and faithful and work hard, as the young man does, and the powers that be will protect you—elsewhere, al-Tanūkhī complains bitterly that, in his own times, the ruling classes are mean and effort goes unrewarded[12]), nor does he ask why what is ultimately the star role in it should have been given to a problematic historical personage, the mother of the caliph al-Muqtadir, who brings about the happy ending but who, in al-Tanūkhī's time, was not yet generally regarded as the model of a public benefactor as was the Zubayda of the *Nights* version.

Mahdi is not the only person to have treated this story as historical. Two centuries after al-Tanūkhī, and also in Baghdad, the great scholar and preacher Ibn al-Jawzī (d.597/1201), an active participant in the Sunnī revival—a project to restore the caliph to an active role and unite all Muslims in sound belief and social solidarity, which had been gaining in coherence and momentum over the previous century or so—incorporated al-Tanūkhī's version of the story of the merchant and his courtship into his vast history, *al-Muntaẓam*, as part of his obituary of the mother of al-Muqtadir under the year 321 AH.[13] *Al-Muntaẓam* is, it seems to me, evidently intended as a vehicle of Sunnī revival[14] and it appeals to a broad constituency rather as did Ibn al-Jawzī's mass sermons, which were by no means simple-minded harangues, but literary exercises aimed at the congregation's hearts and imaginations.[15] Al-Muqtadir's mother, this obituary implies, was a virtuous and tragic figure, tortured by her son's successor to make her disgorge her wealth which, the story of her slave girl's love affair suggests, she employed to bring about the happiness of the people, so linking the caliph's household to ordinary Muslims in benevolence and gratitude and in a healthy social order—an idea very applicable to the kind of caliphate that Ibn al-Jawzī was himself trying to help build. Yet the Queen Mother had been regarded much more equivocally by sources closer to her in date, often as an example of the baneful influence of women on government. Ibn al-Jawzī's remodelling of her image to convey a positive meaning—a coherent and functional ideological vision—is paralleled elsewhere in *al-Muntaẓam*, for example in his portrait of Hārūn al-Rashīd. This is based on materials in a very different type of earlier source, the largely unromantic, politically orientated 'History' (*Taʾrīkh al-Rusul wa 'l-Mulūk*) of al-Ṭabarī (died 314/923); but it eliminates the ambiguities inherent in al-Ṭabarī's juxtaposed and often conflicting accounts, presenting Hārūn not as a man of evident weaknesses with greatness thrust upon him but instead as a figure of simple, sincere faith, a devotee of humble ascetics, whose ruling passion is the desire to be a worthy caliph and to defend orthodoxy.[16] This is a trenchant simplification, yet it is closely modelled on the concluding passages of al-Ṭabarī's account and shows a clear interpretative intent.[17]

Even when he fails to name them, Ibn al-Jawzī usually preserves a certain transparency towards his sources, as in the last-mentioned case; and one example in particular of a portrait of a caliph composed by him seems to offer the tantalizing possibility of uncovering layers of ideology in a range of different sources, ending with an ideological programme which may, perhaps, originate with the caliph himself. The caliph al-Muʿtaḍid (279–89/892–902) and the image of him presented in the Arabic sources has been the object of two recently-published studies, one by Fedwa Malti-Douglas[18] and another by Hugh Kennedy.[19] Kennedy deals with contemporary sources for al-Muʿtaḍid's military career before he came to the throne; Malti-Douglas discusses aspects of his image as ruler in later sources. Kennedy suggests that al-Muʿtaḍid may himself have commissioned a chronicle of the five-year campaign which he and his father led against a long drawn-out rebellion of black agricultural slaves (the Zanj) and Shiʿite sympathisers in southern Iraq, his aim in doing so being, ultimately, to legitimate his own dubious claim to the caliphate.[20] In other words, Kennedy singles out caliphal propaganda as an intrinsic part of the historical content of the contemporary sources, which are preserved in fragmentary form in al-Ṭabarī's 'History'. Malti-Douglas is concerned with image-making as a form of retrospective historical thought, and concludes: 'Different writers, different sources, present different images of al-Muʿtaḍid.

One almost feels at times as if they are carrying on a debate about the nature of this caliph and of caliphal authority in general.'[21] One would dearly like to see if it is possible to tie the two ends of the process together: the caliph's promotion of his own image, and later writers' use of images of him as a means of reflecting upon the exercise of power. Ibn al-Jawzī's access to early sources, together with the ardour of his search for Sunnī heroes and his sensitivity to any potentially useful propaganda content, may offer one line of approach.[22]

Before looking at the image of al-Muʿtaḍid which *al-Muntaẓam* promotes, it should be noted that Ibn al-Jawzī, once he has reached the post-Prophetic period, sticks firmly to an annalistic scheme consisting of: main events of each year, followed by obituaries of notable persons (preponderantly persons of religious standing or moral distinction) who died during that year.[23] New caliphal reigns are prefixed to the events/obituaries scheme; they open with a summary of the caliph's characteristics and rule and are followed by anecdotes in illustration of his character. These serve to colour the reader's understanding of the subsequent events of his reign (the reverse of the procedure employed by al-Ṭabarī, whose regnal portraits follow his chronicle of each reign). Dated events in a caliph's life come under the year in which they occurred, and do not form part of the reign-and-character summary. Thus details of al-Muʿtaḍid's military activities before and after he became caliph do not form part of Ibn al-Jawzī's free-standing portrait of him, which is what we are concerned with here.[24]

Ibn al-Jawzī's introductory description of al-Muʿtaḍid is a dry listing of his parentage, date and place of birth and accession, physique, the motto on his signet ring and of the names and functions of his chief officers of state. It ends with brief praise of the energy and experience he brought to a weakened and bankrupt caliphate, and with a four-line accession poem, written by his cousin, Ibn al-Muʿtazz.[25] This poem appears routine, but in fact its last line is the key to the series of anecdotes that follow: 'You have brought peace of mind to all, and security to those who went in fear', it says.[26] The anecdotes go on to show how.

The anecdotes are not anchored to any particular time. They illustrate essential characteristics of the caliph, and relationships between the caliph and his advisers. They centre on a limited number of themes and return to these themes several times, adding an element of progression. Thus the series opens with Ibn al-Muʿtazz's poem proclaiming the caliph's care for his people and closes with a second poem, also by Ibn al-Muʿtazz, this time an elegy on the death of the caliph's beloved slave girl,[27] following a poem on her by al-Muʿtaḍid himself. The caliph's mourning displays both his tender side, his care for one particular person and his self-control: he puts aside his grief when gently reprimanded by his vizier.

There is a similar symmetry and progression between the first anecdote in the series and the two which precede the closing poem. In the opening anecdote, which Ibn al-Jawzī credits to al-Tanūkhī via his son ʿAlī, al-Muʿtaḍid goes hunting, taking some soldiers with him.[28] He hears a watchman cry out, and has him summoned: the man complains that some of the soldiers have stolen cucumbers (*qiththāʾ*) from his field. The caliph immediately has the soldiers imprisoned and next day has their heads cut off in the same field. Later, he asks the courtier ʿAbd Allāh Ibn Ḥamdūn whether he is popular with the people. Reluctantly, Ibn Ḥamdūn admits that they deplore his bloodthirstiness. The caliph justifies himself: since becoming caliph, he has never spilt blood unlawfully. The men he had executed were not the soldiers at all but a group of robbers. He imprisoned the soldiers to warn them against the slightest misbehaviour. Ibn Ḥamdūn now prompts him to repair his image. How, he asks, are the people to know what the caliph really did and why? The caliph reasons out the necessary steps for himself. He releases the soldiers, after briefing them so as to make sure that they will spread the true version of events.

In symmetry with this story, which shows the caliph learning his craft as ruler and discovering, under the guidance of a courtier, how to apply the common touch effectively, is a variant at the end of the anecdote sequence.[29] Here, the caliph orders a black man to have his head cut off for stealing a bunch of unripe dates, then turns to his companions and says: 'Do you know what the people say/will say? They will say no-one in the world is harder-hearted than this caliph, for the Prophet said: "There shall be no cutting off of hands for fruit or dates"[30]—still less any cutting off of heads.' He then explains that the black man was one of the Zanj rebels whom he and his father fought. He was given a safe-conduct, but betrayed his trust and murderously attacked a man. Al-Muʿtaḍid swore then and there that he should one day pay the penalty, and has now fulfilled his oath and his duty. Immediately following this is an account of how a group of men are denounced to al-Muʿtaḍid's vizier for seditious talk. The vizier advises that some should be hanged and others burnt. The caliph is revolted by his cruelty which, he says, 'has cooled the flames of my anger'. He continues by giving the vizier a lesson both in political theory and in practical statecraft: 'Do you not know that the people *(al-raʿiyya)* are given in trust to their ruler *(sulṭān)*, who will be called upon by God to answer for them? And do you not know that none of the people say this kind of thing unless driven to it by injustice or misfortune to themselves or their fellows? Enquire into their circumstances. Let those who are poor be given money from the treasury, and frighten only those whom this makes insolent.' In these stories the caliph renders justice confidently and without recourse to stratagems. He will have justice done whether the people approve or not, and whether or not his vizier likes it.

All this is very noble, exemplary, and indeed almost impersonal. However, at the heart of Ibn al-Jawzī's portrait are two long anecdotes in which al-Muʿtaḍid cultivates and manipulates his gift of the common touch. Ibn al-Jawzī acknowledges 'al-Muḥassin', i.e. al-Tanūkhī, as his source for both of them. In both, the elements of mystification, suspense and surprise which are seen in miniature in some of the examples just described, are greatly developed. The very plots of the anecdotes, the elaborateness with which details are spun out and the neatness with which they suddenly lock together, impress themselves on the reader as a kind of projection of the ruler's subtle mind and command of the situation.

The two stories are probably too well-known to need retelling here in full. In the second, a merchant vainly tries to recover a very large sum of money owed to him by one of the caliph's military commanders.[31] Even the vizier can do nothing for him, and in desperation he is considering appealing to the caliph himself when a friend offers to help. He takes him to meet an old tailor in the market and tells him his story. The merchant is terrified that this will expose him to the vengeance of the commander, but the tailor calmly goes with the two men to the commander's house and arranges terms of payment. The old tailor is, in fact, the caliph's eyes and ears, directly charged by him to send him a secret signal whenever he sees any evil-doing, great or petty, ever since the time he saved a woman from a wicked Turkish soldier by giving the call to prayer at the wrong time, which instantly alerted the vigilant caliph. There are two significant aspects to this story. One is the homely human touch. The woman's husband had sworn to divorce her if she spent a night away from home; the untimely call to prayer saves her marriage. The other is the military theme. The caliph has the soldier hideously tortured and killed; the story spreads throughout the army and thereafter all the army, great and small, go in fear of the tailor and do his bidding.

This story depicts an ideal order in which the military are obedient to the humblest of civilians, and the caliph too makes himself obedient to the pious tailor. It is for the tailor to tell the caliph, through the call to prayer, whether he needs to exercise his might; but thanks to the fear he has instilled, this never again proves necessary.

The story immediately before this one shows the caliph manipulating rather than honouring a man of the people. He is relaxing with his courtiers but suddenly jumps up, puts on his robes and seizes his caliphal spear as a poor old man is dragged in.[32] The caliph scowls horribly at him and asks: 'Are you the draper who said what you said yesterday?' The old man faints with terror, and when he has recovered, the caliph continues: 'How dare you say in your souk that the Muslims have no-one to take care of them? Where then am I? I have no other concern!' In fact the old man had merely been grumbling about the *muḥtasib*, a petty official whose job was to supervise fair trading and who had evidently failed in his duties. The caliph promises to put matters to rights and sends the old man away. His courtiers are amazed that he should trouble himself with such trivialities, 'all for the sake of a phrase commonly used by the vulgar, who do not even assign it any particular meaning'; but al-Muʿtaḍid explains (I use D. S. Margoliouth's translation of the version in al-Tanūkhī's *Nishwār al-Muḥāḍara*, cut to fit the variants/omissions in *al-Muntaẓam*):[33] 'You do not know what may be the consequences of such a saying. If that sort of thing circulates among the people … they are emboldened to repeat it … such a thing easily instils disaffection … The most effective way of dealing with such a case is to stop the evil at its source.' After this confrontation, the draper, says al-Muʿtaḍid, will spread and exaggerate the story of the caliph's omniscience and justice, and everyone will be convinced that the caliph watches over great and small.

Clearly, this story is the twin of the story of the tailor and the call to prayer, except that it takes an opposite view of the social order. Here it is the people, not the military, who need to be controlled, and the representative of the people who is the caliph's tool is not the caliph's voice of conscience but his dupe.

In its original version in al-Tanūkhī's *Nishwār*, this story is considerably more cynical. The old draper is dragged in while the caliph is in the middle of a drinking session; the caliph goes back to drinking once he has dealt with him and has significantly more to say about his technique of impressing the popular imagination. But does this earlier version, which was in circulation a generation or so after his reign, bring us closer to the real al-Muʿtaḍid and his statecraft, perhaps even to being able to say that he developed a deliberate policy of propagating such myths about himself? Al-Ṭabarī, who was alive during the reign of al-Muʿtaḍid, records no myths of this kind about him as ruler, only, as Kennedy notes, the suggestion that the war against the Zanj in which he took part before he became caliph was a holy war (al-Tanūkhī says nothing about this, but it is picked up by Ibn al-Jawzī).[34] Stories of this kind are not to be found either in al-Masʿūdī, a generation later. Most notably absent from al-Masʿūdī, who elsewhere makes heavy use of symbolic motifs and premonitory dreams, are al-Muʿtaḍid's premonitions, recorded by al-Tanūkhī, of the disasters threatened by the Daylamites, who were to subjugate the caliphs within the next forty or so years, and by the improvident character of his son al-Muqtadir, who was ultimately to succeed him and is credited with having caused the ruin of his dynasty.[35] Absent too are the veridical dreams in which a heavenly voice identifies to al-Muʿtaḍid the perpetrators of as yet unsuspected crimes and enables him to enforce what may truly be called divine justice.[36]

This complex of motifs is, however, central to Ibn al-Jawzī's portrait of al-Muʿtaḍid, and figures prominently in the material on al-Muʿtaḍid found in Ibn al-Jawzī's main source for it, the writings of al-Tanūkhī. Ibn al-Jawzī plainly made his selection from them in such a way as to be able to present an unblemished picture of the caliph; but occasionally we get a glimpse of other considerations guiding his choice. Al-Tanūkhī's alleged eyewitness sources for such stories are, of course, contemporaries of the caliph, chiefly courtiers and statesmen who really existed, but some of his sources are humbler. The story of the draper is immediately followed, in al-Tanūkhī's *Nishwār*, by an eyewitness report, told to him by the aged bailiff of his own paternal great-uncle, with whom he was on close terms, of how al-Muʿtaḍid meted out summary punishment to soldiers who had stolen some melons from him when he was on his way to market. The bailiff was then a young man and al-Muʿtaḍid was still only a young soldier.[37] This story gains in credibility, for al-Tanūkhī if not for us, by virtue of the family link and because it is told by an unsophisticated old man who only learned after the event that the author of this exemplary justice was no ordinary general. It is evidently a foreshadowing of the story of the stolen cucumbers, which follows it in the *Nishwār*,[38] and which Ibn al-Jawzī preferred, probably because it is more dramatic, has more themes in common with the other anecdotes selected by him, and is attributed to a historical witness famous enough for most of his readers to have heard of him, Ibn Ḥamdūn, a member of a dynasty of court companions and purveyors of caliphal anecdotes.

Two centuries later than al-Tanūkhī Ibn al-Jawzī seized upon such tales as perfect illustrations of his ideal of an orthodox caliph connected to his people by his obedience to the divine requirement that he watch over his flock and deal out justice to all. This was an ideal favoured by the mainstream religious thought and by the political developments of his day, and which he had reason to believe might be realised in the flesh. In al-Tanūkhī's time, however, the idea of the caliph as being in a workaday sense a nexus between God and his people was new.[39] It was not a reflection either of current political realities or of earlier caliphal political programmes. The picture of al-Muʿtaḍid as embodying godly rule reaching out to all the people, expressed ironically on occasion, but always with a straightforward appeal to the imagination, seems to be a piece of image-making which pleased al-Tanūkhī because it contrasted with what he saw as contemporary decadence: poor leadership, resulting in debased values and a dislocation of the social order.[40] This myth of al-Muʿtaḍid was probably inspired by eyewitness accounts of his energy and eye for detail (which gave rise also to tales of his cunning and cruelty, also found in al-Tanūkhī); but, close in date to its subject though it is, the lack of corroboration in other early sources suggests that it is an example of extrapolation and creation, of wishes projected on to a figurehead, rather than a product of caliphal policy or propaganda. Al-Tanūkhī's image of the benevolence of al-Muqtadir's mother (which, again, is balanced by stories which show her in a less creditable light) belongs to the same order of idealism and needed little editing by Ibn al-Jawzī to provide grist for the latter's ideological enterprise (it may be worth noting that he was a protégé of his own caliph's Queen Mother).[41] The difference between the meaning of near-identical materials as they occur in al-Tanūkhī's writings and as they are used by Ibn al-Jawzī—and it is an important one—is one of intent. Al-Tanūkhī tacitly condemns his own times but suggests no programme for remedying them, whereas Ibn al-Jawzī for a while thought that he was saluting the dawning of a new age and used moralized history to establish a political genealogy for the revived caliphate.

Are there any conclusions to be drawn from a comparison such as the above for the reading of medieval Arabic literature and historiography generally? That medieval Arabic 'authorship' as exercised at the level of selection, arrangement and implicit suggestion may be highly creative has already been demonstrated in respect of a number of major 'authors' who may be classed either as historians or as men of letters; for convenience, I refer to Hilary Kilpatrick, *Making the Great Book of Songs: compilation and the author's craft in Abū l-Faraj al-Iṣbahānī's Kitāb al-aghānī*, an exemplary study, and to its comprehensive bibliography.[42] A further consideration is that medieval authors may sometimes be assumed to be developing large-scale patterns of thought and not just a series of smaller ones. I have suggested this elsewhere in respect of several writers, including al-Tanūkhī; in the case of Ibn al-Jawzī it is worth noting, in addition to the points made above, that he several times uses the obituary sections of his regnal annals to highlight the virtues of the mothers or consorts of caliphs. It seems likely that this device serves to redeem the reigns of caliphs who are not themselves wholly satisfactory from Ibn al-Jawzī's viewpoint, and that it is meant to suggest a continuity of virtue in the ʿAbbasid caliphate as a political institution; see, for example, the obituary of Shujāʿ, the mother of al-Mutawakkil (232–247/847–861), whose charity to an ʿAlid gives rise to a miracle and counteracts al-Mutawakkil's own anti-Shiʿite policies (which are wrong not because the Shīʿites have a valid political claim, but because the descendants of the Prophet should be revered).[43] Ibn al-Jawzī is regarded as a useful and reliable source mainly for slightly later periods than this, and for his own times, but on such evidence his historical scheme has deep roots in his handling of the ʿAbbasid caliphate as a whole and his treatment even of his own period should probably be viewed with this in mind. One of the fundamental techniques on which it relies is the interweaving of romance and quasi-hagiography in the obituaries and regnal prefaces with hard data in the annalistic sections, a method developed and systematized, as we have seen, from a less tidy scheme already employed by al-Ṭabarī. Neither the scheme itself nor the interplay of sources and techniques has, however, been subjected to the degree of scrutiny that modern historians have applied to al-Ṭabarī and his peers.[44] Yet a fuller understanding of paradigms, whether those of classical Arabic historiography (e.g. al-Tabań) or their successors (e.g. Ibn al-Jawzī), also requires an understanding of paradigm shifts, or 'narrative transformations'. Ibn al-Jawzī's firmly and purposefully selective use of al-Tabań and al-Tanūkhī is a case in point.

## Notes

1. Mark Zvi Brettler, *The Creation of History in Ancient Israel* (London and New York: Routledge, 1995), especially pp. 18–19, 94.
2. Brettler, *Creation of History*, p. 78.
3. Brettler, *Creation of History*, p. 46.
4. Brettler, *Creation of History*, p. 78.
5. Richard G. Hovannisian & Georges Sabagh, eds, The Thousand and One Nights *in Arabic Literature and Society* (Cambridge: Cambridge University Press, 1997).
6. Muhsin Mahdi, 'From history to fiction: the tale told by the king's steward in *The Thousand and One Nights*', in: Richard G. Hovannisian & Georges Sabagh, eds, The Thousand and One Nights *in Arabic Literature and Society*, pp. 78–105.
7. Husain Haddawy (trans.), *The Arabian Nights* (based on the text of the fourteenth-century Syrian manuscript edited by Muhsin Mahdi), (London: Everyman's Library, 1992) (first published New York: W. W. Norton & Company, 1990), p. 228: One Hundred and Twenty-First Night; Muhsin Mahdi, ed., *Kitāb Alf Layla wa-Layla min uṣūlih al-ʿarabiyya al-ūlā* (The Thousand and One Nights From the Earliest Known Sources, Arabic text), (Leiden: E. J. Brill, 1984), p. 121.

8. Al-Tanūkhī, *al-Faraj baʿd al-Shidda*, ed. ʿAbbūd al-Shāljī, Beirut: Dār Ṣādir, 1398/1978, IV, chapter 13 (on reunited lovers), pp. 358–69.
9. Haddawy (trans.), *Nights*, pp. 236, 237.
10. Summarized by Julia Ashtiany [Bray], 'Tanūkhī's *al-Faraj baʿd al-shidda* as a literary source', in Alan Jones, ed., *Arabicus Felix: Luminosus Britannicus. Essays in Honour of A. F. L. Beeston on his Eightieth Birthday* (Reading: Ithaca Press, 1991), pp. 111–13.
11. Mahdi, 'From history to fiction', pp. 81, 82.
12. Al-Tanūkhī, *Nishwār al-Muḥāḍara*, ed. ʿAbbūd al-Shāljī, Beirut: Dār Ṣādir, 1391–3/1971–3, I, pp. 8–9, trans. D. S. Margoliouth, *The Table-Talk of a Mesopotamian Judge* (London: The Royal Asiatic Society, 1922), pp. 5–6.
13. Ibn al-Jawzī, *al-Muntaẓam fī Taʾrīkh al-Mulūk wa ʾl-Umam*, eds. M. & M. ʿA. Q. ʿAṭā (Beirut: Dār al-Kutub al-ʿIlmiyya, 1413/1993, XIII), pp. 321–9. This version, which displays small variants on the *Faraj* version, is assumed by al-Tanūkhī's editor ʿAbbūd al-Shāljī to derive from al-Tanūkhī's other main work, *Nishwār al-Muḥādara*, of which several parts are now lost, and is reproduced by him from Ibn al-Jawzī at *Nishwār al-Muḥāḍara* (Beirut: Dār Ṣādir, 1391–3/1971–3, IV), pp. 177–90. Ibn al-Jawzī's use of the story is discussed by H. F. Amedroz, 'A Tale of the Arabian Nights Told as History in the "Muntaẓam" of Ibn al-Jawzī', *Journal of the Royal Asiatic Society*, 1904, pp. 273–93.
14. This aspect of Ibn al-Jawzī's *Muntaẓam* is not broached in the two most recent surveys of Islamic historiography. Tarif Khalidi, *Arabic Historical Thought in the Classical Period* (Cambridge: Cambridge University Press, 1994) and Chase F. Robinson, *Islamic Historiography* (Cambridge: Cambridge University Press, 2002). For Ibn al-Jawzī's role in the Sunnī revival and his links with the caliphal family, especially the mother of al-Nāṣir (reigned 575–622/1179–1225), see H. Laoust, 'Ibn al-Djawzi', in H.A.R. Gibb *et al.*, eds, *The Encyclopaedia of Islam*, second edition, Leiden: Brill: 1960–2002, III, pp. 751–2.
15. On the literary and imaginative qualities of Ibn al-Jawzī's sermons, see Merlin Swartz, 'Arabic rhetoric and the art of the homily in medieval Islam', in R. G. Hovannisian & G. Sabagh, eds, *Religion and Culture in Medieval Islam (Fourteenth Giorgio Levi Della Vida Biennial Conference)* (Cambridge: Cambridge University Press, 1999), pp. 36–65.
16. Ibn al-Jawzī, *Muntaẓam*, VIII, pp. 318–28.
17. Compare al-Ṭabarī, *Taʾrīkh al-Rusul wa ʾl-Mulūk*, ed. M. J. de Goeje *et al.* (Leiden: E. J. Brill, 1897–1901, III), pp. 740–57 (especially year 193/809, concluding portrait of Hārūn al-Rashīd), trans. C. E. Bosworth, *The History of al-Ṭabarī*, vol. 30: *The ʿAbbasid Caliphate in Equilibrium. The Caliphates of Mūsā al-Hādī and Hārūn al-Rashīd A. D. 785–809/AH 169–193* (Albany: State University of New York Press, 1989), pp. 305–25.
18. Fedwa Malti-Douglas, 'Texts and Tortures: the Reign of al-Muʿtaḍid and the Construction of Historical Meaning', *Arabica*, 46 (1999), pp. 313–36.
19. Hugh Kennedy, 'Caliphs and their chroniclers in the Middle Abbasid period (third/ninth century)', in Chase F. Robinson, ed., *Texts, Documents and Artefacts. Islamic Studies in Honour of D. S. Richards* (Brill: Leiden and Boston, 2003), pp. 17–35, especially pp. 26, 29, 32–5.
20. Kennedy, 'Caliphs and their chroniclers', pp. 26, 34–5.
21. Malti-Douglas, 'Texts and Tortures', p. 336.
22. Malti-Douglas, 'Texts and Tortures', pp. 334–6, discusses the image of al-Muʿtaḍid presented by Ibn al-Jawzī in his *Akhbār al-Adhkiyāʾ*, but not in *al-Muntaẓam*. Some of the materials are common to both.
23. These generally include a number of people of humble or apolitical standing, and of women.
24. Ibn al-Jawzī, *Muntaẓam*, XII, pp. 306–27. For highlights of al-Muʿtaḍid's military activities before he became caliph, see *ibid.*, pp. 211, 224 and 229 (years 267, 269 and 270 AH).
25. Ibn al-Muʿtazz (247–296/861/908) was equally famous as a poet of genius and as an unfortunate political pawn, the 'caliph of one day', who perished when an attempt to put him on the throne in place of al-Muqtadir failed.
26. Ibn al-Jawzī, *Muntaẓam*, XII, p. 307. The quotation consists of lines 5–7, 10 of a 17-line poem in the metre *madīd*, rhyme *-īnā/ūnā*, see Ibn al-Muʿtazz, *Dīwān Ashʿār al-Amīr Abī ʾl-ʿAbbās*, ed. Muḥammad Badīʿ Sharif, Cairo, nd. I, pp. 517–18.
27. Lines 1–4, 7 of a 7-line poem in the metre *khafīf*, rhyme *-īmā/-ūmā*, Ibn al-Muʿtazz, *Dīwān Ashʿār al-Amīr Abī ʾl-ʿAbbās*, I, pp. 7–8.
28. Ibn al-Jawzī, *Muntaẓam*, XII, pp. 307–8.
29. Ibn al-Jawzī, *Muntaẓam*, XII, pp. 324–5.

30. The *ḥadīth* is widespread, see A. J. Wensinck *et al.*, *Concordance et indices de la Tradition musulmane* (Tunis: Dār Saḥnūn and Istanbul: Dār al-Daʿwa, 1987), (reprinted from Leiden: Brill, 1965, V), p.425, s. v. *qaṭʿ* and p. 545, s. v. *kathar.*
31. Ibn al-Jawzī, *Muntaẓam*, XII, pp. 317–21; al-Tanūkhī, *Nishwār*, 1, pp. 312–18, trans. Margoliouth, *Table-Talk*, pp. 164–8, and *Faraj*, II, pp. 389–95.
32. Ibn al-Jawzī, *Muntaẓam*, XII, pp. 315–17.
33. Al-Tanūkhī, *Nishwār*, I, pp. 326–8, trans. Margoliouth, *Table-Talk*, pp. 172–4.
34. See, e.g. the references in note 24 above.
35. Al-Tanūkhī, *Nishwār*, I, pp. 319–21 and *ibid.*, pp. 287–91.
36. Ibn al-Jawzī, *Muntaẓam*, XII, pp. 311–13, related from al-Tanūkhī; this is followed by a tale of only seemingly supernatural prescience, also related from al-Tanūkhī. In al-Tanūkhī's *Faraj*, in place of dreams that enable him to solve crimes, al-Tanūkhī has dreams and portents that show al-Muʿtaḍid that he is destined for the throne, *Faraj*, I, pp. 172–5 and II, 209–12. Fedwa Malti-Douglas has studied the image of al-Muʿtaḍid as a detective as it appears in Ibn al-Jawzī's *Akhbār al-Adhkiyā'*, 'The Classical Arabic Detective', *Arabica*, 35 (1988), pp. 59–68, 71–3.
37. Al-Tanūkhī, *Nishwār*, I, pp. 329–30, trans. Margoliouth, *Table-Talk*, pp. 174–5.
38. Al-Tanūkhī, *Nishwār*, I, pp. 331–3; not translated by Margoliouth.
39. It is, however, presented powerfully in abstract terms by the Andalusian Ibn ʿAbd Rabbih (246. 328–860–940) in the introductory passage of the first chapter of *al-ʿIqd al-Farīd*, ed. Ahmad Amīn *et al.* (Cairo: Maṭbaʿat Lajnat al-Ta'līf wa 'l-Tarjama wa 'l-Nashr, 3rd printing, 1384/1965, I), pp. 7–9. The pious reformer al-Muhtadī may have attempted some such programme during his short reign (255–6/869–70), see Hugh Kennedy, *The Court of the Caliphs. The Rise and Fall of Islam's Greatest Dynasty* (London: Weidenfeld & Nicolson, 2004), pp. 288, 294, and justice and accessibility to the people were Persian kingly ideals which had been held up to the caliphs by their advisors since late Umayyad times, see J. D. Latham, 'The beginnings of Arabic prose literature: the epistolary genre', in A. F. L. Beeston *et al.* ed., *The Cambridge History of Arabic Literature. Arabic Literature to the end of the Umayyad Period* (Cambridge: Cambridge University Press, 1983), ch. 4, pp. 154–79.
40. See reference at note 12 above.
41. See note 14 above, second sentence.
42. Hilary Kilpatrick, *Making the Great Book of Songs: Compilation and the author's craft in Abū l-Faraj al-Iṣbahānī's Kitāb al-aghānī* (London and New York: Routledge/Curzon, 2003).
43. Ibn al-Jawzī, *Muntaẓam*, XI, pp. 346–50 (obituaries for the year 246); see also *Muntaẓam*, XI, p. 238.
44. See note 14 above, first sentence.

# Narrative Strategies in Popular Literature: ideology and ethics in tales from the *Arabian Nights* and other collections

ULRICH MARZOLPH

## Introduction

Research in the eighteenth- and nineteenth-century manuscripts of the *Arabian Nights* has unveiled their curious characteristics.[1] Although the history of the *Arabian Nights* can be traced back to the ninth century CE,[2] 'anything likely to be regarded as a Vulgate text of the *Arabian Nights* was not created until late in the eighteenth century'. Moreover, the eighteenth- and nineteenth-century Arabic manuscripts were compiled 'in direct response to the European demand for complete editions that had been initiated by the enthusiastic reception' of Antoine Galland's first translation of the *Arabian Nights* into a European language (1704–1717). In order to create 'complete' redactions of the text, the subsequent compilers of these manuscripts have exploited a large range of sources additional to the previously available 'basic' stock of *Arabian Nights* tales, whatever that might have been.[3] As David Pinault in his study *Story-Telling Techniques in the Arabian Nights* points out, the redactors of those manuscripts followed a practice that had been approved for centuries of storytelling.[4] The range of material these compilers exploited is vast, besides anecdotes and stories of all kind comprising geographical and historical literature. So far only parts of the narrative repertoire of the *Arabian Nights* have been studied in relation to their sources, such as—most recently—the small corpus of fables inserted after the tale of ʿUmar ibn al-Nuʿmān.[5]

Among the hundreds of anonymous narrative compilations in Arabic manuscript tradition preserved in libraries in the West and the Near East that might have served as a source of inspiration for the Arabic compilers in one way or other, one is of particular importance. While most relevant texts bear comparatively recent dates, the unique manuscript published in 1956 by Hans Wehr under the title *al-Ḥikāyāt al-ʿajība* ('Wonderful Stories') is different. According to paleographical evidence it was probably compiled as early as the fourteenth century.[6] If this dating holds true, it would make the *Ḥikāyāt* older than the oldest extant manuscript of the *Arabian Nights*—the Galland manuscript that is supposed to date from the fifteenth century.[7] While some scholars have seen the *Ḥikāyāt* as a fragment of the monumental compilation of narratives attempted by the tenth-century author al-Jahshiyārī,[8] otherwise lost, it is highly interesting to note that they contain a number of tales also encountered in later redactions of the *Arabian Nights*. Rather than dealing with al-Jahshiyārī's authorship, which to my opinion is rather far-fetched, I propose to discuss here some of the tales common to both the *Ḥikāyāt* and the *Arabian Nights*.

Of the eighteen tales contained in the *Ḥikāyāt*'s only preserved first volume, four correspond directly with tales included in the *Arabian Nights* or, to be exact, in the Macnaghten edition (Calcutta II) as well as the so-called 'Zotenberg's Egyptian recension' (ZER).[9] These are the tales of the *Barber's Brothers*,[10] *Jullanār the Sea-born*,[11] *Jubayr ibn ʿUmayr and the Lady Budūr*[12] and *Abū Muḥammad Lazybones*.[13] A fifth tale—the *Story of the Forty Girls*—is represented in the *Arabian Nights* in an abridged form.[14] Yet another tale from the *Ḥikāyāt*—the *Story of Sūl and Shumūl*—is known both from a sixteenth-century Egyptian manuscript and from a Tübingen manuscript probably dating from the fourteenth century. In the latter the story is broken up into nights, probably so as to be inserted into a redaction of the *Arabian Nights* then under preparation.[15] Of these tales, I have chosen three that relate to my topic in different ways.

As a disclaimer, I should mention that I understand the term *strategy* in a wide sense. In the following, the term is employed to denote a relation between textual arrangements and the effects they have on the meaning of a given tale, whether intended or implicit. I will discuss these textual configurations as resulting from narrative strategies employed by the storytellers. An analysis of the development of a given tale originating from a cultural area and historical period different from that of the tale's readers may reveal narrative strategies crucial for our present access to understanding the tale, such as has been superbly demonstrated by Patrice Coussonet in his detailed study of the tale of *ʿAlī the Cairene and the Haunted House in Baghdad*.[16] More importantly, a comparison of details in different versions may uncover the ideological intentions these narrative strategies work to propagate, or the political or moral 'messages' inherent in the tale. In cases where the objectives of storytellers are impossible to know—all the more so since the story-tellers concerned here remain anonymous—close scrutiny of narrative strategies may help us to begin to infer some of the objectives hidden in the texts. With these theoretical remarks in mind, I propose to discuss different versions of three tales as examples for three different types of narrative adaptation: the tale of *Abū Muḥammad Lazybones* as an example for different interpretations in vaguely contemporary versions; the tale of *Jullanār* as an example for an Eastern tale gone West; and, finally, the tale of the *Forty Girls* as a highly adaptable scheme preserving its main idea even in reduced versions.

## Different Interpretations in Vaguely Contemporary Versions: *Abū Muḥammad Lazybones*

The Tale of *Abū Muḥammad Hight Lazybones*, in Richard Burton's rendition, or *Abu Mohammed, the Sluggard*, in Gustav Edmund von Grunebaum's wording,[17] is essentially the tale of an absurdly lazy young man who with the help of a magical monkey becomes incredibly rich. The tale begins with the caliph Hārūn al-Rashīd looking for a large jewel to be put in a particular place of the new crown his wife (or, in the *Ḥikāyāt*, his sister) has had prepared. As Hārūn's treasury does not hold any fitting jewel, he is told that the only person likely to meet his needs is the said Abū Muḥammad. Summoned to the caliphal palace, Abū Muḥammad displays his riches and when questioned about the sources for his wealth, becomes what Tzvetan Todorov has labelled an 'homme récit;'[18] he tells the caliph (and, by extension, the reader or listener) who he is by telling his story. The tale is then narrated in the first person, as Abū Muḥammad relates how he became rich in his youth.

Young Abū Muḥammad is so lazy as to drive his mother mad. He eats only when his mother brings him food, and he would rather burn in the sun than move into the shade. The one and only occasion on which he ever gets up is in order to ask a merchant about to depart for a journey to buy some goods for him. The merchant accepts but later forgets about his promise and only on the return journey buys a worn-out monkey for Abū Muḥammad. This monkey turns out to be a magical creature, who manages to accumulate tremendous riches in the name of Abū Muḥammad by fetching jewels (or pearls) from the bottom of the sea. The merchant, upon his return, hands everything over to Abū Muḥammad, who becomes the richest man in town. Abū Muḥammad soon realizes that the monkey is in fact a powerful demon (*mārid*), when the monkey makes him assist in acquiring a girl he has been unsuccessfully wooing for a long time. When Abū Muḥammad breaks the magical spell protecting the girl by marrying her, the demon abducts her. Only after a strenuous journey in search of her involving mention (and sometimes practice) of magical tricks, he is reunited with the girl and both return home.

This general outline fits both versions of the tale, but they also contain several differences. Generally speaking, the tale is constructed in four parts: (1) a prologue introducing the protagonist and the circumstances leading to story-telling; (2) a first part in which an apparently undeserving protagonist becomes rich with the help of a magical creature; (3) an interlude separating the lovers; and (4) a second part in which the lovers are reunited and the demon is destroyed. The *Ḥikāyāt* version, for example, starts with the caliph Hārūn al-Rashīd strolling around town with his vizier Jaʿfar. When Hārūn witnesses Abū Muḥammad's tremendous wealth he returns home in an angry mood only to be faced with his sister's request for the large jewel. His wrath is increased further by the fact that his own treasury does not hold any fitting jewel and he is thus forced to ask Abū Muḥammad for help. This introduction enables the narrator to have Abū Muḥammad summoned to the caliph immediately. In the *Arabian Nights*, Abū Muḥammad rather entertains the messengers lavishly first, then takes up the caliph's friendly invitation.

Besides the variation in the introductory passage, there are a number of significant differences between the two versions: (1) in the elaboration of Abū Muḥammad's laziness, the *Arabian Nights* version has his mother deliver the money to the merchant, but he does this all by himself in the *Ḥikāyāt*. (2) In the *Arabian Nights*, the merchant is reminded of his promise to Abū Muḥammad in a conscious act of remembering; in the *Ḥikāyāt* the ship suddenly stops moving and is only released when the merchant remembers his promise. (3) In the *Ḥikāyāt*, the magical monkey dives for pearls in Oman, a place so near to Abū Muḥammad's hometown in Southern Iraq that the episode is directly followed by the merchant's return; whereas in the *Arabian Nights*, the monkey dives for jewels at an unnamed island first and because the riches he acquires initially are comparatively modest, he is given another opportunity to accumulate wealth in compensation for rescuing the merchant and his companions from the cannibal Negroes in Zanzibar. (4) When his bride has been abducted by the evil monkey-demon, Abū Muḥammad receives help and advice from a friendly Muslim demon without any particular reason in the *Ḥikāyāt*; in the *Arabian Nights*, he instead earns the gratitude of a clan of magical white snakes by killing a black snake he finds fighting with one of them. (5) Most significantly of all, the final episode in the *Ḥikāyāt* is extremely short. Here, when Abū Muḥammad reaches the demon's palace after a short journey through magical realms, he finds the demon already destroyed and his beloved peacefully reading the Qur'an. In the *Arabian Nights*, Abū Muḥammad is by contrast submitted to a complicated procedure involving a magical flight on the back of a demon, an encounter with the mythical saint Khiḍr,[19] a journey to the City of Brass,[20] and the conscious application of a magical talisman.

André Miquel[21] has identified the underlying message of this tale as dealing with the question of power. When destiny allows even such a ridiculously lazy person as Abū Muḥammad to accumulate riches larger than those of the caliph himself, the caliph's rule by analogy is shown to result from destiny. The central theme would thus be Fate: God's absolute capacity to decide whatever He wants, or, in Miquel's profane formula, the 'caprice du hasard'.[22] This theme is tackled in both versions, albeit with different tendencies, and it is here that one might ponder about the working of narrative strategies. In both versions of the tale, the prologue and the first part account for about half of the total text while the other half is occupied by the interlude and the second part. In the *Arabian Nights*, however, the tale's final part accounts for about a third of the total text (eight of twenty-three pages), compared to a sixth of the total text (three of eighteen pages) in the *Ḥikāyāt*. This gives the *Arabian Nights* version a climax towards the end, stressing the work of destiny in its incomprehensible and magical dimension. The narrator of the *Ḥikāyāt* version, on the other hand, has constructed the final part in a rather pragmatic manner: it is short, contains few details, and in having God kill the demon in response to the distressed girl's sincere prayer it stresses human responsibility in contrast to a fatalistic surrender to the incomprehensible working of Fate. Human responsibility is also pointed out in the tale's initial scene: while Abū Muḥammad leans on his mother to meet the merchant in the *Arabian Nights* version, he gets up and walks by himself in the *Ḥikāyāt* version. Similarly, in the *Ḥikāyāt* the forgetful merchant remembers to fulfil his promise not by chance, as in the *Arabian Nights*, but through the magical standstill of his ship, constituting a strong call to keep his promise and act responsible. The strategy of varying minor details such as these in the end adds up to major modifications in the tale's implicit message. While both versions accept God's ultimate authority and the inexplicable workings of Fate, the *Ḥikāyāt* version supplies the human factor with a higher degree of responsibility for action within the given frame.

A variation in tendency such as the one pointed out here does not, of course, generate a new literary genre, yet it might modify any given text to such a degree as to leave a different impression on its listeners and, hence, generate new levels of meaning. René Basset, the first one to study the tale of Abū Muḥammad (in its *Arabian Nights* version), regarded it as a recent and badly constructed concoction of motifs also appearing in other tales.[23] While the sheer fact that the use of many motifs is not restricted to this particular tale certainly holds true, Basset's evaluation misses the point that tales are never told without an intention. A version such as that of the *Arabian*

*Nights*, with its elaborate focus on the strange and the wonderful, may be regarded as stressing awe and admiration of the miraculous workings of God's creation—aspects that later formed the basis of a chiefly entertaining genre. The version of the *Ḥikāyāt*, on the other hand, in stressing human responsibility underlines the educative message that even the smallest amount of human activity and responsibility will be rewarded. In order to drive this point home, both the initial irresponsible laziness of the hero as well as the ensuing rewards are exaggerated in a fashion typical of popular literature. Stripped of these popular distortions and boiled down to its essential message, the *Ḥikāyāt* version becomes a pronounced didactic tale.

While both versions of the tale discussed so far are considerably ancient, it is interesting to note what the compiler of the so-called Wortley-Montague manuscript (now in the Bodleian Library at Oxford), which was probably produced in the eighteenth century, has made of this tale.[24] His version is both heavily abridged and stripped of the initial eponymous passages. Here, we encounter a young beggar who buys a dog-faced baboon with the little savings he has. Back home, the monkey changes into a handsome young man exclaiming (in Burton's antiquated English): 'Query me no questions, concerning whatso thou shalt see, for good luck has come to thee.'[25] After the hero Muḥammad has acquired the bride, here the sultan's daughter, and disabled the talisman protecting her from the demon, instead of her being abducted, it is he who is thrown out of his magnificent home and reduced to his former poverty. When strolling around town, a friendly North African (Maghribī) sorcerer hands him a magical note addressed to the Lord of the demons with the help of which the latter is persuaded to punish the mischievous *jinnī* and return Muḥammad to his wife. Besides abridgement, what has happened here can best be characterized by the term rationalization. The tale's essential elements are preserved, but while the initial argument—the hero's absurd laziness and his deserved compensation when acting responsibly—is flattened, the final reward—marriage with the sultan's daughter and acquisition of the rule—is heightened to extremes. Both tendencies, in contrast to the previous stress on either Fate or self-responsibility, work for a rational understanding of the tale inasmuch as the magical ingredients are neglected. The monkey's wonderful capacities, the destruction of the girl's talisman and even the young man's adventures in search of his bride are not elaborated. Instead of the workings of magic, the focus in this eighteenth-century version is on authority (of wealth, knowledge and power). Even the mischievous *jinnī* is not destroyed by magic. The helpful sorcerer does not activate his magical powers; instead, he practices his authority by writing a note to the Lord of the demons—notably of undisclosed content. The latter, in turn, rather than resorting to magic, punishes the *jinnī* within the framework of a rationalized hierarchy, a kind of justice system, that also reigns in the world of demons.

## An Eastern Tale Gone West: *Jullanār*

The second tale to be discussed, the story of the mermaid Jullanār, will be considered from a different angle. As both versions of the tale in the *Ḥikāyāt* and in the *Arabian Nights* are more or less identical, instead of comparing their realization in the Arabic versions, I propose to discuss a late eighteenth-century German version as an example of narrative strategies adapting the Eastern tale to the Western value system. The tale of Jullanār is composed of two parts. Jullanār is only the protagonist of the first one, while the second part elaborates on the adventures of her son Badr (*Ḥikāyāt*) or Badr

Bāsim (*Arabian Nights*). Because the tale's second part does not feature in the European adaptation, we may leave it aside for the present discussion.

Shahriyār (*Arabian Nights*: Shahrimān), king of the northeastern Persian province of Khurāsān, is childless despite his many wives and concubines. One day he is offered an extremely beautiful slave-girl who refuses to speak. He falls in love with her and, while neglecting his other wives, dedicates all his time to her. She finally speaks to him when she becomes pregnant and informs him that she is the daughter of the king of the ocean. As she is about to give birth, she summons her family by ways of magic. Soon after the boy's birth Jullanār's family returns to the sea, and the child is initiated into the life under water by his uncle. The boy grows up, is educated in the arts, and after his father's death becomes king. From this point onward, the Arabic versions focus on the young man's adventures in finding (and, as one might say, winning over) his bride.

The German version I propose to contrast with the Arabic versions is contained in an anonymous collection published in 1801 under the title of *Feen-Mährchen*, or 'Tales of the fairies'.[26] It introduces the young ruler as an Oriental named Ahmed who, although his harem is full of beautiful women, is craving for love rather than sensual pleasure. One night Ahmed overhears a female voice lamenting the separation from her beloved, and finds out that he himself is the object of her love. The young woman, Geldena (a distortion of Galland's 'Gulnare'), a princess of an underwater kingdom, is at first forced to return to the sea with her companions. She returns to land the next day, is caught and immediately brought before Ahmed. Even though Geldena does not speak, Ahmed falls madly in love with her. He sets all his wives free and marries her. Only when she gives birth to a son does she summon her family. Her father, the king of the underwater world, then releases the magic spell that made her speechless. In a lengthy passage, her father explains that Geldena has transgressed the rules of their world by falling in love with a human. Accordingly, her family has been forced to repudiate her. Now that her human husband has proved his true devotion to her, they are allowed to accept her again. Ahmed and Geldena's newborn son is then taken away by his uncle for an education under the sea. He is returned to his earth family two years later when Geldena is giving birth to a second child, a daughter. Another year later all of them visit the dying king of the underwater world, and while Ahmed marvels at the abundant wealth of the marine realms, he is bewildered by not noticing signs of grief among the dying king's family. After their return to the world above, they live—as the text makes us understand—'happily ever after'. Geldena never visits the underwater world again.

In the Arabic versions this story has a second part, which is about twice as long and, hence, goes into much more detail.[27] In consequence, the first part is reduced to a mere introduction, and the only time when the initial protagonist Jullanār enters the scene again is towards the end of the story's second part, when after numerous magical encounters her son appears to be finally subdued by his female opponent, leaving his mother no recourse but to go to war in order to free him. Even though the introductory passage is linked to the following part in several other ways, one might easily imagine the second part as an independent story. The German adaptation, in contrast, develops the introductory passage into a fully-fledged story in its own right. Moreover, it introduces a number of traits and arguments, which root the tale firmly within the contemporary German value system. At the beginning of the eighteenth century Galland had introduced the *Arabian Nights* into the French world of feudal order and courtly manners. A century later, and in a bourgeois German context, the value system is different: instead of considerations about the feasibility of arranged marriages, the concept of individual love is now key; instead of chance, it is her love that brings Geldena to the king; it is her love that causes her to be repudiated by her people; and it is her husband's love that makes her family finally accept the situation. The recent comparison between Galland's original French text and its German translation by Johann Heinrich Voss (1781–1785), vaguely contemporary with the *Feen-Mährchen*, has extracted similar tendencies ruling the German translation.[28] Whenever Galland would elaborate on courtly atmosphere, as his work addressed the French readers at court, Voss would transfer the like passages to the context, manners and intellectual horizon of the German urban citizens constituting his own audience. Similarly, instead of wealth in the *Arabian Nights*, it is now social responsibility that counts in the *Feen-Mährchen.* The wonders of the marine world are depicted with a certain awe, but eventually they serve only as a matrix for further reflections: the inhabitants of the underwater world dwell in gold and silver, yet they part with their wealth freely (notwithstanding in exchange for food); moreover, they do not grieve for things gone by. The latter trait—found also in another tale of the *Arabian Nights*, the tale of *ʿAbdallāh the Fisherman and ʿAbdallāh the Merman*[29]—is stressed repeatedly in other tales of the German collection in which human foibles, above all exaggerated emotions, are criticized. These characteristics are typical of the literature of the time, which was imbued with the culture of the Enlightenment. Other tales in the collection explicitly contrast the 'former dark ages' with the present (1801) 'enlightened days'. Obviously, the Oriental tale, like its contemporary European literature, serves as a background against which other ideas may be tested and developed.[30] In this particular case the German narrator introduces and underlines moral as well as social concepts in order to develop the underwater world into a kind of future vision for humanity, as a utopia built on the value system of Humanism.[31]

## Elaborate and Reduced Versions of a Plot: the *Forty Girls*

The third tale from the *Ḥikāyāt* to be discussed is a peculiar one. It will serve here to demonstrate how the use of similar motifs in different contexts may express varying objectives and, hence, once more reveal the workings of narrative strategies. The tale of the *Forty Girls* features a young man, the youngest of three princes, who is repudiated by his father for having interpreted the latter's dream as an evil omen. Released by his compassionate executioner, the prince reaches a castle that is inhabited by forty warrior girls. At first, the prince hides in their castle and although they suspect his presence, they are unable to find him. In order to track him down, one after the other the forty warrior girls stay at home. When meeting him, each of them falls in love with him and fails to betray his existence to the others. Finally, their leader meets him, also falls in love and declares him her exclusive lover. One day, as the girls have to depart for some business, their leader entrusts to him the keys to the treasury so that he may divert himself. Only one of the doors is not to be opened. Needless to say, curiosity leads our hero to that particular door and when looking into the room through a crack, he notices a beautiful mare. He soon realizes that the mare knows human speech, as she invites him to free her. Even though at this very moment his beloved arrives, he follows the horse's advice and flees. This is as much of the story as is relevant for the present discussion.[32]

In the *Arabian Nights* the equivalent to this story constitutes the third and final episode in the *Third Qalandar's Tale.* After having been shipwrecked at the Magnetic Mountain and later having inadvertently killed a young man living in hiding, the protagonist meets ten one-eyed men in mourning. When he asks the men about what has happened to them, instead of answering they sew him into an animal hide. He is picked up by a giant bird which subsequently drops him on a high mountain. From there, the young man reaches the palace of the forty girls with whom he lives a joyful life for some time. When the girls have to leave him for a period of forty days they entrust the keys to him, but forbid him to open the fortieth chamber. When he finally opens the forbidden door on the fortieth day, he finds a winged horse. Climbing onto the horse's back, he is transported back to the place of the ten mourning men, and the horse whips out one of his eyes with its tail before it leaves. Lamenting the lost pleasure, and not even permitted to compassionately join the group of mourners, he starts to roam the world.

Claude Bremond has pointed out closely related variants of the latter version in the first tale of the Persian poet Neẓāmi's (died 1202) *Haft peikar-e Bahrām-Gur* and in the fifth tale of the equally Persian *Sindbād-nāme*.[33] These tales, both of which are older than any of the Arabic ones, in their turn have given rise to numerous popular adaptations of the theme 'Repenting anything that cannot be changed is of no use', or, as the Persian saying goes, *Pashimāni-ye goẕashte sudi nadārad*.[34] These tales usually follow this structure: (1) gain of a fairy wife, (2) transgression of taboo and (3) irretrievable loss of fairy wife. In Arabic, two of the tales collected by Enno Littmann in Palestine and Egypt contain closely related episodes.[35] In one of these, corresponding to one of the Palestinian folk-tales published by Hans Schmidt and Paul Kahle, the narrators do not contend themselves with having the protagonist submerge in eternal grief; rather, they have the king, who listens to his tales, feel perfectly justified to have the protagonist executed because of his stupid action.[36]

In another variation of the same theme found in the Būlāq edition—obviously resulting from a lacuna in the manuscript that served as the basis of this edition—the *Third Qalandar's Tale* appears in a highly reduced form in which the originally separated second and third episodes are merged.[37] In this condensed version the protagonist watches a group of people prepare an underground mansion, as in the second episode. As soon as they leave he uncovers the mansion's lid, enters, and then suddenly wanders through 39 beautiful gardens, as in the end of the third episode. When opening a door he encounters the magical horse that brings him to the ten mournful youths and whips out of one his eyes with its tail. Notwithstanding the weak motivation for the protagonist's mourning, this version by way of its Persian translation, prepared in the Qajar period, was also popular as a separate chapbook in mid-twentieth century Iran and might have given rise to further variations of the theme in oral tradition.[38]

As the available texts show, the motif of the horse hidden in the forbidden chamber offered itself predominantly in order to illustrate the particular theme of 'pleasure lost' or, as Claude Bremond has put it, 'Hélas sur le passé'.[39] The protagonist at first experiences what Robert Irwin terms a 'joyous [...] celebration of sex'[40] which in the narrator's perspective obviously consists of extensive sexual relations without feeling responsible for the consequences in terms of emotional bondage or offspring.[41] The protagonist's responsibility is then put to the test by pointing out a taboo and thus granting him the potential to transgress it, a test he inevitably fails (both for psychological and structural reasons). In the *Ḥikāyāt* version, the protagonist's unfaithfulness is balanced by the fact that the leader of the forty girls is in fact a witch who has unjustly held her own sister—the enchanted horse—prisoner. As the ethics of success (discussed in relation to the *Arabian Nights* by Peter Molan)[42] permit an unjust act to be countered by another one of the same kind, the hero not only escapes unharmed but also is rewarded with women, children, wealth and power. In the *Arabian Nights* version, the protagonist's transgression is justified by nothing other than his own curiosity. In consequence, he is reduced to his former state of misery after living through the utmost joy in the castle of the girls.

While both versions employ similar motifs, the arguments they elaborate are different and so, consequently, are the narrative strategies employed. In the *Ḥikāyāt* version, the tale of the *Forty Girls* constitutes an integral part of the narrative. It is linked to the tale's introduction by the hero's wandering in the desert, which eventually leads him to the castle of the girls. Moreover, it is linked to the tale's further development in that the horse has a crucial role in advising and helping the hero. Any dramatic turn of events after the transgression of the taboo would hinder the tale's further flow. In fact, as in the *Arabian Nights* and other popular versions, it would lead to a final moral lesson and would thus prevent the narrative's continuation such as developed in the *Ḥikāyāt*. In the *Ḥikāyāt* version, the tale of the *Forty Girls* is rather less a tale of transgression but more a tale about the acquisition of a helpful animal. The actual method of acquisition is not exactly typical of the genre, where friendly behaviour towards the supernatural in need—as in the case of the fight between the black and the white snake in the tale of *Abū Muḥammad*—appears to be more frequent.[43] In the *Arabian Nights*, by contrast, the tale of the *Forty Girls* is but one of the general tale's three episodes that are not logically linked with each other but rather constitute single units. While the tale might exist separately, as in fact it does in the popular versions mentioned in both Arabic and Persian, it is linked here to the preceding episode by means of a common moral, whose overlapping point could read: 'Destiny cannot be escaped'. But while in the earlier episode, the hero unwittingly acts in order to fulfil the ordained Fate, in the third episode he suffers from a fated transgression. Even though it is tempting to interpret the protagonist's action as an individual act of unfaithfulness, the presence of the ten mourning youths in the frame story makes it clear that transgression of a taboo is an inevitable human characteristic.

## Conclusions

According to folklore theory, tales—whether written down or orally performed—gain their meaning in the individual performance.[44] In other words, each performance creates a different tale. While performance in oral tradition means the recitation of a tale to a listening audience, performance with regard to literature refers in the first place to a given tale being fixed in writing, and only in the second place implies the reading of a tale by a specific individual. A researcher's perspective in reading tales written down further complicates matters. Not only the producer's and the recipient's perspective matters, but also the researcher's gaze and expectation. It is the researchers' task to find a balanced judgement burdened as little as possible with presuppositions or biases. They have to remain aware that any of their readings is but one possibility of supplying meaning to a text whose context at the time of production is largely unknown.[45] For the producer, narrative strategies are one way of achieving meaning. In consequence, close examination of narrative strategies may contribute to an understanding of why a tale has taken the shape it has and, more importantly, of its 'meaning'. Similar readings have been undertaken earlier, and many more are needed in order for us to arrive at an adequate evaluation of the art of storytelling in classical Arabic tradition.

The medieval Arabic tales discussed above belong to collections whose authors remain unknown. Moreover, it is quite likely that the tales included in the collections originate from a variety of sources and that more than one author contributed to their final form. This situation makes it impossible to reconstruct an authorial intention at work throughout the whole collection. In particular, the *Arabian Nights* make it difficult to extract a coherent intention, as their heterogeneous character as an *omnium-gatherum* (Irwin) over the centuries has permitted the integration of just about each and every kind of tale, including myths, religious legends, historical anecdotes, romances of chivalry and love, folk- and fairy-tales, animal fables, humorous tales and jokes. That said, it remains possible to uncover the ideological agenda, be it political or moral, of a tale through an attentive scrutiny of narrative strategies employed. As for Arabic folk literature Western readers, with their specific cultural notions such as authorship, individuality, originality and plagiarism, need to be aware of the reign of different concepts in pre-modern Arabic storytelling. Even so, although the *Arabian Nights* may at times appear as a haphazard collection put together for the simple joy of numerical integrity, the narrative universe they offer is not only marvellous and attractive but also revealing and instructive. Close readings can help to decipher the rich layers of cultural notions embedded in its tales.

## Notes

1. For a survey of Arabic pre-eighteenth-century, hence 'pre-Galland' manuscripts, see Marzolph, Ulrich, 'Re-locating the Arabian Nights', in *Philosophy and Arts in the Islamic World. Proceedings of the Eighteenth Congress of the Union Européenne des Arabisants et Islamisants held at the Katholieke Universiteit Leuven* (September 3–September 10, 1996). ed. U. Vermeulen/D. De Smet, *Orientalia Lovanensia Analecta*, 87 (1998), 155–163 (for the following quotations); recent contributions on specific manuscripts include *Tausend und eine Nacht. Neue Erzählungen. Die in anderen Versionen von '1001 Nacht' nicht enthaltenen Geschichten der Wortley-Montague-Handschrift der Oxforder Bodleian Library*. Aus dem arabischen Urtext vollständig übertragen und erläutert von Felix Tauer. Frankfurt am Main, Insel, 1995; Chraïbi, Aboubakr, *Contes nouveaux des 1001 Nuits: Étude du manuscrit Reinhardt* (Paris: Maisonneuve, 1996); Grotzfeld, Heinz, 'Proto-ZÄR-Handschriften von 1001 Nacht in den Gothaer Beständen: Die textgeschichtliche Bedeutung der Handschriften Ms. Orient. A 2638 und A 2637", in *Wilhelm Pertsch–Orientalist und Bibliothekar: Zum 100. Todestag*. ed. by Hans Stein (Gotha: Forschungsbibliothek Gotha, 1999), pp. 91–108.
2. Abbott, Nabia, 'A Ninth-Century Fragment of the "Thousand Nights": new lights on the early history of the *Arabian Nights*', *Journal of Near Eastern Studies*, 8 (1949), 129–64.
3. For an interpretation of what 'basic' tales in the *1001 Nights* might mean see Mahdi, Muhsin: 'Exemplary Tales in the *1001 Nights*', in Campbell, Kay Hardy *et al.*, *The 1001 Nights: Critical Essays and Annotated Bibliography* (Cambridge, MA: Dar Mahjar, 1985), pp. 1–24, also in Mahdi, Muhsin, *The Thousand and One Nights* (Alf Layla wa-Layla) *from the Earliest Known Sources*, Part 3: *Introduction and Indexes* (Leiden: Brill, 1994), pp. 140–63.
4. Pinault, David, *Story-Telling Techniques in the Arabian Nights* (Leiden: Brill, 1992); see also id., 'Būlāq, Macnaghten, and the new Leiden edition compared: notes on storytelling technique from the *Thousand and One Nights*', *Journal of Semitic Studies*, 32,1 (1987), 125–57.
5. Osigus, Anke, *Ein Fabelzyklus in 1001 Nacht. Literatur- und textkritische Analyse*. PhD dissertation, Münster, 2000.
6. *Das Buch der wunderbaren Erzählungen und seltsamen Geschichten*. Mit Benutzung der Vorarbeiten von A. von Bulmerincq herausgegeben von H. Wehr. Wiesbaden 1956 (Bibliotheca Islamica 18) (edition of the Arabic text); *Das Buch der wundersamen Geschichten. Erzählungen aus der Welt von 1001 Nacht*, ed. U. Marzolph (München: Beck 1999) (complete German translation); see also Grotzfeld, Heinz & Sophia, *Die Erzählungen aus 'Tausendundeiner Nacht'* (Darmstadt: Wissenschaftliche Buchgesellschaft, 1984), pp. 75–80; Irwin, Robert, *The Arabian Nights: A Companion* (London: Allen Lane, 1994), pp. 82–3.
7. For the divergent opinions concerning the dating see Grotzfeld, Heinz, 'The Age of the Galland Manuscript of the Nights: Numismatic Evidence for Dating a Manuscript?', *Journal of Arabic and Islamic Studies*, 1 (1996–97), 50–64.

8. cf. Grotzfeld (as in note 6), 16 f., 74 f.; Irwin (as in note 6), 82.
9. The Alif Laila or Book of the Thousand Nights and One Night. Commonly known as 'The Arabian Nights' Entertainments', edited by W. H. Macnaghten, 4 vols (Calcutta 1839–42).
10. Wehr & Marzolph (as in note 6), no. 3 = Chauvin, Victor: *Bibliographie des ouvrages arabes ou relatifs aux arabes* (Liége: Vaillant-Carmanne), vol. 5, pp. 157–64, no. 81–6.
11. Wehr & Marzolph (as in note 6), no. 6 = Chauvin (as in note 10), vol. 5, pp. 147–51, no. 73.
12. Wehr & Marzolph (as in note 6), no. 10 = Chauvin (as in note 10), vol. 7, pp. 93 f., no. 374.
13. Wehr & Marzolph (as in note 6), no. 11 = Chauvin (as in note 10), vol. 6, pp. 64–7, no. 233.
14. Wehr & Marzolph (as in note 6), no. 5 = Chauvin (as in note 10), vol. 5, pp. 200–3, no. 117.
15. Wehr & Marzolph (as in note 6), no. 8 = Chauvin (as in note 10), vol. 7, pp. 107–12, no. 379bis; Grotzfeld (as in note 6) 80–2; Seybold, C.F., *Geschichte von Sul und Schumul. Unbekannte Erzählung aus Tausendundeiner Nacht* (Leipzig, 1902). A number of further correspondences between tales in *al-Ḥikāyāt al-ʿajība* and non-ZER manuscripts of the *Nights* are mentioned in Marzolph, Ulrich and Richard van Leeuwen, *The Arabian Nights Encyclopedia* (Santa Barbara, CA: ABC-Clio, 2004), s. v. '*al-Hikâyât al-ʿajîba*'.
16. Coussonnet, Patrice, *Pensée mythique, idéologie et aspirations sociales dans un conte des Mille et une Nuits: Le récit d'Ali du Caire* (Cairo: Institut français d'archéologie du Caire, 1989) (Supplément aux Annales islamologiques 13).
17. Grunebaum, Gustave Edmund von, 'Greek Form Elements in the Arabian Nights', *Journal of the American Oriental Society*, 62 (1942), 277–92.
18. Todorov, Tzvetan, 'Les Hommes-récits', in *Poétique de la prose* (Paris: Seuil, 1971), pp. 78–91.
19. Franke, Patrick, *Begegnung mit Khidr: Quellenstudien zum Imaginären im traditionellen Islam* (Stuttgart: Steiner, 2000).
20. Pinault 1992 (as in note 4), 148–239; a comprehensive survey of studies on the concept of the City of Brass is given in Marzolph, Ulrich, 'Messingstadt', in *Enzyklopädie des Märchens* [henceforth EM] vol. 9 (Berlin/New York, 1999), cols 599–602.
21. Miquel, André, *Sept contes des Mille et une Nuits; ou Il n'y a pas de contes innocents* (Paris: Sindbad, 1981), pp. 143–63; id.: 'Histoire et société', in Bencheikh, Jamel Eddine *et al.*, *Mille et un Contes de la nuit* (Paris: Gallimard, 1991), pp. 9–78, at 41–3.
22. Miquel 1981 (as in note 21), 148.
23. Basset, René, 'Notes sur les Mille et une Nuits. VI. Histoire d'Abou Mohammed al-Keslan', *Revue des Traditions Populaires*, 14 (1899), 20–37, at 20.
24. The quoted edition is *Arabian Nights*, with introduction and explanatory notes by Richard F. Burton. Reprinted from the original edition [...] 1885, 16 vols (Beirut: Khayat, 1966), vol. 9, pp. 165–88; Tauer (as in note 1), 34–42.
25. Burton (as in note 24), 38; Jonathan Scott has here 'Ask me no questions' (*The 'Aldine' Edition of the Arabian Nights Entertainments*, vol. 4, L. 1890, p. 221), while Felix Tauer renders the passage apparently quite literally as 'Erforsche nicht, was du siehst [...], denn das Glück ist schon zu dir gekommen!'
26. *Feen-Mährchen. Zur Unterhaltung für Freunde und Freundinnen der Feenwelt.* Textkritischer Neudruck der anonymen Ausgabe Braunschweig 1801. Herausgegeben und kommentiert von Ulrich Marzolph (Hildesheim, Zürich, New York: Georg Olms, 2000), no. 12.
27. For a discussion of the tale's Arabic versions see Walther, Wiebke, *Tausend und eine Nacht: Eine Einführung* (Munich: Artemis, 1987), pp. 95–104.
28. Wieckenberg, Ernst-Peter, *Johann Heinrich Voß und 'Tausend und eine Nacht'* (Würzburg: Königshausen & Neumann, 2002).
29. Chauvin (as in note 10), vol. 5, pp. 6–7, no. 3; for interpretations of the Arabic versions of this tale see Gerhardt, Mia I., *The Art of Story-telling: A Literary Study of the Thousand and One Nights* (Leiden: Brill, 1963), pp. 263–9; Miquel 1981 (as in note 21), 111–42.
30. Balke, D., 'Orient und oriental. Lit.en (Einfluß auf Europa und Deutschland)', in *Reallexikon der Deutschen Literaturgeschichte*, vol. 2 (Berlin etc. $^{2}$1965), pp. 816–60.
31. See also Irwin (as in note 6), 211.
32. The further turn of events has the prince, with the help of the magical horse, marry another princess and find out that his former beloved, the leader of the forty girls, the enchanted horse, and the princess are three sisters. Later, he is reunited with his former beloved together with his forty sons, already grown-up, and eventually even meets his father who forgives him and entrusts his own kingdom to him.
33. Bremond, Claude, 'En deçà et au-delà d'un Conte: le devenir des thèmes', in Bencheikh *et al.*, 1991 (as in note 21), 79–258, at 143–7.

34. See e.g. Marzolph, Ulrich, *Typologie des persischen Volksmärchens* (Beirut: Deutsche Morgenländische Gesellschaft, 1984), nos. *832 A, *832 B.
35. Littmann, Enno, *Arabische Märchen und Schwänke aus Ägypten* (Mainz, 1955), pp. 31–5, no. 4; id.: *Arabische Märchen: Aus mündlicher Überlieferung gesammelt und übertragen* (Leipzig, 1957), pp. 42–56.
36. Littmann 1955 (as in note 35); Schmidt, Hans & Paul Kahle: *Volkserzählungen aus Palästina: gesammelt bei den Bauern von Bir-Zet* (Göttingen: Vandenhoeck und Ruprecht, 1918), no. 50.
37. The only Būlāq-text currently available to me is an undated reprint from Cairo, where the passage in question in given on p. 56 (night 15).
38. Marzolph, Ulrich, *Dâstânhâ-ye Širin. Fünfzig persische Volksbüchlein aus der zweiten Hälfte des zwanzigsten Jahrhunderts* (Stuttgart: Steiner, 1994) (Abhandlungen für die Kunde des Morgenlandes 50, 4), no. XLIV; see also id., 'The Persian *Nights*: Links between the *Arabian Nights* and Iranian Culture', *Fabula*, 45 (2004), 275–93, at 285–6.
39. Bremond (as in note 33).
40. Irwin (as in note 6), 164.
41. On this aspect, see also Marzolph, Ulrich, 'As Woman as Can Be: The Gendered Subversiveness of an Arabic Folktale Heroine', *Edebiyât*, 10 (1999), 199–218.
42. Molan, Peter D. 'Sindbad the Sailor: A Commentary on the Ethics of Violence', *Journal of African and Oriental Studies*, 98 (1978), 237–47.
43. See Lindahl, Carl, 'Dankbare (hilfreiche) Tiere', in EM (as in note 20), vol. 3, cols 287–9.
44. For a survey of folklore theory on performance see Ben-Amos, Dan, 'Kontext', in EM (as in note 20), vol. 8, cols 217–37; Braid, Donald, 'Performanz'. *ibid.*, vol. 10, cols 730–4.
45. See Honko, Lauri: 'Folkloristic Studies on Meaning', *Arv*, 40 (1984), 35–65; Röhrich, Lutz: 'Zur Deutung und Be-Deutung von Folklore-Texten', *Fabula*, 26 (1985), 3–28; Kottinger, Wolfgang: 'Hermeneutik', in EM (as in note 20), 841–5.

# The Art of Interruption: The *Thousand and One Nights* and Jan Potócki

RICHARD VAN LEEUWEN

It was Richard Burton, the famous, or perhaps notorious, translator of the *Thousand and One Nights*, who said: 'Without the nights, no *Arabian nights*'. What he meant to say was that the division into nights is an essential characteristic of the *Thousand and One Nights,* without which the work would lose its structure, its coherence and its *raison d'être* as a work of literature. It would be no more than an amorphous collection of tales of varying genres and artistic standards, gathered from various sources. Moreover, the nights-division came to be the most evident influence of the *Thousand and One Nights* on European imitators and authors inspired by the work, both with regard to form and content. How did the nights-division in the *Thousand and One Nights* become so crucial to the work, and why did it have such a powerful impact on the imagination? And why was it so attractive to European authors who used the *Thousand and One Nights* as a model?

It may seem strange that the nights-division has such an important part in creating coherence in a literary work. After all, it is a form of interruption, a form of breaking up something which is whole, which seems to challenge the continuation of the narrative and the unity of the work. However, this fragmentation is only one aspect of what may be called the 'art of interruption'; that is, the usage of interruption as an artistic device, as a means to structure a work of art, to multiply its dimensions and meanings, and to imbue it with rhythm and movement. Interruptions are also associated with boundaries, transitions, perspectives, empty spaces, intervals, separations, connections, gaps, breaches, differences, jumps, divergences, opposites and contradictions. In all these senses, interruptions add something to a literary work. To narrate is to establish relationships between various components, but to be able to do this the continuum to which these components belong has first to be broken up. Only then can new meanings be created from existing ones.[1]

In the following we will discuss the functions of the nights-division in the *Thousand and One Nights* as part of a generic system. First we will examine the function of interruption in a literary form for which it is especially characteristic: the frame story and, more specifically, frame stories that serve as instruction pieces for rulers. Subsequently we will discuss the relationship between this genre and the *Thousand and One Nights* and the function of interruption as a narrative device in its most characteristic form: the night. Finally, we will analyse the use of a similar technique in one of the most important European 'imitations' of the *Thousand and One Nights*, the novel *Manuscrit trouvé à Saragosse* by the French/Polish author Jan Potócki.

## Frame Stories

The tradition of frame stories can be traced to the very beginnings of Arabic prose literature, in re-workings of collections of fables such as *Kalīla wa-Dimna* and in *adab*-collections of various kinds. Its roots should probably be sought in Persian and Sanskrit literature, in which the framing of stories to form a collection of tales was a common artifice. Examples, apart from *Kalīla wa-Dimna*, are such works as the *Panchatantra*, the *Kathasaritsagara*, the *Nonthouk Pakaranam*, the *Sindbādnāma*, the *Ṭūṭīnāma* and the *Hazār afsāna*. Some of these works were translated into Arabic at an early stage (Ibn al-Muqaffa'; 750) and traces of others can be found in various tales and romances. Part of them should be reckoned among the genre of the collections of tales for the instruction of princes, which became well-known in Arabic literature and which generally reveal Persian roots, such as the *Sindbādnāma*, *King Jalīʿād and his vizier Shīmās* and *Kalīla wa-Dimna*. It is collections of this type that concern us here.

The *Sindbādnāma*, whose history predates the ninth century (Persian version 1190; possibly earlier Arabic version[2]), can serve as an example of this type of cycle and as a comparison with the *Thousand and One Nights*, as it is not only structured as a frame story but also contains an important additional element: the time factor. In this cycle, as the result of a divination a prince is forbidden to speak for ten days. He is lodged in the harem of the palace and is subsequently accused by the queen of having attempted to seduce her. As he will die if he speaks he is unable to defend himself, and the ten viziers of the king tell exemplary stories to postpone the prince's execution, while the queen tells stories to convince the king of his guilt. After ten days, the prince is delivered from his predicament.[3]

In the *Sindbādnāma* the use of a framework to link a number of stories creates what can be called a 'situation of dialogue'; that is, a juxtaposition of several viewpoints, which serves as a mechanism to generate meanings and visions of life. In general, meaning is derived from an exchange of visions, of observations from different points, of compromises between differing views.[4] In the frame story this is not only achieved by the dialogue within the frame, between the sultan and his vizier, but also by the relationship between the frame and the stories. The stories are a response to people, statements or events mentioned in the frame. The frame provides the perspective from which the tales should be read and the repeated transition between the frame and the tales creates the split level which makes the perspective possible. The tales comment on the same event, contrasting views from different angles. The dialogic situation gives the tales their meaning and the context for their interpretation.

As a mechanism for the generation of meanings, the juxtaposition of viewpoints enhances the cycle's character as an initiation into new forms of knowledge. The prince is taught about the world and life in a systematic, deliberate way, to prepare him for his future task. The frame makes the conveying of the information even more systematic, since it provides the cycle with a sense of ordering and coherence. The prince is confronted with an alternative reality, outside his scope of reference, in the form of a set of stories which contain the essential truths of this reality which represent the backbone of a vision of the world which is sanctioned by tradition and experience, and which the prince has to know before he can take on his role in society as a ruler. The stories are a symbolic boundary that, once the prince crosses it, will transform him from an innocent youth into a wise statesman. The frame turns the initiation into a ritual.

Apart from these general functions of the framing technique, there is one additional element in the *Sindbādnāma*: the division into ten days. The interruptions between the stories are not merely intended to secure the regular transition from stories to frame and *vice versa*, they also introduce time as a structural principle. This additional component has several functions. First, it places the cycle in the regular pattern of time, suggesting progress and the possibility of change and intervention. The temporal division suggests that there is a beginning, a middle and an end. This not only provides the narrative with a convenient structure, but also has its consequences for the interpretation of the story. The introduction of beginning and end suggests a specific coherence in which each element is part of a process. As there is an ending, the events between beginning and end are no longer fragments; they are rather part of a whole determined by the interrelationships between events—causality, repetitions and a general sense of order. The time-frame causes a confrontation between a meaningful whole and a whole which consists of a mere succession of its components. Here we find one of the essential functions of the device of interruption: time schemata give coherence and meaning by their pattern of fragmentation. They give the narrative its tension and its structure, and they place shattered fragments into a new, meaningful configuration.[5]

The time-frame also introduces the element of contingency into the cycle: the stories are not merely lessons to instruct a prince/reader in any time or any place; they are intended to influence a course of events; to intervene in the sequence of happenings and to prevent some events from happening. Each story can intervene in real life; it can save or kill the prince or the reader. The climax gives all stories of the cycle their final significance. The aim is to disclose the truth, to unravel reality on the basis of allegories that, by showing its underlying 'unreal' truth, will in the end influence reality. The hidden truth can be discovered in the form of fiction, as if only fiction can reach below the misleading surface of reality.

Finally, the time-division enhances the resemblance of the cycle to a rite of initiation. It strengthens the ritual character of the cycle, as it creates the framework for the classical stages of the initiation process: the separation of the prince from society, a temporary 'liminal' period, and his re-incorporation with a different social status. In the cycle of the *Sindbādnāma* this ritual is represented quite clearly: the prince is removed from his regular environment and a taboo is imposed on him to underline his liminal status. This liminality is emphasized by the events that generate the narrative sequence: the prince is pending between life and death; it is uncertain if his initiation will succeed; if it does not, he will have to pay with his life. Since he is in a liminal position, he cannot speak for himself, but in fact it is exactly his inability to speak which leads to his confrontation with the metaphorical representations of his new world. It is the stories told during his liminal 'absence' that are the true initiation. The ritual character of the initiation is further stressed by the fixed period of the liminal situation; within ten days it has to be decided whether he will be re-incorporated or killed.

If we turn to the question of genre, it seems that the *Sindbādnāma* conforms to a specific type of narrative. A genre can be defined as a coherent set of visions, expressed in a coherent narrative form, shaped by a dialogical process, and intended to record certain visions of reality, which are thus handed down to the next generation in a structured representation. Genres are means to establish order and hierarchies in information and meanings, they represent rules, opinions and visions of reality which are related to specific narrative forms. These forms and the conceptual structures that they represent are never fixed but always subject to change. Because they are shaped by dialogism, they are continually adapted to new visions and new circumstances. They can become obsolete or, more probably, swallowed by new genres, which develop from the old ones. They always convey an interpretation of reality, a specific representation of the world.[6]

The cycles mentioned above share a number of generic characteristics. They have a common formal structure, based on the technique of interruption and the interference between stories and frame. They represent literature as a form of initiation, a form of explaining the world in metaphors. The dialogical dimension is made clear in the story itself as a debate between power and wisdom, good and evil, rationality and irrationality, and the ideology which they convey is simple and basic: a wise man will trust only his reason and will not give in to his primary instincts. Everything is aimed to sustain his authority and to avoid destruction. His power is identified with the interests of the state and the dynasty, which can only be preserved by wisdom and prudence. Above all, a wise man does not heed the advice of women and should not tolerate their meddling in affairs of the state. In brief, it is the ideology of a thoroughly patriarchal society from which women are excluded as a force of evil. If they participate in the 'dialogue' at all, they are sure to represent chaos, lust, irrationality and deceit.

It is not difficult to link the *Thousand and One Nights* to this generic pattern. The work consists of a frame and cycles of embedded stories associated in a way similar to the instructive tales for princes; it has the dialogic situation, the temporal deferral and the function of an initiation. The tales are intended to instruct people, to protect them against deceit and to teach them how to behave in certain situations. It is clear that the compiler of the work was inspired by the well-known cycles of tales and fables and, in fact, to the many interpretations of the function of the tales incorporated into the frame story, such as the stories of the 'Bull and the ass' and the 'Merchant and the genie'; we could add that they refer to similar types of collections of fables and exemplary tales. Nevertheless, it is clear that what we have here is something different. To see what the differences are, we can compare the frame story of the *Thousand and One Nights* with the cycle of *King Jalīʿād and his vizier Shīmās*, which is incorporated into some versions of the *Thousand and One Nights*. It is probably of Persian origin and dates back to before the tenth century.[7]

When King Jalīʿād is about to die he instructs his son Wird Khān about the proper conduct of a prince in life and in affairs of the state. He entrusts the prince to the care of the brilliant and perspicacious Vizier Shīmās. In spite of his careful upbringing, Wird Khān becomes recalcitrant and refuses to heed the advice of his viziers. He refuses to give up his addiction to women and neglects his royal duties. To warn him, the viziers tell him parables and stories, hoping to make him repent and mend his ways, but on the advice of his wife Wird Khān has the viziers executed and dedicates himself to his passions. Soon, the empire is threatened by a neighbouring sultan and it seems that destruction is unavoidable. When catastrophe draws near, Wird Khān finally realizes the predicament he is in. When he goes out in distress, he accidentily finds the son of Shīmās and appoints him vizier. In spite of his tender age, he succeeds in saving the empire.

Apart from the structural and generic resemblances, some differences immediately emerge. Shahriyār and Wird Khān are both symbols of absolute power who learn to combine their passions with a rigid discipline; but whereas Wird Khān delivers himself to the destructive wiles of women and has his viziers killed, Shahriyār has his wives killed to prevent them from undermining his authority. Whereas the viziers of Wird Khān tell stories to lure him away from his lustful and treacherous wife, in the frame story of *Thousand and One Nights* it is a woman who tells stories to restore the sultan's relationship with women. While Shahriyār uses his power to—literally—eliminate women from his life and thus brings the empire on the verge of collapse, Wird Khān ruins the empire because he uses his power not to rule, but to relish his bodily passions and exclude state affairs from his life. Whereas Wird Khān is saved by the intelligence of a young man and turned away from the advice of his women, Shahriyār is saved by an intelligent young woman. Whereas Jalīʿād in the end punishes his women by having them executed, Shahriyār decides to spare the women of the empire. Thus, while it is clear that both cycles are construed after the same pattern, it is through an inversion of roles that a different work is created which adds something to the conventions of the genre.

Both these two cycles and the *Sindbādnāma* are built around various sets of oppositions, men and women, private and public, harem and council hall, power and passion, wisdom and rashness, good and evil, absolute authority and the value of advice. These oppositions are structured by interruptions, the juxtaposition of exemplary tales, the interplay between the frame and the stories and, in the case of the *Sindbādnāma* and the *Thousand and One Nights*, a temporal pattern. However, there is one important difference in the temporal 'interruptions' in the two works: whereas in the *Sindbādnāma* the time-division is used as a structuring mechanism, enhancing the formal and conceptual strength of the cycle, in the *Thousand and One Nights* the main form of interruption, the nights, has much more depth. The nights are meant not merely to provide a time-outline, increase tension, suggest order, realism and narrative structure; it is also given a meaning itself, which contributes to the meaning generated by the work as a whole. The night is a metaphor of the oppositions that are the basis of the story. They impregnate the cycle with a new dimension of meanings, exploiting the possibilities of the generic pattern explained above.

## Nights

Apart from other forms of interruption, in the *Thousand and One Nights* it is the night which represents the function of interruption in the most radical way in the frame story. In a general sense, the alternation of night and day reflect the essential duality in our existence, which was of course much stronger felt in the Middle Ages. The day is meant for work, obligations, social responsibilities, the maintenance of rules, regulations and social order; the night, conversely, is meant for pastimes, one's private life, the pursuit of personal pleasures, social meetings, family life, love and passion. But, to add another dimension, the opposition between day and night, light and dark, is also the opposition between the seen and the unseen, clarity and mystery, openness and closedness, the rational and the irrational, purity and sin, control and chaos. This is why taboos, wantonness and crimes are associated with the night: night is the time when social control disintegrates and the forces of passion and sin are unleashed. It is the time for the pursuit of love and sexuality, legitimate or illegtimate. It is the time for secret undertakings, for theft and murder. It is the time for a flight from reality, for fantasy, for the prevalence of the imagination, for visits to metaphorical worlds, for dreaming.[8]

In the *Thousand and One Nights* the duality of night and day is very adequately illustrated by the nightly escapades of Caliph Hārūn al-Rashīd. At night, the caliph sheds his official guise and normally dedicates himself to his private pleasures. Sometimes, however, the instability of the night and the transformation of his role make him restless. He goes out in disguise, hiding his regular, daytime identity, to inspect the circumstances of his subjects. As a rule he discovers some kind of irregularity which manifests itself during the night and which he sets straight when he has assumed his normal identity as caliph the following day. Here night and day represent different worlds, imposing different identities and different roles. At night the caliph is no longer the caliph; he is either involved in the intricacies of his personal life, or he is losing his peace of mind, since the frame of reference of his status has become invisible, or he has to disguise himself as another person. Most of all the different identities of the caliph represent the different parts of his personality, the dualism reflected in the alternation of official life and private life, public duties and private passions, a sense of order and a sense of freedom, the security of social control and social status and the insecurity of chaos and anomalies.

In the *Thousand and One Nights* we can see how the night is used as the quintessential form of interruption, combining the technical aspects of the concept of dialogue, the temporal dimension, and the metaphorical dimension which it provides. The symbolical connotations of the night are represented in several stories included in the collection, such as the story of the 'Porter and the three ladies of Baghdad', the story of the 'Mock caliph', which plays upon the duality of day and night and character, the story of 'Qamar al-Zamān and Budūr', the story of '‘Ajīb and Gharīb', the story of '‘Azīz and ‘Azīza', the story of 'Bulūqiyā', the story of the 'Second calender' and the story of 'Maryam the belt-maker'. These stories contain interruptions as a structural device linked to temporal divisions, such as days and nights, or they utilize nights and sleep as a meeting-point between different realms of reality, the points where transition is possible from the domain of the real to the domain of magic and the supernatural. Nights add a dimension to narratives, to reality, and to the relationship between the two.

The same duality imbues the frame story of Shahriyār and Shahrazād. In the case of Shahriyār, however, the separation between the two realms becomes blurred. By deceiving him with a black slave, the queen not only confronts him with the uncertainties of his nocturnal identity, she also shatters his vision of himself in his daytime appearance, as the all-powerful king. The night has intruded upon his day, undermining his authority and spreading disorder and chaos. What seemed to be the realm of his unquestioned power now turns out to be based on deceit and lies. While he thought himself the model of power, in fact he was a mere toy of his wife, who mocked his dignity and replaced him by the lowest of creatures. In Shahriyār's view, this is the rule of chaos and irrationality, the rule of women. As in the case of Wird Khān, the night has swallowed the day, and the balance between the two components of life, the two components of the sultan's personality, has been disturbed.

The response of Shahriyār is quite simple. After having become convinced that the adultery of his wife is no accident, but rather the manifestation of the true nature of women, he decides to use his formal authority to restore order in his private life. This authority is not only re-imposed on his daytime life as a ruler, but also on his nocturnal life. Order is maintained by a regime of violence: by executing his wives every morning, he prevents them from appropriating the 'official' part of his life and personality, from undermining his authority and endangering hierarchies. He takes control of the realm of the night, excluding the forces of chaos, except those which spring from his own passions. This is more than a restoration of the *status quo ante*, it is a reversal of the situation produced by the act of adultery. Shahriyār fails to restore the regular duality between the components symbolized by day and night, but instead has the day swallow the night, imposing the daytime regime on the night. There is no alternation of light and dark, there is only the one-dimensional force of control. Shahriyār has usurped the domain of the night; the rational part of his personality has usurped the domain of his emotions; his Ego has disciplined his Id. His character has refused to comply to its multiple, or at least dual, nature, and the result is a monolithical personality with a distorted view of itself and the world. It is a personality that can only preserve its wholeness, balance and coherence by the use of violence and the disturbance of the natural course of life and its reproduction. It is a regime of continual interruption causing stagnation and eliminating the forces of movement, renewal, and transformation. Every day a Shahriyār is 'born' which is identical with the Shahriyār of the day before, with all his absolute power intact. The progress of time has no meaning, since change has become impossible. Life has become an endless repetition, as a cyclic structuring from which no escape is possible. Since there is no change or progress, the empire is doomed. After all, the regular mechanisms of reproduction are destroyed, and there will be no-one to succeed Shahriyār, who is only interested in cloning himself day after day.

The cycle of stagnancy is broken by Shahrazād, who is not only the saviour of her sex, but also of Shahriyār and the whole empire. She creates a world in which sexuality, emotions and imagination are tightly interwoven, and which can substitute the ritual cycle installed by Shahriyār. By telling her stories, Shahrazād leads Shahriyār back to an awareness of historical time, in which causality, advance and continuity are restored. She removes the permanent interruption of life every morning and replaces it by another sense of order, which is not based on a ritual measurement of time, but on a conception of time which is based on fluidity and meaning. She juxtaposes Shahriyār's world with another reality, the reality of fantasy and the imagination, carefully structured to instruct and to convey a message. The two worlds are separated by the regular interruption, the appearance of daylight, but Shahrazād convinces Shahriyār that her stories have a bearing upon life in daytime, that the two realms are separate, but linked to each other. She restores the duality in Shahriyār's personality, while at the same time bringing the two components in harmony and establishing a new form of continuity.

The treatment of Shahriyār's aberration by Shahrazād has all the components of a rite of initiation, as in the case of the instructive tales for princes. Shahriyār has excluded himself from a normal relationship with society. He places himself in a situation of isolation, a liminal state in which the passage of time is suspended and the forces of reproduction are discarded. Shahrazād's stories provide him with the metaphors which symbolize the state in which he finds himself, the nature of his former status, and the status he will acquire. As in the case of the instructions for princes, the metaphorical world which she creates symbolizes the boundary which Shahriyār has to cross in order to deserve his new status. He has to internalize her lessons, but also to transform his personality to admit the world of the imagination, of women and emotions. Only then can the regular passage of time be restored and can Shahriyār be re-incorporated into the domain of normal social relationships. Shahrazād makes full use of the possibilities offered by the dialogic mechanism of interruption. In fact, the whole text of the *Thousand and One Nights* is nothing more than the account of an interruption, a long dialogic confrontation with the readers. Stories are interruptions, which place us in another perspective *vis-à-vis* our reality and experiences.

## The Art of Interruption and Jan Potócki

The basic form of the frame, as it was used in the cycles of instructive tales for princes, contributed to the literary value and expressive power of the *Thousand and One Nights* and the elaboration of the narrative contents and function of the frame. The frame story is no longer a vessel containing parables, nor a grid to order a collection of tales. It has become a story on itself, with its own complex configuration of characters, motifs and metaphors. The interruption becomes itself a container of metaphors. The night is no longer a means of measurement, or even of progress, but rather a symbol of the primordial dialectic of life, a fundamental dualism that is part of human nature. The *Thousand and One Nights* is essentially a comment on this fundamental interruption, an effort to find an answer to questions of multiplicity, dichotomies and dualism. In the end, Shahrazād has restored Shahrayār's personality by showing him the interaction between night and day, the complexity of the world and its fundamental unity.

The relationship between the Persian and Arabic collections of instructive tales for princes and the *Thousand and One Nights* is an example of the fluidity of generic patterns, both in form, narrative functions and ideological concept. Apparently, the compiler of the *Thousand and One Nights* knew cycles such as the *Sindbādnāma* and *King Jalīʿād* quite well and decided to use these models to create something new. He used the technique of inversion to play upon the old themes of misogyny and male authority, and to imbue stereotypes with new dimensions, to give them a new contents and a new function. The result is a form of parody: the work refers to its models in various ways, but the sense of irony and the wilful divergences turn it into a comment on the texts which it follows and on the ideology which inspired them. Women are no longer only a force of evil, they are also a force that brings equilibrium to the life of the king. The inversion of gender roles has of course the most powerful parodical effect. It is through her role as saviour of her sex that Shahrazād has acquired her almost mythical image. But this could only be achieved by referring to the patriarchal ideology of male superiority and authority, as it is contained in the tradition of the cycles of instructive tales for princes. Shahrazād not only saved women from the obsession of Shahriyār, but also from their ideological imprisonment in the generic pattern of a type of literature.[9]

The generic characteristics show the flexibility of texts and genres: a basic pattern can be used in various ways and adapted to various views of reality. The pattern of the frame story with inserted tales seems to be an especially strong foundation for the play with generic conventions, as can be shown by the many imitations of the formal structure of the *Thousand and One Nights* in European literature. The genre seems to have withstood the transition from one literary culture to another; it could be used to express new and different worldviews, while retaining its basic formal technique: the device of interruption. To illustrate this, we will proceed to discuss a text which can be regarded as one of the many metamorphoses of the *Thousand and One Nights*: the novel *The Saragossa Manuscript/Manuscrit trouvé à Saragosse* by the Polish author Jan Potócki. In this text the narrative structure is primarily based on the technique of interruption.

## The *Saragossa Manuscript*

Potócki's novel, which was written in French probably between 1792 and 1803 and which was published in various fragments and versions, contains an account of 66 days from the journal of Alphonse van Worden, who is travelling from Flanders to Madrid, where he will join his regiment in the service of the Spanish king. During the journey, Alphonse crosses the Sierra Morena, an unsafe and uncanny area, where he has some mysterious adventures. He spends the night in a seemingly deserted inn, where he is approached by two Moorish girls who say that they are his cousins and who exhort him to convert to Islam. The next morning he finds himself under a gallows between two corpses of—as he is told later—two notorious criminals. Undeterred, Alphonse joins a company of gipsy-smugglers, who roam around the Sierra Morena, and meets several other travellers who tell him the stories of their lives and their philosophies. The chief of the gipsies, a cabbalist and his daughter, a mathematician, the Wandering Jew, and others tell stories that teach Alphonse the principles of martial arts, the history of religion, mathematics, cabbalism, geometry and moral and erotic codes. The stories are each day interrupted by the night and resumed the next evening, and some are embedded in other stories.[10]

Of course, this very brief summary does not do justice to the complexity of the novel, but it gives an indication of its relationship to the *Thousand and One Nights*. This relationship is not only proved by internal evidence within the text but also confirmed by historical references. As shown by his travel account, Potócki had already read the *Thousand and One Nights* when he journeyed to Constantinople and Egypt in 1784. He even included some Oriental anecdotes in his journal. Later he mentioned 'Oriental tales' related to him by his friend Muhammad bin Othman, a Moroccan ambassador to Spain, suggesting the possibility of publishing them. On his trip to Morocco, in 1791, he asked a Moroccan student to purchase a manuscript of the *Thousand and One Nights* for him, a task in which he did not succeed. Finally, he wrote an Oriental tale, *Le voyage de Hafez récit oriental*, which was published in 1792. It is clear, therefore, that Potócki was familiar with the *Thousand and One Nights* and fascinated by the text, and that he considered imitating it, preserving the Oriental 'physionomy' while making it appealing to a Western audience.[11]

The link between the *Saragossa Manuscript* and the *Thousand and One Nights* is already established at the beginning when Emine and Zibbedee, the two Moorish girls, tell their lifes-stories to Alphonse in a nocturnal scene steeped in eroticism. The scene evidently calls to mind the story of Shahriyār and Shahrazād, with Alphonse in the role of the sultan. Throughout the novel Alphonse retains this role: he is the one who listens, and ultimately all stories are told to and for him. This 'opening scene' is followed by several references to stories of the *Thousand and One Nights*, either in the form of motifs—such as the loss of an eye after illicit love-making, a boy dressed up as a girl, empty palaces, dreams and visions or in thematic parallels—such as stories of love and adventure, stories for instruction, the play with illusions and the supernatural. In brief, the *Saragossa Manuscript* is a text that cannot be understood without reference to the *Thousand and One Nights*. It is so fundamentally interwoven with its model that it derives part of its significance from it. Even if the stories themselves sometimes diverge to such an extent that the parallels seem to be lost, the structural links are so strong that the *Thousand and One Nights* is always present.

However, apart from these obvious parallels, the intertextual relationship between the *Saragossa Manuscript* and the *Thousand and One Nights* is established, overwhelmingly, by the concept of interruption in the form of a time-frame. It should be remarked that apparently Potócki had a preference for what a French critic called the '*découpage temporel*', or temporal divisions. His large historical studies of Russia and the Slavs (*Histoire primitive de Russie*, 1802; *Fragments historiques*, 1796; *Chroniques memoires*, 1793) consist mainly of chronological tables and columns filled with data, without a narrative or linear structure. The histories are meant to show a synchronic survey of events, forcing the reader to find his way through history by jumping from one category to another in a labyrinthine way.[12] Another quotation ironically illustrates this link between embedded stories and chronologies:

> J'ai beau faire attention aux récits de notre chef, je n'y puis plus rien comprendre. Je ne sais plus qui parle ou qui écoute. Ici, cést le marquis de Val Florida qui raconte son histoire à sa fille, qui la raconte au Bohémien, qui nous la raconte. En vérité, cela est très confus. Il m'a toujours paru que les romans et autres ouvrages de ce genre devraient être écrits sur plusieurs colonnes, commes des traités de chronologie.[13]

Clearly, the structure of the interrupted, embedded, stories appealed to Potócki because of their suggestion of synchronicity and simultaneity, and their labyrinthine representation of the lives of the characters. Life, as history, is not a linear narrative; it consists of various narratives that unfold simultaneously.

The nature of interruptions in the *Saragossa Manuscript* can be categorized as follows: first, the alternation between night and day: each chapter covers one day; secondly, the beginnings and endings of stories, within the day-night framework; thirdly, when characters meet each other, as a rule their life-stories are related, sometimes within another story; fourthly, stories are interrupted to give comment and to show responses; fifty, interruptions often occur as a motif in stories. This scheme fits quite well with that of the *Thousand and One Nights* and it seems that, through its model, the *Saragossa Manuscript* is tightly linked to the wider tradition of literature in which entertainment and instruction are combined. This link is strengthened when one considers the functions of the specific type of interruption, which is based on a temporal division, as in the *Thousand and One Nights*: the time-frame accentuates the sense of a coherent structure founded on a regular time-sequence and the idea that the combination of storytelling and events will lead to a denouement. This sense is reinforced by the theme of travelling, since the destination of Alphonse's journey is a substitute for the verdict or execution-threat in the *Thousand and One Nights*. These two basic concepts create the impression that the stories have a meaning that gradually builds up, to be revealed in the end. The seemingly endless excursions explore the domains of knowledge and life in their manifold appearances. The 'truth' which will be disclosed in the end is thus thoroughly buttressed by evidence from outside the story, taken from other stories which are not linked by simultaneity or continuation, but by coming together within the time-sequence imposed by the frame.

Here, as in the *Thousand and One Nights*, the combination of the time-frame and the structure of the journey gives the story the pattern of a process of initiation. This initiation is achieved by the interaction between stories and frame, structured according to the phases of a rite of passage. Alphonse has abandoned his home and his community and he is taken out of his former life to assume a new life and a new role. As a traveller, he enters the second stage when he reaches the Sierra Morena, a mysterious, unpacified and unsafe mountain area, which reflects the liminal phase in which Alphonse now finds himself. He is stripped of his former status and reduced to a marginal figure. From now on he is only a listener being prepared for his future status as an officer of the Castilian king, and as a prominent member of the Moorish Gomelez family. Alphonse is deliberately kept in the liminal state by the sheikh of the Gomelez and his helpers, as the journey does not consist of a linear crossing of the Sierra Morena, but rather of a slow circling over the mountains. This lingering is intended to provide sufficient time for Alphonse to complete his 'education'.

Alphonse is the equivalent of Shahriyār, who is also deliberately kept in deferment—to complete a transformation. In both cases, this transformation is realized through storytelling within a time-frame, which ultimately leads to a form of release and the establishment of a new harmony. As in the case of Shahriyār, Alphonse, too, is not only educated in the scholarly sense; he is given a new vision of the world, he is given a new personality, which is in harmony with the hidden components of his soul. He is taught how to live properly and how to reconcile seemingly contradictory elements of his personality. The other focal point in the novel—Alphonse's Shahrazād, so to speak—is the sheikh of the Gomelez, who is the instigator of the avalanche of stories. From his hiding place he directs the storytellers and storytelling, carefully combined with the inexplicable events which arouse Alphonse's puzzlement and open his mind to unknown mysteries and knowledge. The sheikh is the invisible centre of an apparently uncoordinated configuration of stories that is built to create the conditions for Alphonse's release from his liminal status. Although the skeikh relates very little himself, he is the genius behind each meeting, each story.

The journal of Alphonse, as it is given in the *Saragossa Manuscript*, is thus the account of an interruption, of the freezing of the regular course of life, of the deferment of the continuation of a journey, and of the substitution of both by a time and space consisting of stories. These themselves are in turn interrupted, as they do not consist of realities which are part of a continuum, of a homogeneous, autonomous space, but fragments which have to be linked to another space through the frame and the 'real' experiences of Alphonse. The fragmentation gives historical depth, multi-dimensionality and perspective and provides the opportunity to link the abstract, the theoretical and the metaphorical to a consistent here-and-now. It is only through the juxtaposition of these domains and reality that a meaning can be distilled out of the apparently amorphous mass of stories. The time-frame creates the sense that the stories provide information and clues to interpret the narrative, that they can influence the course of events and induce Alphonse to specific actions. This is stressed by the feeling of Alphonse that the boundaries between stories and reality are blurred, that he cannot definitively determine which stories are really 'true' and which are only part of a vision or an illusion. The stories penetrate into reality, they have a meaning for Alphonse's vision of the world and for his deeds. The stories are shaping Alphonse's mind and perhaps also his destiny.

## The *Saragossa Manuscript* and the Idea of the Night

As in the *Thousand and One Nights*, the time-frame of the *Saragossa Manuscript* is intended as a structuring device and the night is endowed with a meaning of its own. In fact, the concept of the night, as opposed to the day, is perhaps the main *leitmotiv* of the narrative, the key to the disclosure of the secret. The model for the concept of the night, as a narrative component, is provided by the famous night at the Venta Quemada inn, when Alphonse has just entered the Sierra Morena and has his dream-like love-experience with his two Moorish cousins. After his awakening among the corpses beneath the gallows, he quite naturally wonders which part of his experience was real and which part was produced by his imagination. The boundary between reality and fantasy is blurred and Alphonse has entered a state of uncertainty. This is a crucial point of the novel, which determines the narrative tension throughout the story and gives it its unity and dramatic depth. It confirms that Alphonse has assumed a liminal status.

The imposition of the liminal status on Alphonse has two important consequences. First, Alphonse's experience of wonder that urges him to know the truth behind the mysterious events. He realizes that his familiar vision of the world cannot give explanations for what happens to him and that another world, with a different logic, hides behind the world he knows. His experience opens his mind to new perceptions and prepares him for the knowledge he is going to receive; it opens his mind to scepticism and doubt, dissociating him from his previous world of certainty. Second, through the story of his Moorish cousins, Alphonse receives the first glimpse of a new identity. It becomes clear that his vision of himself represented only a fragment of his true self and that there are other people hiding inside him. There is another past which becomes manifest in him and there is another future lying in front of him. For the first time, Alphonse is given a choice: the girls ask him to convert to Islam and to marry them, to be able to join the Muslim Gomelez family. It seems, however, that in order to do this he has to give up his previous identity, substitute one identity for another and renounce everything he has stood for in the past. It is a choice between two seemingly opposing, irreconcilable worlds that are marked by mutual exclusion. The stories that follow are intended to help Alphonse in making his choice, by showing examples from the real world, by showing him how life can be, how many guises it can take on, that the world is not monolithic and one-dimensional, but complex and multi-faceted. Whatever his decision will be it will be taken on the basis of a wide and variegated knowledge. Alphonse will be a new person, with new insights and new experiences.

The night is associated with seduction and eroticism. Alphonse is seduced by the two girls with their exotic beauty, but the promised enjoyment is linked to the proposed choice. The Muslim identity is described as a paradise of worldly pleasures, beauty and abundance, as opposed to the rigid morality of Catholicism. Because Alphonse is imprisoned in his liminal state he is not strictly bound by moral prescriptions, and he is allowed to be introduced to the pleasures that are apparently connected with his new identity. However, the pleasures are followed by punishment and the reminder that life is linked to death and that physical pleasures are part of the transitoriness of matter and beauty. Thus, the motif of seduction and eroticism seems obvious as a connotation of the night, but here it pervades all the other connotations, as it is related to the liminal zone that the night represents, the possibility of choice, the opposition of two worlds, and the difference between illusion and reality. What is new is seductive but it is inevitably accompanied by fear and horror.

Alphonse's experiences at the Venta Quemada sets a pattern for the concept of the night which is adhered to in many different forms throughout the novel. They are followed up by new meetings with the two cousins, by a meeting with the sheikh of the Gomelez and a visit to an underground stronghold. These events are always accompanied by illusions, sleep, dreams, seduction and mysteries. It is at this 'nightly' level of the novel that the story is led to its plot, as if the illusory world of the night is the 'real' setting of the story, and the 'reality' of the day is just a container of stories, discourses and fantasies. Two other people have similar experiences at the Venta Quemada and relate these to Alphonse, thus giving a view of the same event from a different perspective, confirming it as a confluence of reality and fantasy, seduction and punishment. Whether it is explained as an act of the devil, or as one of the dimensions of reality, at least the accounts make Alphonse realize that his experience is not meaningless; that it is related to his life.

In the inserted stories, too, the concept of the night is systematically sustained. Many, perhaps even most, characters in the stories have nightly visions of ghosts, dead people and the devil, and hear voices, etc. Night, sleep and dreams interrupt the regular course of their lives to plunge them into a different domain, in which the hidden components become visible and actions during daylight are reconsidered. Here, too, the night is associated with seduction and punishment, lust and sin, but also with mystic rituals, cabbalism, and drugs. The night is a boundary between the real and the imagined, which one cannot cross of one's own free will, but which imposes itself as a reality, with an invisible, but ultimately stronger presence. Behind this boundary are meetings, explanations, instructions and experiences that would be unattainable in real life.

The night, then, determines the underlying ordering of the narrative, the structure of the stories, and the potentialities of the development of the narrative. It contains the thematic structure and the dominant motifs of the story. This effect cannot be dissociated from its primary function as a form of interruption, a dividing line, a boundary between different domains. The predominance of the night, in the concept examined above, determines the main interest of the novel, which is built on a set of dichotomies, which are represented by the alternation of day and night, symbolizing clarity and mystery, but also by the opposition of fiction and rationality, fantasy and scholarship, illusion and philosophy, masculinity and femininity. The world is not a homogeneous, coherent whole, it consists of an essential duality which pervades all our lives, all events, all our visions of reality. And in the case of Alphonse, this duality is ultimately represented as the clash between two religions, two civilizations, which are both linked inseparably to the history of Spain: Islam and Christianity.

In the *Saragossa Manuscript* Christianity is represented by Alphonse's solid upbringing, his sense of virtue and his loyalty to his family and the Spanish king. His worldview is steeped in religion and traditional values, and it is difficult for him to see reality except from the perspective of Christian morality. His steadfastness is tested by his two Moorish cousins, who instigate him to give up his faith, throw away the crucifix that hangs around his neck and become a Muslim. The reward is not only a night of pleasure and love, but also a marriage to the two beautiful girls and the opportunity to become the head of the Gomelez family. The Gomelez, Alphonse is told, are a tribe that entered the Iberian Peninsula with the Islamic invasion and mixed with an ancient, local, Spanish tribe. They settled in an underground labyrinth of caves, where they found a rich gold-vein that enabled them to acquire enormous wealth and to influence politics from their remote hideout. They built a network of relations covering Spain and the Muslim world, and prepared an Islamic revolution. The two girls tell Alphonse that he is a member of this family, from his mother's side, although he did not know it, and that the sheikh of the Gomelez wants him to succeed him after his death. The family is threatened with extinction and Alphonse seems to be the only one capable of saving it.

Alphonse becomes aware of his complex identity and although he remains adamant in his refusal to become a Muslim, he is tempted by the charms of his cousins and fascinated by their story. He has the impression that a conspiracy, probably inspired by the devil, is taking place around him, which ensnares him in a net. In the meantime, he listens to stories that add a Jewish component to his knowledge of the world, told by the Wandering Jew, the cabbalist and his daughter Rebecca. Emine and Zibbedee keep tempting him and allow him to taste of the pleasures that await him if he accepts their proposal. Simultaneously, however, they test his strength of will and his loyalty to his promises. In the end, Alphonse decides to continue his journey and to present himself before the king, as he initially intended. Meanwhile, Emine and Zibbedee have become pregnant by him; the daughter who is born becomes a Christian lady in Spain, the son becomes a Muslim bey in Tunis.

The process of Alphonse's initiation is clear: he is shown the kernel of a new identity inside himself; he is pressured to chose between two loyalties, two lives, two worlds, two selves. In time, Alphonse acquires sufficent wisdom and life-experience to denounce the obligation to choose: he follows the path of his destiny, but cedes to the Gomelez family part of what they require. The result is a synthesis which satisfies all parties and which suggests a world in which Christian and Muslim components are somehow harmoniously put together. Two worlds have been placed in their correct relationship, not one hidden inside the other, as a potentially dangerous ulcer, but one beside the other with revitalized amicable, even familial, links. The Muslims are accepted as part of the history and heritage of Spain, although the sovereignty of Christianty and the king is not affected. The 'phantom' of the Orient is exorcised and relegated to its legitimate realm.

The delay between Alphonse's first meeting with his cousins and his awareness of his new identity is partly the result of his uncertainty whether the meeting has happened in reality or has sprung forth from his imagination. This uncertainty is sustained throughout the novel, creating the space for the inserted stories, which are in a way a comment on the mysterious events of the night. It is as if the night is a boundary between reality and illusion, between rationality and irrationality. The events of the night are presented as inexplicable, while during the day various explanations of reality are proposed, which correspond to rational—or at least enlightened—theories. The mystery is gradually disclosed; illusions are gradually stripped of their fictitiousness and what remains is a world which is not free from strange elements, but which is nevertheless reshaped according to a coherent vision of reality. The supernatural is systematically reduced to the natural; the intervention of ghosts is re-ascribed to human agency; and the imagination is given its proper place within rational comprehension.

Alphonse's initiation is systematically linked to his introduction to the pleasures of sexuality and love. His two cousins not only give him the opportunity to explore the carnal aspects of love, they also show him the feminine side of his identity. His Christian background, the discipline imposed on him by his father, represent a patriarchal world, whose codes are governed by concepts of bravery, loyalty and steadfastness. Emine and Zibbedee make him conscious of another part of his background, originating from the family of his mother and related to the antithesis of his father's authority:

the Gomelez family and the realm of Islam. Thus, the growth to adulthood is accompanied by the shaping of a complete identity, supplementing the familiar aspects of patriarchy with visions of feminine elements.

The metamorphosis of Alphonse consists, then, first of a new consciousness of the Muslim component of his identity and, secondly, of his ability to separate fact from fiction, to reconcile imagination and reality.

## Conclusions

In the foregoing we have argued that generic conventions are flexible and are developed by authors or compilers to present a vision of society, making use of literary patterns which are part of a tradition, but which are transformed to accommodate to new outlooks and tastes. First, we have examined the relationship between the *Thousand and One Nights* and works which may have served as its models, such as the *Sindbādnāma* and the story of *King Jalīʿād.* The resemblances can be found in fundamental formal elements (the frame story; the technique of interruption) and in ideological purport (the patriarchal view of society and its inversion). Second, we investigated the way in which these elements were employed by a European author in the eighteenth century to utilize the connotations of the *Thousand and One Nights* and the generic system to which it belonged.

It is clear that the *Saragossa Manuscript* represents a conscious effort to relocate the *Thousand and One Nights* in a new context. The novel inherited many motifs, themes and structural elements of the *Thousand and One Nights,* and even reflects its parodic inversions: it is the hiding Muslim sheikh, on the verge of losing his power, who challenges the all-powerful, monolithic authority of Christianity, not by taking up arms or waging war but by creating a transformation through storytelling, through the power of the word, the imagination, and the mind. However, the content of the narrative has undergone fundamental changes to suit the outlook of a new era and a new historical context. The *Saragossa Manuscript* contains a systematic outline of the state of knowledge and thought of the eighteenth-century Enlightenment, with its mixture of rationalist, scientific and speculative reasoning. By doing this the novel depicts the transition to a new historical epoch, the disappearance of the Spanish *ancien régime* and the beginning of new manners of thought. The novel shows the functioning of the concept of genre as a reflection of historical circumstances: it is part of a dynamic process of transformation, it is shaped by dialogic processes between cultures, between texts and between characters, and it gives a coherent representation of reality, or a vision of the world.

Perhaps the most enduring generic feature of the works discussed here is the use of interruption as a literary technique. As our discussion of the symbolic meaning of the 'night' in the *Thousand and One Nights* and the *Saragossa Manuscript* shows, the device of interruption is used not only as a formal artifice but also as the key to a more profound interpretation of the narrative. An understanding of the nature of the night reveals the complexity of life, the possibility that every unity consists in fact of a multiplicity of elements, separated from each other but also related to each other in a complex way. It is this lesson that Shahriyār learns from Shahrazād's stories and it is also the lesson taught to Alphonse in the *Saragossa Manuscript.* Both Shahriyār and Alphonse are taught the meaning of boundaries, which separate and link at the same time and which define the meaning of various different domains. They learn that the different components of reality can be integrated into a harmonious vision of life, the male and female elements, the supernatural and the natural, the rational and the irrational, discipline and emotions.

Perhaps the most essential dichotomy in the texts is the one between imagination and reality that can be reconciled through a metaphorical representation of reality. In the *Saragossa Manuscript* the relationship between the two components is most aptly symbolized by the outcome of Alphonse's peregrinations through the real and imaginary worlds: his cousins bear him a son and a daughter; male reality impregnates female fantasy, enabling the imagination to interfere with reality, to manifest itself in the real. This is the onset of a cycle in which both revitalize the other and by which the most important interruption is eliminated: the looming extinction of the dynasties of Shahriyār and Gomelez, and their respective societies. This dynamism is achieved by storytelling, represented not only by the chain of tales within the cycles but also by the cycles themselves: the *Saragossa Manuscript* can be seen as a male version of its female model, imbuing Oriental fantasy with European rationality, and ensuring its survival as a reservoir of generic conventions.

## Notes

1. See: C. Hilmes & D. Mathy, eds, *Die Magie der Unterbrechung* (Bielefeld, 1999).
2. The cycle is incorporated into the *Thousand and one nights*, probably in one of the later versions, with the title *The Craft and Malice of Women.*
3. About the *Sindbādnāma*, see: D. Comparetti, *Researches Respecting the Book of Sindbâd* (London, 1882); K. Campbell, 'A study of the romance of the seven sages'. *PMLA*, vol. 14 (1899); B.E. Perry, 'The origins of the Book of Sindbâd', *Fabula*, vol. 3 (1960); M. Epstein, *Tales of Sendebar* (Philadelphia, 1967); H.R. Runte, J.K. Wakeley & A.J. Farrell, *The Seven Sages of Rome and the Book of Sindbâd* (New York, 1984).
4. For a discussion of the concept of 'dialogue', see; M. Bakhtin, *The Dialogic Imagination, four essays* (Austin, 1994); see also: G.S. Morson & C. Emerson, *Mikhail Bakhtin: creation of a prosaics* (Stanford, 2001).
5. See: F. Kermode, *The Sense of an Ending: studies in the theory of fiction* (New York, 1967).
6. For a discussion of the concept of 'genre', with its components of formal convention and the reflection of world-views and its fluid nature, see: M. Bakhtin, *The Dialogic Imagination: four essays* (Austin, 1994).
7. See: H. Zotenberg, 'L'Histoire de Gal'ad et Schîmâs', *Journal Asiatique*, 8th series, vol. 7 (1886); a version of the story is included in the later versions of the *Thousand and One Nights.*
8. For a discussion of the symbolism of the 'night', see: A. Alvarez, *Night* (London, 1994).
9. A similar line of thought is developed by Ferial Ghazoul, in: 'Mimesis and meta-mimesis', *Nocturnal Poetics: the Arabian Nights in comparative context* (Cairo, 1996). Ghazoul sees the *Thousand and One Nights* as a parody of the *sīra* genre.
10. I have used the most complete edition to date, by R. Radrizzani: J. Potócki, *Manuscrit trouvé à Saragosse*, Librairie José Corti, 5th impression, 1992.
11. J. Potócki, *Voyage dans l'empire du Maroc fait en l'année 1791* (Paris, 1997); id., *Voyage en Turquie et en Égypte*, ed. S. Plantureux (Paris, 1999); for biographical and bibliographical data, see; D. Triaire, *Potócki* (Arles, 1991); J. Herman, P. Pelckmans & F. Rosset, *Le* Manuscrit trouvé a Saragosse *et ses intertextes* (Louvain, Paris, 2001); F. Rosset & D. Triaire, *De Varsovie à Saragosse; Jean Potócki et son oeuvre* (Louvain, Paris, 2000); the only publication about Potócki and the *Thousand and One Nights* which I was able to consult is: M.T. Giaveri, 'Le Mille et una Notte di Jean Potócki', in L. Heller-Goldenberg, *Les Mille et une nuits dans les imaginaires croisés* (Köln, 1994).
12. Rosset Triaire, pp. 117, 133–4, 137.
13. *Manuscrit trouvé à Saragosse*, p. 310; 28th day.

# The House of Fiction and *le jardin anglo-chinois*

PETER L. CARACCIOLO

## I

> HAD China been accessible to Mr. 'Capability' Brown, ... I should have sworn [he] had drawn [his] happiest ideas from the rich sources which I have tasted this day ... being enchanted by scenes perfectly similar to those I had known [in England], to the magnificence of Stowe, the fairy-land of Painshill.[1]

The sense of *déjà vu* experienced by Lord Macartney, when in 1792 the British Embassy to the Ch'ien-lung Emperor was shown some of the summer palace at Jehol, was increased two days later. It was then that Macartney viewed the wilder area to the west: 'it is one of the finest forest scenes in the world ... if any place in. England can be said ... to have similar features ... it is Lowther Hall in Westmoreland'.[2]

Macartney was unaware that his Chinese translators were graduates from a college founded by Fr Matteo Ripa, the first European to visit Jehol and bring back a detailed report to early eighteenth-century Europe. The creator of Jehol, Kang Hsi (the greatest of the Ch'ing emperors and a Manchu enthusiast for Chinese culture), had put the Neopolitan priest to work with Chinese artists in engraving copper plates of 'selected views of his northern pleasure ground'. On the emperor's death Ripa obtained a passage home by an East Indiaman. In 1724 at London his fame led to audiences at the court of George I, and dinners with the directors of the East India Company. At least one set of Ripa's engravings passed into the hands of Alexander Pope's patron, Lord Burlington, to whom the poet was to address his celebrated epistle on Gardens. The British Museum copy of the Ripa album bears the Chiswick House book-plate, and in the 1720s and 1930s the Burlington circle was absorbed in creating the informal gardening styles which were to develop into the great eighteenth-century parks. That the Ripa album was known to the Burlington circle by the mid-1920s is implied by Pope identifying a relevant type of Chinese park as 'both very vast and very wild'.[3]

Significantly, when Pope and Kent liberated Stowe from Bridgeman's fortress-like geometry, they arranged that a serpentine river should descend into the lake through a glade. To such evidence Patrick Conner adds an anecdote that the China House—in 1738 apparently the earliest such pavilion in England and perhaps the work of Kent—once stood in an old pond on this very Alder River near the Shell Bridge.[4] The charming Chinoiserie buildings that subsequently decorate later eighteenth-century parks (for example, at Kew) were more obvious pastiche. The Manchu influence on the eighteenth-century landscape garden implied by the Ripa evidence points to something of greater, indeed, fundamental significance, a question of meaningful structure, at once aesthetic and geopolitical.

Among the urban Han Chinese grassy expanses stirred uneasy memories of incessant raids by nomads upon civilization; for their Manchu conquerors, on the other hand, grass-lands evoked much the same associations of pastoral and the 'sylvan war' (hunting) which the lawns of the eighteenth-century landscape garden inspired in the European mind.

Such affinities have led continental historians to talk of *le jardin anglo-chinois.* Yet from even as early as the beginning of the new century (when, in *The Prelude* Book VIII, Wordsworth dismisses 'Gehol's famous Gardens') it is clear that the degree of connection between the English landscape garden and the Manchu park was gradually being forgotten. In this cultural process I suggest we may see reflected a comparable amnesia concerning the way in which another and contemporaneous Eastern influence, *The Arabian Nights*, helped to shape the development of the English novel.

## II

With the publication in 1697 of Charles Perrault's *Histoires ou Contes du Temps Passe Avec des Moralitez*, 'the fairy tale clearly emerged as a distinct literary genre'.[5] This collection of folk stories created a vogue for tales of marvels in the Court at Versailles and the fashionable literary circles of Paris. The nature of this interest helps explain the welcome given Antoine Galland's translation of *Alf Layla wa layla* and accounts for the gentrification one finds there in his *Mille et une nuits.* Like the collectors of fairy stories, Galland's target audience was adult and cultivated. Although Perrault and his imitators elsewhere in Europe drew on folklore, they did not hesitate to improve on their sources, transforming roughly expressed tales of a bygone age into smoothly written narratives acceptable to polite literary tastes.

Galland's diplomatic adjustments of style, manners, psychology and closure (which at moments bring these Eastern tales close to the literary innovations of the Enlightenment) preserved the *Nights*' essential vitality, rapidly making this brilliant collection immensely influential. In London the Grub Street translations of the *Nights* first appeared around 1706. By the middle of the second decade of the eighteenth century the English version of the Arabian collection had already reached its third edition. In the early 1720s a journal called *The Churchman's Last Shift* began the weekly serialization of 'Sindbad the Sailor'. The *Nights* obviously lends itself to part-publication, and in 1723 the *London News*, a thrice-weekly news-sheet, began serializing *The Arabian Nights' Entertainments*—its 445 instalments ran for three years. A generation or more of readers were being acclimatized to new ways of storytelling far more elaborate and sophisticated than the European fairy tale, which in turn helps to shape the eclectic, expansive structures of the novel genre.

Alas, as was the case with the eighteenth-century landscape gardens, it was informed critics of these literary developments who were lacking. In both spheres of aesthetic creation, experiments with a new form were judged by reference to models (be they ancient or modern) that were almost exclusively Euro-centric. A few literary commentators, recognizing the need to get beyond Aristotle, do follow up some of the suggestions Fielding makes as how to approach those experiments of his, that were helping to establish the new literary form. But comparison of his masterpiece, *The History of Tom Jones* (1749), with solely the work of European writers (illuminating as it is) does not reach far enough. Distracted by a plethora of Oriental pastiche, most critics had little time for fairy-tales, let alone the *Nights*, and so they neglected those clues as to arabesque influence provided by the novelist himself when discussing his comic-epics-in-prose. The nearest that any other eighteenth-century commentator comes to understanding the quite extraordinary achievement that is *Tom Jones* (and how it relates to a story such as the Arabic tale of the Little Hunchback) is Lord Monboddo. Apparently stimulated by his interest in Indo-European linguistic structures, this scholarly Edinburgh lawyer comments in *The Origin and Progress of Language* (1776):

> The *History of Tom Jones* ... has more personages brought into the story than any thing of the poetic kind I have ever seen; ... all those personages have characters peculiar to them, in so much, that there is not even an host or an hostess upon the road, hardly a servant, who is not distinguished in that way. In short, I never saw any thing that was so much animated and as I may say all alive with characters.[6]

In praising the multitudinous and inclusive life of Fielding's novel, Monboddo unwittingly identifies a key parallel between *Tom Jones* and the Arabic story-cycle: the sense that the world is full of stories, and that the common and appropriate destiny of experience is to be rendered into tales.

## III

One of the clearest links between eighteenth-century landscape design (especially the architectural features located in these gardens) and the literary manifestations of oriental influence is made explicit in the image that Henry James famously used to celebrate the accommodating structures of the novel—'the House of Fiction'.[7] The late nineteenth-century master inherits this trope from Walter Scott's 'The Prefatory Letter' to *Peveril of the Peak* (1822). There, in a debate between the novelist and Dr Dryasdust the historian, Scott defends his practice of basing his romances upon history by likening it to:

> ...a Turkish kiosk rising on the ruins of an ancient temple. ... Not quite correct in architecture, strictly and classically criticised; but presenting something uncommon [and] fantastic to the imagination, on which the spectator gazes with pleasure of the same description which arises from the perusal of an Eastern tale.[8]

Scott derives his comparison from Richard Hole who, in his *Remarks on the Arabian Nights* (1797), observed that 'the Voyages of Sindbad' might not unjustly be 'denominated The Arabian *Odyssey*':

> It seems, indeed ... to bear the same resemblance to that performance as an oriental [mosque.] The constituent parts of the first may be separately considered as to their effect and beauty: each forms a little whole by itself, [such features] irregularly placed ... But in the Grecian temple all parts harmonize together, and compose one simple and magnificent whole. The same kind of Saracenic masonry ... is discoverable in [Spenser's] *Fairy Queen*. It constitutes a different order of poetic architecture from that of the classical Epic; and its inferiority must be allowed, though it possesses some peculiar and appropriate beauties.[9]

Building on the fact that the sacred architecture and gardens of Classical Antiquity and Islam are decorated with literary inscriptions, Hole's comparison sheds light on the flexible geometry of both 'Sindbad the Sailor' and *The 1001 Nights*. For the structure of English versions of the frame tale or the Sindbad cycle can vary. However, among the narratives collected in *The Nights* one does find story-groups that are admirably well constructed. At different periods both the tightly symmetrical and more amorphous forms have influenced English narrative. The changing cultural and geopolitical circumstances of all such appropriations invite closer scrutiny; but space being limited, I shall concentrate on the way in which, in *Tom Jones*, Henry Fielding uses the most intricate of these story-cycles, concluding with a necessarily brief glance at the degree to which Fielding's practice has been a model for subsequent British writers, some of whom have been poet-gardeners.

## IV

These traditional architectural comparisons made by Scott and Hole seem particularly applicable to Fielding's *Tom Jones* for a number of reasons. It is not just that one of the early masterpieces of the English novel begins and ends in a great house set in just such an eighteenth-century landscape garden as Pope and Kent (apparently inspired by Ripa's engravings of Jehol) had been creating in the previous decade. Even more telling is the paradox that while Fielding presents an immense and lively panorama of mid-eighteenth-century England, critics have been puzzled about how to describe the novel. Two different solutions have been proposed: one architectural, the other folkloric. Some commentators conceive of *Tom Jones* as built like 'a Palladian Palace'.[10] To others the plot of *Tom Jones* is not a 'real life' story but a folk-tale disguised with realism. William Empson sees that 'the machinery of the happy ending derives from the fairy tale, as Fielding perhaps recognized' (720). Unfortunately Empson's brisk rationalism prevents him from getting as close as he might to the truth when he argues that the author of *Tom Jones* was clearly following a plot derived 'from a complete dated skeleton' (720). Another brilliant twentieth-century poet took a somewhat different view, seeing the inspiration for Fielding's plot as very much alive. Kenneth Rexroth even goes so far as to suggest that 'Tom is ... the typical Chinese hero, and the novel could easily be restated in Chinese terms and setting' (676). Such a comment, at least initially, leaves one feeling that the sinological enthusiasm of this celebrated American translator has got the better of him.

For it is not to the Middle Kingdom but the Middle East that Fielding primarily directs our attention. In Book VIII, chapter IV of the novel we are introduced to 'one of the pleasantest Barbers that was ever recorded in History, the Barber of Bagdad, or he in *Don Quixote* not excepted' (267). True, the novel's editors have identified this Bagdadian as originating in the *Arabian Nights*—Sheridan Baker even placing him, correctly, in the continuation of 'the story of the Little Hunchback'.[11] Unfortunately, the editors do no more than summarize his peculiarities. Yet when Tom Jones calls for a barber, the talk he has with 'little Benjamin Partridge' runs over four chapters. These chapters, leading as they do to the hilarious imbroglio in the Inn at Upton, might be described as the epicentre of the work. Indeed, the repercussions of the curious alliance into which Tom and the garrulous Barber Partridge enter reverberate throughout the novel. Far from having just a local significance, these arabesque allusions turn out to be a crucial element in the novel. (The structural importance of this overt allusion to the *Nights* is subsequently reinforced by a second explicit reference to the art of the Arab story tellers, this in a sly hint which Fielding lets drop in the paragraph concluding chapter I of Book XVII).

There being scores of parallels between the Hunchback cycle and Fielding's novel, I shall simply sketch the common features, returning to the differences later.

Despite problematic relations with the opposite sex, both young men fall in love. Unfortunately the lovers' attempts to make contact are frustrated, the delay being caused by a barber each has engaged. Unnecessarily, these barbers offer medical treatment, for both are also surgeons. Shameless gossips, although proclaiming their reputation as men of 'gravity' and extraordinarily long-winded, they press their company on the young men in their travels, acting more or less as servants. Although the barbers protest that they act out of concern for the safety of the young man, the reluctant objects of their care grow increasingly irritated. At last, when urged to return home, the young men resort to violence. Through their servants' mismanagement both young men are caught in sexually compromising situations by the girls' fathers or others *in loco parentis*.

Among other parallels are verbal echoes. At various points, the same words and rhetoric are used as when both barbers deplore the young men's 'haste' and cite authorities against it (*TJ*, 267; *LH*, 266–7, 269–70). In other instances synonyms, figurative language, different idioms or an ancient tongue have been deployed to vary the rendering used by the English translator of Galland's French. Both know-alls are superstitious, the one believing in astrology, the other in dreams. Inquisitive to excess, both unwittingly find themselves in the vicinity of an execution; both exasperate as much as they amuse the magistrates they encounter.

As with *Tom Jones*, so in the Arab story the young man does not encounter the barber-surgeons until relatively late in the action—in each case their meeting is roughly a third of the way into the larger narrative, by which point in the comparison it is clear that the novel's subtitle 'the History of a Foundling' could serve as well for the Arab tale. After all, both barbers are intimately associated with the fate of a small creature whose apparently insignificant status belies what will turn out to be his importance in the community. At the beginning of the plot the foundling is abandoned by those who should have taken care of him. In the Arabic text, the little hunchback having choked on a morsel that his hostess has pushed into his mouth, the tailor's wife bundles him up to look like a child and, claiming he is sick of 'the small-pox', leaves him at the Jewish physician's.[12] In *Tom Jones*, it is eventually revealed that his father having died of 'the smallpox' (Book XVIII ch. VII, esp. p. 612, also p.41), Tom's unmarried mother had arranged that Jenny Jones and the unwitting schoolmaster—who subsequently becomes the barber-surgeon Partridge—will be taken for the parents. Meanwhile the unwanted baby is bundled up and left for Squire Allworthy to discover in his bed (29). The hilarious way that, in 'The Little Hunchback', a succession of respectable townsfolk endeavour to shift the burden of responsibility onto their neighbours' shoulders and then think better of it (223–5)[13] is mirrored in Fielding. Summoned by Allworthy the maid Deborah Wilkins, a devout Christian, is all for handing the child over to the Parish when Bridget the Squire's sister intervenes (Book I, ch. I, esp. pp. 29–30). Given the name of Tom, the boy grows up to be Allworthy's favourite. However, in socioeconomic terms, being born out of wedlock apparently of no kin (and especially when turned out of his benefactor's home), Tom Jones could be seen, metaphorically speaking, as dead as the little hunchback appears to be. Later on, with the youth's arrest on a false charge of murder, Tom also becomes the novel's analogue to both the little hunchback and those innocent townsfolk in the Arabic cycle who are charged with his death, a death that, in fact, never occurred.

The claims to knowledge concerning the young man's paternity made by both barbers are rightly suspect. Finally, however, these meddlers do play an important role in the restoration of both foundlings to their proper place in the community. However, as Fielding has telescoped the two Arab narratives, rather than re-enacting the dramatic surgical intervention of the tale, Partridge takes his place in the comically identical order in which the reversed chain of conscience-stricken witnesses alter their testimony about the Foundling (*LH* 226–8, 304–5; *TJ* Book XVIII, ch. VI–VII).

The telling symmetry of this reversal is underlined in Book XVIII, chapter III. There, the Squire comments: 'I consider him as a Child sent by Fortune to my Care. I still remember the innocent, the helpless Situation in which I found him. I feel the tender Pressure of his little Hands at this Moment' (602). If we check back, we discover that this echoes the third chapter of Book I, in which Mr Allworthy 'had now got one of his Fingers into the Infant's Hand' (30).

This process of clarification accompanies the fresh testimonies in the course of which, with Tom's release from prison, it is evident that the novel also shares with the Hunchback cycle the motif of life-giving tales. In the climactic recognition-scene the Sultan welcomes back his little favourite; similarly apprised of his innocence and parentage, Tom is acknowledged by his uncle Allworthy as his heir; and the foundling is allowed to marry Sophia.

I do not want to suggest that in the Arabic cycle or Fielding's *History of Tom Jones* there is anything like an allegory, yet something more than simply profane love is involved. Sooner or later in both narratives, as the result of the working conscience on the better sort of people, altruism tends to overcome the instinct for self-preservation. The metropolis (or a similarly cosmopolitan community) is, after all, the place where the citizen (Muslim, Jew or Christian) has the opportunity of learning civilized values. This sense of the narrative as a moral education is, of course, more pronounced in the novel.

From the scores of parallels between the Arabic stories and *Tom Jones*, it is clear that the novelist found the vivid details of ordinary urban life provided in the Hunchback cycle more exciting than any fantasy about the genies. Nevertheless, there is something of a tease about the manner in which, at the close of chapter I of Book XVII, Fielding distinguishes between his art of the novel and the advantage enjoyed by Arab and Persian storytellers with their '*Genii and Fairies*' (570).[14] For there is almost no resort to the supernatural in the Hunchback cycle.

The lameness of the Bagdadian lover Fielding transmutes from a physical into a psychic want, the consequences of a legal disability, complications of the sort which can be better explored through the greater realism of the novel genre. Apart from this change, the most egregious difference between the young men is that while in the past the Arab lover has eschewed women, Tom (having apparently inherited some of the Little Hunchback's '*joi de vivre*') finds it difficult to resist the ladies' charms. But then in his first novel, *Joseph Andrews*, Fielding (with the help of a crypto-Buddhist parable) had already created a hero who is a chaste lover.[15] By this time it should be also evident that the novelist is not following the arabesque model slavishly. The very deficiencies in the way the young Bagdadian is described (he is scarcely more characterised than his beloved) prompts Fielding to further invention.

As many critics have pointed out, Tom has something of the unworldly good nature of the typical hero of the fairy tale—I was tempted to say the Western fairytale. But Tom is not the traditional third son of European fairy story—as, for example, at the beginning of Defoe's *Robinson Crusoe* (1719) we find him entering the English novel. Here, rather, memories of Rexroth's comparison with the Chinese novel return, prompting me to suggest that Tom resembles another fairytale-prototype. Certainly there are aspects of Tom's plight that are familiar from one well-known tale: the death of his parents exposing their child to the ill will of a wicked step-parent and half-sibling. Such is the family resemblance that Tom can be seen as a male version of none other than Cinderella.

## V

The story of Cinderella is surely the best-known fairy story in the world, a tale that has been a wonder for more than a millennium. Apparently a product of the Silk Route, to this day variants are among the most told tales in the Middle and Near East.[16] The form of the story popular today in the West, of course, comes from the skilled retelling of the tale by Perrault, in his *Histoires ou Contes du temps passé* (Paris, 1697).

The origins of this tale are not known. However, in *Folk-Lore* (March 1947), Arthur Waley pointed out that 'the earliest datable version of the Cinderella story in the world occurs in a Chinese book', written around 850 CE,[17] but the Cinderella figure is not simply parachuted into *Tom Jones*. Fielding is too eclectic, too much the synthesizer. At certain points in the novel, the young lovers seem to share the central role in the re-enactment of this tale. Both young lovers, losing their place in their family, attend nocturnal jollifications; true, it is not the Ball of the fairy-tale, but at the sordid inn at Upton. Nevertheless (as in the Cinderella story), an article of clothing left behind distinguishes true love from false. Sophie's 'singed fur muff' (352–53, also pp. 135, 146) parodies the only clue that the Prince is allowed to Cinderella's identity: her lost shoe (or in a English variant tantalizingly close to Fielding a glove that fits her).[18] The glass footwear we are familiar with, of course, is Perrault's brilliant misreading which Robert Samber preserves in his translation of the Frenchman's tale, *Histories or Tales of Past Times*, published in London in 1729.

These arabesque and folkloric characteristics Fielding combines with more canonical literature, features of Jonsonian humours and comedy of manners as well as neoclassical pastoral and the domestic epic.

Such a mixture of literary kinds is what we find discussed in *Joseph Andrews* ($1741^2$), the first instance where Fielding's reference to the *Nights* helps readers follow his experiments with 'comic-epic-in-prose'. These remarks, with their suggestion that the novelist well understood the *Nights* and its nature as a collection of different narrative genres, occurs at the beginning of Book III of *Joseph Andrews*. There, in a chapter praising fictive biography, we find the *Arabian Nights* placed on a scale of works ranging from burlesque through fantasy, picaresque and satire, a scale from Cervantes, Scarron, Le Sage to the more sophisticated psychological analyses of a master of French eighteenth-century literature. Here the value of Galland's version becomes clear; thanks to his astute gentrification the *Nights* can be placed tellingly next to Marivaux's *History of Marianne* and *Le Paisan Parvenu*.[19]

## VI

What the *Nights* uniquely offered to the author of *Tom Jones* and later generations of novelists for whom his masterpiece served as a prototype was a largely secular model of capacious, densely populated protean fictions employing an expressive amalgam of prose and verse, realism and fantasy, comedy and tragedy. Recycling old bits and pieces of ancient stories from different cultures to make new more intricate narratives, these tales within tales still have the capacity to respond to the needs of increasingly complex societies, both at home and abroad.[20]

By the end of the century references to the *Nights* are widely deployed by the Irish and Scottish novelists. On the Celtic periphery, where the Enlightenment literally contends with Romanticism among populations who still believe in the fairies, such arabesque allusions are not confined to the urban and domestic world of the Hunchback cycle.

In the *Waverley* sequence there are regularly arabesque allusions; not as many as there are references to Shakespeare, it is true. However, following the example of Fielding, Scott places these Arabian allusions strategically. References to the *Nights* provide essential clues about the structure, atmosphere, characterization, themes and genre to which most conveniently the whole sequence seems to belong.

It is true that in *Waverley* (1814) Scott rejects the fashionable conventions of the Gothic and the sentimental; his novel is 'neither a romance of chivalry nor tale of modern manners' (ch. 1, p. 3), but the reader should not miss the hint that *Waverley* escapes being contained by any *one* of these particular categories. This is because, on the model of the *Nights*, Scott here attempts to comprehend a range of such genres. The later dismissal of 'Prince Hussein's tapestry' (ch. 5, p. 42), as its tone should warn us, is also a tease. The story of Prince Ahmed and the Peri Banou (where the magic carpet is found) to some degree offers a suggestive likeness to the adventures of Scott's hero as Waverley leaves an eighteenth-century formal garden to venture into the Highlands. Led by romantic feelings into an unfamiliar wilderness, both the British and the Arab protagonist discover the underground abode of 'the daughter of one of the most powerful and distinguished genies'—as this Persian tale puts it (635). While the charms of the new love tend to eclipse the young man's memories of a previous attachment, her male relatives threaten the civilized, if corrupt, world. A thread of such Eastern allusion connects the first references to the *Nights* with one of the finest touches, an episode of genuine sublimity towards the close of the novel. Here a celebrated Arabian formula is pronounced at a moment when clan loyalties could not be more passionately felt. On being condemned to death, Fergus thinks of his leaderless people but he quickly realizes that, to the clan, Waverley cannot be 'Vich Ian Vohr' 'and these three magic words ... are the only "Open Sesame" to their feelings and sympathies' (ch. 40, p. 336). The 'Forty Thieves' allusion recalls tragically the hidden yet genuine riches of Highland sentiment and culture which were now doomed—without letting the reader forget that from their cavernous hideouts these backward Gaelic marauders had threatened the progressive settled English-speaking world. Scott's vision of where the future lies for his countrymen is rigorously pragmatic.

By this stage in the reception of the *Nights*, there is ample evidence that the potential of such references was easily recognized by the novelist's contemporaries. Although alert to the fact that the *Nights* is only one thread among Scott's tapestry of allusions in *Waverley*, the anonymous reviewer in the *British Critic* (August 1814) singled out for praise the arabesque elements in the pattern. Such references were recognized as being particularly apt to Scott's design of serving his native country by interpreting her to England.[21] This was an essential task, as the Celts joined the English in forging the British Empire.[22] The nation's writers found in the *Nights* means with which they were able to express the United Kingdom's new geopolitical role. They extended their arabesque references to those other story-groups in the *Nights* that could be used to reflect the growth of Empire, its policing and defence—as well as the more problematic consequences of its 'civilizing' role.

Later, when Victoria had become Empress of India R. L. Stevenson shrewdly exploits the imperialistic dynamic inherent in *The 1001 Nights* themselves. The Arab conquests in Persia and beyond are imaged in 'The Ladies of Baghdad' through the Petrified City discovered by Zobeide on her eastern voyage. In turn the *Nights*' reference to *jihad* is used adroitly in *The Master of Ballantrae* (1889) to suggest how Clive's victory over the French at Plessy helped the British to secure dominion in New World as well as the Old.[23]

In this global arena the little hunchback fails to assume the subtly dominant role he plays in *The History of Tom Jones*. Allusions to the related stories of the Barber and his Brothers, on the other hand, multiply throughout nineteenth-century literature. In a groundbreaking article, Leonee Ormond drew attention to the various ways in which authors such as Thackeray employ such references to expose the follies and vices of the age.[24] In *Vanity Fair* (1847–1848) the story of one of the Barber's Brothers helps introduce a notable cluster of arabesque allusions. These frame a devastating critique that the novelist makes of an elegant but vicious metropolitan society which after Wellington's triumphs on both the Continent and subcontinent had grown bloated on the profits of the Honourable East India Company. An equally potent example of such arabesque allusion explodes in Conrad's *Secret Agent* (1907), where a gruesome link with a bloody misadventure of another of the Barber's Brothers points up the threat posed to society by anarchy and state terrorism.[25]

The *Nights* continue to play an important role in the strategies adopted by a whole range of writers (popular no less than highbrow) confronting the challenges of the new age. Arabesque influences are detectable in work as diverse as H. G. Wells's fiction (the mainstream as well the scientific romances), Yeats's *A Vision* and Joyce's experiments; indeed his anti-novel is even more of an 'Aludin's cave' (108: 27) than *Ulysses*.[26] The evidence indicates that 'The Hunchback's Tale' is one of three specific *Nights* tales of death and revival underlying the dream structure of *Finnegans Wake*. With its Christian broker and Jewish doctor, the Hunchback's tale testifies to 'the cultural melting pot' of the Arab cities, to a cosmopolitanism offering a worldview apt for the modern age.

Paradoxically, however, as the twentieth century wore on, the activities of the Barber's brothers could be disowned by a certain type of English author—even when there are grounds for believing that the writer concerned was in reality alert to the arabesque elements in the poetic heritage of the novel—at least subconsciously.

## VII

> It was left to Fielding, who had not himself the poetic mind ... to construct a fictional form which could attract the poetic imagination. *Tom Jones* was to prove the archetype not only of the picaresque novelists. James and Joyce owe as much to it as Dickens (Graham Greene, 'Fielding and Sterne', 1937).[27]

There is something wilful about Greene's blindness here to the poetic in Fielding, a writer he goes out of his way to recognize as a seminal influence; so much so that one is driven to wonder if there might be debts in Greene's own work which he is reluctant to acknowledge.

Significantly Graham Greene's attitude to the *Nights* is ambivalent. Deploring 'a general refusal to grasp the importance of fantasy in [his own] work', Greene reminds us, 'I'm a story-teller, unlike writers of the previous generation'. Indeed, his narratives, filled with action and suspense, commonly wearing an uncomplicated look, do seem to derive from the linear aspects of the *Nights* rather than from their more involved patterns, which attracted the Modernists to them. Nevertheless, from his early works to the more recent, beneath the appearance of apparently straightforward realism, Greene's structures are often surprisingly arabesque, especially in the later fictions. Variations on the frame tale of the *Nights* in particular tend to reappear throughout his *oeuvre*. While some references remain explicit, more and more are submerged. However, in Greene's late masterpiece something other than just teasing of the reader seems involved. In *Monsignor Quixote* (1982, pt. II, ch. 4) the censorship of the innocent priest by his reactionary bishop leads to a sublime use of the imaginary meal that the Barber's Sixth Brother pretends to share with his Barmecide host. From a story cherished by the Victorians and their successors Greene creates that deeply poignant scene. Long past midnight, without the prescribed bread and wine, the sick Monsignor Quixote falteringly celebrates his last mass, and moved by love for his old philosophical sparring-partner the communist mayor, Sancho, receives Holy Communion.

Greene has been prepared to accept the possibility that aspects of Cervantic studies might have subconsciously influenced his *oeuvre*.[28] To the suggestion that the arabesque might similarly be operative, Greene's response was courteous if somewhat equivocal: 'I doubt whether I ever read [the *Nights*] through to the end'. (Such a reaction was understandable in the aftershock of the bomb that in December 1988 blew PanAm Flight 103 out of the skies over the Scottish town of Lockerbie.) Subsequently, when reminded that the story of the Little Hunchback appears very early on in the Routledge edition (which he identified as the translation he acquired in the 1930s), Greene's position softened: 'I have read *The Arabian Nights* in the Mardrus and Mathers translation. I still possess the four volumes, but as I probably read it all some fifty years ago I have very little memory of any details'.[29]

Whereas the nineteenth century produced around half-a-dozen translations from the Arabic (whether directly or otherwise) into English, the modern period so far has managed barely half that number. Of these, there is only one version that as yet can compete in comprehensiveness with the efforts of Lane, Payne and Burton: Initially appearing privately (1923, repr. 1929), Edward Powys Mathers' translation from the French of Mardrus, eventually found a wider audience in a trade edition that Routledge published (1937). Rival publishers reacted somewhat in the way that their predecessors had done to each reworking of the *Nights* in the nineteenth century, battening onto the success enjoyed by the new edition.

During the inter-war period many writers found that the Mardrus and Mathers acted on their own memories like Proust's 'Madeleine'. Bordering on the world of the archetypes, in Borges's words, the book of *The Thousand and One Nights* is 'so vast that it is not necessary to have read it, for it is part of our memory'.[30] Such pervasive influences might go practically unregarded until activated by, for instance, visits to the cinema.[31] Reminders of childhood experiences of being read to, taken to the Pantomime or of some other potent encounter with the *Nights* could easily have prompted the adult Greene's purchase of the Madrus–Mathers.

## VIII

The turn to romance observable in his later fiction can also be related partly to the appearance of new translations of the *Nights*. In 1954 Allen Lane brought out N. J. Dawood's 'The Hunchback, Sindbad and Other Tales' as their Penguin no. 1001. By the mid-1960s there were no fewer than six different paperback versions of the *Nights*. This *embarras de richesses* coincided with the Anglophone discovery of the Latin American writer for whom the *Nights* has had the greatest significance. In 1960 Jorge Luis Borges was joint winner of the International Publishers Prize. Two years later samples of his work appeared on both sides of the Atlantic, Weidenfeld and Nicholson bringing out *Ficciones*, New Directions *Labryinths*, while selected stories were broadcast on the BBC.

The evident impression that Borges's subtly arabesque 'Sud' (*A Personal Anthology*, 1967) made on Greene's *The Honorary Consul* (1978) invites a comparison that in returning us to the images of the House of Fiction and *Le Jardin Anglo-chinois* sheds further light upon the relation between aesthetics and geopolitics. The epicentre of Greene's shift into fantasy, that extraordinary story 'Under the Garden' (*A Sense of Reality*, 1963) shares many of the features that characterize two other celebrated gardens created during the second half of the twentieth century. One, like Greene's dream vision, is a purely literary masterpiece, Borges' 'The Garden of Forking Paths'.[32] The other, being the work of Britain's outstanding concrete poet, Ian Hamilton Finlay, has transformed Stonypath, a small property on the Southern Uplands of Scotland into 'Little Sparta', which in the manner of the eighteenth-century poet-gardener is something vastly more than just a neoclassical landscape.[33] There are further obvious differences in scale and elaboration between the three creations, but the dozen or so parallels are noteworthy.

A reading of these stories or a visit to Stonypath involves the exploration of a garden that combines Oriental and Western traditions: 'word, letter, sign and symbol reverberating throughout the landscape'—as they do in Chinese, Islamic and Neoclassic traditions.[34] The magnitude of this magic space varies, sometimes appearing to the imagination to be immense and associated with the Ocean itself; in Greene's oneiric-fantasy a pond is transformed into 'the sea of the unconscious'. This garden is richly enigmatic, full of stories within stories calling out to be decoded. The inscribed structures of the emblematic labyrinth—cave (Greene), pavilion (Borges) or temple (Finlay)—are alike places of initiation for artist as much as audience. Dedicated 'To Apollo his music his missiles his muses' the riddle of the Garden Temple at Little Sparta is the most easily explicated: 'considered in geopolitical terms, it challenges the state of Western culture in a north-westerly outpost of contemporary Europe'.[35] The more private concerns in all three works are framed by global conflict, with references ranging form World Wars I and II to the nuclear standoff. At a key moment in the struggle, a coded message about an enemy offensive is conveyed in a form combining the literary and visual arts. The literary references involve what in the past were regarded as subordinate genres: Novel, News, and the *Nights*; indeed in both 'Under the Garden' and Little Sparta it is the same tale that is recalled, conjuring up images of Aladdin, the treasure cave and the magic lamp. Finlay's Heroic Emblem picturing a Japanese battle ship *Ijn Djinn Yamato* celebrates the United States' hard-won victory in the Pacific War. With the destruction of European hegemony, world dominion has passed across the Atlantic—at least for the moment. Given the imperialist dynamic inherent in the Arabian collection itself, perhaps it was only to be expected that the fabulously gifted author of *Midnight's Children* and *The Moor's Last Sigh* should be drawn to re-locate to New York.

## Acknowledgements

For help in preparing this essay, I am grateful to Evelyn Fishburn, Judith Hawley, Javed Majeed, Wen-chin Ouyang and the RNIB.

## Notes

1. See Patrick Conner, *Oriental Architecture in the West* (Thames and Hudson, 1979), p. 103; also Peter L. Caracciolo's article-review of Conner's often enlightening study in 'Stately Pleasure Domes', *The Literary Review*, No 13 (4–11 April 1980), pp. 36–7. On the related topic of Robert Sayer's publication of *The Emperor of China's Palace at Peking* (London, 1753), see Mara Miller, 'A New Source of English Garden Design,' in *Apollo* (March 1984), pp. 181–4, and Mara Miller, *The Garden as Art* (Albany: SUNY, 1993), pl. 4.
2. *An Embassy to China, Lord Macartney's Journal*, ed. J.L. Crammer-Byng (Longman, 1962), p. 132.
3. See Conner, pp. 31, 42.
4. See Conner, ch. 4; with the China House reproduced in plates 17 and 18 compare Ripa's depiction of the smaller pavilions on the island palace complex in the Imperial Gardens at Jehol in pl. 16.
5. As we are reminded by Robert Irwin during his discussion of fairy tales in *The Arabian Nights A Companion* (Allen Lane, 1994), pp. 99–102.
6. Volume III of *The Origin and the Progress of Language* (1776) by James Burnett, Lord Monboddo cited in *Novel and Romance 1700–1800 A Documentary Record* edited by Ioan Williams (Routledge, 1970), pp. 291–2.
7. The image of the million-windowed house of fiction occurs in the Preface to *The Portrait of a Lady* (1908).
8. Border Edition (1893), I lxxiv: citations from Scott's novels are to this edition.
9. Richard Hole, *Remarks on Arabian Nights Entertainments* (Cadell, 1797), pp. 17–18. On this distinction between Western and Islamic architecture, see, e.g. John D. Hoag, *Western Islamic Architecture* (Studio Vista, 1963), esp. pp. 8–9, 29.
10. Thus Dorothy van Ghent, cited in one of the essays appended to Sheridan Baker's edition of *Tom Jones* (New York: Norton, 1973), p. 702. All citations here, whether of Fielding's novel or the twentieth century critical commentaries by the likes of William Empson and Kenneth Rexroth are to this edition.
11. See *Arabian Nights Entertainments*, edited by Robert L. Mack (Oxford: World's Classics, 1995), pp. 222–395. All references are to this text.
12. Here *Tom Jones* seems nearer to *Alf Layla wa Layla* than to Galland or his Grub Street translator. In Husain Haddawy's translation (based on the Arabic text edited by Muhsin Mahdi), the tailor's wife pretends the 'dead' Hunchback is a child stricken with the smallpox, *The Arabian Nights* (Norton, 1990), p. 208. Had Fielding heard a version of this memorable story closer to the Arabic original? On the novelist's interest in Oriental culture and his financial connections with the East India Company, see Peter L. Caracciolo, 'Afloat on the Sea of Stories,' in *Comparative Criticism XX* (Cambridge University Press, 2000), pp. 2–20, esp. pp. 7, 16–17.
13. For an illuminating analysis of this tale, see Mia Gerhardt, *The Art of Story-Telling* (Leiden: Brill, 1963), pp. 411–16; also the perceptive comments in Irwin, *passim*.

14. A genie and a fairy intervene in a tale immediately preceding that of the Little Hunchback. The parallels between *Tom Jones* and The story of the amours of Camaralzaman and Badoura (*The Nights*, pp. 357–440) are also examined in my forthcoming essay 'Oriental Fielding'.
15. 'Afloat on the Sea of Stories', pp. 2–7.
16. Neil Philip, *The Cinderella Story* (Penguin, 1989), p. 40
17. See Iona & Peter Opie, *The Classic Fairy Tales* (Oxford University Press, 1974), pp. 120–1.
18. Philip, p. 2.
19. *Joseph Andrews* (Norton, 1987), p. 146.
20. For more on this point see 'Introduction' to *The Arabian Nights in English Literature* (hereafter cited as *ANEL*) edited by Peter L. Caracciolo (Macmillan, 1988), esp. p.16. For a penetrating study of the way these stories are generated see Ferial J. Ghazoul, *The Arabian Nights: a structural analysis* (Cairo, 1980).
21. See 'Introduction' to *ANEL*, pp. 11–15.
22. On the Scots, Ulstermen and to a lesser extent the Catholic Irish as empire-builders, see Linda Colley, *Britons: Forging the Nation 1707–1837* (Pimlico, 1994), pp. 127–34.
23. Robert Louis Stevenson, 'Adventure of Chevalier Burke in India', *The Master of Ballantrae* (Penguin, 1994), p. 129. See also 'Afloat on the Sea of Stories', pp. 3–5.
24. As well as Leonee Ormond's, see Cornelia Cook's essay in *ANEL*: respectively, chapters 7 and 8. More generally Muhsin Jassim Ali's *Scheherezade in England* (1981) is a perceptive study of eighteenth- and nineteenth-century English responses
25. See Peter L. Caracciolo and Robert Hampson, 'Conrad, Collins, Dickens and the Barber's Fourth Brother, *Notes and Queries* (1989) NS, XXVI, ii, pp. 193–6.
26. See the illuminating essays on these authors by Robert Hampson and Warwick Gould in *ANEL*: respectively, chapters 9 and 10.
27. Graham Greene, *Collected Essays* (Bodley Head, 1969), p. 86. Citations from Greene's fiction are to the Penguin editions.
28. Graham Greene, *Ways of Escape* (1980; Vintage reprint 1999), p. 258.
29. Personal communication.
30. Jorge Luis Borges, *Seven Nights* (Faber, 1986), pp. 50, 57.
31. As film critic at *The Spectator* for five years in the 1930s Greene was hardly unaware that directors such as Robison, Lubitsch and Fairbanks Jr made versions of the *Nights*. The potent impact of the Arabian collection on earlier forms of popular entertainment, especially Pantomime, is discussed in *ANEL* (pp. 1, 44, 154, 230–1, 236). Notable here is Greene's *A Gun for Sale* (1936) where discretely overarching allusions to the pantomimes of Aladdin and Sindbad point up the presence of a nocturnal weaver of therapeutic tales at an important crisis in the novel (pp. 21, 53, 159, 160; see also chap. 5).
32. Translations of 'The Garden of Forking Paths' appeared in both the 1962 Weidenfeld and New Directions selections. According to his nephew Nicholas Dennys, Greene possessed a large Borges collection.
33. For an account of this visionary garden, see Yves Abrioux, *Jan Hamilton Finlay: a visual primer* (Edinburgh: Reaktion Press, 1985).
34. Thus Charles Jenks, *The Garden of Cosmic Speculation* (Frances Lincoln, 2003), p. 44. This work celebrates the collaboration between the author and his wife Maggie Keswick that resulted in the most philosophical of all recent experiments in *Le jardin anglo-chinois*.
35. Abrioux, p. 132.

# Traces of the *Thousand and One Nights* in Borges

EVELYN FISHBURN

## 'Los siglos pasan y la gente sigue escuchando la voz de Shaharazad'

'Los siglos pasan y la gente sigue escuchando la voz de Shaharazad'; the centuries go by, and we are still hearing the voice of Scheherazade: with this simple sentence Borges pays tribute to the enduring impact of the *Arabian Nights* in shaping our present culture. Elsewhere, in *Seven Nights* he states provocatively that we do not need to have read 'this vast book' to be influenced by it, for 'it is part of our memory'. What appears to be no more than an elegant throwaway line is actually quite a powerful statement: as ever, Borges is questioning monolithic concepts by disturbing accepted connotations of East and West, and opening up a debate about acculturation and transculturation in words that predate that terminology. He refers to the *Nights* as 'a vast dream of Islam that invaded the West', dismantling in its wake the edifice of the rationalist rhetoric of Boileau and clearing the path for Romanticism to sweep over Europe. In his words, 'the Romantic Movement began when someone, in Normandy or in Paris, read Galland's translation of *The Thousand and One Nights*'.[1] For Borges, the *Nights* are not so much an exotic other as a constitutive component of our culture.

Borges continually uses the *Nights* in his ironic stance against categories, asking 'What are all the Nights of Scheherazade next to an argument of Berkeley', or commenting that Scheherazade is 'less inventive than Allah', provocatively conjoining fiction with philosophy and religion.[2]

Our literature continues to bear the traces of the *Nights*, as has been amply demonstrated during the workshops of the AHRB Project on Genre Ideologies and Narrative Transformation. In what follows I shall address some aspects of the presence of the

*Nights* in Borges. As is perhaps too well known, Borges started reading Burton's translation in secret as a young child;[3] he has since studied most of the principal translations and written on their comparative merits and demerits with recognized insight, a topic that goes right to the heart of the subject of this project, cultural transmutations, and one that I would have found fascinating to pursue were it not that it has been so admirably dealt with in the writings of scholars such as Peter Caracciolo and Robert Irwin.[4] Borges's essay 'The Translators of the One Hundred and One Nights' discusses a number of different versions of the *Nights*, addressing the highly relevant question of how fiction shapes ideologies and ideology fiction. Although the focus of his interest is in the qualities of the translations,[5] he also makes some comments on their faithfulness to the agreed source language. But his knowledge of the source was not first-hand: he took his first lessons in Arabic shortly before his death in Geneva.[6] His short story 'Averroës' Search' can be read as a self-ironic fictional elaboration of this situation: the attempt to cross cultural boundaries with the limited tools of one's own culture. Seduced by his reading of Burton and Lane and some other Orientalists, the Borgesian narrator of 'Averroës' Search' thinks he can dream up an Islamic scholar's vain efforts to comprehend a culture other than his own, but in the end he realizes that he has created merely a self-reflecting false image of an Islamic scholar (Averroes), on a self-deluding endeavour such as his own. Until I came to prepare this article, I had never thought of the link between this story and Borges's undoubtedly authoritative writings on the *Nights*. It is not a matter of now questioning his erudition or insight into the translations he discusses nor, of course, of disputing his claim regarding the presence of Islam in Western culture, but of showing his acute awareness of the complexity of the (postmodern) problem of how to embrace the 'Other' while still respecting its difference, that kernel of otherness which defies appropriation and translation.

The *Nights* are mentioned explicitly in several Borges stories: in 'Tlön, Uqbar, Orbis Tertius', 'The Garden of Forking Paths', 'The Zahir', 'The Man on the Threshold', 'Brodie's Report' and 'The Book of Sands', while particular tales from the *Nights* are alluded to in others. Critics have rightly pointed out that they appear at key moments in the fiction to open it up to an alternative fantastic interpretation.[7] I should like to qualify any overarching conclusion by examining the diversity in the role allusion to the *Nights* plays in Borges. This is part of a larger project; for this article, let me focus on 'The South', a story in which the presence of the *Nights* is most insistent as it is mentioned at four different moments, all associated with the relationship between fiction and reality. The first explains that it is impatience to peruse a copy of Weil's version of the *Nights* which is the direct cause of the accident suffered by the main character, Johannes Dahlmann; the second links his feverish nightmares to the awesome illustrations of Weil's *Nights*; the third refers to Dahlmann's train journey, when he decides to start reading the first volume of the *Nights* to prove that he has overcome the trauma of his illness. On this occasion he finds he has no need of fantasy because he feels happy travelling through the Buenos Aires outskirts, yet later on in the story it is exactly the opposite: in a country store, mocked by some aggressive drinkers, Dahlmann does need the escape fantasy offers and turns, once more, to the *Nights*. This story is unusual in that Borges himself has offered three possible explanations of its highly improbable plot line: one, that it happened as narrated, making the allusion to the *Nights* a realistic detail concerning a bookish protagonist; two, that the ending was a nightmare, bringing the story back to realism from Todorov's uncanny moment of hesitation; three, that it expressed the innermost wishes of the Borges-like protagonist:

to die in a knife-fight.[8] The allusions to the *Nights* inflect this last allusion differently, with a suggestion of *dédoublement*.

It is interesting to note that there are changes in the autobiographical beginning of the story. In real life, one Christmas Eve Borges suffered a similar accident to Dahlmann's when he rushed up the stairs to meet 'une jeune fille chilienne tres belle' (in Bernès' version of Borges's account of the incident).[9] He hurt himself, septicaemia set in, and he suffered prolonged feverish nightmares. Why change the beautiful Chilean to a copy of the *Nights*, and why particularly to Weil's version? The second question is easy to answer: because of Borges's meticulous attention to detail, for Weil's version has, indeed, some truly gruesome illustrations. Within the fantasy, this is a realistic detail. Critics are too ready to assume that Borges is 'making up' his allusions; usually, precisely the opposite is the case, in that the allusion is invoked with great precision and, of course, imagination, as in this case. But what of the other references?

I shall leave it to psychoanalysts to elaborate on the change from the beautiful Chilean to a volume of the *Nights*; for literary purposes it introduces with the marvels of the *Nights* the topic of the relationship of life and fiction. The last two references to the *Nights* are more precise on this: measured against the joy of life, Scheherazade's miracles have become 'superfluous': 'Happiness distracted him from Scheherazade and her *superfluous* miracles' (F 149, my emphasis), but when life becomes threatening, 'he opened the volume of *The Arabian Nights as though to block out reality*' (F 152, my emphasis), and the magic of fiction becomes an alternative to reality, a means of escape from its horror and a strategy for survival. Through these references to the *Nights* Borges is weaving several of his ideas about fiction into his own fiction such as its dangers, its dreamlike qualities, its redundancy and its consolation but most particularly his belief that literature does not reflect reality but is something added to the world: 'una cosa más agregada al mundo, no su reflejo [not a mirror of the world, but just another thing added to the world's contents]' (310).[10]

If we think of the key concepts associated with Borges's fiction we will surely come up with the following: infinity, the labyrinth, entertainment (divertir), mirrors, duplication, embedding and centrality. It is interesting to look at these well-worn borgesian themes from the transcultural perspective of the *Nights*.

## Infinity

There is no canonical text: the movement from orality to writing, the *Nights*' uncertain but widespread origins, and open-ended and many-layered composition, receiving accretions, interpolations and imitations make this an infinite text.[11] Such a literary *oeuvre* in permanent transformation underlies Borges's story 'The Immortal' which, oddly, does not seem to mention the *Nights* as one of the many transmutations of the eternal, total book. And yet, it does, in an almost cryptic reference, namely, to the 1835 Bulaq edition of the *Nights*: 'in the seventh century of the Hegira, on the outskirts of Bulaq, I transcribed with deliberate calligraphy, in a language I have forgotten, in an alphabet I know not, the seven voyages of Sinbad and the story of the City of Brass' (192).[12]

The reference to Sinbad is particularly opportune in the context of inter-and transtextuality in 'The Immortal', first, because the Sinbad cycle is one of the many accretions to the *Nights*, a proof of its loose structure and secondly, because of its association with the *Odyssey* (Sinbad encounters and blinds a giant in his third voyage, an incident which echoes Odysseus' encounter with Polyphemus, as noted by Borges in *Seven Nights*).

Borges loved the open-endedness of the title 'The Thousand and One Nights', that is, a thousand, standing for infinity, having still one Night added to it, and played with this openness. He re-wrote some of the *Nights*, namely, 'The Chamber of Statues' and 'The Story of the Two Dreamers', removing the religious admonishing of Galland's version and introducing a more metaphysical flavour.[13] With proverbial tongue-in-cheek, Borges attributed the latter tale to Gustav Weil, its translator.[14] Even more controversially, he repeatedly attributed his own invented story, 'The Two Kings and the Two Labyrinths' to Burton, and to the *Nights*.[15]

Borges added to the *Nights* in other ways, too. For instance, the manuscript of 'Brodie's Report' in the eponymous story was found hidden inside a copy of the first volume of Lane's translation, with a suggestion that in time this story will become integrated into the Lane text. Borges is here continuing in the tradition of the medieval copyists, who often intercalated their favourite stories.[16] *The Book of Sand*, so-called because 'neither sand nor this book has a beginning or an end ... No page is the first page; no page is the last' (91),[17] most epitomizes the idea of the total and endless book. Its association with the *Nights* is suggested when the narrator chooses to hide it 'behind some imperfect volumes of the *Thousand and One Nights*'. I read the word 'imperfect' as a reference, precisely to the open-endedness of the *Nights*, the fact that, as mentioned, there is no canonical text.

## The Labyrinth and its diversions in the *Nights* and in Borges

The opening image of all the volumes of Richard Burton's translation of the *Nights* has a figure strongly suggestive of a labyrinth construction (it is not, strictly speaking, a labyrinth, but very evocative of one).[18] This figure is obviously related to the intricate pattern of self-proliferating stories within stories that are endlessly told by Scheherazade. As we all know, Scheherazade constructs her labyrinth of stories to prolong her life but when she reaches the symbolic centre she is saved; such a happy ending does not occur in Borges's fiction, where there is often a moment of illumination, or its delusion on reaching the symbolic centre of the labyrinth, but either madness, or death, inevitably awaits.

In a traditional labyrinth you have to turn, and turn, and turn again until you find the centre (or the way out). These turns are *diversions* (Latin *divertere*) which mean both to amuse and to turn aside. The *Nights*' mission was to draw attention away from a serious concern (diversion) through entertainment (diversion). The title, *The Arabian Nights Entertainments* makes this clear. Borges repeats the claim for himself: 'My tales, like those of the *One Thousand and One Nights*, are intended not to persuade readers, but to entertain and touch them' (345). Yet what form does this entertainment take? For Scheherazade, as mentioned, it is a life-saving operation; her tales are what delays the moment of her execution. She weaves her labyrinthine web of tales to enthral and entrap the King with the happy outcome we all know. The same initial situation obtains in 'The Secret Miracle' where Hladik, the main character, has also been condemned to death by a dictator more vicious and implacable than Shahriyar, namely Hitler, and he too thinks of resorting to fiction to delay the moment of his death.[19] But unlike Scheherazade, Hladik has no captive interlocutor; as Foucault points out, he tells stories that are not to be heard, or even read, by anyone.[20] His is a purely private means of survival. From the moment he is sentenced to death he escapes into various fantasies, among them endless atrocious death scenes. Yet 'Sometimes, impatiently, he yearned ... for the blast that would redeem him ... from his vain imaginings' (158). Hladik's occasional wish for death simply not to have to go on imagining life-saving plots is a despondency we do not hear from Scheherazade. When Hladik realises that these fantasies are clearly not working he switches tack in desperation, and asks God to grant him a year to perfect his circular drama *The Enemies*, a play he had written earlier and left unfinished. 'Painstakingly, motionless, secretly, he forged in time his grand invisible labyrinth' (160), repeating endlessly the frame story with death-delaying variations. He believes that through his fiction he will be able to give sense not only to his life but also justify God's existence.

One of the questions we may ask is 'why do tellers tell tales and what do tales tell about the tellers and their world'. There is, very obviously, a dark shift in the 'entertainment' motif from the *Nights* to 'The Secret Miracle', responding to their different cultural contexts but there is also an important element of continuity uniting the texts in their shared belief in the enduring power of narrative. Of course, this belief is triumphant in the *Nights*, and cruelly and self-mockingly ridiculed in Borges's twentieth-century fiction, for Hladik dies a bare two minutes after the appointed time.

However, 'The Secret Miracle' can also be read differently, as a gloss on the Koranic verse which serves as its epitaph:

> And God caused him to die for an hundred years, and then raised him to life. And God said, 'How long hast thou waited?' He said, 'I have waited a day or part of a day' (Qu'ran, 2:261, qtd. Hurley, 157).[21]

If we take an epigraph to be the gateway to the main text, we will find in this one an ironic inversion of the secret miracle of the story where the two minutes' delay in Hadlik's execution seemed to him as a year, allowing the fulfilment of his wish. I am proposing here that we read in this epigraph an invitation to consider the magic of the story as its central element. By directing us to the Islamic traces of the story a possible trajectory is established from the Koran to the *Nights* through the link made by Borges mentioned earlier, when he declared Sheherazade's tales to be 'less inventive than Allah's'.

This reading is obviously not unequivocal, but seen and understood from the vantage-point of 'that vast dream of Islam', so rich in miracles, it becomes a convincing layer of interpretation and, I suggest, a not undeserving continuation of the *Nights*.

## Embedding and centrality[22]

If I had to choose the one feature of the *Nights* most closely linked to Borges and most frequently mentioned by him it would be the Night that is embedded at the centre of the work, 'magic among Nights' in which the King allegedly hears his own story related in one of Scheherazade's tales. This assertion by Borges is quoted in every study of the *Nights* that I have come across (and even, most recently, in a travel book on Sicily);[23] however, Borges's specular interpretation of this Night which arguably has influenced many subsequent readings of the *Nights* has been the object of much dispute and merits separate discussion.[24] For my purposes here, the accuracy of the details is not of primary importance; what is significant is the reading of this Night that Borges constructs and which focuses, in 'The Garden of Forking Paths' on centrality as the privileged site of revelation: 'I also recalled that Night at the centre of the *1001 Nights*, when the queen Scheherazade (through some magical distractedness on the part of the copyist) begins to retell, verbatim, the story of the *1001 Nights*, with the risk of returning once again to the Night on which she is telling it—and so on, *ad infinitum*' (125). This Night, with all its attributes, is referred to repeatedly as Night 602, which is clearly not at the centre of 1001 and yet Borges artfully glides over this anomaly, 'reading creatively', as always.[25] The idea of a sovereign mid-point, whether in theology, cosmology, architecture or literature, once carried a generally recognized iconological significance[26] and is still, today, an important element in structural criticism. The weight that Borges attaches to this 'central Night' coincides, strikingly, with that ascribed to the centre in 'ring composition' where it is considered 'so important, [that] it can carry the meaning of the whole'. In some ring composition, 'The meaning does not accumulate with the progress of the piece, it fans out from the middle'.[27] It is from this perspective of central accent that I should like to consider the *Nights*—let me insist on this: the *Nights* as filtered through Borges's reading—*and* suggest, somewhat playfully, a transmuted manifestation of this structure in his own fiction, namely in 'Emma Zunz'.

My argument will be that both the *Nights* and 'Emma Zunz' are constructed around a pivotal mid-point in which a groundbreaking revelation takes place, although with different outcomes. I see this as an example of thematic transmutation and structural continuity. The idea of a magic Night of revelation occurs several times in his fiction: in 'The Garden of Forking Paths' when it is the memory of this central Nights that allowed the sinologist Albert to decipher Ts'ui Pen's perplexing novel, and to see it as a metaphor of our labyrinthine universe, and in 'Tlön', where the Night of Nights is recalled as the Night when 'the secret portals of the heavens open wide and the water in the water jars is sweeter than on other nights' (71).[28] The vertiginous emotion engendered by this magic Night is recalled by the narrator as he leafs through a book of precisely 1001 pages, the eleventh volume of an Encyclopaedia classifying the total history of an unknown planet. In 'Emma Zunz' there is also a central Night, of vertigo and revelation, although of a more intimate order.

Revenge, forced intercourse and false accusations of seduction are shared topics in both narratives. In the *Nights* the initial revenge is public, large-scale and passes uncommented. When the King witnesses the amorous antics of his harem he has the faithless Queen killed, and participates in the killing of all his concubines and their 'Mameluke' lovers. He then continues to take his revenge: every virgin he marries at night is decapitated in the morning. In 'Emma Zunz' the idea of revenge is also immediate, as in the *Nights*, but its execution is premeditated, carefully planned, and highly complex. Emma, the heroine, devises a plan to avenge her wrongly accused father, news of whose death (suicide is suggested) has just reached her, by killing the man who had framed him and who is now her employer, Loewenthal. Emma artfully hides her plan under another plan in which she will kill her employer pleading the excuse that he has raped her.

The layout of the two narratives differs quite substantially. In the expansive *Nights* we have an initial story, generating the next story, generating the next. Borges wrote of these ramifications, 'the effect is superficial, like a Persian carpet'.[29] In his own story the same proliferation of tales of revenge occurs, although more economically: here the different versions do not unfold horizontally or consecutively but vertically, embedded in the same surface tale. Let me explain: Emma's revenge for her father is nested beneath the outward and publicly believed story of her self-defence; moreover it is inferred rather than spelt out; that is to say, not so much stated in the narrative as suggested.

However, near the heart of the story (I refused to count the lines, but they may well correspond to the ratio 602:1001), while the virginal Emma is having intercourse with a sailor to provide herself with the necessary evidence for her defence, in 'a time outside time' there is pivotal episode, when the story turns on its axis. In a (near)palindromic sentence, '*pensó, (no pudo no pensar)*—she thought, she could not help thinking) Emma experiences the shocking insight that her father must have done to her mother 'the horrible thing being done to her now' (217). At this crucial moment yet another layer is added: this is the contradictory motivation to avenge her mother for the abuse she has suffered from her father and, by extension, to avenge herself. Her false plan has become true: she has become conscious of suffering sexual abuse and Lowenthal, her employer and her father's betrayer, is the indirect cause of it. In the *Nights* these would have been separate proliferating stories, which are here subsumed into one multi-layered core story.

But while the tales of revenge unfold differently there is an element of continuity, which evolves around a central moment of insight in both narratives. The story that the King hears on Night 602 (in the versions by Burton, Payne, Littmann, and Lane, [where it is summarized in a note], to name just those I was able to trace) concerns a Prince who is blackmailed by an imprisoned Damsel to make love to her while her Ifrit is sleeping, else she will accuse him of seduction; he complies and is then made to leave his seal ring as a memento to add to her collection of illicit lovers. The Damsel is seeking revenge for the Ifrit's abuse from all the men she encounters (a point which may be seen as a significant trace in my reading of Emma Zunz). The story replicates almost exactly the King's own experience in the frame story, with the plausible danger, according to Borges, of its endless repetition. (The King and his brother were also both forcibly seduced and made to leave their seal rings by a Damsel seeking revenge on the Demon who had imprisoned her.)

A similar *regressus* occurs in 'Emma Zunz', where one plot reflects another, and another and another. Both experiences, the King's and Emma's, are examples of the devise known as *mise en abyme*, which occurs 'when the work turns back on itself, and appears to be a kind of *reflexion*'.[30] Semantically the word 'abyme' evokes ideas of depth, of infinity, of vertigo. First used in connection with literature by Gide, the phrase stems from heraldry where a shield containing in its centre a miniature replica of itself is said to be *en abyme*. In the heraldic example the figure at the heart of the shield may be combined with other figures, but does not touch any of these figures.[31] The tale in Night 602 reflects but does not touch the frame story. This is not so in 'Emma Zunz' where the 'figures' made up of each plan of revenge are compressed and expressed by the same overall figure, the false outward plot which eventually becomes true.[32]

Not only the disposition but also the effect of self-embedding in the two narratives may be seen as different. Night 602 offers the possibility of an illuminating insight, which foresees the happy ending of the *Nights*. The King in this tale condemns his son to death for having lost his seal ring, in the same circumstances as Shahriyar, the King in the frame story, but his Vizier delays the execution in case he comes to regret his decision, which the King does when the Prince's innocence is revealed. King Shahriyar, therefore, may see himself not only reflected in the Prince's adventure with the Ifrit's Mistress but also in the Prince's father, the other King, with Scheherazade and her tales performing the same task as the Vizier, namely, saving him from killing an innocent victim, herself.[33]

Emma's insight during the intercourse at the centre of her story is also magically revelatory in that it enhances her awareness of what is happening to her, but her illuminating moment, unlike Shahriyar's, has no positive effect upon the initial plot, no effect at all: she carries out the killing of Loewenthal exactly as originally planned. The self-embedded layers in 'Emma Zunz' are identical in their manifestation in that the initial plan has not changed by one iota.

Foucault, quoting Borges, notes of *The Arabian Nights* that 'the mirror structure is explicitly presented here: at its centre, the work holds up a mirror ... in which it appears as if in miniature ...'.[34] This borgesian image of self-embedding has been transmuted in Borges's own fiction into a centre which also holds up a mirror, but refracted on it are different images of the same story of revenge.

What does all this say about the *Nights* and 'Emma Zunz'? The differences separating these two narratives are taken as a given of what occupies these series of workshops, namely, how stories transform and are transformed in time and across cultures. What I have found of particular interest is how despite all obvious transformations a shared structural element remained, highlighted by Borges in his reading of the *Nights* and writing of his fiction: I refer to the destabilizing effect of the *mise en abyme* at the centre of both narratives as a moment of illumination and self-knowledge.

Regarding the specific topic of this article, the interface between the *Nights* and Borges, it would seem that readings of Borges's fiction from the *Nights* offer a fruitful source of new interpretations or, perhaps less ambitiously but more fun and more borgesian, new shades of meaning in the same interpretation.

## Notes

1. *Seven Nights*, tr. E. Weinberger, London, Faber, 1986, 46–55. On this point see also N. Eliséeff, *Thèmes et motifs des Mille et une nuits: Essai de classification* (Beyrouth, 1949). Elisséeff comments 'il y a dans les lettres une crise grave: nous sommes alors entre les deux phases de la Querelle des Anciens et des Modernes, ... le public est las d'entendre raisonner des Latins et des Grecs'.
2. *Seven Nights*, 57; *Borges, el memorioso: conversaciones de Jorge Luis Borges con Antonio Carrizo* (Mexico: Fondo de Cultura Economic, 1983), 11, respectively.
3. 'An Autobiographical Essay', in *The Aleph and Other Stories* (New York, E.P. Dutton, 1970), 209. For a study of Borges and the Orient see Julia A. Kushigian, *Orientalism in the Hispanic Literary Tradition* (Albuquerque, University of New Mexico Press, 1991), particularly 19–42.
4. P. Caracciolo, ed., *The 'Arabian Nights' in English Literature. Studies in the Reception of 'The Thousand and One Nights' into British Culture* (London, Macmillan Press, 1988); Introduction and Chapter 6; R. Irwin, *The Arabian Nights: A Companion* (London, Allan Lane, 1994). See also: E. Kristal, *Invisible Work. Borges and Translation* (Nashville, Vanderbilt University Press, 2002), 25–30; and A. Louis, *Jorge Luis Borges: oeuvre et manoeuvres* (Paris, L'Harmattan, 1997), 318–64.
5. N. Helft & A. Pauls, in *El factor Borges* (Buenos Aires, 2000), 108–109 *et passim*, Alain Pauls is right in his comment that Borges focuses on the context of the translations rather than the original yet Borges discusses the *Nights* origins and early editions and comments on 'the faded flavour of the original'.
6. See P. Tornelli, 'Algunos motivos árabes e islámicos en la obra de Borges', *Borges Studies on Line*, 2001.
7. Regarding 'The South', see R. Irwin, *Companion*, 285; R. Piglia, *Crítica y ficción* (Buenos Aires, Siglo Veinte, 1990), 151.
8. See J. Bernès, Borges, *Oeuvres Complètes* (Paris, Gallimard (coll. La Pléiade), 1993), v. 1, 1596–8.
9. For an account of this accident as a spur to his fiction writing, see Borges's 'Autobiographical Essay'.
10. References to Borges's fiction will be to A. Hurley's translation, *Collected Fictions*, and will appear parenthetically after each quotation. When not otherwise stated, reference to Borges's non-fiction will be to *The total library. Non-fiction 1922–1986. Jorge Luis Borges*, edited by Eliot Weinberger, tr. by Esther Allen, Suzanne Jill Levine & Eliot Weinberger (London, Allan Lane, 2000).
11. In *Seven Nights*, Borges declared the notion of infinity to be inherent in the *Nights*.

12. According to Robert Irwin, the Bulaq text became the source of most subsequent printed versions of the *Nights* (*Companion*, 44).
13. For a discussion of the changes made by Borges, see Kristal, 71–4.
14. In Borges, J.L., Ocampo, S. & Bioy Casares, A., *Antología de literatura fantástica* (Buenos Aires, Sudamericana, 1967), 404–5, but not in *Collected Fictions*, 56–7; cf. footnotes on 531.
15. Bernès gives detailed information on the chequered history of this invented tale in V. I, 1640–1. For a detailed discussion of the relationship between 'The Two Kings and the Two Labyrinths' and 'Ibn Hakam al-Bokhari, Murdered in his Labyrinth' see Pablo A.J. Brescia, 'De policías y ladrones: Abenjacán, Borges y la teoría del cuento' in *Variaciones Borges*, V 10, 2000, 145–66, particularly 159 footnote 22. See also S. Boldy, 'Éramos pocos y parió la abuela: más versiones borgeanas', *Revista Canadiense de Estudios Hispánicos*, 6.2 (1982): 257–62.
16. See Irwin, pp. 42–62, particularly 58–9.
17. A book of an infinite number of self-proliferating pages was anticipated as a *single volume* in the 'The Library of Babel'.
18. For a full discussion of this point see P. Caracciolo, *The Arabian Nights*, xiii–xvii.
19. Reality has provided us with a more nightmarish example of a death delaying tactic than fiction could ever dream up. I am thinking of the musicians in Auschwitz who played every night to save their lives.
20. See M. Foucault, 'Le langage à l'infini', *Tel Quel*, 15 (1963) 47, also 45, 48. Strategies for postponing fictional death in modern literature are discussed by Wendy B. Faris in *The Georgia Review*, Winter, 1982, 811–30. I am indebted to Lois Zamora Parkinson for alerting me to this article.
21. As quoted in *Collected Fictions*, 157.
22. On embedding, see T. Todorov, 'Narrative Men', in *The Poetics of Prose* (Oxford: Blackwell), 67–79. It is noteworthy that most of the main collections of Borges's fictional work have a story of the same name embedded in it, which in turn embeds a story of that same name and they all make some allusion to the *Nights*. They are 'The Garden of Forking Paths', 'The Aleph', 'Dr. Brodie's Report' and 'The Book of Sands'. This observation adds a structural significance to the link between *regressus* in Borges and the *Nights*.
23. Peter Robb, *Midnight in Sicily. On Art, food, History, Travel & Cosa Nostra* (London, 1999). Robb adds: 'Something odd was going on here. The oddness was that all this literary filtering and indirection from Arabic to English to Spanish to Italian came back to the old Arabic starting point'. The Borges quotation regarding the magical Night appears in the context of his having been Sciascia's 'great enabling influence', 275–6.
24. I expand on this issue in an article in preparation on 'Readings and Misreadings of Night 602'.
25. Night 602 is mentioned in 'The Translators of the 1001 Nights', in 'When Fiction Lives in Fiction' and in 'Partial Magic of the Quixote'. It is also alluded to indirectly in the poem 'The Metaphors of the 1001 Nights'.
26. Fowler, *Triumphal Forms* (CUP, 1970), p. 23.
27. Mary Douglas, unpublished lecture on 'Ring Composition, Ancient and Modern'. In 'ring composition' there are matching parallels on each side of a middle chiasmus, the point of return to things previously mentioned, or things resembling them, in reverse order. I am not here making a case for either the *Nights* or 'Emma Zunz' as examples of ring composition, but am borrowing from it the concept of a weight-carrying central point for my discussion of Borges's insistence on 'the magic Night at the centre of the collection'. I am extremely grateful to Prof. Douglas for kindly making available to me her unpublished FD Maurice Lectures, 2002, and for discussing ring composition with me, particularly for clarifying that there is more to ring composition than a load-bearing centre.
28. The Night of Nights, or The Night of Power is a Koranic concept (see chapter xcvii.3) and is mentioned in Night 596, 'The Tale of The Three Wishes or the Man who longed to see the Night of Power'. This tale introduces the cluster of stories on the Malice of Women, featuring Night 602. Of interest to the Project topic of narrative transmutations is the note in Lane, which points out that this same belief in a Night of revelation existed in medieval Europe regarding Christmas Eve, E.W. Lane, *The Thousand and One Nights, commonly called 'The Arabian Nights' Entertainment* (London, 1839), III 180.
29. Quoted both in 'When Fiction Lives in Fiction' and in 'Partial Magic of the Quixote'.
30. L. Dallenbach, in *The Mirror in the Text* (Oxford: Polity Press, 1989), 172. Dallenbach discusses the various examples of *mise en abyme*, which Borges lists in 'Partial Magic of the Quixote'.

31. Dallenbach, 8, and fn7 189.
32. Borges offers another extreme case of self-embedding in 'On Exactitude in Science'.
33. D. Balderston, in *Out of Context*, Durham and London, Duke University Press, 1993, 151 footnote 7, was the first to draw attention to a footnote in Enno Littmann's translation, which points out the *regressus*. See also V. vi. 199, footnote 3 in Burton's translation (Benares, 1885).
34. Dallenbach, *Mirror*, 169.

# *A Thousand and One Nights* at the Movies

**ROBERT IRWIN**

Although Edward Said did produce an article, 'Jungle Calling' that discussed the appearance of Johnny Weissmuller in the Tarzan films, he did not tackle the presentation of the Arabs and Islam in any sustained fashion either in *Orientalism* or in *Covering Islam*.[1] He only briefly commented on film very briefly in *Orientalism* as follows: 'In films and television the Arab is associated either with lechery or bloodthirsty dishonesty. He appears as an oversexed degenerate, capable it is true of cleverly devious intrigues, but essentially sadistic, treacherous and low'.[2] But this is too much of a throwaway generalization to be remotely satisfactory and it is not obvious that such a verdict would apply to such films as *The Thief of Bagdad* (in either the Fairbanks or the Korda version), *King Richard and the Crusaders, Kismet* (the 1955 version with Howard Keel), *Lawrence of Arabia* or *The Lion of the Desert*. Said did not address broader issues concerning the presentation of the Orient in popular culture. It is possible that he thought the matter too trivial for serious discussion.

A fuller account of Orientalism in the cinema has been left to others—most notably Ella Shohat in a well-known essay 'Gender and Culture of Empire'.[3] In this essay she made an explicit link between serious, academic Orientalism and popular Orientalism: 'Western popular culture ... has operated on the same Eurocentric discursive continuum as such disciplines as philosophy, Egyptology, anthropology, historiography and geography'.[4] It is evident from the general tenor of her article that she finds the one form of Orientalism as blameworthy as the other. However, I found her discussion of particular films inadequate and inaccurate. In a review in *The Times Literary Supplement* of *Visions of the East: Orientalism in Film* (the volume in which her essay appeared) I wrote as follows:

> The Douglas Fairbanks version of *The Thief of Bagdad* (1924) is singled out by Shohat as one of the films 'which claim to initiate the Western spectator into an unknown culture' and in which 'the spectator is invited on an ethnographic tour of a celluloid- "preserved" culture'. In such a manner, the Middle East 'becomes the object of study and spectacle'. Such a solemn academic approach to the Fairbanks romp may seem overblown, even bizarre. But why should not the citizens of Fairbanks's Old Baghdad be blessed with an ethnography, in just the same way as the Munchkins of Oz and the winged men of the *Flash Gordon* films? The citizens of the Fairbanks city work and stroll amid eerily tall buildings built in the German Expressionist manner; the interiors of their houses conform to Art Nouveau principles; they take their shade under ink-plume cypresses which might have been drawn by the pen of Dulac. These citizens seem prosperous and hard-working. (Even Ahmed the thief comes, in time, to recognize the value of hard work.) By the end of the film, a foreign invasion has been repelled. There does not seem anything in the topography, ethnography or the brief snatch of celluloid Baghdad's fantasy history which would legitimize a colonialist annexation of the city.[5]

The history of the *Thousand and One Nights* on film is nearly as old as the history film itself. In 1897 Antoine Lumière showed the first film ever in the Indian salon at the Grand Café at the Boulevard des Capucines in Paris. This film showed workers leaving the Lumière factory, but fantasy soon supplanted realism. In 1902 Thomas Edison produced a film version of *Ali Baba and the Forty Thieves*, directed by the comic actor Ferdinand Zecca. Soon after it came Georges Méliès's *Palais des Mille et Une Nuits* (1905). Then Zecca did an *Aladdin or the Marvelous Lamp* in 1906; thereafter the floodgates were opened. There is a Popeye version of *Aladdin*, a Fairbanks junior version of *Sinbad the Sailor*, Phil Silvers starred in *A Thousand and One Nights* (1945) (as a bespectacled Abdullah the Touched One). There have been *Nights* films starring Dorothy Lamour, Abbott and Costello, Eddy Cantor, the Three Stooges, Mickey Mouse, Gene Kelly, Steve Reeves, Micky Rooney, Christopher Lee, Howard Keel, Tom Baker, Patrick Troughton, Fernandel, Maureen O Hara, Krazy Kat, Terence Stamp, Woody Woodpecker, Peter Ustinov, Tony Curtis, Lucille Ball, Bugs Bunny, Roddy McDowall and Elvis Presley. So the first point is that the *Thousand and One Nights* genre includes hundreds of films.[6] The second point is that most of them have been forgotten and deserve to be so.

Still, there at least half a dozen masterpieces among the rich mulch of trash—from the wonderful early German films such as Lubitch's *Sumurun* (1920), Pabst's *Der Mude Tod* (1921) and *Geheimnisse des Orients* (1928) to Pier Paolo Pasolini's *Il Fiore della Mille e Una Notte* (1974). I have found only two or three *Arabian Nights*-type films produced by Arab film-makers, but doubtless there are others. Arab films in the genre include Nasser Khemir's *Les Balisseurs du Desert* (1984) and his *Ṭawq al-Ḥamāma al-Mafqūd* ('The Lost Ring of the Dove,' 1999), described by Viola Shafik as 'a colourful and exotic *Thousand and One Nights* picture-book of a film'.[7]

All literary adaptations for the screen have their problems. When one is producing or discussing the film script of a novel, then one normally is dealing with contractions of the original text. Of course, skilled scriptwriters do not merely excise and abridge, they also find ways of saying things visually, when there is no time available to squeeze that material into the dialogue or voice-over narration. Apart from the necessary compression, there are also industrial–commercial pressures to vulgarize literary sources. Usually the film, when it is released, is a disappointment—for example, the film of *Captain Corelli's Mandolin* comes to mind—usually but not always. Margaret Mitchell's *Gone With the Wind* and Nick Hornby's *High Fidelity* do not seem to have suffered much, if at all, from their transfer to celluloid.

However, all this is quite irrelevant when one comes to consider film versions of stories in the *Nights*. Here no one is trying to compress the literary material, for the stories in question are invariably quite short (if, indeed, there is a particular story in question, something that is certainly not always the case). The script-writing hack does not have to steel him- or herself to throw away great chunks of dialogue. On the contrary; there is so little in the original material, that the script-writer actually has to invent more verbiage in order to pad out the action of the story—and if he can come up with an extra subplot or two, so much the better. So it is that *Nights* films appear with stately or sluggish dialogues, roving tours of crowded bazaars, musical numbers, comedy scenes and extraneous fights with monsters. They were not there in the medieval Arab story, but they are necessary in the film. There are no worries about vulgarizing a literary masterpiece—it was perceived by of as a vulgar folk- or fairytale compilation anyway. And no worries about accusations of not being faithful to the text, for very few people have ever actually read a text of the *Nights*.

On the contrary, and this is crucially important, most people today who have an image of the *Nights* or think that they know about the *Nights* derive that image and that knowledge from films—or just possibly video games or pinball machines (and the Orientalist iconography of a pinball machine is often derived from a particular film). The film version of the *Nights* is the present-day reality, whereas the texts are mere ghostly presences and, as such, hardly more than a matter of academic interest. To clarify the reference to pinball, by the way, the Man in the Moon pub in London's Kings Road used to offer its customers an opportunity to play on a classic Williams pinball-machine, 'Tales of the Arabian Nights'. Spread out on the machine's gaudily painted playbar, one discovered the filmic iconography of the *Nights*, divorced and free-floating from particular stories. The iconography will register with people who have never opened the book of the *Nights*: the Roc's egg, harem girls, scimitars, genies, minarets, the cyclops, the prince disguised as a beggar, the basket full of serpents, the rope which turns into a ladder, the all-seeing eye. This visual clutter of oriental knick-knacks can be put to any purpose—either as functional parts of the story or serving merely to decorate it. This applies to the films as much as to the pinball machines.

An investigation of the way *Nights* has been transferred to celluloid involves two slightly different types of film. First, one can consider films that are indeed recognisable as screen adaptations of the or a text of the *Nights*, no matter how distorted—for examples, Zecca's *Ali Baba*, Fairbanks's *Thief of Bagdad* (based on 'Prince Ahmed and the Peri Banou'), Pasolini's *Fiore* and the Disney studio's version of *Aladdin*. Zecca's *Ali Baba* of 1902 followed the original plot very closely and unimaginatively, but added dancing girls from the Paris Opera.

*The Thief of Bagdad* (1924) was directed by Raoul Walsh, under the supervision of its star and producer, Fairbanks. The latter had the Prince Ahmed role, but he had to be demoted from prince to street-rogue in order to satisfy US democratic sentiment. While medieval Arab shopkeepers, artisans and peasants were apparently quite happy to identify with princes, modern Western audiences are not usually thought capable of such an empathetic leap. The plot of the film was based, but very loosely, on the *Nights* tale of 'Prince Ahmed and the Peri Banou', as found in Galland. It was designed to be a grandiose successor to Fairbanks's previous epic hit *Robin Hood* and as a showcase for Fairbanks's balletic acrobatics. The adjective 'balletic' is used advisedly, for the athletic star danced his way through the plot. Fairbanks himself had been much impressed by Diaghilev's Ballets Russe and, generally, Ballets Russe sets and costumes, particularly those designed by Bakst for the bloodily erotic ballet version of *Scheherezade*, exercised an immense influence on films in this early period. The Diaghilev–Bakst ballet *Scheherezade*, first staged in 1910, was perhaps the biggest ballet ever mounted up to that time. Although it used Rimsky-Korsakov's music, it ditched the original Sinbad the adventurer story-line in favour of the erotic and sadistic *Nights* frame-story of how King Shahriyar discovered that he was being betrayed by his wife with the Golden Negro. The first decade of the twentieth century was the heyday for sadistically erotic readings of the *Nights*, for this was a time when people were enthusing about Mardrus's wretchedly overripe translation of the *Nights*. (Additionally Oscar Wilde's *Salome*, and especially Reinhardt's staging of it, had a considerable impact on stage and cinema versions of the Orient.) Baksts's sets and designs drew for their inspiration on Persian miniatures, on paintings by Repin and Vrubel, on ethnic costumes of the Caucasus and by art of Beardsley and Moreau. The choreography seems to have been influenced by the visit of a Siamese dance troupe to St Petersburg in 1900. Once again one must be struck by the mad eclecticism of staged versions of the *Nights*. Even so, Proust said that he had never seen anything so beautiful as the Ballets Russes's performance of *Scheherezade*.

To return to Fairbanks's *Thief of Bagdad*, Ahmed (Fairbanks), the thieving protagonist, is a can-do, get-up-and-go character. In this earnestly moralistic film, Ahmed learns that 'Happiness must be earned'. (Actually this is a most un*Arabian Nights* like theme. The medieval Arab storytellers preferred to dwell on undeserved good fortune—as in the cases of Aladdin and Ali Baba). Fairbanks was a Horatio Alger with a turban and scimitar and his film was a showpiece for American pep, grit and know-how. Fairbanks in the 1920s was trying to lose his pre-war aristocratic image and, instead, he was trying to present himself as a real jock, a straight up-and-down guy. Actually he had highly cultivated tastes. It was not just a matter of his admiration for the Ballets Russes, but also his enthusiasm for German expressionist films. It was Fairbanks's travels in Europe and his interest in the works of figures such as Robert Wiene and Fritz Lang which had made him want to make the *Thief* in the first place.

As far as American know-how was concerned, this was really special effects and many of these, for example the flying carpet, were lifted from German films. Set design, which was also Germanic, was masterminded by one of the great yet obscure figures of cinema history, William Cameron Menzies (1896–1957). Menzies, who had previously previous worked with D.W. Griffiths and with Lubitsch, applied himself to adapt Lang's expressionist effects. Expressionist films (for examples, *The Cabinet of Caligari* and *Destiny*) were ostentatiously designed films, which made great play with play of light against dark and the use of landscape and architecture to symbolise or express in a stylised fashion Man's inner states. Expressionists were preoccupied with Fate and with the monstrous and the supernatural. It is easy to see how well this essentially German subject matter could be married to the stories of the *Thousand and One Nights*. Reinhardt's stagecraft was particularly influential on Menzies. Max Reinhardt (1873–1943) was the leading proponent in theatre of the *Gesamtkunstwerk*, the total work of art, incorporating acting, choreography, music, lighting, design—everything. (The

*Gesamtkunstwerk* was itself very much a nineteenth-century notion, with shades of Wagner and Scriabin.) Reinhardt—and Menzies after him—experimented with new lighting techniques. They directed vast crowds of histrionically gesturing extras so that their movement was unobtrusively disciplined and expressive. They set their scenes in vast sets with towering stylized architecture. In *The Thief of Bagdad*, Menzies heightened a dreamlike impact of the architecture by having polished black floors, and then brightly lit bases to the vast buildings so that they seemed to float above the ground. Fairbanks and Menzies certainly studied the Reinhardtian touches in the earlier German films with Oriental backgrounds, *Sumurun* and *Der mude Tod*. Incidentally, Expressionism also had a definite impact on the *Arabian Nights* musical, *Kismet*, (1944), directed by William Dieterle. Dieterle had started out as an actor with Reinhardt.

As we have seen, Shohat cited the *Thief of Bagdad* as an example of a whole genre of colonial films, which claimed to initiate the Western spectator into an unknown culture, to appropriate that culture and to legitimize its colonial annexation. However, it is clear that such ambitions were quite alien to the makers of *The Thief of Bagdad*. Fairbanks and his team had no interest whatsoever in the real Middle East, nor more generally in ethnography. They believed in American values and they were enthusiastic about Russian ballet and the German Expressionist style. They were not trying to compile an imperialist encyclopedia of the Orient. More generally, prior to the Second World War—prior, that is, to the vast expansion of American oil companies' interests in Saudi Arabia and prior to establishment of the state of Israel—America's political and economic interests in the Middle East were perfectly negligible.

Pasolini, who was the most faithful of all film men to work with the *Nights*, took several authentic *Nights* stories but rearranged their structure (intelligently). 'I have made a realistic film full of dust and the faces of the poor', claimed the Marxist Pasolini.[8] Happily, it is not too grindingly earnest and realistic and the film can be viewed as a commentary on the nature of popular culture, storytelling and the role of dreams in that culture. Ray Harryhausen, the producer of the Sinbad films, once remarked that *Nights* films are always expensive to make, because one has to build the sets of the *Arabian Nights* cities. Pasolini avoided this, as he found his buildings and natural settings ready made in Eritrea, Yemen and Nepal. Similarly, his cast was, for the most part, cheap and locally recruited. His was a people's *Nights*, featuring the *ragazzi di vita*. Pasolini delighted in pre-industrial, unWesternized societies and their pre-capitalist innocence.

*Il fiore della Mille e una notte* (1974) opens with the voyeuristic scene of the Shaykh and Shaykha (naturalized jinns) looking down and admiring the boy, Nur al-Din and the girl, Zumurrud, who in turn are admiring and fondling one another. Pasolini here challenges the audience, and reminds them of their own voyeurism as they watch his film. Voyeurism seems to be a latent theme in many *Nights* films. The filmmakers are winking at their clientele, reminding their audiences what they are doing, and, in a sense, including the audiences within their films. Painters of the Italian Renaissance sometimes made use of a similar device. For example, Botticelli used to paint himself looking out of the painting, inviting us to join him in it.

Besides being a filmmaker Pasolini was a distinguished, if controversial, poet and novelist and he took a much more literary approach to his task than any of his predecessors. In keeping with the authentic tradition of *Nights* stories the hero, Nur al-Din is a shiftless weed, while Zumurrud is the one who wears the trousers. Pasolini retained the Chinese box-structure of the *Nights*, although he made a selective re-arrangement of *Nights* stories within the boxed framework of tale-within-tale. Most interestingly, at one or two points he actually has the stories explode outwards, so that a character in one story may influence events in the story of the character who is telling the story about the first character. At one point in the film, a gardener talking to the misanthropic lady Dunya, who thinks that she has been warned off men by a dream, makes the following remark: 'Sometimes dreams are bad teachers and that is because they seldom end on the night they start. The whole truth is revealed in many dreams'. Obviously, the gardener is commenting on the boxed sequence of tales in which the gardener himself is only another character. The film's concluding line re-emphasizes this key point, '*La verità non sta in un sogna ma in molti sogni*' [The truth does not lie in one dream, but in many dreams'].

Then there is the Disney *Aladdin* (1992), which when I reviewed it for *The Times Literary Supplement*, I commended for actually improving the original rather defective plot.[9] Again the hero has to be turned into a lovable rogue, a streetwise kid from the wrong side of the tracks (whereas the original Aladdin was certainly not streetwise). The Djinn has been gifted with a great verbal performance from Robin Williams, but has been divested of menace and mystery. He is lovable and comic. There are unsatisfactory aspects to the film. Medieval Arab storytellers were always happy to include strong, bold and even violent female protagonists in their stories. In the original story of Aladdin, Aladdin's bride actually tricks and kills the magician, but in the squeamish, sanitized, bogusly politically correct Disney version, the princess sings of her vaguely feminist aspirations (her mission-song), but thereafter Princess Jasmin is merely to be wooed and courted; she is just the pretty prize that Aladdin and Jaffar are competing for. Roughly the same applies to the Harryhausen Sinbad films, in which the beautiful girl is at best a sidekick, but essentially she is man's reward for coming through all those dangerous adventures and, as such, she is worth more than the gold and rubies or the magic amulet Sinbad thought he was questing for. (So it would seem that modern film-makers in the West are more medieval in their attitudes to women than were medieval Arabs.)

However, to award ticks and crosses for a film's fidelity to the original *Nights* would be a dubious and tedious business. The second category of films, which is a much larger group and one that is more challenging and interesting to study, are films that are not in any serious sense adaptations of a *Nights* story, but rather draw upon the visual iconography of the *Nights*, on a kind of mock oriental language and a limited but ever-popular range of plot motifs and character types. *The Arabian Nights* then has become a kind of storytelling brand name. George Méliès's *Palais des Mille et Une Nuits*, Korda's *Thief of Bagdad*, The Harryhausen films and Disney's *The Return of Jafar* all belong to this curious and little-understood genre.

As far as the visual iconography as concerned it at first drew heavily on Victorian materials: John Martin's canvases of Biblical catastrophes, Doré's engravings of scenes from the Bible and the *Nights*, as well as the work of other illustrators of the *Nights*, such as Dalziel. Orientalist paintings may have inspired some sets. Dulac's Persian miniature style illustration to the *Nights* were certainly drawn upon by Cameron Mackintosh, the brilliant designer who turned some of the scenes in the Fairbanks *Thief of Bagadad* into a grisaille version of Dulac illustrations. The film iconography of the *Nights* doubtless also drew on the wardrobe and props of burlesque and pantomime, although this is hard to document. Eventually, however, visual iconography of *Nights* films became mostly autocannibalistic, as film-makers plagiarized earlier films in the genre rather than going to outside sources such as books or paintings. The German *Adventures of Baron von Munchausen* (1941), an extravagant Nazi prestige project which can be regarded as a *Nights* film, and the Disney *Aladdin* both stole from the Korda *Thief of Bagdad.* Even so, the diligent Disney animators also conducted research on illustrations to Victorian editions of the *Nights.*

A viewing of the three Sinbad films made by Harryhausen suggests that the '*Nights* feel' of these three films is not just a matter of visual cueing—of turbans, scimitars, domes and minarets and of princesses oddly dressed as belly dancers with pointy golden bras. One becomes aware that the dialogue is mostly in 'Orientalspeak'. Orientalspeak is a delightful language that is surprisingly easy to learn. Orientalspeak is guttural and the more villainous one is the more guttural. Orientalspeak is a stately, solemn language, laden with proverbs and invocations of Destiny. The following examples all come from *The Golden Voyage of Sinbad*: 'Is it not written that a wise man will try to realise his dream?' 'Captain, he who walks on fire will burn his feet.' 'He who seeks for pearls must not sleep … Walls have ears and ears have eyes.' 'Fate, Destiny have brought us together'. 'You have the belief of Destiny for that is what has brought us together'. 'There is an old proverb "trust in Allah, tie up your camel".', 'She finds favour in my eyes'. 'He who is patient obtains'. 'Don't throw stones into the well that you drink from'. 'Magic purges the soul, Achmed. The night are its ears and the day its eyes.' 'Destiny is invisible, yet visible'. 'A man's destiny lies in his own hands. A live dog is better than a dead lion'. 'It is written that the Fountain of Destiny lies within easy march'. And how about this from the Korda *Thief of Bagdad*?: 'In the fullness of the years a liberator shall come upon ye. And this shall be the sign of him. He shall be the lowest of the low and he shall come mounted upon the clouds'.

'Destiny', apart from serving as padding in a leaky old horsehair armchair of a script, is invoked by the scriptwriter when he cannot think of a sensible motivation for what his characters are doing. When there is no reason for what Sinbad decides to do, well then he does it because it is his Destiny. Indeed Destiny is that which is 'written'. The association of the Orient with proverbs and wise maxims goes back to the seventeenth century and the labours of Pocock and Erpenius on the *Fables of Luqman* and, a little later, Antoine Galland's *Les Paroles remarquables, les Bons mots et les Maximes des Orientaux* … (1694). As for the style of Orientalspeak more generally, it draws on that of the other great collection of eastern storytelling, the Bible, as well as on the translationese of Edward William Lane, Richard Burton and Edward Fitzgerald—and perhaps a touch of James Elroy Flecker too. Its stateliness and occasional inversion of the natural word order successfully suggests the pastness of the Orient.

So, when one turns *Nights* material into a film, one has to stretch it out a bit; but obviously something else is going on. The original *Nights* stories were composed for adults—adults, moreover, who were fairly familiar with the world of the bazaar, mosque and desert in which those stories are set. But the *Nights* films are aimed at children in the West. (The Pasolini film is a rare exception.) The children know almost nothing about the medieval Middle East and probably have little interest in it. The medieval stories were set in familiar territory; the films are set in Exoticland.

Edward Said has written (in *The World and the Critic*) about how the *Nights* features in the poems of Tennyson and Wordsworth as something to be put aside when one leaves the enchanted world of childhood.[10] The film-makers are similarly keen to ring-fence the *Nights* as something especially for children. This is made most explicit in the Korda *Thief of Bagdad*, in which the true hero is not the youthful Prince Achmed but the actual child, Sabu, who at one point is hailed by a mysterious conclave of ancient sages as the future Sultan of their never-never land. The old Sultan of Bagdad in this film (and his carbon copy in the Disney *Aladdin*) with his irresponsibility and passion for mechanical toys is a lovable elderly child. In the *Seventh Voyage of Sinbad*, the genie's deepest wish is to become a real boy.

The films are designed to feed childish imagination but, as the films are aimed at a juvenile audience, there also is a considerable freight of teaching about ethics, popular psychology, good citizenship and so on. Today's cinema peddles a secularized kind of piety. Disney's Aladdin has to recognize himself as what he is and not to present himself as something other than he is. The quest films that are notionally about finding treasure are often really about discovering one's true identity, or acquiring a sense of worth, or learning to love—that kind of thing. Fairbanks's Thief learns that 'Happiness has to be earned'. (The original Arab storytellers, on the other hand, seem quite happy with the concept of unearned happiness and unearned treasure.)

In general, youth is celebrated and pitted against age: dashing young Sinbad invariably faces an older villain—an evil stepmother in *Eye of the Tiger* or the rapidly aging sorcerer Koura played by Tom Baker in *The Golden Voyage of Sinbad*. Disney has got us used to the idea that fairy-tales are only for children, and the *Nights* film-makers are turning adult stories into films for children (unlike the rare fairytale films aimed at an adult audience, such as Cocteau's *Beauty and the Beast* and Neil Jordan's *The Company of Wolves*).

In the real world most people dislike and fear thieves. Films love them. Fairbanks and Sabu are both thieves and so is the Disney Aladdin. The modern film cult of the thief happens to have its precedent in ninth- and tenth-century Bagdad in the writings of al-Tanūkhī and Abū Dulaf and the literature devoted to the Banū Sāsān and the rogues of the *Maqāmāt* and the shadow plays of Ibn Dāniyāl. The medieval Arab literary cult of the thief and the rogue is not our concern here, but it seems clear that the thief in *Nights* films stands for something quite different from his knavish Arab prototype. The film thieves laugh and are gay, they snatch and scamper about, they climb trees and scramble up magic ropes, they bounce about on great oil jars and they climb over walls into other people's gardens. In effect, then, they are children, young men who have not accepted responsibility and have not been absorbed into the humdrum world of work.

The Arab storytellers were not so prejudiced against the world of work: merchants, shopkeepers, bakers, fishermen and porters feature quite frequently as protagonists in their stories. Now consider Sinbad, for his destiny is a curious thing to marvel on and worthy to be graven with a needle on the edges of one's eye. Early on in *Sinbad and the Eye of the Tiger*, Sinbad shouts 'Hoist the mainsail!' and soon his ship is scudding across the sea in search of adventure and danger; but the original Arab Sinbad never shouted 'Hoist the mainsail!' He did not know how to splice the reef knot, or how to shimmy up a rope to the crow's nest with a scimitar clenched between his teeth. He had not a clue about the things sailors do and know. The original Sindbād al-Baḥrī was a merchant. He was engaged in commerce, not treasure-hunting. His adventures were on the whole unsought by him. Now, what is the significance of Hollywood's transformation of Sinbad from an unheroic merchant into a swashbuckling sailor? The audience for Sinbad films, whether the children or their parents, are far more likely to have had experience of trade and shop-keeping than of tacking through a tropical storm or beating off a man armed with a cutlass. Still, what is served up to them is the sword-fighting, questing sailor. It is not entirely clear why the transformation has taken place. Perhaps the quest element is the key here. Although the quest is hardly unknown in eastern literature, it is perhaps more central to the western tradition of storytelling—take, for example, the Quest for the Grail, whose mystery has been unmasked by Tzvetan Todorov. What is the true Grail? The Grail is precisely the story of the quest for it. What is Sinbad questing for really? Not the fabulous treasure of gold and pearls, not that princess who is worth so much more than the gold he thought he was looking for, not even the discovery of his own worth and identity. No, the real quest is for the STORY of which he is a part. In more banal terms, the quest is what keeps things moving. As Pasolini said of his film, 'The Protagonist of this story is in fact destiny itself'.

John Clute's *Encyclopedia of Fantasy*, in its brief entry on Quests, notes how the quest normally has a male protagonist and how he has collect 'plot coupons' on the way. 'Plot coupons' include maps, magic amulets, travelling companions who serve as helpers. There is also the 'plot voucher'—a wild card issued early on in the story that will be of crucial use to the protagonist when the climax comes.[11] As for the climax, it is noticeable how often it is that the plot of a *Nights* film reaches its climax in a vast subterranean cavern. In *Nights* films this corresponds to the shoot-out in the deserted warehouse in crime films. There may well be something Freudian about the climax in the cavern. There has been a tendency among film-makers to broaden the stories out topographically. The set designers favour a cultural eclecticism that is most enjoyable. Harryhausen has used bits and pieces of legends and iconography from Pharaonic Egypt, ancient Greece, Hinduism and Cambodia. The palaces of the Alhambra are a popular location. The Alhambra's Court of the Lions, the Cuarto Dorado and the Generalife stood in for old Baghdad in *The Seventh Voyage of Sinbad*, whereas *The Golden Voyage of Sinbad* made do with the Court of the Myrtles.[12]

One can spend hours, days, weeks and years analysing plot structures and protagonists. But all this may be beside the point. Sinbad's function is to pursue the quest, but what is the function of the quest itself? Very often the quest is designed as a structure that will serve as a showcase for special effects: Edison and Méłès were both desperate to demonstrate the wonders of cinema. Edison's *Ali Baba* of 1902 had colour effects. For Georges Méliès, in particular, it was more than a window on the world, it was rather a vehicle for trick photography, including such devices as stop motion and superimposition. Méliès worked as a sorcerer before and behind the camera. Then consider the Fairbanks flying carpet. Then think of the marvellously animated and delicate silhouettes created by Lotte Reiniger for *Die Abenteuer des Prinzen Achmed* (1926), the world's first full-length animation picture. And what about the automated Kali and giant djinn's foot in the Korda *Thief of Bagdad*, and the heads growing on trees in Von Baky's *Adventures of Baron von Munchausen* (shades of the island of Wāqwāq!). The Korda *Thief* and the Von Baky *Munchausen* were conceived of as set-piece demonstrations of what could be achieved through the artistic use of colour—still a novelty in the 1940s. They were also affirmations of the possibility of making fantasy films with sound tracks. It had been thought that the coming of sound had finished off the fantasy film—until *Snow White and the Seven Dwarfs* and the *Wizard of Oz* and then *The Thief of Bagdad* proved otherwise. The Korda *Thief* had music by Miklos Rosza. It also used back projection, front projection, blue screen models, stop-frame animation and trick shots with painted glass; and consider the lumbering, animated monsters and fighting skeletons of the Harryhausen films and the feverishly inspired animation of Disney's *Aladdin*. Technology has customarily been the prime mover in cinema's handling of material from the *Arabian Nights*. In all the films just mentioned the medium is the message—this sort of film work is, in effect, using magic to create stories that are about magic.

In recent decades there has been a tendency to discuss cultural Orientalism as if it consisted of a (probably dark) canon of masterpieces by mainly dead white males—

Flaubert, T.E. Lawrence, Conrad, Delacroix, Gérôme, Matisse, Verdi—the cultural big hitters. Moreover, the critical literature on *Nights* films (such as it is) refuses to acknowledge that the films are fun or indeed any good at all. However, it is questionable whether it makes sense to remove these films from the context of popular entertainment and then analyse them as something that is only and utterly serious.

*Nights* films are an important part of popular Orientalism, and they need to be considered as part of a broader cultural phenomenon that includes such diverse things as Turkish cigarettes, Flying Carpet Travel Agents, Flying Carpet Dry Cleaning outlets, cinemas called the Alhambra, Egyptian music halls, Orientalist sheet music, camel jokes, the Genie in advertisements for brass polish, three wishes jokes, Wilson, Keppel and Betty's Egyptian sand dance, Kettelby's 'In a Persian Market', the Bonzo Dog Doo Dah Band's 'Ali Baba and his Camel', Fry's Turkish Delight, the posters for conjuring and circus shows, Tommy Cooper's fez, night-club versions of the Dance of the Seven Veils, Chu Chin Chow and the storyboard of the pinball machine already alluded to. And novels of course—novels such as Robert Hichens's *The Garden of Allah*, E.M. Hull's *The Sheik* and P.C. Wren's *Beau Geste*,[13] and comics such as *Tin Tin and the Crab with the Golden Claws.* Such popular entertainments may not offer the academic or the intellectual very much, but what about the wider public? From where did they get their image of the Orient? What sort of image was it? What did non-academics make of non-academic examples of Orientalism? The inevitable temptation for an intellectual is to try to make a phenomenon such as popular Orientalism subsidiary to something more intellectual—that is to say, to make developments in popular Orientalism follow on after developments in academic and intellectual and literary Orientalism. It is sometimes tempting to think about *Nights* in film in this way. For example, there may be an inclination to link developments in the 1930s genre of Orientalist film-making to academic presentations of the Islamic world by, for instance, Gibb and Massignon. However, there is little evidence to support the idea that Méliès, Korda or Harryhausen were constrained by an Orientalist discourse and limited in their vocabulary and references to a particular archive that had been generated by intellectuals, or which constrained the ways in which intellectuals think. Of course, the film-makers worked with a set of clichés, stereotypes and audience expectations. Our task should be to look at those clichés, stereotypes and expectations with fresh eyes—like a child entering the cinema for the first time.

Just as in the much earlier Orientalist writings of John de Mandeville and Guillaume Postel, the Orient is portrayed in films and in other areas of popular culture as a place of fertility, wonder and delight, a place of beautiful women, wise men and great treasures that may be won by the adventurous. Because most *Nights* films are aimed at children, the Orient it presents is remarkably innocent—on the surface at least. The Orient, which in other contexts may well be seen as threatening, alien and Other, has to be presented for entertainment purposes by film-makers as familiar and ultimately safe, for all its swishing robes and its marvels.

## Notes

1. Edward Said, 'Jungle Calling', *Interview Magazine* (June, 1989) reprinted in *Reflections on Exile and Other Essays* (Cambridge, MA: Harvard University Press, 2000), pp. 327–36.
2. Said, *Orientalism* (London: Routledge & Kegan Paul, 1978), pp. 286–7.
3. Ella Shohat, 'Gender and Culture of Empire: Towards a Feminist Ethnography of the Cinema,' in Matthew Bernstein & Gaylyn Studlar, *Visions of the East: Orientalism in Film* (London: I.B. Tauris, 1997), pp. 19–66.

4. Shohat, 'Gender and Culture', p. 57.
5. Robert Irwin, 'The Theorists of Baghdad', *Times Literary Supplement*, May 30, 1997, p. 18
6. Some of these films are discussed by Jack G. Shaheen, in *Reel Bad Arabs: How Hollywood Vilifies a People* (New York: Olive Branch Press, 2001).
7. Viola Shafik, *Arab Cinema: History and Cultural Identity* (Cairo: American University in Cairo Press, 1998).
8. Pier Paolo Pasolini, 'Pasolini on Film', in Paul Williams, ed., *Pier Paolo Pasolini* (London: British Film Institute, 1977), p. 75.
9. Irwin, 'There's the rub and there too. The elusive meaning and history of the Aladdin story, *Times Literary Supplement*, December 4, 1993, pp. 14–15.
10. Edward W. Said, *The World the Text and the Critic* (London: Faber & Faber, 1984), p. 271.
11. John Clute, 'Quests', in John Clute & John Grant, eds, *The Encyclopedia of Fantasy* (London: Orbit, 1995), p. 796.
12. Robert Irwin, *The Alhambra* (London: Profile, 2004), pp. 15, 176.
13. On these novels, see Claud Cockburn, *Bestseller: The Books Everyone Read 1900–1939* (London: Sidgwick & Jackson, 1972), pp. 51–72, 138–47.

# *Thousand and One Nights* at the Komedie Stamboel: Popular theatre and travelling stories in colonial Southeast Asia

MATTHEW ISAAC COHEN

The Komedie Stamboel is celebrated as the first Malay-language professional theatre company of the Netherlands Indies (now Indonesia).[1] The core repertoire of the Komedie Stamboel during its first year of existence consisted of tales from the *Thousand and One Nights*. Fully ninety per cent of the performances in the Komedie Stamboel's first ten months of existence (January–November 1891)—when it was resident in the port city of Surabaya in eastern Java—were dramatic adaptations of stories from the *Nights*. This indeed is how the company got its name: Komedie was the Malay (as well as Dutch) term for commercial entertainment, while Stamboel was the common Malay (as well as Dutch) designation for Istanbul, the capital of the Ottoman Empire—symbolic of the Near and Middle East in the popular imagination. So formative was the Komedie Stamboel that the company's name later became generalized to an entire popular theatrical genre, with scores of professional and amateur companies functioning throughout western Indonesia until the 1950s.

This article explores some of the reasons for the founding of a theatre dedicated to performing *Thousand and One Nights* stories in late nineteenth-century Indonesia and then explores the changes in repertoire and generic expectations that accompanied the shift of the Komedie Stamboel from a resident to an itinerant theatrical company during a roughly three-year (or 1001-night) period of 1891–1894. My particular interest will be in the modern well-travelled tales that entered the repertoire, and how these transformed in relation to the generic expectations established in relation to the *Thousand and One Nights* plays.

The *Thousand and One Nights* came into Southeast Asia through European languages, and were associated with European modernity. The identification of Komedie Stamboel with the *Nights* allowed it to exist as a truly popular theatre cutting across various class, racial and religious lines. This identification also presented certain generic limitations, however. It compounded the theatre's reputation for crudity, bawdiness and the risqué, stigmatizing this theatrical genre for decades to come.

## Cultural Consumption in the Indies

Picture, if you will, a young Javanese man named Mengadoerradjin from the city of Solo.[2] Evidently well-travelled and with some education as well as money, he is writing a letter to the Surabaya daily *Bintang Soerabaia* in late November, 1891—the same year the Komedie Stamboel was founded and the very same week that the Komedie Stamboel played in Solo for the first time. Perhaps Mengadoerradjin went to see the Komedie Stamboel perform himself; it is almost certain he witnessed the company's circus-like tent being erected in the *alun-alun* square north of the royal court. (This tent was described as 'quite fine'—*rajin*—in Surakarta's Malay-language newspaper.) As he writes, Mengadoerradjin might even be humming one of the theatre's versatile characteristic tunes, said to be impossible to get out of your mind. Devotees were known to sing these tunes in their sleep.[3]

At Mengadoerradjin's writing desk is a composition book into which he has pasted decorative illustrations he has cut off the back of matchboxes. He writes about his hobby—which he characterizes as a recent craze in Batavia, Semarang and Surabaya—with genuine enthusiasm for the pictures and (more importantly) their meanings. Some interpretations are obvious, others more esoteric. A crown placed below a globe means that the king is subservient to the world. A picture of Christ above a globe means that the religion is above the world. A picture of a lion means that someone with money is as strong as a lion. A picture of a lion holding a sword means that the memory of someone with money is as sharp as a sword's blade. A picture of a king's head means that someone with money has power like that of a king. The words around the edge of the one-*ringgit* coin also benefit from explanation, he continues: *God Zij Met Ons* (literally 'God be with us' in Dutch) means in fact 'power, strength and sharpness belong to the way of the Prophets'.

This sort of appropriation of culture, involving a reframing (cutting and pasting), resetting (into a blank book) and creative (though possibly contested) interpretation was characteristic of a cultural moment in the Indies. It was a moment of possibility, in which urban populations were rapidly growing, rail-lines were being laid down, steamships transforming oceanic travel and trade and education were opening up new horizons of expectation. Minke, the journalist–narrator of Pramoedya Ananta Toer's bildungsroman *This Earth of Mankind*, emblematizes the wonder of the age and the transition away from an agrarian feudal society to a market-orientated, urban-centred, modern society, speaking as a youth growing up in Surabaya in the 1890s.

> One of the products of science at which I never stopped marvelling was printing, especially zincography. Imagine, people can reproduce tens of thousands of copies of any photograph in just one day: pictures of landscapes, important people, new machines, American skyscrapers. [...] Trains—carriages without horses, without cattle, without buffalo—had been witnessed now for over ten years by my countrymen. And astonishment remains in their

> hearts even today. The distance from Betawi [Batavia] to Surabaya can be travelled in only three days! [...] Power was no longer the monopoly of the elephant and the rhinoceros. They had been replaced by small manmade things: nuts, screws, and bolts. [...] The forces of nature were beginning to be changed by man and put to his service. Machines will replace all and every kind of work. [...] Modern! How quickly the word had surged forward and multiplied itself [...].[4]

The moment shared by Mengadoerradjin, Minke and the Komedie Stamboel was the arrival in the Indies of the modern, the age of the world picture, in Martin Heidegger's terms. Heidegger identifies five essential phenomena as characteristic of the modern age—science, machine technology, the objectification of art as an expression of human life, the valuation of culture as the highest good of man, and the loss of the gods. In the modern era, the world can be represented as a picture, a structured image knowable in its entirety from a human (i.e. not divine) perspective.[5]

The Komedie Stamboel played a decisive role in securing, organizing and articulating of a modern world view in nineteenth-century Java and other islands of Indonesia. It marks a genuine break with the traditional ethos and worldview most prominently displayed in *wayang kulit*, shadow puppet theatre.[6] Wayang kulit enacts a stratified world of gods, demons and humans, in which characters are inherited types rather than novel creations. Performances are contingent on ritual functions and dedicated to ancestors and tutelary spirits; the puppeteer is both entertainer and ritual officiant. Stories might be new creations based on the characters and situations of oral tradition, but resolutions are fixed: there is always a return to the *status quo*. The Javanese language used in wayang kulit is often purposefully archaic and obscure, demanding linguistic expertise from the audience. The Komedie Stamboel presented a new model for representation, both in theatre and in real life.[7] As commercial entertainment performed in readily accessible Malay language in public theatres, it was not contingent on expert spectators, local religious practices or place spirits. Plays were typically narrative transformations of literary sources, but the companies were free to take substantial liberties with sources as these were not fixed by the legacy of a performing tradition. It was, in other words, a site for play.

## The *Thousand and One Nights*

The Komedie Stamboel began in Surabaya in 1891 when Yap Goan Thay, a Chinese entrepreneur, bankrolled a company of impoverished Eurasians to perform dramatic versions of *Thousand and One Nights* tales. Performances were after the style of the Parsi theatre of Bombay (which is first documented as having visited Java in 1883) and European light opera, as performed by touring European companies at Surabaya's Schouwburg theatre. The most famous figure associated with the company by far was the Eurasian actor–manager Auguste Mahieu, who had a fine tenor voice and remarkable talent as a comic actor. One report had it that 'in every play in which Mr Mahieu performs spectators just can't stop laughing because he is so hilariously funny. When he acts in "Aladin", people laugh until their stomachs hurt. There are those who say that Mr Mahieu possesses a magical *Pengirutan* charm [*jimat*]'.[8] Mahieu eventually bought the company from Yap Goan Thay and functioned as owner as well as artistic director.

The choice of the *Nights* as the dramatic staple was based on many factors. Individual tales and selections of the *Nights* had been translated into Malay and Javanese poetry and prose, published as books in Batavia, Semarang and Singapore and serialized in vernacular newspapers, since the 1870s.[9] A deluxe, lushly illustrated and multi-volume edition of the *Nights* was published in Batavia starting in 1891; these volumes were said to be greatly appreciated by devotees of the Komedie Stamboel.[10] The Javanese translations, in particular, were evidently motivated by a perceived need on the part of Dutch scholars for 'suitable' Javanese reading matter for use in schools and as belletristic exemplars for aspiring Javanese authors.[11] Much Arabic and Persian literature was translated into the languages of the Indonesian archipelago following the rise of the first Islamic city-states in the fifteenth-century. Most translations were religious and philosophical texts, but there were also romances such as tales of Amir Hamza, Mohammad's uncle, believed to have been known in Indonesia as early as the fifteenth century.[12] The *Nights*, however, were transmitted to Southeast Asia through Europe. The original source might have been Arabic, but the Malay and Javanese translations that appeared during the colonial period were mediated through European languages—usually French by way of Dutch. (A cognate pattern is apparent elsewhere in Asia, including Thailand, where the *Nights* provided a source for royal dance and drama starting in the 1870s.[13]

The link to European culture was reinforced not only by the source literary texts, but also by the prevalence of *Thousand and One Nights* plays in the repertoire of Dutch amateur theatrical groups and visiting European companies. More often than not, the *Nights* were played as farce and parody, and as an opportunity to dress up in romantic 'Oriental' attire. A typical example was the musical extravaganza presented by Harry Stanley's English Comic and Burlesque Opera Company during their long run in Surabaya's Schouwburg theatre in 1891, 'Blue Beard or Harlequin Ali Barber and Sinbad, the Wig Ked Coarse-Hair'.[14]

There is a strong element of the farcical in the Komedie Stamboel's *Nights*. Mahieu, as already mentioned, was in his element as a comic actor: he was said to be so funny in the role of Aladdin that a spectator at one show wet herself from laughter. Clowns, often playing the roles of servants, were major draws. The very costumes worn were funny. The spectre of pan-Islamism haunted the upper echelons of the colonial bureaucracy, but the clothing styles and odd public behaviour of Turks and Arabs were viewed as outlandish by the masses.[15] The Komedie Stamboel's original target audience was Chinese, who enjoyed a higher economic status but lower legal rights and privileges in the colonial hierarchy as the Komedie Stamboel's predominately Eurasian cast. This audience probably took a subversive pleasure in seeing Eurasians dress up in ridiculous costumes, deemed by one European observer to be more like dress-up costumes for children than proper stage attire, and perform songs and dances for their amusement. Prior to Mahieu's purchase of the company from Yap Goan Thay, the actors were even required to dress off-stage in 'white jackets and pants, red scarves as waistbands and red fezes with stars on them'.[16] Some found this dress code attractive, but others found it plain odd.

The *Nights* tales were not completely dissociated from Javanese culture, of course. The long presence of Islam in the archipelago meant that Java shared a common body of supernatural lore with the world of the *Nights*. Figures such as *jinn* and *ifrit* were known (and usually feared). It is also possible that the Komedie Stamboel's modern audiences identified with the spirit of adventure and possibility of the translocal, Islamic mercantile community of the medieval transoceanic mercantile depicted in the *Nights*.[17]

The *Nights* presented theatre workers with numerous opportunities to demonstrate the marvels of theatrical technology. This had been a selling-point of popular theatre of the Komedie Stamboel type for decades, as manifest in this announcement for a Parsi theatre play. A typical Komedie Stamboel notice reads:

> On 24 February, we shall perform the story of Ali Baba. In a new arrangement, there will be numerous cannons mounted on Ali Baba's ship, and furthermore his brother Kasim will be realistically cut in two with a knife, after the manner of a magician.[18]

The Komedie Stamboel's Ali Baba was a grand spectacle, likened in one promotion to an Ali Baba production at Amsterdam's Paleis voor Volksvlijt (Palace of Industry).[19] The Komedie Stamboel's dramatization was not the 'original' tale—Arabic redactions make no mention of an episode in which Ali Baba flees the captain of the forty thieves by ship and engages him in a dramatic sea battle. But this version of the *Nights* became the norm for Malay theatre spectators in Java and elsewhere in Indonesia: when a touring Bangsawan company from Malaysia presented an Ali Baba which 'intentionally cut' the sea battle, the performance was roundly condemned for its departure from the accepted version.[20] It was not to everyone's taste. When the Komedie Stamboel performed the play in Singapore in 1894 a local English-language newspaper stated that 'the play was creditably mounted and the scenery and stage effects good, though at times of a highly sensational character, and the audience in our opinion might well have been spared the painfully realistic murder of the man found in the robber's cave'.[21]

A large part of the appeal of this spectacle resided in the ability to create stage pictures through scenery, focused lighting, special effects and movement. Realism in pictorial representation had only been recently introduced into the Indies' mass culture. Commercial travelling panorama shows inspired local artists to create their own versions of this art. Lithographs and illustrated books were available for purchase, and very occasionally newspapers featured pen-and-ink drawings of foreign vistas. The sight of perspectively accurate representations of foreign vistas and familiar scenes in drop curtains regularly brought salvos of applause. A Komedie Stamboel fan writes a letter of appreciation in 17 verses to the newspaper.[22] Two verses read:

> The clothes were like pictures from an almanac,
> In which the story of the Turkish king is told.
> [The almanac is] treasured by natives
> And published by van Dorp from the city of Semarang.
>
> There were screens with pictures on them,
> The front curtain would open and the picture would change.
> All spectators were amazed
> That the pictures appropriately followed the plot.

The comparison of the stage image to mechanically reproduced pictures was typical. Another poem written in appreciation of an 1892 performance of 'Siti Senimbar' in Yogyakarta reads that the eponymous heroine was 'as pretty as a picture, causing the hearts of spectators to race'.[23]

Yet the *Nights* stories carried with them a 'coloured' reputation among polite circles. This only compounded the reputation the company's actors and actresses had for criminality, prostitution and violence. The news that the troupe was planning to move in the course of an 1892 run in Batavia from Glodok to the more elite residential area of Gambir yielded the following news item in the Malay daily *Pembrita Betawie*.[24]

> We feel that this will result in a decline in the number of spectators as the good people of Gambir tend not to be inclined to spend money on entertainments such as the Komedie Stamboel, which performs plays based exclusively on the *Thousand and One Nights.* These stories do not need to be known by good girls, because nearly all the stories deal with the secrets of relations between the sexes, for example how people having sexual relations hit each another as foreplay, and other such matters. All of this is not the sort of thing to be seen by young women. Better for the company to find other subjects which are more fitting to be seen by all spectators.

## Expanding the Repertoire

The *Nights* constitute one item in a diverse corpus of pre-modern Arabic texts that travelled extensively in the medieval period and after, substantially influencing literature and oral traditions throughout Asia, Africa and Europe. Others included tales based on Biblical sources such as 'Joseph and Potiphar's Wife' and 'Solomon and the Queen of Sheba'; historical and legendary accounts such as 'Alexander the Great'; and chivalric romances such as 'Antar and Abla'. All these texts and more (e.g. the *Disciplina Clericalis,* a collection of parables and extravagant tales) were told and re-told in countless forms, usually undergoing substantial cultural translation in the process.[25] The modern age also had its host of travelling tales—principally what we now recognize as 'fairy tales' or 'children's stories' (such as Cinderella), but also semi-historical accounts (the romance of Napoleon and Josephine) and moralistic tales (Uncle Tom's Cabin). These texts did not displace the pre-modern travelling stories, but joined them in a common ocean of stories. The tales were not only told in written form, they were performed; the popular, commercial theatre above all brought them to the attention (and into the imagination) of the masses in the years before the rise of sound film. What distinguishes these modern travelling stories from their pre-modern counterparts is that the latter tend *not* to be culturally translated to the same degree; a Graeco–Roman toga drama such as *Quo Vadis?* will normally be played in togas whether performed as concert party in Ghana or revue theatre in Japan. This was certainly the case for the Komedie Stamboel; its expansion of repertoire to incorporate modern travelling stories thus also entailed an expansion of expressive means.

The *Nights* remained at the core of the Komedie Stamboel's repertoire for the rest of its existence, but no longer accounted for the majority of plays performed by 1894. Plays such as 'Siti Sanimbar', 'The Gorda's Egg', 'Ali Baba' and 'Aladdin' remained in the repertoire into the twentieth century, but many other *Nights* plays were phased out as others were introduced. A major principal was variety. The company was often praised for variety, and variety in repertoire and style was underlined in publicity.[26] While certain plays exhibited longevity, and were much in demand with audiences, others passed quickly from the repertoire, mirroring and shaping the dynamic fluctuations of popular tastes. Most plays could (in theory) be enacted in a single night, but some, such as an adaptation of the celebrated pan-Islamic novel, 'Secrets of the Court of Constantinople', were performed as serials over the course of two or more nights.[27]

A look at the plays presented in an actual run gives a sense of the variety. The Komedie Stamboel presented the following plays during the course of a 25 day run in August–September 1894 in the small coastal city of Cirebon (western Java): 'Siti Senimbar'; 'Zaheer Zaman'; 'Ali and the Magical Fiddle'; 'Sleeping Beauty'; 'Machmoed or the Fisherman and the Jinni'; two comic farces titled 'He is Not Jealous' and 'He is Too Jealous'; 'The Roc's Egg'; 'Ali Baba and the Forty Thieves'; 'The Son of the

White Tiger'; 'The Somnambulist'; 'The Punishments of Hell'; 'Bluebeard'; 'Aladdin and the Magical Lamp'; 'The World Star'; 'Genoveva'; 'The Three Jealous Sisters'; 'Kamarel Zahman and Badur'; 'The Hunchback and the Loquacious Barber'; 'Siti Safira'; 'Damsie, The Fallen Angel'; 'Amgiad and Assad: The Two Misidentified Princes'; 'Snow White'; a reprise of 'Ali Baba'; 'Love and Artifice'; and a reprise of the 'Somnambulist'. These plays were adapted from a variety of sources. Less than half of them are *Nights* plays. A number are new plays written by Mahieu; five are based on European literature. At least one, 'Earth Star', also known as 'Badarel Dunia', is based on a play introduced to the Indies via a touring Bangsawan troupe from Malaya (which in turn drew inspiration from a touring Parsi company from India).[28]

The need to find other subjects for performance was experienced even during the first ten months of the Komedie Stamboel's Surabaya residency. It was felt by some that Surabaya audiences were growing bored of the same old *Nights* plays performed nightly with the same stock of costumes and scenery; a *Bintang Soerabaia* reporter suggested adapting tales of Sheikh Abdul Mulia or Abdul Muluk to increase ticket sales—a suggestion which was never picked up on.[29] The majority of the new plays performed in 1891 seem to have been adaptations of European novels and new comical farces of the sort popular among Dutch amateur theatrical groups. These were performed as experiments—with mixed results. An adaptation by actor–manager Charles O. van der Laan[30] of the Faust tale, titled 'Tatool-Achmat or The Faust of Arabia' (premiered 22 September 1891), merited the following review in Surabaya's Dutch language daily.

> The performance last night by the Komedie Stamboel of the 'Faust of Arabia'—a faithful imitation [*getrouwe nabootsing*] of the German Faust—was very fine and seemed to have been to the taste of the fairly large public in attendance, which otherwise is composed of a majority of Chinese spectators, but this time consisted exclusively of Europeans. John Chinaman appears not to desire a performance of the devil's realm. The actors and actresses acquitted themselves well of their difficult task, made even more difficult as most of them have never seen the 'Faust' enacted. These play lies outside of the *genre* of tales of the 1001 Nights, which so far the Komedie Stamboel has drawn upon for her performances. The tableau vivant at the conclusion was also attractively arranged.[31]

Mahieu also wrote his own plays, which were popular among audiences. Some of these plays could be quite controversial. This was clearly the case for a theatrical telling of an event from the pages of the newspaper—the invasion of Lombok. The play was banned before its first scheduled performance, although later it was acted in revised form.

There were also European fairy tales and romances. One of the most frequently performed was 'Sleeping Beauty' known (after the Dutch fashion) as *Boenga Mawar*, or the Rose. This play was 'adapted from a famous Dutch book and is quite appropriate for the theatre'[32] and entered the Komedie Stamboel's repertoire in 1893. The play was set against a European background, with actors clothed in Spanish costumes.[33] A much abbreviated summary is provided in a notice.

> A childless king prayed to God for an offspring. His prayer was granted by God and a short time later his queen gave birth to a girl named Boenga Mawar. The king was so filled with joy that he gave a party, inviting all the good fairies [translated as both *peri* and *dewa*, or Hindu gods, in the summary] to it. There was one evil fairy among the fairies who was upset that she was not invited to the party. All the good fairies came to the party and one by one

> gave their gifts and departed. One granted a long life, another fortune, a third good luck. In short, all gifted Boenga Mawar with different sorts of virtues. After this, the evil fairy was announced. 'Everything given Boenga Mawar is for nought,' [she said], 'because when she reaches 16 years of age she will stab herself on a pointed object and sleep for a hundred years.' The king becomes depressed upon hearing this and he orders everyone in the palace to discard all sharp objects. But when Boenga Mawar reaches the age of 16, she injures her hand on a sharp object and goes into a deep sleep, along with everyone else in the palace. Following this, a prince arrives and wakens everyone.[34]

The play is said to be enjoyable as it is 'very fine and lively, with sung poetry or *pantun* and fine music'. A fan poem praised the play for the liveliness and precise choreography of its party scene.[35]

> The play of Boenga Mawar
> Depicts a gathering of fairies at a big party.
> The voices are lively like at a market
> And nobody who comes takes a misstep.

Following the Komedie Stamboel's 1894 performances of 'Boenga Mawar' in Batavia, it was said that 'many residents of Batavia were so crazy for the actress playing Boenga Mawar that they constantly see the image of Boenga Mawar in their mind's eye'.[36] The production also was a good vehicle for the comical and vocal talents of Mahieu—who (of course) played the young prince. The cast was not uniformly excellent. Reviews of 1893 and 1894 performances of the play in Cirebon reports that while Mahieu (playing the prince) sung and acted well, the chorus singing from back stage was occasionally out of tune.[37] A special theme song written for the play, Setamboel Boenga Mawar, was released by Yap Goan Kioe as a perforated organ roll in 1895.[38] So popular was this story that not only did it enter the repertoire of other Malay popular theatre troupes, a later troupe under Mahieu's direction was named after it—Komidi Stambool Boenga Mawar. The popularity of 'children's tales' such as 'Sleeping Beauty' was later used to demonstrate the 'childishness' of the Malay/Indonesian popular theatre and Indonesians in general. But in the period under consideration, these sorts of plays clearly appealed every bit as much to 'Natives' as to 'Europeans'. Audiences seemed to genuinely enjoy 'Genoveva'; its Occidental exotica and the spectacle of a prancing deer yielded admiration and loud applause.[39] A Dutch reviewer stated of 'Bluebeard' that 'it was very much to our tastes. It was a comic spectacle play and evoked frequent peals of laughter from the audience'.[40] Much of the performative appeal of these plays was in their mixture of horror, wonder and comedy, founded on a prescience of the tale's ultimate outcome.

> Wednesday evening we attended the performance of 'Bluebeard', one of the best plays yet performed. The actors and actresses enacted their rolls very well. The scene between Bluebeard's two servants, in which they unsuccessfully tried to clean a blood-stained key with brandy was most charmingly played. When the chamber of horrors with the seven wives was opened and revealed to the public, spectators reacted with horror. Sister Anna was also not wanting: she waved to the brothers, who rushed in at precisely the critical moment and properly disposed of Bluebeard and the executioner.[41]

I have already noted the influence of Bangsawan. A number of plays added to the repertoire in 1893 and 1894 show signs of influence of other Malay theatrical troupes. Mahieu adapted 'Hawamajelis, the Sun-Princess' for the stage in a production that premiered in Batavia on 3 August 1894. An advertisement states that the tale is drawn from 'Hindu tradition'.[42] But this play (also known as 'Hawai Majlis') had also been a staple of the popular theatre repertoire in Malaya since at least 1887[43] and can in fact be traced back to the Parsi theatre.[44] The entrance of these plays into the repertoire (the most famous being perhaps 'Jula-Juli Bintang Tiga') was an attempt to compete with these foreign troupes. A reviewer of one such Bangsawan troupe noted that 'the Komedie Stamboel adapts its plays from the 1001 Nights, but the Bangsawan bases itself on chronicles of the ancestors, selecting beautiful literature and pleasing the hearts of spectators'.[45] Such critiques could be responded to quickly with the addition of new plays.

The plays performed by the Komedie Stamboel demonstrate the predominance of (even obsession over) certain themes—innocence threatened and protected, sins committed and punished, love and jealousy, exiles who regain their domains. One also notices the many fantastic creatures and objects—magical lamps and violins, white tigers, gods, sun-princesses, genies, hunchbacks, horned kings. This is the stuff of legend and myth, to be enacted with all the means available to melodrama and pantomimic farce.

## The *Nights* and Artistic Reputation

The Komedie Stamboel began to refer to itself as 'Opera' in July 1893, appending this designation to its name. This change in nomenclature reflected aspirations to high art. One report speculated that this was an attempt to avoid paying the *pacht wayang*, a tax for native entertainments paid to (normally Chinese) tax farmers.[46] It opened the company to the charge that it was overstepping its propriety in its self-representation, but it also created new connections between the Malay popular theatre and European high art. Previously, commentators noted with pride that the Komedie Stamboel was a distinct cultural product, not a simple imitation of European opera.[47] But with the form identified as 'opera', actors were henceforth counselled to watch European opera in order to improve their acting skills.[48]

Much debate of the troupe's quality focused on the language used in dialogue. Reports vary according to the tastes and inclinations of observers. The Dutch journalist and cultural observer S. Kalff reports in an impressionistic essay of 1893 titled 'Een avond in de Komedie Stamboel' [A Night at the Komedie Stamboel] that a 'spectator must know fairly good Malay, as well as high Malay, in order to follow the plot of a play'.[49] Others spoke more harshly of the speech style of the dialogue, and indeed the historiographical record of posterity emblematizes the Komedie Stamboel as a 'low Malay' or 'bazaar Malay' art form. Letters, reports, and articles debated these matters.

> The Komedie Stamboel is indeed praised and very much appreciated by the populace of Betawi, but the language and dialogue are criticized by the newspaper 'Hindi Ollanda' as its Malay language is very awkward. According to proper Malay language use, the words *batina* (female) and *jantan* (male) are only used for animals, while the words *prampuwan* (woman) and *laki laki* (men) are used for humans, but in this theatre the words *batina* and *jantan* are used for humans.[50]

The language critique of the Komedie Stamboel often emerged in comparison to touring Bangsawan troupes from Malaya. 'The language of the Bangsawan theatre is more refined than that used in the Komedie Stamboel. For Bangsawan theatre tends not to use the foul language often used in the Komedie Stamboel'.[51]

The troupe's reputation for rough language and crudity accounts for much of the suspicion over political plays and Shakespeare adaptations produced by the troupe. The adaptation of Shakespeare, true crime stories and the agitprop drama composed on behalf of the Indies League are properly the subject of another work. These were all development of the late 1890s, and my focus in this article has been on the first part of the decade. But such was the reputation of the Komedie Stamboel for trivial fluff and rough comedy that just the idea of Shakespeare performed as *komedie stamboel* was enough to turn the stomachs of some. 'The Merchant of Venice—in the Komedie Stamboel, o gods!' exclaims Jan Fabricius in his sardonic commentary on a Sinar India performance of the play.[52] 'Who knows: the event could turn out to be a high point in Shakespearian history', Fabricius states with heavy sarcasm, but *we* (Fabricius' Dutch readers) know that the performance by necessity will turn out otherwise. Apparently, seeing the culture god of the European pantheon served up by a theatre that was so closely associated with the *Nights* could only be understood by some as travesty.

The shift from the *Nights* to a more eclectic repertoire was not without its moments of humour. It was the practise at the conclusion of a play for one of the actors to appear before the footlights and announce the next night's performance, as the tableaux vivant that concluded a night's entertainment was being arranged behind a drop curtain. At one performance, Moll, a clerk from Bogor turned comedian, appeared in the 'blackamoor' costume he had worn while playing an African slave in the story of Aladdin.

> Moll, who superbly executed the difficult role of the deaf-mute African, came before the footlights to announce the programme for the following evenings. His speech, charmingly delivered in broken Dutch mimicking an African, went more or less as follows: 'Ladies and Gentlemen, tomorrow there be good play. Faust, that be Dutch, the King of Arab, (I cannot speak Dutch), and a tableau of Paris burning. I be born near the Frenchman. And the day after next, there is the violin if you do play him fast, he dances; if you do it slow, he sleeps. And with a tableau ... Lho! I does forget ... Oh yes, about the burning up of the Krakatau. Now, Ladies and Gentlemen (bowing deeply), bottoms up! If I be free, I come back. If no, forget about it!'[53]

The comedy in Moll's speech, which intermixes Dutch malapropisms with Malay and the occasional low Javanese word, comes from his attempt to frame subjects including European high art and history (Faust, the 1873 fire of Paris) in contention with subnormal linguistic abilities. The improvizational talents of this clerk-turned-comedian were greatly valued and evoked hilarity—from those among the audience who understood Dutch. The Dutch laughter was barbed. It was not only laughter due to enjoyment of 'charming delivery'. It was also laughter evoked from the perceived impossibility of weaning Malay popular theatre from the comedy and sensationalism of the *Nights*. Mengadoerradjin might have believed that *God Zij Met Ons* means 'power, strength and sharpness belong to the way of the Prophets', but a Dutch colonial would be certain that it meant 'God be with us'—with 'us' referring to the Christian colonizers. There were limits in colonial contexts to the appropriation of stories and other texts. Many of those colonial limits remain as imprisoning structures for 'post-colonials' today.

## Notes

1. This article is based primarily on newspapers housed in the National Library (Jakarta), the Royal Library (The Hague), the University Library of the University of Leiden and the library of the Royal Institute of Linguisties and Anthropology (Leiden). Kind thanks to all these institutions and their staffs.
2. This account is based on a letter published in *Bintang Soerabaia*, 1 December 1891.
3. *Bintang Soerabaia*, 12 December 1893.
4. Pramoedya Ananta Toer, *This Earth of Mankind*, tr. by Max Lane (London: Penguin Books, 1990), pp. 17–18.
5. Martin Heidegger, 'The Age of the world picture', in *The Question Concerning Technology and Other Essays*, tr. by William Lovitt (New York: Harper and Row, 1977), pp. 115–54.
6. A classic formulation of ethos and world view in *wayang kulit* is provided in Clifford Geertz, 'Ethos, world view, and the analysis of sacred symbols, in *The Interpretation of Cultures* (New York: Basic Books, 1973 [1957]), pp. 126–41.
7. On this point, see Benedict R. O'G. Anderson, 'Language, fantasy, revolution: Java 1900–1950', in Daniel S. Lev & Ruth McVey, eds, *Making Indonesia* (Ithaca: Southeast Asia Program, Cornell University, 1995), pp. 26–40.
8. *Bintang Soerabaia*, 14 November 1893.
9. Representative volumes in the KITLV collection in Leiden (The Netherlands) include *Serat Sewu Satunggal Dalu* (Semarang: G.C.T. Van Dorp, 1875); A.F. van de Wall (tr.), *Hikajat Sinbad* (Batavia: Ogilvie, 1876); Mas Prawirahadijaya, *Cariyos Lalampahnipun Sinbad* (Batavia: Ogelfi, 1881); R. Brons Middel (tr.), *Hikajat Orang Terbangoen dari pada Tidornja* (Batavia: Albrecht and Rusche, 1888).
10. Matthew Isaac Cohen, 'On the Origin of the Komedie Stamboel: Popular Culture, Colonial Society, and the Parsi Theatre Movement', *Bijdragen tot de Taal-, Land- en Volkenkunde* 157/2 (2001), pp. 339f.
11. Theodore G. Th. Pigeaud, *Literature of Java I* (The Hague: Martinus Nijhoff, 1967), p. 257.
12. Pigeaud, *Literature*, p. 213.
13. Mattani Mojdara Rutnin, *Dance, Drama, and Theatre in Thailand: The Process of Development and Modernization* (Chiang Mai: Silkworm, 1996).
14. Cohen, 'On the Origin', p. 337.
15. On pan-Islamic paranoia, see C. van Dijk, 'Colonial fears, 1890–1918: Pan-Islamism and the Germano-Indian plot', in H. de Jonge & N. Kaptein, eds, *Transcending Borders: Arabs, Politics, Trade and Islam in Southeast Asia* (Leiden: KITLV, 2002), pp. 53–89.
16. *Bintang Barat*, 13 July 1893.
17. Cohen, 'On the Origin', pp. 347f.
18. *Bintang Soerabaia*, 23 February 1892.
19. *Bataviaasch Nieuwsblad*, 9 May 1894.
20. *Bintang Betawi*, 9 September 1901.
21. *The Singapore Free Press*, 19 February 1894.
22. *Bintang Soerabaia*, 17 August 1892.
23. Tan Tjiook San, 'Sair Komedi Stamboel', in *Almanak Bahasa Melajoe boeat taoen 1893* (Yogyakarta: H. Buning, 1892), p. 258.
24. Reprinted in *Bintang Soerabaia*, 17 October 1892.
25. See E. L. Ranelagh, *The Past We Share: The Near Eastern Ancestry of Western Folk Literature* (London: Quartet Books, 1979).
26. See, e.g. *Tjerimai*, 21 October 1893.
27. 'Secrets of the Court of Constantinople' was translated into Malay (probably by E.F. Wiggers) and serialized in *Bintang Barat* beginning in 1882. It was published in book form between 1892–1898.
28. On touring Bangsawan troupes in the Netherlands Indies, see Matthew Isaac Cohen, 'Border crossings: Bangsawan in the Netherlands Indies in the nineteenth and early twentieth centuries', *Indonesia and the Malay World*, 30/87 (2002) 101–115.
29. Cohen, 'On the Origin', p. 344.
30. Charles O. van der Laan was the actor-manager of the Komedie Stamboel during the period August–October 1891; he subsequently acted as Mahieu's co-director. See Cohen, 'On the Origin', for details on the shifting management structure of the Komedie Stamboel in 1891.
31. *Soerabaiasch-Handelsblad*, 23 September 1891; see also Cohen, 'On the Origin', p. 342.
32. *Bintang Soerabaia*, 21 July 1894.

33. *Tjerimai*, 15 August 1894.
34. *Bintang Soerabaia*, 23 April 1894.
35. *Bintang Soerabaia*, 3 August 1893.
36. *Bintang Soerabaia*, 11 June 1894.
37. *Tjerimai*, 11 November 1893; *Tjerimai*, 15 August 1894.
38. *Pembrita Betawi*, 10 January 1895.
39. *Tjerimai*, 29 August 1894.
40. *Advertentieblad voor Tegal en Omstreken*, 6 December 1893.
41. *Tjerimai*, 11 November 1893.
42. *Java Bode*, 3 August 1894.
43. Cantius Leo Camoens, 'The Wayang Parsi, Tiruan Wayang Parsi, Komidi Melayu and the Bangsawan, 1887–1895', *Malaysia in History*, 25 (1982) p. 2.
44. Ram Babu Saskena, *A History of Urdu Literature* (Lahore: Sind Sagar Academy, 1975 [1924]), p. 354.
45. *Bintang Soerabaia*, 2 October 1893.
46. *Bintang Barat*, 27 July 1893; *Bintang Soerabaia*, 8 August 1893.
47. *Slompret Melayoe*, 30 August 1892.
48. *Pembrita Betawi*, 29 July 1895.
49. *Java Bode* 15 February 1893. This article was subsequently revised by Kalff and republished as 'Een avond in de "Komedie Stamboul" ', *Indie* 2, 1918–19: 757, 759, 761, 774–8.
50. *Bintang Soerabaia*, 16 September 1893.
51. *Bintang Soerabaia*, 2 October 1893.
52. Jan Fabricius, *Tempo Doeloe: Uit de Goeie Ouwe Tijd* (The Hague: Leopold, 1949), p. 76. Sinar India is the name of Auguste Mahieu's troupe during the period 1899–1903.
53. *Tjerimai*, 15 November 1893. The two plays announced by Moll are 'Tatool Achmat or the Faust of Arabia' and 'Ali and the Magic Violin'.

# Emboldening Dinarzad: the *Thousand and One Nights* in contemporary fiction

STEPHANIE JONES

## Introduction: Tempering the Nights

The ideological questions raised by recent allusions to the stories of Shahrazad—her cameo appearances and reduction to the numeracy of her stories—were first posed over half a century ago by Jorge Luis Borges in his short story, "The Garden of Forking Paths" (1941). As Husain Haddawy points out, enumeration within the *Thousand and One Nights*—of everything from people, to numbered flagons of wine and legs of mutton—secures the fantastic elements of the tales to a sense of the everyday, catalyzing the suspension of disbelief.[1] However, following Borges, the numbering of the *Nights* themselves has taken on an inter-textual loading to converse effect; a wandering away from the quotidian into philosophies of temporality and theses on history. In "The Garden of Forking Paths", the *Nights* are exemplary of a certain kind of temporally self-defeating innumerability:

> I remembered ... that night which is at the middle of the *Thousand and One Nights* when Scheherazade (through a magical oversight of the copyist) begins to relate word for word the story of the *Thousand and One Nights*, establishing the risk of coming once again to the night when she must repeat it, and thus on to infinity.[2]

The curiosity of Borges's allusion is not in the establishment of the *Nights* as a marker of infinity, but in the ways in which the story puts a line through—almost erases—this equivalence. In the extant manuscripts and famous translations of the *Nights* (of which Borges famously made a life-long study), there are variations and riffs on the frame-story, but there is no such exact event of "magical oversight", no middle-night prompting infinite repetition.[3] But that such a manuscript must have existed is almost a truism of Borges's labyrinthine world view. This manuscript would be inevitable within the differently infinite-text more centrally explored within "The Garden of Forking Paths". The reference to the *Nights* is in one sense an openly admitted red herring. It is offered almost too emphatically as a possibility that "does not correspond, not even remotely" to the text at the centre of the story.[4] The narrator explains how an apparently incoherent and contradictory "novel"—entitled *The Garden of Forking Paths*—is finally comprehended as a presentation of a metaphysic of time. The work's contradictions make sense if it is first understood that the writer is simultaneously pursuing every possible choice of the protagonist; every conceivable and hard to conceive of happening. This work is not merely a "rhetorical exercise", but an expression of belief in "an infinite series of times, in a growing, dizzying net of divergent, convergent and parallel times". Against a "uniform, absolute time", this text "simultaneously" expresses every probability and infinite possibility.[5] Curiously, this other text is closer to the radical notion of the spreading (rather than closer circling) infinity of which the *Nights* has more often been posited as exemplary within contemporary literatures. But this, of course, is not the end of the intricacy of Borges's tale. Returning his story to its own literary qualities—of plot, pace, suspense and character—reveals the difficulties arising from deployments of the *Nights* as either a self-involving and/or infinitely multiplying trope and talisman of infinity.

The stories of Borges, like the stories of the *Nights*, are vulnerable to a hyper-abstraction that glosses the specificity of the tales themselves. "The Garden of Forking Paths" is a story about temporality and textuality—but this is not what sustains the reader's attention. The meditation on the infinite-text is itself told within a confessional letter, which is presented by the omniscient narrator as a corrective to an anecdote within another (fictionally-factual) text—*A History of World War I*, which tells the story of an "insignificant" four-day delay to a British mission, apparently caused by heavy rains. The narrator of the corrective letter is Yu Tsun, an English-speaking Chinese spy for the Germans, who "throws an unsuspected light over the whole affair" of the delay.[6] The substance of "The Garden of Forking Paths" is the narration of this letter, which details Yu Tsun's realization that he has been discovered; and his consequently desperate plan to convey information about the location of British barracks back to his command in Germany before he is captured. He does so by murdering a man simply because he is called Stephen Albert—his surname indicating to the Germans "the secret name of the city they must attack" (the bombing of the city "Albert" thus causing the delay in British operations put down to heavy rains).[7] In an extraordinary (or ordinary-Borgesian) coincidence, Albert happens to be a Sinologist whose life's work has been the study of the texts left by the ancestor of Yu Tsun himself. Albert, unaware that he is about to be killed, explains how he came to an understanding of the infinite-text; which explanation is retold with admiration and poignancy by Yu Tsun—his murderer—in the letter.[8] The atmosphere of Borges's story is not itself one of energizing infinite possibility, but of bizarre fatefulness and despondency. In this sense of predetermination, the allusion to the *Nights* is more oblique but more telling than the explicit (but discarded) reference.

The grip of Borges's story is not in the trajectory of text within text, but in the literary tension between ideas of the infinite and this extraordinary sense of predestination. The implications of this tension might be teased out if the infinite-text is understood as a Lacanian "symbolic object". In his work towards a theory of ideology—in which he concentrates on the unconscious, subjective and inter-subjective experience of totalitarian rule—Slavoj Žižek explicates Lacan's recognition of "the material presence of a fragment of reality … remnants which cannot be reduced to a network of formal relations proper to the symbolic structure, but [which are] paradoxically, at the same time, the positive condition for the effectuation of the formal structure".[9] In Borges's story, the infinite-text is precisely such a "leftover": it is that which is both "radically contingent" to the plot and also the "pure material element" which "guarantees … the structure of symbolic exchange" between the characters.[10] In its paradoxical, irreducible and mere presence, it embodies

> … the greatest mystery of the symbolic order: how its necessity arises from the shock of a totally contingent encounter of the Real—like the well-known accident in the *Arabian Nights*: the hero, lost in the desert, quite by chance

> enters a cave; there, he finds three old wise men, awoken by his entry, who say to him: "Finally, you have arrived! We have been waiting for you for the last three hundred years".[11]

So Yu Tsun, having identified a random "Albert" in the phone-book, arrives at his house late at night and is greeted without surprise as the expected descendent of the author of the infinite-text. However, the affinity between Borges's story and the *Nights* is not fulfilled by Žižek's example. This is completed at a more encompassing level. Like Borges's tale, the frame-story of the *Nights* inscribes both a sense of infinite play and a sense of fated completion. It is not simply that the story of Shahrazad's immense story-telling feat properly, roundly, concludes (literary tradition is unanimous that Shahrazad is successful in averting the Shahrayar's determination to take a virgin every night and kill her the following morning in revenge for being cuckolded by his wife and in mad disillusionment with all women). It is that the story stabilizes and maintains the symbolic order, rather than subverts or diverts. As Edward Said comments in his *Beginnings, Intention and Method*:

> The Prophet is he who has *completed* a world-view .... Islam views the world as a plenum, capable of neither diminishment nor amplification. Consequently, stories like those in *The Arabian Nights* are ornamental, variations on the world, not completions of it; neither are they lessons, structures, extensions, or totalities designed to illustrate either the author's prowess in representation, the education of a character, or ways in which the world can be viewed and changed.[12]

For Said, the *Nights* are exemplary of a powerful completion and an inconsequential incompletion. He reminds us that Shahrazad imagines and talks, not with intent to go on forever, but only long enough. Averting Shahrayar's murderous plan does not equate to an ability or a will to undermine or overcome. Shahrazad seeks relief, equanimity and maintenance, not triumph or chaos, or a new history or tempo. However, against her abstraction into a sign of just such anti-ideological proliferations, a return to the substance and teleology of the frame-story is not without radical potential. But this potential, I would argue, has been realized in recent literature not so much through the figure and extraordinary ability of Shahrazad herself, but more fully in the seemingly vague and peripheral role of her younger sister, Dinarzad. In Žižek's Lacanian formulation, Dinarzad may be read as the radically anterior "symbolic object" that both mediates and manifests the impossibility of the ideological tension within the frame-story of the *Nights*. "Dinarzad" or "Dunyazad"—meaning of this world, this very tangible place—may be read as lending political and secular weight to her name.[13] As will be explored in the third part of this essay, she can be read as the material paradox that both determines and disrupts the symbolic order.

Using Žižek's Lacanian formulation, the idea of this paper is to explore the "original" role—the core concept—of Dinarzad as it has been historically reinscribed. But more fully, it is to examine how Dinarzad has been given body and voice across a range of contemporary fictions: from the Borgesian (but emphatically North American) work of John Barth to a brief short-story by the Pakistani writer Intizar Husain; from the troubled feminism of the Algerian writer, Assia Djebar to the elliptical literary structures of the Indian novelist, Githa Hariharan. The idea, however, is not to concentrate on how Dinarzad has been appropriated towards particular themes of national fiction, but rather to seek the nub of her cross-cultural imaginative possibility. Towards this analysis, the following section moves from Borges to Franz Kafka, Salman Rushdie and through the mediating work of the less-known novelist, M. G. Vassanji, to trace how one strain of trans-national inter-textual narrative moves around Shahrazad as a trope of infinite proliferation. More particularly, tracking allusion to the *Nights* through this genealogy of texts reveals the on-going conversation between (the ideology) of the *Nights* and (the ideology) of the novel. For while re-writings of Dinarzad counterpoint historical variations on the *Nights*, they may be read more fully and precisely—and in the name of *both* sisters—against recent abstractions of Shahrazad as she has been deployed within and against the novel genre.

## Part One: Abstracting Shahrazad

Walter Benjamin writes that "in the stories which Kafka left us, narrative art regains the significance it had in the mouth of Scheherazade: to postpone the future".[14] The relationship across centuries between these tellers of tales is in the use of suspension and deferral to both comprehend and challenge the threat of a mad and maddening rule. Within Benjamin's thinking, this move is a politically admirable counter to both fervent teleological temporalities and the secular empty time of modernity. But it is difficult to decide which storyteller is more successful in their defiance—or indeed whether their measure of success is comparable. When the abstraction of their method is returned to the body of their story, the parallel is harder to sustain. The sinister bureaucracy of Kafka's world is frightening because it is geared exclusively to its own self-perpetuation, without a defined God-head to give logic or meaning to the system. In Kafka's novels, the nameless K. is unable to escape or penetrate this world, becoming an emptier (more exhausted and confused) cipher than at the beginning. The triumph of the tale is not in the *denouement*, but in the ridiculous and ridiculing tempo; a gift of sensibility to the reader, numbed and unaware of their own and others' place/lessness in totalitarian systems and histories. Conversely, a triumph of sorts is guaranteed—is even inevitable—for Shahrazad in her role as restorer and bolster of a given order with an unquestioned God-head. From a cipher, one of an anonymous series of women defined only by their virginity, she emerges indefatigably Shahrazad, her name resounding across centuries of pages of literature. It is ironic, then, that in the cause of impugning ideologies that oppress, Shahrazad has been returned to a cipher within recent literary productions.

The Shahrazadean one thousand + one ( + one ...) is a recurring signifier of infinite metamorphoses, exciting possibilities and the power of fiction across Rushdie's texts. *Haroun and the Sea of Stories* (1990) most particularly and unambiguously inscribes the good necessity of story playing on story *ad infinitum* against the evil of historic and mythical monologisms.[15] More complexly, in *Midnight's Children* (1981) Saleem Sinai's identity is compromised at birth, not only because he is swapped as a new-born with his alter-ego Shiva, but because he is one of 1001 children born at the moment of India's independence.[16] While Saleem is the most unreliable of narrators, the description of his unwitting telepathy—his transformation into a radio transmitter for the other 1000 children—powerfully signifies, not just his symbolic relationship to the teeming nation, but also a more terrifying bloating and fragmentation of identity. Similarly, in *The Satanic Verses* (1988), through his public persona as the radio's "Man of a Thousand Voices and a Voice", Saladin Chamcha's identity slips in and out of the fictions of his professional work—even as the text itself rejoices in the broader, anti-fundamentalist significations of a thousand + one ways of telling the world.[17] Rushdie's deployment of the trope oscillates between joy in the expansive and hybrid nature of identity and history; and those moments of terror that a comprehension of the every-collapsing, ever-malleable must entail. Within Rushdie's work, the *Nights* signifies narratives of both subversion and aversion. However, in the very mode of his writing—teetering with adjectives, gleefully splicing and splitting—he implies that the freedoms of infinity and the certainty of incompletion are to be more finely valued than deplored. Underlining this reading, Rushdie's celebration of the *Nights*—rather than his equally provoking and often more poignant narrative of loss—has itself become a contemporary myth on which other writer's play.

Like the South-Asian/British/American Rushdie, the South-Asian/East-African/Canadian M.G. Vassanji defies purities in his work—any complacently self-contained idea of a national, religious, racial or communal construction of a people. And like Rushdie, Vassanji's pursuit of history leads him to figures verging on exile. But the slippage of the migrant into a metaphor for the alienations of modernity or the liberations of globalisation are, in Vassanji's work, referred back to his Ismaili people's particular world view. In his novel *The Gunny Sack* (1989), this view is filtered through/prompted by the contemplation of items contained in an old bag. The frustrations of conjuring a seemingly whole history out of this jumble becomes, in the narrator's mind, a process of wooing the right story at the right time out of the bag; which he characterizes early in the text as a kind of sacky "Shehrazade". In *The Gunny Sack*, the one thousand + one possibilities signified by each evocative but silent object suggests both ever-alternative versions of history, and the constant, tantalizing slippage of certainty into ellipses at the most crucial and climactic point. Vassanji's Shehrazade, however, is "a home-grown type, a local version".[18] This parochial Shehrazade defies the complete absorption of the novel into a tradition of writing utilizing the myth. As the narrator petitions his dowdy "Shehru" for the stories he wants, Vassanji asks the reader to value the specificities of the African and Ismaili histories he is telling. In his later novel *Amriika* (1999), Vassanji goes even further in disassociating his work from the tradition of texts utilizing the Shahrazadian myth. His very deliberate inter-textual reference to Rushdie's work continues the trope, but in a defiantly lower register.

*Amriika*, spelling out an Indian-accented America, may be read allusively with Kafka's Prague-German accented, unfinished novel about *Amerika* (1924). The pronounced spelling of the title apparently signifies Vassanji's intent to create what Gilles Deleuze and Felix Guattari—in their work on Kafka—term a "minor" literature: to deploy "the polylingualism of one's own language" towards an "absolute deterritorialization" of English. But Vassanji's text is also clearly intended to be more major—in the sense of more accessible—than his previous novels. The lives told are not always "magnified and intensified within an estranging temporality", nor strangely pared down "to connect immediately to politics".[19] Trading between the reflexive narrative necessary to his sense of history, and the more linear and traditionally presumptive effects of his chosen genre, Vassanji's novel plays out his particular Ismaili ancestry of trade and negotiation. But this doesn't suggest a loss of integrity, nor read as an inadequate or less revolutionary minor sensibility, but rather works into a central theme on the necessity of compromise itself. So between Kafka's pared, alienating, recessive narrative effect and Rushdie's excessive, all-claiming language—between iconic work of modernist literature and iconic work of postmodern literature—Vassanji insists on a moderate historical sensibility that is suppressed at one extreme and overwhelmed at the other.

Kafka himself, in naming the protagonist of *Amerika* "Karl", indicates an exceptional move towards an apparently more "major" use of language. Stripped down to their initial K, the protagonists of *The Trial* and *The Castle* define "minor" literature through the "materially intense" effects of a "purely intensive" use of language.[20] The migration of K into Karl in the journey to America—"a new life in a new country"—suggests a self-possession; a relative expansiveness of individual character within a wider geography.[21] Kafka seems eager to work with the new world myth, a freer space that doesn't so urgently require or force a minor perspective—where that view can relax into some of the presumptions of a (self)-mastering consciousness. However, bodily tiredness and the mere effort to keep hold of his meagre material possessions as Karl travels America searching for work—but more immediately and constantly, repeatedly for sleep—take the text into closed, "materially intense" spaces within hotels, apartment blocks and trains. Read as a story about delayed sleep, the text appears to most literally bear out Benjamin's comment on the Shahrazadian nature of Kafka's work. But the multiple energetic beginnings and suspended endings by which Shahrazad postpones her future are missing in *Amerika*. Karl's endless weariness, his running inability to get a good night's sleep, retards the very idea of new beginnings. The cathartic and myth-making functions of literature are themselves postponed and turned into alienating banalities. Against this emptying effect, Vassanji's return of "narrative art" to "the significance it had in the mouth of Scheherazade" appears as energetic post-modern play—a celebratory incarnation beyond Kafka's aesthetic. However, in explicitly defining his text against Rushdie's *The Satanic Verses*, Vassanji deliberately curtails the endlessly multiplying potential of this effect. Shahrazad appears in *Amriika*, not—as in *The Gunny Sack*—as an explicit structuring metaphor, but as an opera of the *Nights* to which the narrator is invited but doesn't attend. The aside within an anecdote about a failed love affair both admits and signifies the carefully limited influence of this mode of story telling on the narrative of *Amriika*.[22]

*Amriika* begins with a meditation on "Beginnings ...". Vassanji suggests that a defined beginning is a myth, and that myth—in the mode of Shahrazad's tales—is the only definitive beginning: "a time when invocations worked miracles, angels kept watch over us, and djinns lurked in the grey shadows of the sunset".[23] But the narrator is not just writing this account "to imagine beginnings", but "to sustain them and guide them to my present condition, here in the obscurity of these rented rooms near a beach".[24] He is in exile because of his inadvertent involvement in the bombing of a shop that sold a book criticising the encroachment of mainstream Islam into smaller, divergent practices of the religion. The parallel with the violent reaction—book burnings and the fatwa declared by Ayatollah Ruholla Khomeini—to the publication of Rushdie's anti-fundamentalist *The Satanic Verses* is explicitly made by a character who is angered by the text: "If that other satanic author had received his due—".[25] But while the narrator/Vassanji condemn the bombing, the impetus of *Amriika* is not a complete exoneration of Rushdie's book. This point is emphasised in a complex imitation of Rushdie's own self-conscious style. Naming the controversial text *101 Letters*, Vassanji plays on but limits the trope of the *Nights*. Further, at the point at which the narrator is about to quote from *101 Letters* to demonstrate how it might offend, he stops himself and turns the pause into a self-reflexive interruption, speaking of his fear of even voicing the text.[26] In glossing over the details of the religious argument and turning the moment into a questioning of narrative form, the novel obliquely quotes *The Satanic Verses*. The issue, Vassanji implies with Rushdie, is larger than the specific question of competing theological interpretations. He admits that all narrative is vulnerable to challenge—even to 101 or 1001 parallel, future and legitimate reinterpretations. But that this important diminution of staid objectivity necessarily leads to the expression of an equally dogmatic anti-fundamentalism becomes, for Vassanji, the crux of his novel.

The narrator's suspicion—probably true, although never confirmed—is that the author of *101 Letters* is his best friend, who is evangelical in his campaign against movements within their particular Ismaili community "to purify itself of so-called Hindu idolatry and move closer to a cleaner, mainstream Islam".[27] The title of the book obliquely references the mutable tradition of the *Nights*, in which both structure and story can be traced back to the earlier Hindu story-telling tradition of the *Panchatantra*—a fusion that is pulled-back-apart in Rushdie's *Haroun and the Sea of Stories*, which takes both as separate inspiration, re-combining them in his joyous modern proliferation of myths. However, such insistence on maintaining a syncretic tradition is portrayed by Vassanji as ultimately dogmatic in its anti-dogma. Vassanji is eager that, having discarded the solidarities of traditional religious fundamentalisms and theorised fundamental pluralisms, something real remains. And this, in one reading, is his novel itself—a modulation between a poststructuralist recognition of 1001 versions, and a more traditional exercise in the art of the novel that sustains a beginning to a truly redemptive end. Said similarly moves between the significations of the *Nights* and the art of the novel, but offers a notably different understanding of the counterpoint.

Against his identification of the European novelistic desire "to create an alternative world, to modify or augment the real world through the act of writing", the *Nights*—as already quoted above—are exemplary, for Said, of an always-already "completed" Islamic world view.[28] Said posits the substance of the *Nights* against the abstractions offered by Rushdie and Vassanji—for whom they signify the art of beginnings and ever more alternative beginnings, reaching vastly beyond a politics of anti-fundamentalism to challenge the sacredness of any whole-view. To return to the quote from Benjamin, Said implies that the measure of Shahrazad's success is indeed very different to that of Kafka's. But the comparison of the *Nights* with Kafka's profoundly anti-novelistic novels leads to Said's fuller definition of the art of the novel—or rather the novel as cultural artefact "of bourgeois society". In *Culture and Imperialism*, he argues that the traditional nineteenth century novel expresses "an entire system of social reference that depends on the existing institutions of bourgeois society, their authority and power". The "will to modify or augment" is, then, tightly bound to the energising of secular bourgeois ambition through imperialism: "imperialism and the novel fortified each other to such a degree that it is impossible, I would argue, to read one without in some way dealing with the other".[29] So as the energies of the novel contrast the stasis of the *Nights*, so the *Nights* are redeployed against the calcification of the novel into a categorical genre. In putting these anti-imperialist critics (Benjamin and Said) and novelists (Kafka, Rushdie and Vassanji) together, the conversation between the *Nights* and the novel emerges as dynamic—the very mutually unsettling effect they have on one another prompting a constant, creative questioning of political and moral assumptions. This is a conversation that is being continued under the sign of Dinarzad. But here, the presence and adequacy of the *Nights* in both allusive and adaptive relation to the novel tends to be more focused, more concerned with particular feminine and feminist potentials. The next part of this paper explores the transformations (ellipses and perversions) of Dinarzad to point up the different and more discrete ideological implications of some recent generic (mal)-absorptions of the *Nights*.

## Part Two: Emboldening Dinarzad

In Steve Barron and Peter Barnes's visually sumptuous and narratively impudent television extravaganza, *Arabian Nights* (2000), Dinarzad is missing.[30] The effect is more disconcerting than might be expected. The absence of the quiet sister at the foot of the bed at first seems a small loss within a dramatic reworking of the frame-story of the *Nights*. In reducing the first three murderous years of the tale to a mere threat—not one virgin is actually raped or murdered—Shahrayar has been reincarnated as an ordinarily angry, benign Sultan; and Shahrazad is presented as a soothing prophylactic rather than potential martyr. But it isn't because of our comparative knowledge of the bloodier ancestor of this prime-time Shahrayar that the absence of his prefacing killing spree itself kills any real quality of suspense. For of course the literary quality of the *Nights* has never been dependent on the belief that Shahrayar might actually kill Shahrazad. Shahrazad's stories are reduced to a titillating game, not because the Sultan has no blood on his hands, but because the stories are told directly and exclusively to Shahrayar: in other words, because Dinarzad has been excised.

It is Dinarzad who, every night, prompts Shahrazad to tell her stories—"Please, if you are not sleepy, tell us one of your lovely little tales to while away the night". And every dawn, as Shahrazad's story reaches a critically suspenseful point, it is Dinarzad who acts as prompt and chorus: "Sister, what a lovely story!" Shahrazad replied, "What is this compared with what I shall tell you tomorrow night?" ".[31] While the *Nights* are structured through a technique of immersion—trapping the audience into a bewildering labyrinth of story within story—they are encompassed by a structure of certainty. The artistry of the *Nights* might be said to lie precisely in this movement between involvement in the story and the regular pauses of the framing dialogue—the oxymoronic shock of the expected. However, this movement can be seen to place the audience at a particular distance. It renders the tale—in Said's terms—an "ornament", the discrete artistry of which may be contemplated, but the ordering ideology of which resists interrogation. This resistance is more fully inscribed in the mode of dialogue, specifically in the way in which it avoids the obvious question.

Often the presence of a witness induces shame, either in those witnessed or indeed—as in the frame-story of Shahrayar observing his first wife in the act of sexual betrayal—in the witness themselves. But the presence of Dinarzad in the room with Shahrazad and Shahrayar prevents shame. The structure of request and reply between the two sisters avoids the issue of question and answer between Shahrazad and Shahrayar. This has ideological implications. As Žižek writes of the power of the direct question, regardless of its content:

> It is the form of the question as such which is obscene: the question lays open, exposes, denudes its addressee … this is why the basic, elementary reaction to a question is shame on the bodily level, blushing and lowering our eyes …. Questioning is the basic procedure of the totalitarian intersubjective relationship.[32]

The big questions—of the end of the stories, of Shahrayar's shifty failure to kill Shahrazad—are repeatedly glossed in the frame-story. Giving Žižek's point a twist, Dinarzad provides a means by which Shahrazad can maintain a graceful complicity with Shahrayar. For of course while a totalitarian regime may operate through questioning, this shaming process can be only dangerously, fatally reversed. So in this sense, Dinarzad is that upon which the maintenance and renewal of order rests. But read through Žižek as a Lacanian "symbolic object", it is her mere presence—not even her minimal speaking role—as the third person between Shahrazad and Shahrayar that takes on weight. If the "basic gesture of structuralism is to reduce the imaginary richness to a formal network of symbolic relations"—of dualites and hierarchical binaries—then "the one which *has no* counterpart" signifies the grounding "limit" and thereby the very necessity of the symbolic order. But this "leftover of the real" also "shocks" and disrupts this order through its very radical contingency.[33]

Bringing the implications of this reading into contemporary national discourse, a recent collection of migrant writing has been entitled *Dinarzad's Children: An Anthology of Contemporary Arab American Fiction* (2004).[34] Here, the name Dinarzad takes on a double meaning. She is both "of this world"—staking a claim to America as the immediate, material present—and she is of the world in a more expansive sense. Dinarzad accrues meaning in translation; the confluence in English between "of this world" and "of the world" allows Dinarzad to signify a traveler, a figure of worldliness. Further, as the mother of a diaspora, she is still the sister of Shahrazad—whose name, meaning "of the city", comes to signify the local, the bounded, the homely. The traditional distinction between the wise, sophisticated Shahrazad—with her international tales of adventure—and the virginal Dinarzad seems to have been reversed. Recast as a modern migrant, she comes to emblemize the effort of emerging from quiet, still obedience (to the Sultan, and to sister) into movement and speech. However, in sustained contemporary reworkings of Dinarzad, it is notable that she is barely abstracted. Her symbolic resonance is articulated through her very materiality and particularly the intensities of her woman's body. Although in John Barth's supercilious re-writing of "the story of the story of" the *Nights*, this narrative splays into a spoof of feminist acts of sexual and political awakening.[35]

Implicitly invoking Borges's *Nights* of "The Garden of Forking Paths", Barth's *Dunyazadiad* (1972) regenerates the *Nights* as an infinitely circular text. As Wen-chin Ouyang puts it, the "narrative pattern" of the *Nights* is turned "inside out, outside-in", producing "a text that sounds uncannily familiar but looks positively extraordinary".[36] But Barth backs away from the despondency of Borges's deathly ending to inscribe a patriarchal joke; a betrayal of the possibility—tantalizingly offered—of the text as a generous feminist act. In the epilogue to the *Dunyazadiad*, the author writes of how, if he "should invent a story as beautiful" as the *Nights*, "it should be about little Dunyazade".[37] Setting her up as narrator, Barth lends his Dunyazade a modern colloquial voice that contrasts comically with the monarchical scenes of the *Nights*—but institutes a lacunae between tone and setting that constantly reveals Barth as the ultimate narrator. There is a concentric logic, even metaphysical necessity, to Barth's appearance as the author of the *Nights* themselves. Dunyazade's behind-the-scenes tale reveals that the stories told by "Sherry" were narrated to her by a "Genie" bearing a marked physical resemblance to Barth himself.[38] Genie-Barth is conjured by Scheherazade when, in despair for an idea by which she can save the virgins being raped and killed by the Sultan, she arrives at the cryptic notion—but not a method to match it—that "the key to the treasure is the treasure". At the same moment in the future (invoking the differently infinite-text of Borges's story), Barth happens to write the same phrase.[39] Through this mystical coincidence, the unlikely Genie appears and gives Scheherazade the idea for the stories by telling her of the volumes of the *Nights* on the shelves of his study at home in the future. So the plot develops; when Scheherazade needs a new story, she conjures the Genie with the magical phrase, and he then narrates to her one of her own tales in prosaic fulfillment of Borges's self-encircling *Nights*. A conversation on the art of story-telling develops between Scheherazade and the Genie, who both delight in and "speculate endlessly" on structures of "tale-within-tales-within-tales-within-tales". The meaning of their mantra "the key to the treasure is the treasure" is that it is not the flesh, as it were, of story (which is always already derivative) but the ways into and out of the tales—their relative structure—that is of crucial significance.[40] As Ouyang carefully traces, the central movement of the *Dunyazadiad* is not towards the creation of a substantially new story, but towards the resolution of Barth's own writer's block through the interdiction of his subjectivity into the structuring principle of the old tales.[41] Dunyazade, even in her own narration, is a foil:

> This relation (which to me seemed less important than what the stories were about) interested the two of them no end, just as Sherry and Shahryar were fascinated by the pacing of their nightly pleasures ... instead of the degree and quality of their love.[42]

Dunyazade (of this world, the material present) here argues for substance. Her appeal for Barth—both the ultimate author and the visiting Genie—is her very impatience with the storytelling tradition in which he so delights. The affect of Barth's *Dunyazadiad* is not in the generation of an every more complex *mise-en-abyme*, but in the expression of tension between the self-satisfied, complacent virtuosity of the technique and the demythologizing tone of Dunyazade—although ultimately, I would argue, the one overwhelms the other.

Following the tradition of longer versions of the *Nights*, Barth's Dunyazade is married to Shahrayar's brother, Shah Zaman, at the end of the frame-story. However, this apparently happy conclusion—in which Dunyazade is given a counterpart and resolves into the given order—is perverted in Barth's telling. We learn that Dunyazade is narrating her story to Shah Zaman on their wedding night—while holding a knife to her husband's penis which, under Scheherazade's instruction, she plans to chop off (the sisters having resolved to take simultaneous vengeance on the brothers because the men, having both been cuckolded by their first wives, had shared a vow to take a virgin every night and kill her the following morning. This means—in Barth's comically pedantic tones—that they believe Shah Zaman to be doubly culpable because he carried out a killing spree that lasted as long as Shahrayar's *plus* the length of the telling of the *Nights*). Dunyazade thus relishes telling the orgiastic details of her relationship with her sister and their everyday cuckolding of Shahrayar: "the King per usual spent the day in his durbar, bidding and forbidding between man and man ... ; I climbed in with Sherry as soon as he was gone, and per usual we spent our day sleeping in and making love".[43] However, between Dunyazade's tale and Barth's encompassing epilogue, the story is passed to Shah Zaman, who asks Dunyazade to listen to his own story before she acts.

The second half of the *Dunyazadiad* is narrated by Shah Zaman, who tells of how he was unable to achieve an erection with the first of his intended virginal victims until he determined not to fulfill his deadly intentions, but instead to let her leave his kingdom and found a society of women who would cut of one breast to signify that "in one aspect we're all women, in another all warrior". Shah Zaman avers that instead of raping and killing the virgins, he told them of this "alternative society" and sent them in groups "to organize and populate it"—thus maintaining the impression that he had kept his vow to his brother while pursuing a virtuous and politically radical scheme.[44] The resolution of his farcical moral quandary leaves Dunyazade uncertain; whether the story is true or a lie ("Fictions maybe—but truer than facts", Shah Zaman tries to persuade); and whether she can love and live with Shah Zaman. But before she decides, dawn breaks and the story ends—or begins. The implication that Dunyazade has taken Shahrayar's role and that Shah Zaman has taken Shahrazad's place—a distorted mirroring—has ambivalent ramifications. Dunyazade is lent power, but in the end is returned to the role of listener. Further, the power she has been given as narrator freezes her in a caricature of feminist agendas—the knife poised over the penis. (That the penis is erect even further reduces the political possibilities of her position to a titillation). She is even more fully stultified by being doubly circumscribed by male voices; enclosed by Shah Zaman's and by Barth's own narratives. Where the complex structure of the nights energized Shahrazad, it stifles Dunyazade. In the end, the story is not so much about "little Dunyazade"—the patronizing tone is apt—as it is about Barth himself as the true inheritor of Shahrazad's mantle. He less tells Dunyazade's story than uses her story to tell his own. In the more intense and sober texts that follow, Dinarzad as speaker, as listener—as material dialogic presence—is worked into less double-edged, if often no less fantastically shaped narratives.

In "The Death of Shahrazad" (2002), Intizar Husain imagines the life of the frame-characters after the nights of the *Nights* are over. In his telling, Dunyazad "decided to forsake marriage and motherhood and live in her sister's shadow".[45] Years pass in a few sentences and Shahrazad has granddaughters by her sons. One day Dunyazad suggests the girls ask their grandmother to tell them a story. When day after day Shahrazad begins hesitantly and then finally fails to remember the plot or the right words, it is Dunyazad who continues the telling; "Shahrazad heard Dunyazad's story as though it was her sister's story, and not her own. She was now among the listeners. And the three little girls were absolutely entranced".[46] The tale ends with a tearful Shahrazad explaining to her "dear" Shahryar that while he granted her life, he had taken her stories; that she "lived only" in her stories, so when they ended her "own story ended with them".[47] These end statements involve the idea that Shahrazad was forced to live only in her stories (her life defined and exhausted by her momentous act); and also the idea that it is only through story that we live. However, an interpretation that gathers all the deliberate elements of the text together implies a more specific notion of story-giving and receiving. Taking Shahrazad's stories from her, Shahryar's act was a violation, of her right and ability to give them to her granddaughters.The ellipses over Shahrazad's sons suggest that the stories are something that—properly, naturally, vitally—women give generously to women (Shahryar's theft itself exemplifying why the skills and power of story are the necessary birthright of daughters and granddaughters). In this reading, Dunyazad is the more redemptive figure, her sacrifice of a selfhood allowing her—in a poignant, aged, post-climax—to take Shahrazad's place. Less a full-voiced inheritor than a mere substitute, Husain's Dunyazad nonetheless has imaginative impact. Presented as deliberately reducing her own role in her own life, the light—or the shadowy—presence of the Dinarzad of the *Nights* is given weight. It is the very scant mention of her that takes on meaning. This strategy or literary-loop—the substantiation of Dinarzad through an imagining of the very peripheral or substitutive nature of her life—is also at the centre of Assia Djebar's *A Sister to Scheherazade* (1987).[48]

Djebar's book is divided into three parts. In the first, the liberated, middle-class narrator, Isma, imagines the new life she has chosen for Hajila; the veiled woman she has selected from the city's slums to become her ex-husband's new wife. This man—"the man"—is never named, but is a wisfully distant figure of combative and sexually fulfilling past-love for Isma; and a figure of immediate threat, class-power and frustrated sexual inadequacy for Hajila. In Isma's mind, she speaks to Hajila; telling Hajila of the woman's own sense of dislocation in the man's high-rise city flat and her slow determination to walk in the streets unveiled. The narrative is told in hindsight, after the final dramatic event, so is full of half-intimations that lend an ominous atmosphere.

This is compounded by the emphasis of Isma's imagining. The syntax reminds the reader that Isma is offering—in guilt, in retribution, as a gift of articulation to the uneducated other woman—Hajila's own story to herself. But Hajila is not clearly present; "Here I am speaking to you again, Hajila. As if, in truth, I were causing you to exist. A phantom whom my voice has brought to life".[49] At other points in the text, this idea of Hajila as Isma's creation becomes a fuller mergence of the two women. The power of the writing often lies in the creative ambivalence between Isma's almost sinister possession of Hajila's story, and the striving, empathic feminist narrative that understands all women as facets of one another. This effect is centrally achieved through allusion to the *Nights* frame-tale.

In Isma's mind, the plot—the man's impassivity, his descent back into alcoholism, his acts of morose psychological and finally physical violence towards Hajila—are themselves obscure, muffled in contrast to the detailed imagining of the feeling of unveiling; the texture of the cloth, the clear moments on the streets when Hajila decides to remove the veil, the sunlight, the air. There is a great effort towards female solidarity here, but also a voyeurism and violation that reminds the reader of the narrator's original class-complicity with the man in choosing her own substitute. In the second part of the book, Isma seems to both recognize this complicity and seek solace through the act of telling stories. She offers Hajila fragments of memory and gossip, weaving together stories of women both supported and betrayed by other women. As in the *Nights*, the frame-story is suspended and relief is offered in the paradoxical form of even more elaborate tales of faith and duplicity. But within this scheme, it is difficult finally to determine which woman is Scheherazade and which Dinarzade; an ambivalence that lends coherence of a sort to the elliptical, intense description of Hajila's life and Isma's girlhood memories.

The translation of the novel's title from *Ombre Sultane* to *A Sister to Scheherazade* involves not a just a warning about the shifts in meaning—the creative rewritings—that inevitably accompany translation. It also hints at the disconcerting shifts and evocative slippages of metaphor within the novel itself. Throughout the text, Isma speaks; she is the story-teller, the Scheherazade figure. Hajila, like Dinarzade, sleeps chastely and uncomfortably on the floor below her husband's bed. And like Dinarzade, it is Hajila who is Isma/Scheherazade's accomplice—albeit unknowingly—in helping her to escape the man. But it is Hajila whose life, like Scheherazade's, is in the balance. And Isma, in her own mind, is like Dinarzade; the shadowy figure of support and witness to the more modern perversions and pending moments of violence in the man's house. In mixing her metaphors, Djebar seems to be pointing up the inadequacy of the patterning and parallels of the *Nights* to the real lives of women. In constantly shifting the lines of comparison, she defies the fatefulness that accompanies techniques of allusion. Further, at the centre of the text, the story of Isma and Hajila seems to collapse the distinction between Scheherazade and Dinarzade into one strategic, metaphysical symbol for the power of female collaboration: "And all the fears haunting women today are dispelled, because of the two faces of the sultan's bride".[50] However, in exceeding the metaphor of the *Nights*, she is primarily making a more particular, directed statement about the place of women within Islamic law.

Between the first and second parts of the text, there is an interlude. The narrative voice is located—it still seems to be Isma speaking—but the text is presented in italics, suggesting the greater encompassing and omniscient thematic significance of this section. The narrator offers a definition of the Arabic word *derra* as meaning both the new wife of a man and "a wound": "in our land, the man has a right to four wives simultaneously, as much as to say, four … wounds.[51] Djebar's point here is convoluted. Isma and Hajila are not actually simultaneous wives; the liberated Isma has left the man. So Djebar is turning around the nuances of tradition to explicate a more modern situation—a strategy that risks reducing the relationships between her two main characters to a process of mutual wounding (although Djebar accounts for all possible lines of hurt between the man and the women). But *derra* also offers a way of thinking about the relationship between Isma and Hajila that is not about the successive and mutual acts of wounding that, in Djebar's reading, are sanctified by Islamic law. The term enables Isma's simultaneous presence; it bringsher voice into the room and allows her to speak to Hajila. Used this way, the suggestive confluences of the word between wives and wounding—women hurting women—are partly diverted. Similarly, between the two short sections that introduce Part II of the text, Djebar offers a reading (or translation) that she then subverts.

Part II of the text is comprised of thematically connected fragments of atmosphere and story. The two opening slices of text are also presented in italics, suggesting a continuation of Isma's more omniscient voice and indicating their weightier significance. The first of these sections offers a bare, synoptic rendering of the conversation between Scheherazade and Dinarzade prefacing the first night of the *Nights* (in which Dinarzade agrees to her strategic role as prompt). Djebar then re-writes this same conversation, but with a deeper gloss. She considers how, within Islamic law, any female blood relation of a wife is *haram*, taboo, at least in the wife's lifetime. This recognition suggests a cynical reading of Shahryar's killing spree: "Is that why a man, be he sultan or beggar, threatens with death the woman he has possessed?" Against the creative confusion of metaphor around sisters and wives, Djebar's stark equation of the Shahrayar figure with "the man" and all men is absolute, focused and angry. But as this theme is developed, the saving relationship between the women almost sidelines the man. He becomes a threat that can be dampened by the sheer power of watchfulness, the pragmatic fact of the other female witness: "to be sure, the tales [Scheherazade] spins help save her, but first and foremost it is because her sister has kept watch and woken her in time".[52] Within the short-circling, almost repetitive technique of Djebar's writing, the impressionistic section entitled "The Sister" expands this point. And here again, metaphor encompasses itself. Djebar/Isma insists that it is because she is *haram* that the sister can keep vigil. But then the syntax and the sense shifts, suggesting that the woman who keeps watch *is* the sister:

> She is there just because she is the sister, so taboo to the polygamist …. A woman keeps secret watch beneath the bed: a woman prompts the other with a word at the first sign of weakening. Her voice is ready to fly to the rescue, picking up every dropped stitch in the tale, and this woman is the sister. [53]

But then another switch back: it is because the sister is taboo that she can be

> her double and the one who can never be her rival …. Up above, the sultan's bride spins her tales; she is fighting for her life. Her sister, beneath the couch, rallies the past victims. [54]

These dissonances between the sister (defined by the law) and the sister (as lawless metaphor) might be read in Deleuze and Guattari's terms. Through the "estranging temporality"—the out-of-time of the italicized portions of the text—Djebar gives herself a concentrated space. Within this space, she worries-at her language. The slight but intense and repetitive shifts of definition—the constant rephrasing of the role of the sister/co-wife/woman—generates a "minor" aesthetic against both the easy, "major" (colonial) use of French and against the masterful, patriarchal presumption of certain divisions between women. But more particularly, this creative "deterritorialization" of the language is achieved—almost forced—through the tension between the possibilities of Islamic law and the secular bent of the metaphor. Once again adapting Žižek's Lacanian formula, Dinarzad can be understood as that which both grounds and signifies a limit. It is *because* she is *haram* that she can enter the room; it is *because* she is allowed and recognized within the religious narrative that she signifies the larger, subversive and secular potential of a metaphorical "sisterhood" between women. Djebar's oscillating language posits Dinarzad as both necessary and anterior; both contradiction and impossibility within Islamic law. However, her text does not end with this powerfully feminist and creative impasse. In Part III, it returns to plot and the cohering effects of the frame-tale; resuming the conversation between the *Nights* and the novel.

Again, the interstice between Part II and Part III works around the unstable metaphor of co-wives, through which Isma and Hajila are thought about as either or both interlopers and either or both potentially wounding. However, the italicized beginning of Part III seems at first to present a more stable metaphorical reading of the *Nights*. Isma understands herself as bearing the responsibility of Dinarzade; to awaken her sister, Hajila. But in establishing herself this way, she immediately prompts a series of more abstracted questions—and through this a rising sense of panic—that once again mixes the metaphor between the women. Wondering "what if" the sister had fallen asleep and Scheherazade had been executed; wondering "what if" this "disappeared, voiceless" Scheherazade had then taken up the role of the sister beneath the bed; and "what if" this second sister had forgotten her role; and "what if" so many women—"a third, a fourth, did not take up her post in her shadow, in her voice, in her night"? In wondering "What if this first lapse were the root of our first misfortune?", Isma narrates the *Nights* as a creationist myth for women (a wry subversion of the myth of Eve).[55] As for Borges, Djebar's *Nights* inevitably become a self-encircling infinite. But where for Borges this presents a vast existential and heavily textualized quandary, for Djebar it is about a more crucially immediate oral responsibility. Infinity here is a sign of the material need for mutuality; for ongoing vigilance and (im)-proper action between women. This is born out in the final sections of the novel. Contrasting the fragmented atmosphere of Part II, the text ends by lending an urgent sense of plot to this figurative panic of questions.

Isma contrives to meet up with Hajila in the *hammam*—" a harem in reverse ... Here, women can communicate by signs; here, a split-second glance, a barely perceptible touch, will seal their secret collusion".[56] And again: "*Hammam*, refuge where time stands still. The very concept of enclosure and thus of imprisonment, dissolves or disintegrates".[57] These repeated textual translations/definitions are complemented by the detailed explanation of the techniques and slow-order of bathing; the texture of skin, towels, the sensations of steam and cold water. This concentration has two effects. It reveals an intended, uninitiated readership: a European audience (for Djebar, both a political aim and a publishing necessity). And it focuses the body, the very materiality of women. There is a kind of relief in this, but also what at first seems to be a contradiction with the metaphorical emphasis on voice—on women speaking to, warning, supporting women—that has so intensely motivated the writing to this point. In the *hammam*, women are "purified of the triteness and dissonance of words".[58] Further, the dialogue between Isma and Hajila is brief. Isma hands Hajila a copy of the key to the man's flat, which will allow her to leave the house in order to seek advice and decide whether to continue her pregnancy. While the whole narrative is addressed to Hajila, these are some of the very few words that Isma actually speaks to the other woman. In a sense, the text returns to the original bareness of dialogue between Scheherazade and Dinarzade. The wakening of Hajila—to the freedom to unveil, to reproductive choice—that Isma sees herself as performing is not in fact achieved through the intricate metaphors of story. Unlike Husain's text—in which story is the means of support and rightful inheritance between women—Djebar values the power of the furtive, more physical in-between. The articulation of the lives of Isma and Hajila through the relationship of Scheherazade and Dinarzade finally emphasizes the impact of incipient and surrounding gestures. The very sparsity of words traditionally allowed between women in the presence of men has, in Djebar's narrative, bred another, more elliptical language that operates around and between acts of speech. Through the indirection of the narrative relationship between Isma and Hajila and the fragmentary, evocative structure of the text, Djebar values the ancillary forms of communication that are her birthright. But it is the novel that gives her the very means of making manifest and enriching these forms. Through Djebar, the conversation between the *Nights* and the structures of the novel transcends genre ideologies and creates a language for the inscription of a feminist sensibility.

## Conclusion: Dinarzad's quiet genealogy

Like Husain's story, Githa Hariharan's *When Dreams Travel* (1999) begins decades after the last of the nights of the *Nights*. A middle-aged Shahrzad has died in mysterious circumstances and Shahryar is obsessed with building a monument to his dead wife. The novel opens with Dunyazad—long married to Shahzaman and living in Samarkand, but now widowed—arriving at the palace in grief and suspicion, anxious to discover the truth about her sister's death. Describing the decadence and fastidiousness of palace life, Hariharan slowly evokes both a vague, timeless, classical atmosphere and the historical feudal class structures of a medieval Sultanate. But the plot of this late frame-tale might be shortly stated. While the circumstances of Shahrzad's death remain uncertain, Dunyazad nevertheless agrees (with the complicity of the compelling slave-girl, Dilshad) to arrange a meeting with Shahryar that will give her nephew, Umar, the opportunity to ambush and imprison his father. The intrigue itself is simple, sharpening a generic sense of narrative about power, kingship, fathers and sons; the shift from an old rule of flabby religious observance and monumental architectures (palaces and tombs) to a new religious fervour and equally strong belief in the useful architectures of modernity. This story is full of segues that complicate—both locate and dislocate—the text. Shahryar's monument to Shahrzad implicitly, partially conjures the Taj Mahal; half-dreaming, half-historicising the *Nights* as a product of Mogul India. And the son's splicing of religious stricture with an ascetic modernizing verve gestures towards an unnerving, unexpected ideological association. The apparent divine certainties of statehood—the traditional presumptions of the *Nights*—are shaken-down, rendered uncertain within the novel form; but simultaneously, modern generic expectations founder on the magical co-ordinates of the *Nights*. Ultimately, the story of the state is a holding narrative. The fantastical bulk of the text—like that of the *Nights*—is within/outside the frame-tale.

Like Djebar's *A Sister to Scheherazade*, Hariharan's novel dwells on the daily bodily sensations of women; a pervading language of blood, milk and flesh inscribes both incontrovertible material presence and a devastating sense of mortality. Hariharan's after-story of the frame-tale characters is haunted by the gory, easily-rent physicality of the many beheaded virgins; and her text is heavy with en-framed stories of the quotidian lives of physically abused, wounded and disabled women. But equally, the young Shahrzad is "solidly built—her breasts heavy domes, her legs palatial pillars". And even in her age, she is still a "warrior", that most muscular and physical of professionals.[59] Hariharan's Shahrzad is monumental in her physicality. And indeed, her story-telling effort is imagined as an almost purely physically monumental achievement. Hariharan relishes filling-in the missing scenes of the *Nights'* frame-tale, but she often does so by pursuing a risky strategy of heightening (reducing) Shahrzad to her body, her sex, her intensely-felt lack of sleep; and, in one long scene, one of her pregnancies.[60] Hariharan gives a wearying reality to what is surely the most fantastical and elliptical narrative within the *Nights*: the story of how Shahrzad bore three children without missing one night of life-saving story-telling. However, this story also introduces Hariharan's equal commitment to a circling, dreamy, intricate structure that works in creative tension with the insistent, sensual, kinesthetic quality of her writing. As with Djebar's text, the feminist motivation of Hariharan's novel does not rest with the bodily recuperation of the frame-tale sisters, their robust materiality and entailing vulnerability. Rather, it lies in the balance between these close specificities and an ephemeral, at times abstruse, textual structure.

Like Barth's Sherry, Hariharan's Shahrzad does not bear three sons (as unanimously agreed in the written traditions and translations of the *Nights*). She bears two sons and a daughter. In the *Dunyazadiad*, this slip is the nub of the back-to-the-future impasse: if the "real" Scheherazade bore two sons and a daughter, but the Genie's supposedly authentic transcription of the *Nights* records three sons, then what other, more life-threatening lacunae might there be between the written-version and the unfolding of the future of the past? The point, typically, becomes self-involving. Anxiety is replaced by an almost smug presentation of the impossibility of any "authentic" text. In Hariharan's work, Shahrzad's daughter is both more and less significant. She is barely mentioned—almost an aside, her death in infancy is not dwelt upon.[61] But the substitution of a girl for a boy and the fact of this daughter's absence gains subtle import within a novel that is complexly structured—deliberately over-burdened, even—by a scew, biologically and culturally deviant genealogy of female story-tellers. Unlike Husain's gentle understanding of a proper matrilineage, Hariharan tracks a creative impropriety of heretical, racially and physically aberrant women.

The opening image of the text is of Dunyazad as a man, cross-dressed for travel and safety; lending a new potential to her role as the third, the material in-between. But Dunyazad is not static—even in this more radical sexual incarnation—within Hariharan's text. After the plot of the frame-tale is essentially completed, there is still more than half the book to be read: and in this, women counter, adapt and offer alternative versions of old and new stories. Dunyazad—the "amputated sorceress"—is released from her role as forever "the audience, the prompter, the chorus, the heckler".[62] In Hariharan's text, the cohesive principle of Shahrzad's voice is replaced by a dialectic, in which Dunyazad's memory-stories are trumped by the stranger, more brutal and more fabulously subversive tales of Dilshad. But within this scheme, there is also a crucial third, a presence ultimately without counterpart, who might be identified as Dunyazad's true ancestor/inheritor/sister.

Hariharan has spoken of the pleasures she found in playing through all the possible pairings and quartets of women and men within *When Dreams Travel*.[63] The plot moves (and the atmosphere of conspiracy peaks and recedes) through the shifting affiliations and jealousies between sisters, brothers, husbands, wives. But at the heart of the novel are "Two women, one possessed by a missing story-teller, the other by a muted poet".[64] The invitation is to read the stories that comprise the second half of the text as a parallel seeking: Dunyazad worries (lovingly and jealously) at the memory of Shahrzad, as Dilshad conjures the poetic skill and fantastic biography of her mentor, Satyasama, in ever more extreme tales. But in another reading, it is Dilshad who teaches Dunyazad the art of storytelling. And in yet other narrative strands, it is Dilshad who—taking the transcripts of the *Nights* in payment for helping Umar to the throne—is Shahrzad's descendent. Again, the pairings, parallels and loyalties veer and are manoeuvred through all possibilities. However, the mysterious, worldly, hairy, one-eyed (and in one story, limbless) monkey-woman Satyasama—racially, sexually and linguistically oblique—takes on many incarnations in the novel that stymie and exceed this careful patterning. She enters the text as a *harem* freak, but is fundamentally peripheral to the progression of the plot. Hariharan admits that she cannot explain Satyasama, she doesn't know how or why she emerged in her writing; only that this character seemed somehow necessary in these "times of different fatwas".[65] In the stories told by Dilshad, Satya (Sanskrit, "truth") sama (Arabic, "sky") is persecuted for her higher wisdom in the allegorical tales of the Indian nation and communalism. But in her reiterated physical alterity (there is an almost obsessive concentration on the violations and smelly animal perversions of her body) she has a more (anti-) symbolic meaning. This reaches beyond the translation offered by Hariharan in her own attempt to contain the character in a novelistic convention of national parable. Satyasama is—gruesomely, literally—a material leftover. In Žižek's Lacanian sense, she is both necessary and radically anterior to Hariharan's very feminist symbolic order itself; the disruptive in-between the mutual, empowering recuperations achieved by Dunyazad and Dilshad in their story-telling.

Barth, Husain, Djebar and Hariharan have all found imaginative possibility in lending Dinarzad movement and voice. While their works are of different intensities and effect, there is nonetheless a common underlying sense that in the very empowering relief of articulation, Dunyazad is reduced to her biology; her status as Shahrazad's sister/substitute daughter/imitator. Hariharan's text ends with Dunyazad's imagining of Shahrzad's last dream. The old woman, surrounded by serving girls, envisions all "their futures, curving one into the other, a circle with no beginning or end".[66] The Borgesian conception of the *Nights* is here reconstructed as an ambivalent triumph; generations of women fated to fight the same battle, to voice the same resistance in a kind of thrall to Shahrazad's monumental talent. But there is another genealogy tangential to this circling order. The one pairing (a cross-cultural, racially diffuse ancestral possibility) that is not fully explicated within Hariharan's text is that between Dunyazad and Satyasama. This is left to silence, an inexpressible connection between the ambivalence—the radical anti-biological stand—of both women. There is a defiance in Dunyazad's cross-dressing and Satyasama's inexplicable, broken, sexually inviolable body that connects to the broken, unsustainable (anti-)metaphors of *A Sister to Sheherazade*. While both Djebar and Hariharan take powerful feminist delight in elucidating the *Nights* as a precedent and pattern for women's stories of resistance, they equally and more fundamentally structure their writing around still moments, temporal disjunctures and ellipses; inexpressible moments outside the symbolic order. In a sense, both texts deliberately founder on the original silence of Dinarzad. It is not, at last, her relationship to the ever-talking Shahrazad that defines and empowers Dinarzad. It is Dinarzad's return to her lone, unpaired, unassimilated material constitution that most powerfully disconcerts *both* patriarchal and matrilineal symbolic orders.

## Notes

1. Husain Haddawy, *The Arabian Nights*, 1990 (New York, Toronto: Alfred A. Knopf, 1992), p. xv. Haddawy's text is based upon Muhsin Mahdi's Arabic edition of a fourteenth-century Syrian manuscript. While the *Arabian Nights* or the *Thousand and One Nights* are titles that conjure an unknowably long tradition of translation, tracing back into culturally diverse oral practices, Haddawy's text—as the straightest translation into English of an "originary" manuscript—is a recent authoritative point of reference. I have used his name spellings (Shahrazad, Dinarzad, Shahrayar) for overarching reference to the frame-tale characters. Other spellings appearing in the text follow the contemporary literature under discussion.
2. Jorge Luis Borges, "The Garden of Forking Paths", 1941, *Labyrinths: Selected Stories and Other Writings* trans. from Spanish, Donald A. Yates (New York: New Directions, 1964), p. 25.
3. For a broader examination of Borges's use of the *Nights*, see Evelyn Fishburn's "Traces of the *Thousand and One Nights* in Borges" in this volume.
4. Borges, p. 26.
5. Borges, pp. 27–28.
6. Borges, p. 19.
7. Borges, p. 29.
8. Borges, p. 28.
9. Slavoj Žižek, *The Sublime Object of Ideology* (London, New York: Verso, 1989), p. 182.
10. Žižek, p. 183.
11. Žižek, p. 185.
12. Edward Said, *Beginnings, Intention and Method*, 1975, (London: Granta Books,1997), p. 81 (emphasis Said's).
13. Many thanks to Wen-chin Ouyang for discussions on the meaning of Dinarzad and Dunyazad.
14. Walter Benjamin, "Franz Kafka", 1955, *Illuminations*, trans. from German, Harry Zohn (London: Fontana, 1992), p. 125.
15. Salman Rushdie, *Haroun and the Sea of Stories*, 1990 (London: Granta, 1991).
16. Salman Rushdie, *Midnight's Children*, 1981, (Book Club Associates and Jonathan Cape: London, 1982)
17. Salman Rushdie, *Satanic* Verses, 1988, (London: Vintage, 1998), p. 60.
18. M. G. Vassanji, *The Gunny Sack* (Oxford: Heinemann African Writers Series, 1989) pp. 5–6.
19. Gilles Deleuze and Felix Guattari, *Kafka: Toward a Minor Literature*, trans. from German, Polan Dana (Minneapolis: University of Minnesota Press, 1986), p. 19.
20. Deleuze, p. 19.
21. Franz Kafka, *The Man Who Disappeared (Amerika)*, 1924, trans. from German, Michael Hofmann (London: Penguin, 1996), p. 28.
22. M. G. Vassanji, *Amriika* (Toronto: McClelland & Stewart, 1999), p. 196.
23. Vassanji, *Amriika*, p. 1.
24. Vassanji, *Amriika*, p. 2.
25. Vassanji, *Amriika*, p. 304.
26. Vassanji, *Amriika*, p. 351.
27. Vassanji, *Amriika*, p. 205
28. Said, *Beginnings*, p. 81.
29. Edward Said, *Culture and Imperialism* (London: Vintage, 1993) p. 84.
30. Stephen Barron (dir.) and Peter Barnes (writer), *Arabian Nights* (Hallmark Entertainment Network, 2000).
31. Haddawy, p. 21.
32. Žižek, p. 179.
33. Žižek, pp. 183;185 (Žižek's emphasis).
34. Paulin Kaldas and Khaled Mattawa (eds.), *Dinarzad's Chilren: An Anthology of Contemporary Arab American Fiction* (Arkansas: University of Arkansas Press, 2004).
35. John Barth "Dunyazadiad", *Chimera*, 1972 (London: Andre Deutsch, 1974) p. 55.

36. Wen-chin Ouyang, "Metamorphoses of Scheherazade in literature and film", *Bulletin of the School of Oriental and African Studies*, 66: 3 (2003), p. 417.
37. Barth, p. 55.
38. Barth, pp. 8–9.
39. Barth, p. 11.
40. Barth, p. 24.
41. Ouyang, pp. 415; 417–18.
42. Barth, p. 23.
43. Barth, p. 4.
44. Barth, pp. 50; 49.
45. Intizar Husain "The Death of Shahrazad" trans. from Urdu, Rakhshanda Jalil, *The Annual of Urdu Studies* 18 (2003), p. 525.
46. Husain, p. 527.
47. Husain, p. 529.
48. Also in May Tellimisany's autobiographical novel, *Dunyazad* (2000), wistful meaning is made of the unfulfilled life signified by the name, which is given to the narrator's dead baby daughter. Like her namesake, she is "only ... those few lines on a page", not a completed life. May Tellimisany, *Dunyazad* trans. from Arabic, Roger Allen (London: Saqi Books, 2000), p. 25.
49. Assia Djebar, *A Sister to Scheherazade* trans. from French, Dorothy S. Blair (London, New York: Quartet Books, 1987), p. 85.
50. Djebar, p. 95.
51. Djebar, p. 91 (Djebar's ellipses).
52. Djebar, p. 95.
53. Djebar, p. 98.
54. Djebar, p. 99.
55. Djebar, p. 143.
56. Djebar, p. 148.
57. Djebar, p. 152.
58. Djebar, p. 152.
59. Githa Hariharan, *When Dreams Travel* (London: Picador, 1999), pp. 7; 276.
60. Hariharan, p. 121.
61. Hariharan, p. 39.
62. Hariharan, pp. 23; 37.
63. Githa Hariharan, "The Double Burden: The Continual Contesting of Tradition and Moderntiy": Interview with Joel Kuorrti, *Journal of Commonwealth Literature* 36 (March 2001), p. 6.
64. Hariharan, p. 114.
65. Hariharan Interview, p. 18.
66. Hariharan, p. 276.

# AFTERWORD: BEYOND THE PROJECT

That *The Thousand and One Nights* would have a life beyond the project on Genre Ideologies and Narrative Transformation was never in doubt. What is surprising is not so much the global interest in this body of stories—their allure has been irresistible since 1704 when Galland published the first instalment of his French translation—as the intensity and proliferation of this interest during the three year period of the Project. Perhaps the Project is fortunate in its timing, for 2004 is the tercentennial anniversary of Galland's translation, and in celebration even the general assembly of UNESCO voted to include *The Thousand and One Nights* in its list of commemorative events for 2004–2005. International scholarly conferences were held across the world, from London to Paris, Wolfenbüttel in Europe, and from Rabat in Morocco to Osaka in Japan. Many core members of the Project played a key role in planning and organizing these conferences.

Aboubakr Chraïbi was behind the conference *Les Mille et Une Nuits: du texte au mythe* held in Rabat in 2002, and another conference, *Les Mille et Une Nuits en partage*, held in Paris in 2004. While the proceedings for the former await a firm publication date, those of the latter have appeared in the form of a book: *Les Mille et Une Nuits en partage* (Paris: Sindbad, Actes Sud, 2004).

Ulrich Marzolph has been equally active and productive. He played a central role in the 2002 Osaka conference on *The Arabian Nights and Orientalism in Resonances* as well as the accompanying special exhibit of *Nights* manuscripts and paraphernalia organized by Tetsuo Nishio and Yuriko Yamanaka at the National Museum for Ethnography. The proceedings of the conference will be published as a book entitled *Arabian Nights and Orientalism: Perspectives from East and West* (London: I. B. Tauris, expected 2005). Marzolph himself co-organized with the Herzog-August Library at Wolfenbüttel in 2004 yet another symposium on *The Arabian Nights: Past and Present*. The proceedings of this conference have appeared in special issues of *Marvels and Tales* (18:2, 2004) and *Fabula* (45:3/4, 2004) and will be published again in the form of a book as *The Arabian Nights: A Transnational Perspective* (Wayne State University Press, expected 2006). In addition, the fruit of his long-term collaborative project with Richard van Leeuwen, *The Arabian Nights Encyclopedia*, in two volumes, saw the light of day in 2004.

Robert Irwin embarked on a new adventure, taking part in a series of radio programmes devoted to *The Arabian Nights*, broadcast daily from 17 to 21 May 2004 on BBC Radio 4. His programmes, like his popular book, *The Arabian Nights: A Companion*, which has been republished in a new edition (I. B. Tauris, 2004), were elegant, informative and insightful.

The Project is also fortunate in that it tapped into, consolidated and expanded a network of scholars of the *Nights* whose interests, though diverse, intersect and complement one another. It is precisely because their paths to the *Nights* are so divergent that it has been possible for them to create a genuinely multicultural and interdisciplinary intellectual space where issues of politics of cultural exchange, including those identified by Edward Said as 'Orientalism', and ideological underpinnings of literary transformation may be raised, interrogated and debated in a meaningful, productive way. The literary field surrounding the *Nights*, whether in the Arab world, America, Europe, or even Asia, has changed irrevocably and, more pertinently, for the better. 'Influence studies' have expanded to cover geographical areas outside Western Europe. There are now studies tracing the presence and reception of the *Nights* in, for example, Japanese culture, Balochi, Greek and East African Swahili oral traditions, Afghani performance, and world cinema. They look at the politics of cultural exchange, at the transformations and distortions of translating and rewriting the *Nights*, when, for example, the 'Oriental Tale' is embraced by European fiction or when modern Arab novelists seek inspiration from the *Nights*.

This book contains the articles (some in revised form) that were first published as a special issue of *Middle Eastern Literatures* (vol. 7:2) in 2004, with the addition of one article. It is appropriate that this article, by Stephanie Jones, stresses the importance of the concept 'plus one' when speaking of the *Thousand-Nights-plus-One-Night*. It is, as she says, a 'signifier of infinite metamorphoses'; it hints at an unlimited continuity and at Projects. By the same reasoning it is equally apt that this book, by appearing in 2005, has turned Galland's tercentenary into a tercentenary-plus-one. For all its importance, Galland's translation is merely an instance of the *Nights* manifold manifestations, a *locus* where, rather arbitrarily, one particular form of the *Nights* crystallized after centuries of amorphously floating around, a form that in turn sparked off countless new forms and will continue to do so.

The Editors

# INDEX

For Product Safety Concerns and Information please contact our EU representative GPSR@taylorandfrancis.com
Taylor & Francis Verlag GmbH, Kaufingerstraße 24, 80331 München, Germany

www.ingramcontent.com/pod-product-compliance
Lightning Source LLC
Chambersburg PA
CBHW081357090726
47908CB00011B/2707

* 9 7 8 0 4 1 5 7 5 9 1 5 1 *